## Evil i...

She stopped dead in the ..... her eyes, and took a number of deep breaths. There, in the dark, in the rain, she let her mind go, let it rise up to the clouds and turbulence above.

And she felt *power*.

She was one with the storm, and the storm was hers. She was where she stood but she was also everywhere touched by this great tropical storm. The winds were hers to command, to bend branches or whip through the treetops; the lightning was a plaything, a toy, a weapon if she wanted it to be.

She was aware, suddenly, of a *presence* in the storm, a thing not of it that hid within it and took from the storm's center a bit of its power to give it form. It used clouds to form a skull face, a demon face, and electrical energy to feed it and give it strength and solidity. She did not know what it was, but she knew immediately, somehow, that it was looking for her. Looking, but not seeing, because the rest of the storm was hers. . . .

# Don't miss the first book
# of the CHANGEWINDS saga
# by Jack L. Chalker:
# *WHEN THE CHANGEWINDS BLOW*

"Stunning. . . . The ingenious Jack L. Chalker is back with the start of another intriguing new series."
—*Rave Reviews*

*Ace books by Jack L. Chalker*

**The Changewinds Saga**

WHEN THE CHANGEWINDS BLOW
RIDERS OF THE WINDS
WAR OF THE MAELSTROM
*(coming in October)*

CHANGEWINDS II:

# Riders of the Winds

# JACK L. CHALKER

ACE BOOKS, NEW YORK

This book is an Ace
original edition, and
has never been previously
published.

RIDERS OF THE WINDS

An Ace Book/published by arrangement with
the author

PRINTING HISTORY
Ace edition/May 1988

ISBN: 0-441-72351-9

Ace Books are published by The Berkley Publishing Group,
200 Madison Avenue, New York, New York 10016.
The name "ACE" and the "A"
logo are trademarks belonging to
Charter Communications, Inc.

PRINTED IN THE UNITED STATES OF AMERICA

10 9 8 7 6 5 4 3 2 1

*For Ted Cogswell, and Polly Freas,
and Bea Mahaffey, and Alice "Tip" Sheldon,
and too many other old friends
who left this outplane while I was writing this.
I owe you all, but too many of you are missing
when I return to this reality, and contrary to
natural law, there are far too many vacuums where
once special brightness dwelt.*

# RIDERS OF THE WINDS

# • PROLOGUE •

## The Shape of Things

WHEN THE CHANGEWINDS blow, out from the Seat of Probability and across the worlds they themselves created, they are capricious things, at once random and consistent, yet they obey their own spectral meteorology.

The Changewinds' breath touched the formative Earth when it was but a cooling mass of molten rock, its own formation caused by a previous storm hitting in the void, and within that mass was sufficient moisture to cause the great clouds formed from condensation. The winds had less to draw them, then, so they let it alone for thousands of years. It was one hell of a rainstorm.

The Changewinds returned to touch the new Earth when it was still soup, and the conditions arose for the joining of acids and proteins just so. It was not planned that way; it simply had to happen someplace under the laws of probability, which are the only laws the Changewinds recognize.

Later Changewinds, far weakened this far from the Seat of their origin, none the less gently caressed the still-developing mass sufficient to create the early creatures of the sea and establish the developmental pattern that led in the end to the vast jungles and the reign of great reptiles and amphibians. Another, perhaps stronger, storm dismissed them as coldly and capriciously as they had been made masters of the world, and allowed for the rise of mammals.

Why did the ape line develop better than the rest? Why did one branch develop intelligence and tools and eventually

1

civilization of sorts? Well, why not? It might as well have been them as anything else. And the same sort of thing had happened on a large number of probable worlds between the Earth we know and the Seat, creating both the same sorts of creatures and very different ones. Our world is far from the Seat, and younger; the others developed earlier, as ones beyond developed later than we, but those vast civilizations and worlds which developed in between created a buffer between the younger worlds and the Seat, increasingly dense, protecting our world as mountains and jet streams and seas and air masses protect us from weather, absorbing much of the energy.

A great storm moves across the land wreaking havoc as it comes, until it hits the mountains, the great, impressive barriers of nature. Crossing those mountains requires ten, a hundred, a thousand times the energy of crossing vast plains and oceans. A stubborn, particularly violent storm might make it, but if it does it will be so weakened that it will be quite ordinary to those living on the far side of the range. Or it might be diverted, attempting to go around the mountain barriers, and hitting elsewhere or spending itself in a long, futile journey.

So, too, the Changewinds are weakened and diverted by the worlds between, thus aiding the new humanity from suffering as capriciously as the dinosaurs sudden and terrible extinction. We owe the dinosaurs a debt, for we might have been first, when protections were weaker, and they come later.

But though the storm that crosses the mountains might be a pale shadow of its former self, it is still a storm. It still wets or whitens the ground, changes temperature and humidity, causes slippery roads and accidents and changed plans, or perhaps causes a crop to be saved or a drought to be ended. Even though it is not large or grand, it still might have far-reaching effects, if you must drive on that rainy day on some slippery road instead of on dry asphalt under a comforting sun and blue sky. Without the storm you might not have lost traction on that hill, might not have hit the post or the oncoming car, or been in the path of another, causing a tragic chain.

One little storm, no matter how tiny it may be, can have great repercussions.

A great Changewind storm was a mere ripple in the mathematics of probability by the time it touched Troy, but Troy fell just the same when it succumbed to a pretty ridiculous trick. Another ripple placed Alexander where he could conquer the known world, and took him from that world too young to do more than that. Just a tiny whisper, a slight rippling in the leaves, but Caesar dies because all goes exactly right, and the assassins then are beaten because nothing does. Just a mere sigh of the wind chimes, but a carpenter turned rabbi, one of hundreds of self-proclaimed prophets and messiahs of the times, becomes a force that lasts for thousands of years because everything, even his death, goes right. Such things can happen, even to a single holy man among multitudes in India or an illiterate nomad near Medina in Arabia. For every one that founded a great religion and affected millions there were thousands who did not. Why them? Were they what they claimed, or not? It makes no difference to the Changewinds, except to remember that they worship probability alone, and so any one of these just might have been for real . . .

The winds are like that.

Wars, and peace; revolution and reaction; darkness and renaissance; invention and ignorance . . . all are the same to the Changewinds, and one is just as good as the other. Causes rarely win or lose on their merits, but on the smallest of things.

"For want of a nail the shoe was lost . . ."

The Changewinds touch the ordinary and make them great, and touch the great and make them failures. A Corsican officer becomes Emperor of France. A Hainanese librarian unifies mainland China under a communism of his own unique design. A German Jewish economist believes he finds the key to human history and dominates radicalism but never controls it. The son of a superintendent of schools, a former seminary student, and a Russian Jewish scholar unite in the name of the proletariat they never were and bring a new order to Russia in the name of a man who said that communism might never be possible there. A failed painter of Viennese postcards moves to Bavaria and becomes the leader of a ragtag collection of disaffected radicals and old soldiers and in ten years is acclaimed dictator of a new Germany. The probability of this, all things *considered, is next to none, but so long as it is not zero the winds might manage it.*

*There are still impossible things when the Changewinds blow, but nothing is improbable.*

*And everyone who lives a life is eventually touched by at least a small one, some many times; if not in day-to-day life then in dreams, mythologies, fantasies, gods, and demons, which are echoes, remnants, of those lands through which the winds must pass.*

*All the universes created by the winds exist in time and space distanced enough so that the creatures of those universes live in egocentric ignorance of the nature of their true birth and that which touches and shapes their large and small destinies. This infinite stream of universes rarely touches another reality and even less often overlaps. It does happen, of course. Benjamin Bathhurst walked around a horse in full view of a dozen men and was never seen again. A wild wolf-boy appears mysteriously as a young teen in a German forest. How came he there, and from where? One place has a sudden rain of frogs, and another has a solid churchman explode and burn while sitting in his easy chair reading the paper. From whence came the bolt that ignited him, for there is no hole in the roof? These and many other puzzles do happen, but they are rare enough that rational men might dismiss them as folklore, old wives' tales, or, even when stumped for the most farfetched of rational-sounding solutions, fall back on, "There must be a logical explanation!"*

*Down, though, close to the Seat of Probability, the gravitational force of the First Cause pulls the worlds ever closer, ever more densely packed together. There might, that close in, be hundreds, even thousands of universes all so densely packed that what is the rare and bizarre overlap in the far-off universes of the rational folk is commonplace there, and one might walk from one universe to the other while hardly realizing it.*

*This region, the closest in to the Seat that will support any sort of life as we might know it, is called by its rulers Akahlar.*

*The Akhbreed fell here, a remnant of a powerful tribe, perhaps, in ancient times, from some world farther out, but they were first and they learned to live in and adapt to this land. Their understanding and mastery of the arcane laws that* govern such a madhouse gives them their power over all the others who have fallen since and over those universes that have the bad fortune to overlap. The Akhbreed sorcerers weave no magic in the true sense; they simply have mastery over physical laws and powers bestowed by a far different universe than our own. They maintain the rock-steady loci, great lands held fast by the sorcerers for their kings and people, and they milk the produce of a colonial empire extending over so many worlds that none of the greatest imperialist dreamers could have hoped for such power and domains. Between the loci kingdoms, though, is anywhere and anywhen for countless universes and lands. The Akhbreed navigators can pick their lands and universes and routes, but for the rest it is random, making revolution impossible and resistance futile on any large scale.

There is only one thing that even the Akhbreed fear, and that even the Akhbreed sorcerers must yield before, and that is the Changewind, which blows far more frequently and with far greater severity through Akahlar, since no Changewind, however diminished, could reach the outer universes except first it pass through Akahlar.

For countless centuries those people who must pay tribute to the Akhbreed and place those masters first before their own interests have dreamed and hoped for a deliverer.

For countless centuries the Akhbreed sorcerers have dreamed of the ultimate power, of control and direction of the very Changewinds themselves, a power that would truly make them gods over all the universes everywhere.

This is a tale of a choice of dreams, and a choice of nightmares, down, deep, where the Changewinds blow . . .

# · 1 ·

## A Choice of Bad Roads

CLOUDS WERE RARE in Kudaan Wastes; its blasted appearance, orange, furrowed hills, and deep ravines and lack of much that was the green color of life attested to that. To have two storms in a matter of days was not only unheard of, it was a prescription for disaster, since such parched lands had ground baked so hard it would run off and the flash flood might ensnare anyone or anything anywhere.

This was a small storm, forming with suddenness as such storms usually do, perhaps over some cool spot where sufficient moisture from the last rain had collected and begged to be evaporated by the harsh sun. The clouds swirled and thickened and seemed to take on a life of their own. Small flashes of energy built up within, and from the darkest part of the building thunderhead shone two tiny, deep depressions that illuminated a crimson red from the charges within, as if the cloud indeed was the protective shield or shroud of some dark and loathsome monster.

The Sudog drew its strength from the storm and took control of it, blazing eyes looking down, scouring the land. There was little wind that it did not create and little variation in the heat of the day except where its shadow fell, and so it had a relatively free hand.

It swung first west, until it found the main road leading into the Wastes, taking care not to get too close to the border where the interaction between wedges could cause unpredictable and perhaps fatal weather effects. The desert floor that was usually

7

so flat and featureless was in full bloom, with great blood red flowers hanging from strong green vines that shot out of the soil and into the air and tried to do all that they had to do in the days perhaps even hours, before the moisture dried and they were forced once again into dormancy.

The Sudog wasted none of its energy on them, nor any of the water that kept it cohesive. If floated well over the growths and towards where the road went down deep into a canyon with steep walls and isolated bluffs, its dull red and yellow and purple rock layers thus exposed leaving part of its depth forever in shadow.

There were the clear signs of a disaster here: broken wagons, half-eaten and rotting corpses of animals and some people, partly crumbled rock walls and ledges, showing what a true heavy rain on the down-sloping plain above could do to anyone unlucky enough to be trapped here.

The Sudog floated overhead and looked down for a distance, until the wreckage and remains ceased, then it floated back, away and to the north, back out again over the Wastes themselves where roads were mere trails through colorful desolation.

Twisting, turning, following the trail it discovered a great rock arch on the downward side and there the remains of more violence, this of a far different kind. A new grave on the rim opposite the arch and overlooking it, and much scorching of the very rock itself. Below, some animals, both nargas and horses, and the remains of burnt-out wagons, and a number of bodies of more recent vintage than those in the canyon had been, bodies not drowned but bloodied and mutilated by shot and shell.

It began to follow the trail, but its energy was nearly spent; it was next to impossible to withstand the low humidity of the surrounding air and the scorching heat of the desert sun for long. It felt itself first weakened, then almost coming apart. The eyes faded, the sliver of crimson that might have been a mouth grew dull, then merged with the clouds, which were already turning from dark to white. Its last impression was the mere hint of life farther on, of horses, possibly, and riders, but no details. It was sufficient, however, for the Sudog's master.

There were four horses farther on, had it been able to get just a little bit closer, four horses but with five very different riders. Also along was a narga, a four-footed beast of burden that somewhat resembled a cross between a no-humped camel and a mule, laden with packs.

One was a very fat young woman, looking because of her weight older than her years but still with youth in her face and complexion, with short black hair. The second was a strikingly beautiful young woman in possibly her late teens with long strawberry blond hair and a perfect figure, her eyes painted or possibly tattooed with the flowing lines of sapphire blue butterfly's wings, and a similar, if much more grandiose, design on her chest from her breasts down to her crotch. The effect was neither grotesque nor overdone, but rather exotic.

The third was an older woman but in very good condition, extremely thin and very tall, certainly over six feet in bare feet. Her hair was black, her facial complexion very dark, but little more could be said, since almost all of her body was covered with colorful and exotic designs that seemed to flow into one another and made her appear outlandishly dressed even if she were nude, which in fact she basically was. In fact, they all were.

The final pair sharing a horse were very young, one in her early teens who was thin and fairly plain, the other, no more than nine or ten, almost insufferably cute. They looked grim and tired, though, as did the others, and their faces reflected experiences that had aged them as none of their tender years should have aged, inside.

They had clearly made what they could out of what they had. The two youngest wore what were obviously pieces of blankets with crude holes cut in their middles to give them basic serapelike protection from the sun. Much the same had been done with a full blanket for the fat woman, while the butterfly woman wore a shorter length tied at the neck like a cape. The tall one with the tattoos wore nothing at all save double pistols on a cut-down gunbelt. Both the big woman and the butterfly girl also were similarly armed.

There was some thunder in the background and the big woman stopped and turned to look back. "They're looking for us," she said tensely. "I can feel it. We have to put as much distance as possible between ourselves and this place as fast as we can." Her voice was very low and gravelly, almost a distinctive and not very melodic young man's voice, straddling the octaves between male and female. She spoke in the nonetheless melodic language of the Akhbreed, but the butterfly girl answered in American English.

"Sam, we're all dead tired, and the girls most of all. We've been through a *lot*, and there's maybe only a couple of more hours of sun left. We can only push ourselves so far and God knows where the next water is. If they find us then they'll find us, no matter what kind of distance we make today. Best if we're all at our best. I say we look for a campsite that seems safe." She sighed. "What a mess. No guides, can't use the main trail, and, considering the horses, maybe two days' worth of water tops. And we can't go back to the border 'cause all of those *things* are blooming."

The plants now flowering on the plain were not placid creatures. They had crushed and eaten people, horses, even wagons that had the bad luck to spill some moisture on the plot of ground above them, and who knew what they were like thick, aboveground, and in full bloom?

Samantha Buell, the large woman, did not bother to translate for the others. Charley could understand the Akhbreed language, or enough to get by, but speaking it was beyond her. There was no need to translate; why get the others more depressed than they already were?

"All right," Sam said, "we'll look for a safe place to camp. I think tomorrow, though, we have to track north until we can find some clear way back to the border. With all those wedges changing all the time if we can get someplace else, anyplace, they'll have a real tough time finding us then."

"Do you think those who seek you won't also have that in mind?" the tall, tattooed woman asked sharply. "Even now they will be sending their minions to patrol the length and will use their pet monsters to deter or discourage us from trying it until they can get there. There are always storms on a border, even one such as this, to breed them. Were Boday your enemy she would keep you in the Wastes and off the roads, running, jumping, and hiding, until the water ran out and the horses died; and, afoot and thirsty, all would be as easy to pick as flowers in a garden."

Sam sighed. "You're right, Boday, and that's probably exactly what they *will* do. Damn it, they're not after you, Charley, or the girls. They're only after *me*. The rest of you are in danger only because of me. They couldn't care less about the rest of you."

"Yeah, but they think I'm you," Sharlene "Charley" Sharkin, the butterfly girl, responded. "Even that sorceress or whatever she was thought so. You're the quarry but I'm the target!"

The Akhbreed sorcerer Boolean had arranged it so that Charley, who bore a superficial resemblance to Sam before the weight gain, had come to look, *sans* butterfly tattoos, precisely like her friend. And a combination of a long wait, depression, and Boolean's pet demon had caused Sam to become more than merely fat, so that one would have to be a very good observer and look very close to take Sam and Charley as virtual twins. The idea, to make everyone chase Charley instead of Sam, had worked well—to Charley's dismay. They didn't know if Boolean's demon and the monstrously beautiful but evil sorceress who had vanished while in combat with one another were still alive somewhere else or in another plane or had destroyed one another. If not, then the enemy for whom that sorceress worked had given a pretty accurate description of Charley to her master, and with Boday's butterfly tattoos Charley wasn't exactly easy to disguise.

Charley knew, too, that the others were still somewhat in shock and that the day's labors had helped put off the inevitable horror within the others. Sam, Boday, and the two girls, Rani and Sheka, had been tied down by a marauding gang of animals in the shape of men and brutally raped; the two girls had further been subjected to the loss of both their parents and probably their two brothers in the flood. Charley, with some help from the girls' dying father, had managed to rescue them and eliminate the gang, but she couldn't know just what they had been through and because of the language barrier she couldn't lead them. She could only lead Sam, and then only to a point.

The two girls had barely spoken all day, and Sam was clearly on the edge. Boday seemed normal for Boday, but the artist and alchemist was more than eccentric, and even rape and torture might not have affected *that* very bizarre mind; but for the same reason Boday was the last person Charley wanted in charge of anything. The only control now was that love potion Boday had accidentally consumed that had caused her to fall madly in love with Sam, the first person she saw after coming around, but even that wasn't as absolute as it always seemed in the fairy tales. When somebody who was both mad and dangerous was passionately in love with you, you had to watch yourself even more than otherwise, as they had discovered more than once.

Boday called a halt and pointed to their left. "Up in the rocks there, darlings! Looks like enough room for us and the animals, at least, and there's high ground overlooking the only trail in these parts."

Sam looked up at it. "Might be rough getting all the animals up there," she said worriedly.

"Perhaps. But it will be just as difficult for anyone else to get to us."

It *wasn't* easy, and the final solution was to walk each of the animals up by leading them and not falling down themselves. All of them were exhausted, all had pushed themselves beyond their limits, and as soon as the horse blankets were converted to beds by laying them out on the hard, uneven ground most wanted only to sleep, although they did have hardtack-type biscuits and invaluable canteens and small casks filled with water and wine.

Charley got out the single-shot shotgun and a box of shells. "I'll take the first watch," she told them. "You get some sleep. When I can't take it anymore I'll wake you up, Sam, and then Boday can finish off the night."

"No," Sam told her. "I'll go first. I don't think I can sleep right now. We at least got some rest thanks to that damned spell or whatever that *thing* put on us. I'll be okay. I got to do some thinking anyway."

The sun was still up and casting long shadows against the forbidding landscape when most dropped off into states more approaching unconsciousness than sleep, but for Charley sleep just wouldn't come. She was overtired; she knew that. She also ached in every muscle in her body including some she had never even suspected before, but that only made it harder. She lay there, looking over at Sam, who was just sitting there staring vacantly into the distance towards the setting sun. She finally gave up, got up, and went over and sat beside her friend.

"I can't get off to sleep," she told Sam. "Maybe I should take the watch anyway."

Sam shook her head negatively. "Uh-uh. Take some of the wine. It's not great but it's pretty strong."

"Maybe. The way the animals went at that keg of water, though, I think we should save any liquid until we just have to have it." She sighed. "It's been rough so far, hasn't it? And we only just started."

Sam nodded. "I been thinking about that, and a lot of other things. I just don't know how much more of this I can stand, Charley. Right now I feel—*dirty*. Those filthy, murdering scum playing with my body, getting *inside* of me, getting off inside me, and there was nothing I could do! Nothing! I'm still matted up down there with dried prick juice. And *her*—that—that *thing*—laughing and cheerin' 'em on. I think she was gettin' off on it herself just watchin' 'em."

Charley sighed. "Yeah, I can imagine how you must feel. At least, though, we learned one thing from it all. We learned just what kind of people and creatures work for this bastard out to get you. Somehow I just can't picture this Boolean being real cozy with that dragonfly queen. You didn't get to see her full, I guess, like I did. Half beautiful woman, half some monstrous insect. Nobody's born like that, not even here. You remember your changewind vision? Of the boy changed into a monster by one of those winds?"

Sam nodded absently.

"Well, I think this one was another like that, only maybe only part way, like part of her was covered and part wasn't and somehow it made a new whole. You can almost see how somebody like that is made. A pretty woman like that, changed into half what she was and half monster. Maybe that *is* the only way she can get satisfaction herself now—by watching it. Maybe she's just gettin' even with everybody, 'specially girls, who can still have what she can't. Even so, she worked for the guy with the horns. She told me so. He might look human, but inside he's gotta be an inhuman bastard, worse than she was.

Imagine this whole place, all of it, dominated and run by ones like the dragonfly queen."

Sam shook her head in wonderment. "Maybe. I think I could have stood it for me, but those *children*! How could *anyone* defile kids like that? I wanted to do much worse than kill them. I wanted to roast them, live, over a fire and take 'em apart piece by piece."

Charley looked over at the sleeping girls. "Yeah, and they been so quiet. The little one is so full of hate, though, you can feel it, and the big one—you can't tell about her at all. And while I'm glad we saved 'em, I wish I knew what we'd saved them for. They're gonna slow us down and we'll have to have extra supplies for them and protect them in a fight. It's not good, Sam."

The large woman nodded. "I know, I know. You don't know how I want to give in to Boday, find someplace away from it all and just rot there in peace. But, you're right—we've now seen what the enemy looks like and it's not pretty. If stopping them means I got to reach Boolean, then I got to reach Boolean. Bad as this Akhbreed rule over all these colonies is, when I think of guys like the ones we killed rulin' over all the little kids . . ."

Darkness fell quickly as they sat and talked, bringing a hot, dry wind with it as the temperature cooled down to merely intolerable.

"It's a long way from the mall," Charley sighed.

"You ever think about home?"

"Lots. Particularly Mom and Dad and what my disappearance has to have put them through. I think I could take this better if there was some way to contact them, tell them I'm still alive. And I dream of warm showers in comfortable homes and cars and mall hopping and all the rest. God! For high school dropouts we sure dropped out farther and lower than anybody else."

Sam gave a dry chuckle. "I guess that's right. The funny thing is, though, I don't think of home too much. Oh, yeah, I'd like Mom and Dad to both know I'm still alive, too, and I kind'a have this crazy hope that maybe my vanishing act brought 'em back together or something, but every time I think of home I also think of here. Where the hell was I heading? I can see myself as some butch dyke on the make with some job

sellin' shoes or maybe a waitress. I dunno. I kind'a think I was
on my way to poppin' a ton of pills one night or drinkin'
myself to death. So here I am a really gross fat girl hooked up
with a flaky nutso cross between an artist, a madam, and a
pharmacist, stuck out in the middle of nowhere and bein'
chased by who knows what—and no matter what I feel like I'd
pick here over there. I guess I *am* nuts.''

"No, I think I can see it,'' Charley told her. "You got a few
things here you never had back home. Thanks to that potion
you not only have somebody who cares about you but one you
know isn't gonna back stab you later on or hurt you. And you
don't hav'ta get anorexia or do anything to attract other people.
And you got a purpose here. No matter what, you're
important. In a way, all the powers of Akahlar are tryin' to get
you to Boolean or keep you away from him. That may not be
safe or comfortable, but it sure as hell is a big deal.''

"Maybe,'' Sam responded. "but, deep down, I really wish
you were really the one that was important, the one they
wanted. I really don't want this. It's too heavy for me. I think I
could'a been happy just stayin' with Boday in Tubikosa,
cookin' the meals, doin' the laundry and cleaning, and running
the studio and household. It's crazy. What most girls won't
have no part of anymore back home was all I really ever
wanted. Only trouble was, I never wanted to do it with a guy. I
didn't want to admit that, even to myself. It'd kill my mom.
Hell, even I thought it was evil, one of the big sins. It ain't
until you're tied down and stretched out naked while a bunch
of dirty, slimy bastards play with your body that you see how
dumb that is, what real evil and sin is all about.''

"Poor Sam,'' Charley sympathized. "No matter where you
wind up there's something you can't control lousing things
up.''

"Well, at least likin' girls don't bother me no more. I'm
comfortable with it. That's one thing last night did for me. No
more lies, not to nobody, not even to myself. If other folks
can't handle it that's their tough luck. And if I'm okay with
myself as a fat slob, then that's all right, too. Hell, all them
fantasies about me bein' a glamour queen and what the hell
would it get me, huh? I ain't never gonna be my mom, so I
might as well just be me.''

"I guess that's the best way to think about it," Charley told her, "Me, I never figured on any of this, but I *do* like the men. Jeez! Could I use a good fuck right now! Not like what you had," she hastened to add. "I mean a good one."

"I still need you, Charley," Sam said seriously. "Not as a lover but for your strength. Maybe that's why I was so attracted to you all that time. You're more like my mom than I could ever be. Supermom. Lawyer, activist, mother, church deacon—you name it, she's it. Maybe we had the wrong parents. Maybe they switched us when we were babies or something."

Charley chuckled. "Good trick since we were born two thousand miles apart. I'm not sure I ever wanted to be superwoman, but I sure had ambition, that was for sure. I was gonna be a businesswoman, that was for sure. M.B.A. and all. Maybe create a chain of stores or some kind of design business. Maybe even an architect. I spent so much time in malls I could design the perfect one in my sleep. So I wind up a painted courtesan selling myself for money here. No citizenship, no rights, no nothin'. Can't even speak the cockamamie language except in words and gestures. And chased around while everybody thinks I'm you. At this point all I'm interested in is getting you to the big boy so I can get the heat off me. I can't think beyond that right now."

Sam sighed. "Boy, are we screwed up!" She reached down and started scratching her inner thigh. "Tell you one thing I'd kill for from home, though. Some kind of lotion. I've got chafing like mad from thighs to crotch and under my tits. I sure wish Boday had her kit at least." She looked out in the darkness. "That's odd," she said suddenly in a tone quite different than the one she'd been taking.

"Huh? What?"

"It's glowing over there. Many miles away. Like towns glow on the horizon in the dark anyplace. But there ain't supposed to be no towns in this hole! See it?"

Charley shook her head. "Sam, I was trying to keep this from everybody, but I can't see well at all. I've never had perfect eyes—you remember I needed glasses or contacts to drive—but after watching that magic duel it got suddenly worse. I can't say if it's a little better, a little worse, or just the same now, but with you riding just in front of me today I could see you, only blurry. I could tell it was somebody on a horse but if you paid me I couldn't say if it was really you or a total stranger. After you was nothing but a blurry fog. Maybe six or eight feet clearly, then double that very blurrily, and after that I'm blind as a bat."

Sam gave a low whistle. "I didn't need to hear that. You're in the best shape and you're the only decent shot we got. Damn!"

"You're telling me? Without company I'd be dead meat out here now. Of course, now that it's black as pitch it doesn't make much difference. Maybe when we can get to some civilization it can be fixed, maybe with glasses or something. In the meantime, I'll take the shotgun. You don't need to see much to hit with a shotgun."

Sam turned back and looked at the glow on the horizon. "I'd sure like to know what that is," she said at last. "If it's some kind of small town or mining camp we might be able to contact the authorities. If it's an enemy encampment I'd like to know just what we're facing."

"Most likely some bandit camp," Charley replied. "That's who supposedly lives out here, isn't it? Refugees, exiles, and changelings. At least we have some bargaining if it's bandits. The jewelry and stuff from the train they looted plus we know where a bunch of Mandan gold blankets are hidden. They seem to be worth lives around here."

It was for the Mandan gold blankets that the marauding bands of the enemy was stalking and attacking trains, for they were rare and valuable and the only things that could protect you in a changewind. Why Klittichorn and his minions wanted and needed so many was unknown, but clearly it was a high priority. They would have liked to bring the cloaks in the rock arch with them, if only for protection for themselves, but they were far too heavy to carry on horses that also needed to carry riders, and with all wagons broken or destroyed and only one narga healthy and untouched enough to carry a load, they had to sacrifice the blankets for more water and wine casks. They had managed to haul them a ways, though, and more or less bury them under rock and debris away from the main camp.

"Yeah, but most of that type of person or thing or whatever would be just as likely to enslave us and turn it all over to the enemy," Sam pointed out. "After all, he's playing it as the champion of the colonials and the outcasts. No, let's try and slip by 'em and get to someplace where we can slip across the border into someplace cool and rainy where they never heard of you or me."

"Maybe. But if I could see better I'd sure as hell like to take a peek at them. If they're off a ways, then it's even money we'll be camping tomorrow pretty near them if we keep going that way."

"We'll see. We can't go back—they're sure to be sniffin' all around there by now. We can't go to the border—that's a sure way to get caught out in the open. And if we go inland we don't know where we're goin' or what the hell we're doin' and we run out of water fast. Boday's in pretty good shape. Maybe she'll be our scout."

Charley suddenly felt dizzy. "I think it's finally caught up to me. I'm going to try and get some rest. You remember to wake somebody up when you feel it yourself."

"I promise. Get some rest now. We got another day of that sun tomorrow."

Charley went off and Sam turned back to the lookout. The glow was small and subdued, but it remained constant, not like someone or a body of people on the move and certainly larger than a camp. They had money, but no place to spend it, and little else. She scratched again. God! How she could use a long, hours long, bath! A real soak. They were all dirty, sweaty, itchy, and smelled like warmed-over turds. Right about now they needed some allies more than anything in the world.

"I still don't like the idea of that camp or whatever it was over there," Sam said over what passed for breakfast. She was still dead tired, ached like hell, and felt like she hadn't slept at all—but she knew that she didn't feel any different than the others. "If there's no fork later on, this road seems to be heading right for it."

"Boday is for cutting back a bit and making for the border now," the mad alchemist put in. "There will not have been enough time to bring up a force capable of covering the whole border area and we are certainly beyond the rain and bloom period of those *ghastly* plants. If we continue south, on this trail, we might or might not run into whoever is over there, but we would certainly be easy to find from above, either by something flying or even sentries on the high points. To go by night is suicide. To go by day is suicide. To go in any direction is suicide. To stay here is suicide. Let us make for the border!''

Charley listened to the arguments and finally said, "Well, it's clear we can't stay here but we don't dare go back. Somebody's sure to be hot on our trail. I say we go on, now, as soon as possible, before the sun's full up and there's maximum heat, but if there's a fork or anything that takes us towards the border we go that way. I'd rather know what I was facing and shoot my way through than keep *this* up and die of thirst or worse."

Rani looked up at them and spoke in a dry, soft voice. "I know we don't have much say in all this, but I got to tell you that we won't let nobody, no men, no freaks, take us again. We can shoot. I never was sure I *could* shoot nobody before, but I'm sure now."

Charley didn't feel comfortable, particularly with that comment about "freaks." It was hard to remember these were Akhbreed children, born and raised to be masters of the colonial empires. "Just don't you both go shooting *everybody* you see, and everything," she warned. "The odds are most folks we'll meet are not our friends, but not all will be enemies, either. Wait for one of us before firing."

The girls stared at her sullenly, but said nothing.

"All right, then," Sam said firmly. "We go both ways. North and towards the border first chance if it's a trail that looks like it has even half a chance of being able to take horses. Let's pack up and get moving. No matter what, I think we got to stop at midday and find some shade, for our sake and the horses', so the earlier the start the better."

As they rode along, Charley eased up close to Sam. "Sam— just in case, I think we oughta make clear that we're all heading for Boolean. If, somehow, we get split up and can't find each other, that's where we head."

Sam nodded. "Okay by me. I'm not so sure, though, that we're likely to get split up. Killed, maybe, but not split."

After only a few hours it was as if someone had turned up the thermostat to "broil." If anything, it seemed worse than before, and shade more nebulous and not much help when they could find it. Still, they covered quite a good distance before it was clearly time to stop and take some kind of a break. It was hard even to think under these conditions.

Suddenly Boday called out, "Look, loves! The trail splits, and one of it goes down into a canyon. We dare not hope for water but it looks deep enough for cool shade."

They made for it, feeling in no condition to argue, although Sam noticed almost casually that the fork into the shade was going in the wrong direction. Anything right now for relief, she decided.

It was clear very quickly that this was <u>no ordin</u>ary canyon, but a long and relatively straight side break to a much larger formation. The ground seemed to drop away to their left, leaving them with a very narrow trail to navigate through many switchbacks on their somewhat nervous and very tired and thirsty horses. Charley couldn't see much past the edge but she could see to it, and what she saw made her almost glad she couldn't see just how far a drop it was.

But it was all in the shade, at least for now, and as they descended it really did seem to be getting just a little bit cooler, with a slight breeze hitting them from the side.

"This trail's well maintained," Sam noted. "There's a spot we went over a few minutes ago that you can now see up and in back of us. Some kind of rock slide took it out and now it's back, reinforced with rocks and timber. And there have been animal turds, maybe horses', on and off along the path. They aren't fresh, but they don't look all that old, either."

"We approach the main canyon," Boday announced. "See? It looks almost like a river down there. Small, yes, but water! We shall live if but briefly! There are even some trees and bushes along it."

The horses and narga seemed to smell it, too, and gained some confidence and quickness. Charley decided just to hang on loosely and let the horse do the work, and hoped that the others had the sense to do the same.

It took perhaps two hours to fully descend, and the canyon floor was surprisingly narrow, but there was no mistaking the feel and smell of life and the water that brought it.

The animals had no hesitation in heading straight for the

river and drinking from it, and neither did the riders. The river was fairly wide, perhaps a few hundred yards right here, and it was *fast*. This was white water, and treacherous, but there were points at which it slowed as it was forced to turn and at one such place they just let loose.

The water felt cool but not cold, and it was *wonderful*. They took off their gunbelts and blankets and just waded in, sitting in it, splashing it on both themselves and each other, and generally acting like little kids at the beach. They finally got out, in ones and twos, exhausted but happy, and settled on the sandy silt bar caused by the river's bend. "God! All I need is a comb and I can feel almost human again!" Charley exclaimed. "Wow! Did we pick the right turn!"

Boday's head suddenly jerked up and she grew serious, intent. "Perhaps. Perhaps not. Boday thinks she hears thunder far off, and she remembers the last time we were in a canyon in the rain in this cursed land."

The hilarity suddenly stopped and they all strained to hear. "That's not thunder," Sam muttered at last. "That's—horses, or something like 'em. A fair number, too. Too fast to be comin' down the mountain one at a time. They got to be already down here! *Shit!* And us trapped in a squeeze like this!"

"I knew it was too good to last," Charley responded. "At least we never unsaddled the animals. Get the weapons and horses and let's move ahead as fast as we can. Maybe there's someplace up ahead we can make a better stand than here!"

Boday looked around. "They have moved too far upstream in their grazing! Boday can barely see them, and the riders come from that direction! Get the guns and run downstream as fast as you can! Perhaps we will see places to hide out there! The sight of the horses may stop them and buy us some time!"

The sounds left no room for argument. They grabbed their guns and began running as fast as possible along the river trail. They were quickly out of sight around the bend from the silt bar, but things didn't look much better up ahead and there seemed no choice but to keep running for the next bend well ahead and hope they made it before the riders.

It wasn't until they had made it, and stopped, gasping for

breath, that they realized that the rumble of horses had ceased, leaving only the loud river noise.

"I'd say they found the horses," Charley managed. "What's it look like ahead?"

"Not good," Sam managed. Her weight was really telling on her now and she was gasping and coughing and sounding almost like she was going to die. Clearly she wasn't going to be able to take this for much longer.

"Sheer rock walls and darker and deeper," Sam told her, through coughs and gags. "And what do we have? Four pistols and the shotgun. Maybe enough if every shot counted and we were under cover, but let's not kid ourselves."

Charley thought furiously. "Everybody can swim or we wouldn't be here."

Sam managed to stop coughing for a moment. "In *that*? It's white water, Charley! There's rocks and stuff out there, too!"

"Yeah, I know it's dumb, but you got a better idea? We shoot and give up or we just give up or we jump in and try and make it to the other side. There *is* another side, isn't there?"

Sam nodded. "Yeah, but it's not like a continuous trail."

"The hell with it! If we make it over there we'll figure out how to get back when they're gone! They could be here any minute now, too! They won't be ridin' so fast lookin' for us!"

Sam told the others what Charley was suggesting.

"We'll try it," Rani responded. "I would rather drown than be caught and we made it through worse."

"All right," Sam sighed. "Then everybody throw the guns and gunbelts in the water so they won't know we went in here. The trail's hard rock, there won't be prints. Maybe I'll get dashed against a rock but with these tits I sure ain't gonna sink. Boday, you stick close to Charley. She ain't seein' so good lately. I'll try and stick close to the kids. Aim for that bar over there, but if you miss keep goin' down and hide as soon as you can. We'll regroup on the other side of the bend after they're gone."

Slipping into the water now was no longer the fun and luxury it was only a few minutes before, but at least the idea wasn't completely crazy. This was still part of a bend, where the river was forced to slow, and it was less rough and shallower than at many other parts of the canyon. Still, the water was surprisingly deep not too far out, and soon they were all floating at the mercy of the currents.

Charley felt suddenly weighted down by her waterlogged hair and swore to herself she was going to cut it shorter than Sam's if she ever lived to get the chance. She was also disoriented, and suddenly felt Boday's strong hand take her. The tall woman was much stronger than Charley and had little trouble handling her, although getting to the other side while the current picked up speed was more of a trick. Still, after what seemed like an eternity in wet semidarkness, Charley felt herself being pulled from the water onto sandy silt.

"Down and quiet!" Boday whispered firmly in her ear so she would be heard over the roar of the water. "They come."

They flattened out next to each other, and Charley thought that with their sun-darkened skins and the designs of Boday on both herself and Charley they were probably expertly camouflaged to an observer on the other side of the river. She aligned her head more closely with Boday's and whispered, "Sam? Rani? Sheka?" She cursed herself for her inability to speak this language, even though at least she could understand it.

"Can't see 'em," Boday responded tersely. "Perhaps still in the water, perhaps farther down. Boday sees the riders, though. Five of them. They have our horses, curse their souls! The narga, too. Big, tough-looking men in dark uniforms. Not the local army and not thieves. Well organized. They have the cut of those pigs we killed."

They lay there in silence for quite some time, and finally Boday sighed and sat up. "They are gone, or at least they seem to be. We shall wait here awhile before trying any more things, though. Best to be certain that they will not double back when they do not find us. Boday sits patiently and hopes that her wonderful mate is now doing what she is doing and is safe."

*Yeah, safe,* Charley thought glumly. *Even if we stay away from those guys and link back up, we're up this damned creek without a paddle or a stitch. Stark naked, no weapons, no food, no horses or trade goods. Nothing. Every time we think we hit bottom we fall into a damned mineshaft!*

Sam had slipped into the water and tried to stick as close as possible to the two girls. In the swift current it was impossible for them all to link together, so it was mostly a matter of using her strength to keep up with them and catch them if they lost control.

Little Sheka proved an excellent swimmer, while Rani had real problems keeping control. Allowing the smaller girl to swim free, Sam managed to grab on to Rani and keep her from being carried well away, but at the expense of losing sight of the destination on the opposite shore. By the time Sam was able to get hold of and help guide Rani, with Sheka keeping them close, they were already well past the destination and speeding up through the canyon near the center of the current.

Disoriented, Sam saw a number of rocks jutting up just to their left out of the water and at first she was afraid they would be dashed against them. Thinking fast, though, and realizing that they all had only so much strength, she managed to shout to Rani to grab on and, with a near-supreme effort, got hold of a jagged black spire and stopped both of them. She looked around and saw Sheka had managed not only to hold on but to have something of a protected spot on the other side of the larger outcrop.

It had been Sam's purpose only to slow or stop them so that she could get her bearings, but as she looked around through the white water bubbling and hissing and splashing all around she caught a glimpse of the trail side and saw the horsemen and realized that there was nothing to do now but hang on and stay where they were.

The men seemed to deliberate, looking down at the trail for signs of them and occasionally out at the water itself, but they maintained a slow and steady progress through the canyon, not seeing them and not inclined to stop. Whoever they were, they had their priorities, and perhaps if they'd taken any time at all to see what other than casks the narga was carrying they didn't really care if they found the riders or not. The lead and trailing rider had rifles ready, in case of some ambush or trap, but they didn't look too worried.

Sam let them go on until they were well out of sight down the trail and then some. Oddly, it wasn't all that bad clinging to the rocks right there, although getting safely away from them again might well be a problem. She managed to wriggle herself around so that she was facing downstream, seeing now that the narrow canyon opened up considerably a quarter mile or so farther down and that there was another river bend at that point. The shore, more like a rock ledge, opposite the trail side was closer but the way the river was running it wasn't nearly as accessible. Providing they had enough strength to keep out of the center current, it was almost certainly easier to return to the shore they'd left, and it began to look as if the men were not coming back.

"Put your arms around my neck and hold on!" she told Rani. "Sheka—do you think you can swim towards the trail?"

The girl looked, then nodded. "I will make it!"

"All right, then. Three, two, one, *now!*"

Satisfied that Rani was clinging well to her, Sam let go of the rocks and was back out into the main stream again. It was tough and awkward with the girl, but she managed with a supreme effort to get over and beyond the main current and allowed the water to take her down towards the next curve and out of the canyon. She hadn't expected the rocks and silt to have built up to such a level there and almost got hurt when she suddenly struck bottom, but she managed to grab hold of some protrusions out of the water, steady herself, and slowly make it to the shore. Sheka climbed out a few yards down, and they all collapsed for a while.

Sam suddenly was seized by fits of coughing and gagging once more and felt very sick and very sore, and it was some time before she recovered enough to think straight. She was very near total exhaustion, and knew it, but she also knew that her impulse to just stay there was impossible. Somehow they all had to make it out into the wider canyon where they could find some sort of hiding place to collapse and regroup.

Hardly able to stand but urging the two girls up, she managed to get to the trail and look around at the widened canyon. This, at least, showed promise; there were other side canyons going off here now and lots of uneven ground. Not too far off the trail was a rocky prominence that would provide some cover from the trail and shade from the sun. She urged them towards it, her mind only able to focus on getting to that spot and nothing beyond. She wasn't at all sure she could make it, but not only she but the other two did as well. It wasn't great—hard, rusty-red rock—but their spot would not be visible from the trail itself and it provided a bit of relief. They collapsed there, all of them, and Sam simply passed out.

Farther upstream, Charley was wringing the water out of her long hair as best she could while Boday was studying the land and water. Finally she said, "We cannot stay here. It looks as if this side has a narrow ledge going the length of the canyon, so we will try and use it as our trail and not slip and fall in. They must have been carried farther on. Keep your eyes and ears open, pretty butterfly, and we shall see if we can find them."

Both were in much better shape, both physically and in the amount of effort they had exerted to get to safety, and it was not as much of a struggle for them to press on. This shore, however, was not exactly the nice, wide trail area of the other. In places the ledge above the river narrowed to but a few inches, and was never more than two or three feet wide. It was slow going.

Charley was frustrated most of all by the language barrier, which kept her from even sharing her concerns with her companion. The Akhbreed tongue was complex and polytonal; the same thing said in just slightly different intonations could mean something totally different, or turn nouns into verbs and verbs into adjectives, and the rules for what type of word followed what seemed more intuitive than true rules as in English or Spanish, the two tongues she spoke well. Sam was so linked to her counterpart in this world that she had known the language from the start; Charley had no such advantages. The only version of Akhbreed she could use with confidence was the soft singsong of the Short Speech, taught to the unlucky girls who wound up in the red-light districts of the Akhbreed cities as prostitutes or worse; and its inadequate, submissive, slavelike vocabulary contained only a few hundred words at best. Still, it was better than nothing, and any Akhbreed speaker could understand it.

"Does Mistress think the men saw them?" she asked in it.

The artist shrugged. "Boday thinks slowly today, little one. For now we can but follow this shore and see what we can see. If we do not find them soon, then we might assume that they are caught and then we might have to track them." She sighed. "Boday was made to create delicate and beautiful works of art. She was not meant to be an adventurer!"

They made it out of the narrows and to the major new bend in the river where the canyon opened up. The bend was significant enough and slowed the river enough that clearly anyone swept up in the current, or even the body of such a one, would be washed up at this point. Just the lack of bodies against the silt bar on the opposite bank provided them both with some feeling of relief, but it also deepened the mystery.

Boday was thinking furiously. "We know that they could not have made it to our side, as surely we would have come across them by now or at least at this point. They are not hiding and looking for us around here or we would have been hailed. It is a good bet, then, that the children were not up to the crossing and were caught in the current, which would wash them . . . here. Sam, my darling Susama, would stick with them out of duty. Boday fears the worst, little butterfly. If they are not here, and they are not before here, then they *must* have been captured." She sighed. "We will wait a little while for them just to make certain, but if we wait too long we shall be here all night with empty bellies and a cold trail to follow."

Charley nodded. The logic was impeccable. It seemed like they were always chasing after and rescuing each other. It didn't seem fair, somehow. They were naked and defenseless, lost in a strange and hostile land, and, damn it, *they* needed rescuing.

They sat there and waited as the shadows lengthened, until finally Boday sighed and got up. "We should be able to cross here. They are not coming, that is clear. Come, little butterfly. Let us go and see what if anything we can do for them."

Charley sighed and nodded. The crossing wasn't as easy as it looked, but Boday was right; it was here or a long way farther down. They took one last look around and even risked a few shouts of the names of the missing members, but there was no response but echoes.

Sadly, they turned and started down the trail after the men and horses, not realizing that they were less than five hundred yards from those they sought, passed out in exhaustion just beyond their sight and too deep in slumber to hear their cries.

# · 2 ·

## The Outcasts of the Kudaan

SAM AWOKE VERY slowly and groaned. She hurt all over and figured that there hadn't been a muscle not used or a square inch of surface left unbruised. The very act of attempting to sit up caused pain, but she managed it. Her eyes wouldn't focus right; it seemed pretty dark for where they'd settled in, the sky fairly light and clear but sunless, although it seemed to get a little brighter even as she watched. *What the hell . . . ?*

*My god, it's morning!* she suddenly realized. *It is getting brighter! The sun's coming* up, *not going down!*

Quickly she turned to check on the kids. They were there, huddled close together, still out but looking no worse than they had before. Still, they were bruised and burned by the sun and they looked, well, probably almost as bad as she did. *This can't go on,* she decided. *As much as I like them, if they stay with me they're gonna die. Somehow, if we get out of this spot, I'm gonna have to find a place for them. Maybe I'm a shit for giving my word and goin' back on it, but up to now it hasn't been my doing. If I can find 'em a spot and don't take it, though, their blood'll be on my hands.*

She sat back a moment, trying to get her mental bearings. Morning. It had been late afternoon when they'd slid into the river and crawled away from those guys up to here. *That meant they'd slept the whole damned night through!* Charley and Boday . . . Oh, god! If those guys didn't catch them, and it was a good bet they hadn't since she'd seen the riders go past, then the others had probably spent a lot of time looking for them and still missed them.

She tried to think. She'd swallowed a lot of water in and around that river yet she felt dry, her lips almost cracking. *What if we slept two days? Good god, is that possible?* It might be—there was no way to tell. She hadn't had access to a calendar or a watch in a pretty long time anyway, and they had been through so much and been so exhausted. A day and a half, anyway.

She got unsteadily to her feet and managed to go down to the water at the bend. It was shallow enough right in here that she could go in for a little, wash off whatever was on her, and get some of the water on her face and inside her. It helped, although not as much as she would have liked. She felt weak and nauseous and it was just what she didn't need to feel right now. About the only consolation was that if her stomach had anything in it she'd probably throw it up anyway, so there wasn't much loss. Well, unlike the kids, she had plenty of reserves. Considering she had water, she could probably feed off her own fat for a month. *Days without eating, lots of exercise, and I bet I lost maybe two or three pounds*, she thought grumpily. Would nothing ever go right for her here? Would she never get a lucky break?

Suddenly her depressing reverie was broken by the screams of Sheka, and she jumped up and out of the water and rushed back to the hiding place, not quite sure what the hell she could do but knowing she had to try something nevertheless.

She first saw the two girls, huddled together against the rock and staring in stark terror at something beyond. She stopped, turned, and followed their gaze.

He was about thirty feet away, standing still as stone on a rock ledge that had no obvious way up or down but was still about twenty feet up the canyon wall. He was of medium height, well built and muscular, and he was as naked as they were. He wasn't all that handsome but he had a strong face with a prominent Roman nose and maybe a mouth a little too small for its setting, and if he had any ears at all they were hidden in the weirdest-looking haircut Sam had ever seen. He also—well, it was probably the distance and an illusion, but he didn't seem to have any arms.

Sam looked around, found a couple of rocks, and picked them up. Something was better than nothing. "Who are you?" she called out to him, thankful that she'd been able to drink her fill first. "What do you want with us?"

For a moment the stranger said nothing, then he responded, in a soft, rather gentle voice that was both educated and classical in its way, "I was about to ask you that very question. This is my land, and it is not often that I discover three naked Akhbreed women in the midst of it."

Sam decided to gamble on honesty, considering that she had only two rocks and little else to play any other way.

"Look, sir, in the past few days we have been attacked, almost drowned twice, held captive by some very evil sorts who raped and abused us, lost our family and friends and all our meager possessions, hunted through here by more hard-looking men and forced into this condition."

The strange man thought it over. As the first real sunlight came into the canyon and struck him, his eyes seemed to shine, almost like a cat's, when he turned his head slightly.

"You are from the wagon train that was crushed in the flash flood over on the main highway, then," he said, nodding to himself. "You have come a long way."

She clutched the rocks tighter. "You—know about that?"

"Oh, yes. I have been surveying the region for two days now, ever since word of it came, looking for any survivors who might be in such condition as yourselves. This is not a land easy to live in in the best of conditions, and it is a killer if you do not know and love it."

*You're telling me!* "And have you found any survivors?"

"A few."

"And what do you do with them? Everyone we've encountered in this hell since we got here has been trying to rape, murder, or enslave us."

He sighed. "I am Medac Pasedo. My father is Duke Alon Pasedo of the Kingdom of Mashtopol, who holds the governor's position in this district. We are neither bandits nor murderers, and I am incapable of forcing anything upon you myself, but I am almost uniquely qualified to find and bring to safety any who require it."

"Yeah, I bet," Sheka sneered. "And the son of a duke

forgets his pants, right? And what duke would ever be governor out *here*?"

Medac Pasedo sighed. "I am sorry if I offend your morals, but you are not exactly cloaked in modesty yourselves," he noted. "As for me, I find that any clothing that would not inhibit me would be impossible to remove when needed, such as to relieve oneself. That is for the same reason that I am no threat to you and why one such as my father would accept this sort of post." With that Medac raised what should have been his arms, but were not.

They were wings.

Not mere wings, either, but great, majestic wings, fully feathered. He looked one way, then the other, as if either testing the air or waiting for something, then suddenly jumped off the cliff and began to soar, first down a bit, then up and around, soaring and looping, and then coming down and to a running rest on the river trail.

Sam was so startled she dropped both rocks and just stared.

"By the gods, he's a freak!" Rani muttered. "We're in the hands of the freaks! They'll kill us sure, or make us into monsters!"

Sam turned and glared at the two girls who saw only horror in this man, even though she knew it was how they had been raised. She didn't necessarily trust the guy, but whether or not she did wouldn't depend on if he had arms or wings, hair or feathers.

And, in fact, he *did* have feathers, thick ones, from the top of his head back down his back and ending in a birdlike tail that almost but not quite reached the ground. It had been masked by the shadows on the cliff before but was quite obvious now.

"I cannot do you harm," he said as reassuringly as possible. "Hollow bones. Without them I could never fly. Only in the air am I among the biggest and strongest; on the ground I am fragile and easily broken."

Sam was more curious than fearful right now. The fellow just seemed too genuine to disbelieve, and he certainly was vulnerable. "A changewind did this to you?"

He nodded. "There are far worse fates the winds can mete out than this, although it has its disadvantages, not the least of which that I would be under a death sentence anywhere in

Mashtopol proper except the Kudaan Wastes. Rank and blood does have some privileges. Most of the kingdoms have places like this, refuges for the unlucky and the exiled and the sentenced. We are fortunate enough to also have a king who could not conceive of even his transfigured nephew grubbing for food like an animal. My father, who is still very much a full Akhbreed, has established a comfortable refuge in his governor's quarters for those who merely had misfortune and are not running or hiding for other reasons. I can take you to it, if you wish."

"Don't trust no freaks!" Sheka hissed, and Rani nodded nervously.

Sam whirled on them. "This will stop! *Now!* Did your father die so that you can rot in the sun of this land and your bones be eaten by animals? This is no different than catching a disease, or being crippled in an accident. The sooner you get that through your head the better. Now, I don't know if he's telling the truth or not, but I'm going with him. I'm going with him first because there's no place else to go and I'm in no condition to scrabble naked and unarmed over this land. And I'm going with him because he saw us long before we saw him, and if he meant us real harm he could have brought in anybody or anything he wanted without us even knowing until it was too late."

"You're not our real mother," Rani retorted. "You can't talk to us like that."

"Oh, so it's that way, huh? Okay, then, you're on your own, both of you. You can come, and follow orders, and behave yourselves, or you can stay here and strike off on your own. You're right—I have no call on you, but if you stick with me you behave. If you stay here, well and good, but I got a real good idea that within another day or so you'll wind up back under some bastard's thumb, tied up and used as playthings."

"She is quite correct," the bird man put in. "The canyon area is thick with every sort of dangerous type because it is the only aboveground river within hundreds of leegs. The rest are mere springs and oases that will support few and are not numerous. I know the prejudices of the Akhbreed, for I was born and raised one myself. But if I am a mere freak, this land is teeming with monsters, some physically, many more inside where you cannot see but which is far more deadly and dangerous, as well as every sort of criminal, fugitive, madman, black witch, and blacker sorcerer. They will not touch you if you are with me, as I have the protection of Malokis, High Sorcerer of Mashtopol, as a member of the governor's company, and my father's resources and troops and their knowledge of this land are enough to protect us. Here, you might escape them for a day, perhaps two, but sooner or later they will find you or you will run into them."

He said it with such casual confidence that Sam really believed him, and that made her even angrier at the kids, who were acting very irrationally considering the circumstances. The first real break in a long time and they were screwing it up. And Boolean was counting on *her* to help save this damned Akhbreed culture!

"Let's go," she told him. "They can come, or not. Is it far?"

"Not very. About an hour and a half at a regular pace. You just take the trail until it splits off, the main trail following the river and the other going into a steep-walled side canyon. The imperial seal is on a post at the trail branch to note what it is. Follow that branch and you will quickly come to the ducal residence. It is green there and quite grand, really. You can't miss it."

"You're not walking with us?" Sam asked, suddenly apprehensive about that "protection."

"I cannot possibly walk that distance. I will cover you all the way from the air, and if anyone should challenge you I will be instantly there. I am well known here, and I know most of the vermin who lurk about. There is a certain—agreement— between us. They will not break it for their own sakes."

That told volumes about how things worked around here. She would never have suspected that such a terrible place as this would have a governor, but if there really was one then he was damned sure corrupt as hell. This was not merely a refuge or hideout for unfortunate changelings and those cursed by magic, she remembered Navigator Jahoort saying. It was also a hideout and hangout for criminals and political exiles.

"Uh—you say your father has some troops?" she prompted, hoping against hope.

He nodded. "Yes. Enough."

"Do they wear dull green and black uniforms?"

He frowned. "No. Blue with gold trim, as with all Mashtopol forces. Why?"

"The men we lost everything trying to avoid were in those black uniforms. They stole everything we had."

"That is not good. There should be no foreign or irregular forces in here. My father will want to know this. And they went downstream?"

"Yes."

"I shall have a look for them from on high, if they are still anywhere in the area." He made ready to take off.

"Wait! You said you found some other refugees! Did you find any down here? A tall woman with tattoos all over and a young, pretty girl with designs like a butterfly?"

He started at that. "Um, I am quite certain that had I encountered either of the ones you mention I would have remembered. All the rest were discovered above. You are the first and only in the river canyon area."

*Shit! Well, half a loaf is better than none, but where in hell could they be?* "They were with us when this all started. Yesterday, maybe, or maybe the afternoon of the day before. I don't know how long we were out."

He nodded. "Well, once we have you safely at my father's, I will make certain that the word gets out. If they are anywhere in the district I am certain we will be able to locate them." And, with that, he began to run, picking up a fair amount of speed, wings outstretched; and then, suddenly, he rose into the air, perhaps only a few feet at first, but curving, swirling, and with each maneuver gaining altitude.

Sam sighed and turned to the girls. "Well? Are you coming or not?"

Rani looked at Sheka and Sheka looked at Rani and both sighed. "Yeah, I guess so," said the older girl. And, together, they started off down the trail.

They didn't see the winged man anymore, although they occasionally looked around for him, but the trail division was pretty easy to spot. True to the instructions, right at the division was an imposing stone pillar on which were written in professional carved type some very fancy pictographs—Sam knew how to speak Akhbreed but had never learned to read and write it—and a very fancy seal of metal mounted with strong masonry bolts that had obviously been made elsewhere and brought in.

Rani looked at the words. "Well, at least he's telling this much of the truth," she said, studying the monolith. "It says 'Seat of the Royal Governor, Yatoo Canyon District, Commonwealth of Kudaan, Kingdom of Mashtopol.' That's fancier than the one *we* had."

"Well," Sam sighed, feeling a bit irritated that she had to depend on a thirteen-year-old to read her a sign, "at least we now know where we are." She looked down at herself. "Great outfit to meet a royal governor," she added sourly. A year with Boday had destroyed any sense of modesty she ever had, but she sure as hell was gonna make one great first impression.

The difference in the canyon area was apparent almost immediately. Here was the first tributary they had seen running into the main river. It wasn't much more than a creek, maybe ankle deep and six feet wide, but it was real running water and it was coming from someplace, and it appeared to be supporting a fairly large amount of vegetation. It wasn't exactly a jungle, but there were groves of tall, thin trees and other areas obviously cultivated. The trail passed over a number of irrigation canals that had the remnants of water in them, and there were actually some birds and insects about.

And there were people about in those cultivated areas, doing something that farm types might do, whatever that was. Sowing or irrigating or picking or whatever, maybe fertilizing. They were a strange crop; many of them were less human than *creatures*, at least in appearance, with all manner and variety of strangeness. Ones with saucerlike eyes and others with trunklike noses and ones with fur and tails and some too downright weird to categorize easily. They worked well together, though, and with humans. Both males and females seemed to wear only skirtlike garments, the men solid colors, the women colorful patterns, kind of Hawaiian, like before the missionaries had ruined it. There were enough bare breasts that Sam felt a little more at ease, anyway. They were loose here. Well, how strictly religious could a governor be whose son wore feathers and nothing else.

There was something odd about most of the humans, too, though, that she only realized after they had gone a ways in towards the residence. Many bore ugly scars; others had peg legs or one leg and a crutch, or had one arm or even no arms.

"Worse than I thought," Sheka whispered loudly to Rani. "Gives me the creeps. They're all freaks or cripples or worse."

"You watch that kind of talk!" Sam warned. It *was* a little discomfiting, although she wouldn't admit it to the girls, but it was kind of like touring a hospital's worst wards. You felt sorry for the people and at the same time you were damned glad it wasn't you. That's what this place was, really—a hospital, or, more properly, a sanitarium for those with disfigurements that could never be reversed.

Most of the people seemed to live in adobe apartment blocks that reminded Sam of New Mexican pueblos. Most were three levels with those who could climb on top and those who couldn't on the bottom. Most of the changelings, except those whose very form made it impossible to climb, were at the very top. Sam was startled to see some apparently normal human kids around there playing, and there were in fact quite a few who looked like very sun-darkened but otherwise whole Akhbreed. So not everybody here was in an asylum. Perhaps they were staff.

On the side opposite the blocks of pueblo dwellings was an adobe barracks building, stables, and other signs of a small military outpost, complete with two uniformed soldiers standing guard outside the barracks building. They wore the same blue-and-gold uniforms that the wagon train had expected and was almost fooled by, only this time clean and without bloodstains and bullet holes in them. They looked a little hot to wear, but kind of comic-opera snazzy, too.

The main residence, however, was a knockout. It was *huge*—it was nearly impossible to say how huge, but Sam's old two-bedroom bungalow back home would have fit inside the main entry hall alone. Even though it, too, was the pink adobe, it looked more like a grand hotel than anybody's house.

It went up and out at all sorts of angles, with really high peaks and roofs rising at steep angles and then coming down straight. The whole thing was like a geometry lesson, with every shape represented but the triangle as king. There was lots of glass, too, whole walls or roofs of it, and what looked like greenhouses. It was an exotic yet modernist design. The magazines back home would go nuts over it, Sam thought.

Even the girls were suitably awed. "That's the biggest damned house I ever seen," Sheka said in a whisper. "This guy must be the richest grafter in the kingdom. No wonder he don't mind livin' out here."

Sam could appreciate the thought. Sanitarium or not, she'd gone from absolute bottom to this in a very short period of time—and in the nick of time, too. She felt like Dorothy suddenly at the gates of the Emerald City. She deserved one like this, one break at least. She and the girls by rights should have been captives in some criminal lair right now. Instead . . . Jeez . . .

There was a sudden dark thought. *They* were here, by luck and good fortune, but where were Charley and Boday? Who would be hosting *them* tonight, and under what conditions?

A bare-breasted young Akhbreed woman wearing a red-and-yellow flowered skirt came out from the main doors and walked down to them. She looked very normal, physically, which was a relief to the two kids, and she flashed a big smile akin to an official greeter's for the tourists.

"Hello," she said cheerily. "I am called Avala. Medac said you would be coming. The Lord Governor is busy now, but I will see to you if you will just follow me."

"I am Susama, but most call me Sam. These are Rani and Sheka."

"I am pleased to meet you all," responded the woman, sounding sincerely like she meant it. "Come this way."

They entered the house, now feeling more than a little self-conscious, although none of the people about paid them any notice to speak of. The entry hall was enormous and full of hanging plants and covered by a great angled skylight and really did seem more like a fancy hotel than any home. Of course, Sam thought, this was more than a home, it was sort of the state capitol building as well, and maybe even a bit of a hospital and hotel at that.

Rani and Sheka stuck very close as if they were afraid that some of the people going about their business around them

would attack them or even touch them. Most were Akhbreed
"normal," if that was the right word for it, but, here and there,
there were some of the odd-looking, even bizarre changelings
and some Akhbreed who were maimed or disfigured, and more
than a few who looked not like victims but rather people of
different racial types, some rather bizarre or exotic. Colonial
races, here apparently on an equal footing. What was grotesque to the two girls was somewhat reassuring to Sam. Here,
for the first time in Akahlar, were people of both the master and
subject races, changelings, and people with disfiguring or
debilitating deformities who would have little chance to be
more than beggars in a city like Tubikosa, all mixing with
apparent ease on a more or less equal basis. Maybe this duke
had the negatives of royalty and the rest, but in some ways he
certainly seemed a visionary, even a revolutionary. Here was
the dream that Klittichorn promised to buy Akahlar with blood,
only realized by a member of the established order.

That did give her a little twinge of worry, though. Duke
Pasedo seemed very much the type of man who might be on the
side of the horned wizard and his minions, if not openly at least
secretly. Sam couldn't help but have a nagging worry that in
spite of all this she might well have walked into the front door
of the enemy that sought to kill her.

They were led almost immediately to a wing of the building
that was obviously used as some kind of transient quarters. The
rooms were fairly large and generally resembled a high-class
Akahlar hotel, with large feather mattresses and pillows, a
dressing table, night stand with cold running water, and what
appeared to be a shared toilet. There was even a small balcony
nook just out a glass door, with a table and two chairs looking
out on the canyon area. The finish was adobe, as were all the
buildings, but it felt sound and fairly cozy. No bathtub or
shower was provided; as was the usual custom, there would be
a common bathhouse for that, usually one for each sex,
although as casual as they were around here it might be coed
like the lower-class places she was used to.

The room next door interconnected through the shared toilet,
and Sam got one room and the girls the other. The pair seemed
to be delighted by the room and bed and Sam looked at her own
enviously. Still, first things first. "We haven't eaten—maybe

for days," she told Avala. Curiously, she felt more dizzy and weak than hungry, but she knew what had to be done to get any sense of normalcy.

The woman nodded. "I will have something sent up to you all. It is between normal mealtimes here, but I am sure we can find something filling. I will also have one of the housekeepers send up some clothing now that I have been able to see you and know what is required. Please just relax and remain here for now. All that you require will be sent up to you, and after a day or so, when you are fed and rested once again, I am sure My Lord the Duke will wish to speak with you all. If you have any needs or requests, just push the button by the door there. That will ring a bell and bring someone. Tell them to ask for Avala."

"You have been very kind," Sam told her. "Thank you."

The woman kept smiling. "It is my function," she responded enigmatically, and left.

They were as good as their word and even seemed to have anticipated their arrival. Within just a few minutes a man wearing a sarong of sorts brought in a large tray full of small sandwiches, fruits, raw vegetables, and cakes, then another appeared pushing a small cart with two carafes of wine, a pitcher of dark beer, and another pitcher of fruit juice. Sam appreciated the juice touch; she had never really gotten used to a society where the kids drank wine with meals just like the adults, although it didn't seem to do them much harm.

The two girls mostly nibbled, though, as if their systems had become unused to food, and even Sam had a tough time, although the food wasn't at all bad. Even though they'd passed out for God knew how long on the rocks, none of them felt as if they had had any real sleep in weeks. She forced them to eat what they could by badgering, but it was clear that they were still very tired and still had borderline shock, both physical and mental, and she had little trouble pressing them both to go back and get in bed. They were out in minutes, and she stood there, again looking at them and feeling guilty. She liked them—most of the time—but she had no right to drag them through this. Not anymore, if this Duke could help at all.

She went back into her room and closed the door and sat down, trying to think. The transition had just been too sudden, too great. From that horrible night to fleeing across a scorched desert landscape to losing everything including the only ones in this world that meant anything to her, and now, suddenly, this. She started nibbling again on the sandwiches and drinking some of the beer.

*Maybe I'm in shock, too,* she told herself. *How would I know?* It must have been *something,* since she felt oddly drained, washed out, almost distant from herself and her circumstances. Maybe one day there would come a time when she could just unbottle it all and cry it out for two or three days, but not now. The less she wanted duty and responsibility and all that the more she seemed to get. All that time she had dreamed of Akahlar back home, and many of the dreams were scary, she had still loved it because it was distant; romantic because it was just something from her imagination. Now she was here, and it was real, and it wasn't very romantic at all. Powerful people were still trying to kill her, and every time she found something at least comfortable it had been snatched away. Now even Boday and Charley were out there someplace, separated from her. She hoped they were still alive, still okay, but if Medac couldn't find them or they didn't blunder in here, what then? She would be entirely on her own.

But if they were okay, how could they have missed that big stone monolith with the imperial seal on it? Boday could read the thing, and they'd be nuts not to head for here.

So she was on her own. Now what? This place should feel comfortable, but something about it felt threatening and she couldn't pin it down. If it were a threat of some kind, what could she do about it? There was no place to run, no place to hide.

*It's growing-up time,* she thought nervously. *No magic demon, no Charley, no Boday. Nobody but me. And I'm not even sure who I really am or who or what I can be. Damn it, it's not fair!*

She felt a little giddy all of a sudden. Without really realizing it, she'd been drinking the beer as she sat there, munching on the contents of the tray, and then she'd had some of the wine. It was only when she tried to pour a refill and nothing came out that she realized that it was all gone. There had been a considerable amount of food and drink there and she had gone through it all without even thinking. And, the fact was, the aches had subsided, the nausea she had been feeling had gone away, and although she felt very tired and a little bit drunk she felt, physically, far better. She made her way over to the bed, plopped down, grabbed a pillow, and was out like a light.

She was out cold, but only for a couple of hours; it was just getting dark outside when she awoke, feeling remarkably clearheaded and not half-bad. Usually booze had a terrible effect on her, and quickly. Maybe after all this time in Akahlar, where they drank mostly beer, ale, or wine with meals due to suspect water, and her added weight had increased her tolerance, she thought. Well, something good had come from it.

Much of what went in got processed fast, though, and she was on the toilet for a fairly long time. After, she felt oddly famished, and decided to check on the girls and maybe find out about dinner. She was surprised, but not yet worried, to find the girls' room empty. As far as she knew, they were guests here, refugees as it were, not prisoners. She went back into her room and to the sink and looked at herself in the mirror. The sun had certainly taken its toll; she was tanned about as dark as she could ever remember, but she kind of liked the effect. If you were gonna be fat you should look Italian or something like that.

Her hair was a rat's nest, but there was an advantage to keeping her hair short, even though she knew that fat faces tended to look better with long hair. All you needed was a comb and brush, which they'd provided, a part in the middle, and you looked socially presentable. She needed a bath, or maybe a couple of hours of hot soaking, but until she found out where it was and when it was available there was no sense in wishing for what she didn't have.

Only then did she notice that someone had been and gone while she slept. The remnants of that first meal, what little she'd left, were gone, and there were clean face cloths and other things on the small dresser. There were a couple of outfits, one beige and one cinnamon, made out of the stretch-type material that seemed very common in Akahlar. They were cling-type two-piece outfits that would do nothing to disguise or support her giant jugs or mask her spare tires and blimp ass, but they would fit and they would be reasonably comfortable and, unless you had custom tailors on the premises, were about the only choice when faced with someone with a less-than-average physique. There were also sandals of the extra-large and extra-wide variety and a pair of ankle-length soft skin boots with turn-down tops. She was familiar with the type; they looked decent and would spread for wide feet, but they didn't have much give and had little support inside. They were a bit long and not comfortable, but even though the sandals would feel better they'd look tacky. She had the distinct idea that this was more casual evening wear. She decided on the beige. Considering her tan, the cinnamon would just make her appear still naked.

There was also a small pack of cosmetics and some minimal jewelry that didn't look very expensive or fancy, but she passed on them. She'd never felt any particular need to use them in the past, except when trying to humor Charley back home, and she didn't really feel any need for them now. The right earrings might have helped set off her face a little, but the first and last time she'd had her ears pierced was when she was fourteen and she wasn't about to do it herself.

At last she felt as ready as she could be—but for what? *All dressed up and no place to go,* she thought suddenly. *Well, when in doubt ring the bell.* She went over to the button just inside the door and pushed it. In about a minute there was a soft knock, and she opened it to find a tall, thin, middle-aged man there wearing the usual sarong. He didn't say anything, so she said, "I was told to ask for Avala."

He stared a moment, then pointed to his ears and his mouth. With a start, Sam realized he must be deaf. She looked up into his face and said, very exaggeratedly, "Ah-va-lah." He nodded, held up a hand that said, "Wait," and walked on down the corridor.

Lip reading must be real fun with a multitone language where how you said something was as important as what you said, she thought. For that matter, how had he heard the bell? She looked out and down the corridor and saw a small desk there, and then looked up at the outside of her own room and the other rooms on the hall. They all had lights over the doors and little switches like doorbells next to them. So that's all the "bell" did—flashed the light like a stewardess call button and kept flashing until he saw it and came and turned it out.

Avala came in another minute or two. She was still bare-breasted, but the patterned skirt she was wearing was much fancier, her long hair had been neatly combed and hung on both sides of her shoulders, she had sandals on, and wore a kind of lei around her neck made up of big, pretty pink and gold flowers with greenery linking them. Sam found the whole effect very attractive.

"Hello, how do you feel now?" the woman asked her, always with that cheery smile.

"Fine. You've been almost too good to me. I'm feeling hungry and I need a long bath, but I'll survive."

Avala gave a slight chuckle. "My Lord the Duke is very busy right now, but we can go to the staff dining room. Later on I will show you the public areas of the residence and you can bathe as long as you like. The springs that come out here are hot mineral springs, so we have many bathhouses that are much better than just tubs."

The staff dining room was a large area, nicely styled, that was basically a buffet. You got what you wanted, picked a seat along communal tables, and ate whatever you wanted and as much as you wanted. There were some areas that made special provisions for physical abnormalities, and while they weren't being used then Sam wasn't sure she wanted to see what would fit in those types of seats.

There weren't many in the dining room. While dinner was up now, the bulk of the staff ate at particular times on a schedule and the room tended to open early for "guests" like Sam and various senior staff members who did not fit the regular schedule.

"Where are the two girls that came in with me?" Sam asked as they gathered the food, which looked and smelled tremendous.

"They found you asleep when they awoke and rang for me much earlier," Avala told her. "We have a number of children here and children's facilities, and we also wanted them to be looked over by our treatment staff to make sure they had no ill effects from their exposure. You will be looked at as well, when you feel up to it."

"Any time after a bath," Sam told her, feeling somewhat at ease. The state of medicine in Akahlar wasn't all that good. There weren't any doctors as such, and a lot of trust was placed in alchemists, magicians, and a host of people who were nothing more than civilized and pretentious witch doctors— although some knew their specialties and some of their oddball charms, herbs, rituals, and potions really worked. The trick was, without real standards, finding the good from the charlatan. Still, these people had gone through a lot and seemed to be in decent health, at least as healthy as they could be considering the state of things.

She was amazed and a bit embarrassed by her appetite, and a bit disturbed that she was only partly aware of how much she was eating until it was done. She'd put on the fat herself in that year with Boday, but the demon in the Jewel of Omak had cursed her to keep it until she got to Boolean, but had assured her she would have whatever energy she required if needed. She considered that. She'd just been through several days with little or no food and had managed, in spite of her weight, to ride great distances, hike, climb rocks, swim, and in general do the sorts of things on a sustained basis that she might have expected one in far better shape to have managed. Now her body was demanding payment. The curse was insisting on being maintained.

That made it a little easier, really, since it removed the guilt. *What the hell, if I gotta be fat why not enjoy it?* she asked herself, and did not skip dessert.

The question of guilt settled, she turned her attention to why she felt leery about this place in spite of its wondrous appearance. The staff was one reason. They all seemed eternally cheery, even the ones with handicaps or disfigurements, yet from just listening in the dining room she found that they talked little among themselves and generally about inconsequential things or the events of the day. The problem was, how to get some information without seeming to.

She turned to her companion and guide. "Were you born here, Avala?"

To Sam's surprise, the young woman shrugged. "I am sorry, but I really do not know," the guide told her. "I have been here, on the household staff, doing various things as long as I can remember."

"And before? Your parents? Brothers and sisters?"

Avala shrugged. "I do not remember. They say I was found, long ago, wandering in the desert, unable to tell them anything. I do not even remember that. It does not trouble me. I am happy here and performing a useful function."

So even the "normal" humans around were actually wards. Still, the way the guide and hostess was so satisfied and apparently not even curious about her past enough to wonder about it bothered Sam. A spell, or potion, or even some Akahlarian therapy? It was impossible to say, but from the similarity of the staff it was probably one of the first two.

As Sam was shown around the palatial estate, some judicious questions brought out that Avala had no concept of the world beyond the canyon here, and no interest in it, either. She was interested only in what concerned her life here and totally uninterested in anything outside of this cloistered life. Either she was limited in her mental capacity, which didn't seem obvious or even likely, or the way she was was the way she was *supposed* to be or maybe *compelled* to be, although she was unaware of it. Of course, there was a possible innocent explanation as well, since she seemed neither overworked nor exploited in particular. Suppose she *had* been found wandering in the Wastes, and suppose she hadn't had amnesia but rather tremendous shock. Sam herself would never forget being tied down and gang raped, and she knew that the horrible scars she would have to live with inside were almost certainly magnified in Rani and Sheka no matter how they were hiding it now. Suppose that kind of fate, but sustained over a very long time until the mind just broke, had been Avala's? Suppose the choice was to leave her in a living mental hell or wipe out everything? It would fit the apparent philosophy of this place.

The Emerald Sanitarium of Oz.

The baths were quite nice; natural bubbling hot springs were allowed to flow into chambers. It was sort of like a nature-made hot tub and it really helped the aches and pains. Then clear water rinsed you, and you felt both clean and relaxed, although if you stayed in the bubbling mineral baths too long you had the muscle control of a wet noodle.

When she got back up to the rooms she found Rani and Sheka there, and she had to confess to herself that she was somewhat relieved they had indeed been out doing just what Avala said they were doing. They had seen the "examiners"— no big deal, Sheka assured Sam—and then they had been taken in tow by some girls their own age and shown around some of the outside of the place and even played and got to be kids again for just a little while. They were quite happy about it, although Rani let slip that they had thrown a fit when the first set of examiners had been men and that women were then substituted. "I just—can't—let a grown-up man *touch* me," Rani said, a little apologetically. "I knew that all the men we saw today were just being nice or polite, but I just couldn't *handle* it. Not yet. Maybe not ever. I just keep seeing those— those—*animals.*"

"Me, too," Sheka agreed. "One of these days I'm gonna find a place with no boys at all, not even tomcats or stallions, and *no* freaks, neither, and *that's* where I'm gonna live!"

Sam sighed. "I know it was tough and I know it's going to take a long time to learn to live with it, but you both know that those evil men who did that to us weren't normal men. They were vicious, no better than animals, and they got what they deserved. And you're also going to have to learn that these 'freaks' are just people who had something bad happen to them, something they could no more control than catching a cold, only lots worse."

"That's all funny, comin' from *you*," Sheka said acidly.

Sam stiffened. "What do you mean by that?"

"Well, I never saw *you* makin' friends with no men, and you're something of a freak yourself. I mean, you didn't just live with a girl, you *married* her."

Now what the hell do you say? "You're a little young to explain that, but don't think I don't like some men—nice men—or won't in the future. I may not want to have a romance with them, but I don't want a romance with most women, either. It's normal to be a little afraid right now. These are all strangers, men and women alike. I admit I might be a little nervous for quite a while alone walking down a street with strange men about, but I'll do it because I *have* to. And don't forget their leader was a woman."

"A damned changeling freak!" the girl retorted. "Like the ones crawling all over this place. I don't think I'll feel better until we're out of here."

"Well, you'd better get used to it and make the best of it, because we're stuck here until they can make arrangements to get us not only away from here but safely out of Kudaan. I asked about it and they are generally supplied by a caravan that comes through every week to ten days, and one was here only a few days ago. It also suits me to stay for a bit until I can get some word on Charley and Boday. Either way we'll go with the caravan and then we'll see a certain navigation company and claim our free passage, resupply, and insurance and be on our way. All right?"

Sheka sighed. "All right, all right."

Sam looked over at Rani, who was lying on the bed face up, staring at the ceiling, a rather odd expression on her face. She looked, in fact, like she was going to cry, but was repressing the tears. "Rani—is there anything else wrong?"

"No. It's all right."

"Come on. Tell me. It might help and it can't hurt."

Rani sighed. "It—it was one of the girls we were with today. Her dad came over for her. He—for a moment—I thought he looked—well, like, Daddy." And then she did start to cry, but just a little, for Sheka's sake.

Sam shook her head and said what comforting things she could. Damn it, they didn't just have one whammy, they had two, and the loss of their parents and brothers was perhaps more devastating than even the brutalizing, since it was those very people who could have helped them over the ugliness. Sam got them into bed and turned out the light and went back to her room. She felt a little like crying herself at this point, but at least it wasn't over her own problems this time. Something like this would knock the self-pity right out of you.

The next day, Sam ate a prodigious breakfast and then was off for her own trip to the examiners. They seemed a bit gun shy after the girls; they provided a man and a woman for her, the man well up in years, gray-haired and cherubic, the woman maybe in her forties and with a real professional look and air.

They introduced themselves as Halomar and Gira; he was a healing magician, she an alchemist. They gave her a surprisingly thorough physical, even using a primitive form of stethoscope, and they wanted blood and urine samples. Sam didn't like that part—she knew that body samples were useful to black magic here and that giving some of your own free will was almost putting your life in another's hands, but there was little choice.

Halomar did most of the physical, but it was the woman, Gira, who took the samples and also sat down to ask some questions while the magician took notes on a worn pad.

"Your name is Susama Boday," she said more than asked.

"Yes."

"That is a married form, but both names are feminine."

Sam shrugged. She had decided not to give excuses or long-winded explanations anymore. "Yes, I have a legally registered statement of union at Tubikosa. My wife is still missing somewhere in the Wastes."

"Hmmm . . . It takes courage to do that in a strict place like Tubikosa. I can see why you were leaving. I take it that you are comfortable with it, though, and that you have no self-doubts about your nature and orientation."

*Of* course *I have self-doubts, you asshole! And I'm decidedly* not *comfortable when I'm put on the spot like this and forced on the defensive like I'm some kind of Sheka's freak!*

"Yes," said Sam. "She's also an alchemist, by the way. Want to fool around?"

The alchemist started slightly, then realized she was being baited and regained her cool composure. Still, partly to help his colleague, Halomar decided to step in.

"Were you aware that you were under some rather strange spell?" he asked.

Sam nodded. "It didn't put on this weight but it keeps it on."

"Ah! So that's the basis. It was quite complex. You should be careful, though. It is very strong, and it would take an Akhbreed sorcerer to lift it, and even then with difficulty. You can't keep any weight off at the level you were when it was imposed, but you can still gain, and what you gain if kept over any period of time will become part of the curse and will stick. Your height is seventeen point four krils and your weight is a hundred and two and a fraction halg. In other circumstances we would say that was dangerous.''

Sam did some quick mental calculations. She knew she was around five one—she'd always been damned short—and a halg she figured once was about two and a half pounds. Jeez—two fifty-five, and that was *after* days of starvation and exercise!

"So how am I supposed to keep it there?"

"Exercise daily and vigorously," he told her. "All you can. It is all you can do. Your heart is surprisingly strong, your lungs are moderately clean, and your blood pressure is surprisingly normal for one of your weight. Considering all you've been through, I would say that was incredible. Exercise will certainly help.''

"Your periods—how are they?" the woman asked.

She shrugged. "I used to have 'em pretty bad but they've been mild and just spotty since I gained all this weight. I guess that's the one bright spot in it. My last one was two weeks ago, more or less," she added. "I haven't exactly been paying attention to the calendar." *And the demon who stuck me with the weight also shut down the egg factory, so I haven't been too concerned about it,* she added to herself.

She realized what they were asking for—she had, after all, been a victim of multiple rape—but aside from the fact that it was still a little painful down there she didn't think there were any lasting physical problems from it. It was more the extra layer of fear and anxiety it put into her in even normal, casual circumstances that was the real scar. She had never given much thought to walking alone, even in the evenings, even in the rough district of Tubikosa where they'd lived that year, but now she found it impossible to consider walking anywhere alone that wasn't brightly lit and didn't have people around.

Finally, they asked her about future plans, and there she decided to be very circumspect. She had a reasonable idea by now that these people had no idea of who she was and that she was being hunted by somebody important, but she didn't want to find out whose side they were on by letting anything slip. She had an idea that the magician could tell truth from falsehood, but limited truths would ring no bells.

"I wish to find my companions, if possible," she told them. "Whether or not they are found, though, I will continue on. This curse was a product of a magic charm, no longer any good even if I still had it, produced by a sorcerer to the northwest. I was assured that he or one of his associates could lift it if I got there."

They nodded, and the alchemist then asked, "And then what?"

"Huh? I don't understand."

"Suppose you get there and the curse is lifted—what then? Do you have family, tribe, or profession to call upon?"

It was an unexpected and somewhat disconcerting question since, indeed, she had none of those. How best to answer?

"I am told," she said carefully, "that anyone who triggers this curse can be assured of some employment by the people who can remove it."

"Hmph!" said Halomar. "The sort of way these things work, I wouldn't want to be the object of such a curse. You could well wind up being research subject for new spells or worse. And the children? How will they be provided for?"

She shrugged. "I have always managed to fill my needs. I admit I would like to see them safe and secure someplace, but unless I was absolutely certain it was in their best interests I am prepared to do whatever it takes to raise them to adulthood."

They leaned back and whispered to one another too low for her to hear. Then Gira picked up a piece of paper—a form of some kind—and slid it to Sam. "Please read this and sign it and that will be all, I think," the alchemist said pleasantly.

Sam looked at the pictographic writing, no two characters alike, and again felt embarrassed. "I'm sorry—I know my native tongue but I never learned to read Akhbreed."

The paper was withdrawn. "That is all right." Gira paused for a moment, thinking, then said, "You are in surprisingly good health considering your ordeal. It is customary, after a physical approval, that our guests here do some work in lieu of payment, if they are up to it. Would this bother you?"

"No," Sam replied. "In fact, I was feeling kind of guilty about taking all this with no way to pay it back as it was. What sort of work?"

"We have some wide agricultural holdings here, making the desert bloom in the only part of the region where it *can* be made to bloom. In this we not only make ourselves self-sufficient in food and cloth but also experiment with new ways of growing things. This is spread out along the river and is planned so that something is always being harvested and something else planted. Now we are harvesting *enu* groves in a small valley about nine leegs from here. It is physical work but requires no special knowledge or skills."

Sam nodded. "Sounds fair, I guess." She didn't really like the idea of hard physical work but, what the hell, it was only for four or five days and she owed it.

"Very well. I will have Avala outfit you and take you there. Avala herself began with us there and she knows it well. Thank you."

Sam got up, then shook hands all around, and Gira showed her to the door where Avala was waiting outside. "Susama has volunteered for the picking crew. Will you see that she gets there and gets what she needs?"

Avala bowed slightly. "Of course. Come, it will be good to get out in the air for a while."

Gira watched them go, then shut the door and went back over to her colleague.

"She is something of a survivor, but toughness is not a good measure of her best interests," Halomar noted.

"I was thinking the same thing," Gira agreed. "She is illiterate, without family, tribe, or skills. By her own admission here she lived entirely as a housekeeper for her missing mate who is, or was, both artist and alchemist and sufficient to be a provider for both. Her sexual orientation makes it unlikely she will settle in any conventional family scheme, and she is hardly the type for courtesan work. The best she could hope for would be some sort of menial job. Otherwise, she'll be a social outcast anywhere. She certainly has a low self-image; even with her weight she seems to go out of her way to make herself look plain and unattractive. If there weren't the matter of the curse the decision would be simple."

Halomar nodded. "I agree, particularly in light of the children. Even in the best of circumstances those children would have no future with her, a fact even she tacitly acknowledges. But those children are torn up inside, as you well know, and have no anchor in family or in law. At best they would wind up of necessity being slipped some potion and working as whores to support Susama, whose background is in that seamier side of life anyway. Their hurt and prejudices are deep. I do not think Directors were wrong in fearing that eventually they might suicide without support and a stable family life. As for Susama's curse, I said that exercise will control it and she is surprisingly healthy as she is."

"Yes, that is why I thought immediately of a field worker. It is good exercise and is something constructive she can do. Avala knows enough to make certain she gets the potions that will ease the strain and aid the transition to real work."

"And precondition her as well. I believe we would be criminals if we let those children go off with her, but unless we also take in Susama it would be very difficult to do."

"Yes, I thought the same."

"If she were to have her memories and personality permanently erased and a newer, simpler one built," Halomar suggested, "she would fit in perfectly as a permanent field worker—planting, picking, and the like—and get heavy daily exercise to boot. With the aid of some careful guidance and hypnotics or spells she could almost certainly be reoriented sufficiently to be happy in a heterosexual relationship. Of course, we've already agreed that erasure is the only hope of saving those children."

The alchemist sighed. "Exactly my thinking. We have done it so many times before with poor unfortunates that it would not be at all difficult to handle gently and unobtrusively, but we would have an embarrassing, even awkward, situation if then her mate walks in. In that instance, it could be quite— *difficult*—for the Duke."

"We could cover," responded the magician, "but it is best to play it a bit cautiously. It is five days until the next caravan— Crim's, I believe, which is a good choice, since Crim won't care or ask questions one way or the other. If neither or both of the missing pair are located within that time it's safe to assume that they never will be. You and I both know this country, and the additional time will give us an opportunity to test her in this role without committing anyone. Of course, the final decision is His Grace's, but I will recommend treatment on the morning five days from today if the conditioning tests are satisfactory and nothing else develops."

"Five days seems more than safe," Gira agreed. "I'll write it up for the Directors and His Grace today."

# · 3 ·

## Of Brigands, Scoundrels, and Slaves

BODAY STEPPED AND suddenly froze, her face a mask of revulsion. She looked down and said, disgustedly, "We are still following them. Perhaps we follow *too* closely. The horse dung is still *very* fresh."

Charley suppressed something of a giggle. She looked up and around and saw a large stone monolith with carving and a fancy seal on it. "See, Mistress—the way goes in two, and what is that?" She hated the demeaning Short Speech but it was all she had. Boday knew no English and Charley's mouth simply wouldn't form Akhbreed. She was only thankful that her ear for languages and liking for music allowed her to understand—mostly—what was being said. To be in this position and effectively mute was inconvenient; to be essentially deaf would be intolerable.

Boday finished wiping what she could against the dry grass near the river and came up to look. "It appears to be an Imperial seal," she said, marveling. "It says that there is a Governor's residence down there. Difficult to believe in this desolation that anyone would *bother* with a Governor."

"Does Mistress think they might go there?" It was a real hope.

Boday sighed and thought about it. "There is more fresh dung going straight, and we know now that it is most certainly the riders with all our belongings and horses and perhaps Susama as well. This is too far along. Why would they have come here instead of waiting for us? No, the evidence points to them being captured by the riders. They go slowly because of their extra load anyway. Boday is thinking! Ah! What we must do is follow the riders for now, while there is still daylight. If we fail to catch up with them, at least sufficient to see if they do or do not have Susama and the girls, then we will return here and beg the Governor's help."

"Might he not help now, Mistress?"

Boday shook her head. "No, any Governor of a place like this is either in deep disgrace or he is the ringleader for all the criminal bands in the area. We might well be forced to him out of sheer hunger or desperation, but until we must Boday would like to avoid it. There is no sign of any recent horses save those we follow, so it is unlikely that this Governor's people found them and took them in, but it is quite likely that they had their hands in the raiders who attacked the trains. If so, one good look at you, my little butterfly, and you will quickly meet your horned pursuer. Never mind that he will then see through the deception. That will simply make my Susama the obvious target and our own fates will be most unpleasant. No, while Boday could happily eat one of her missing horses, she is tough, she can do without for now. We know where this place is now. We can always fall back on it as a last resort."

Charley nodded, seeing her logic. This was the Kudaan *Wastes*, for Pete's sake! Who would a Governor govern, and why? But an Akhbreed noble who had both official standing and criminal connections out here, with no other authority around, would be an ideal ally for Klittichorn. Damn it, if they just didn't think she was Sam this would be all suddenly very simple!

So they continued on, moving well past the cutoff, although Boday noted that here and there breaks in the rugged landscape showed distant groves and greenery, and more than once they passed small, expertly engineered gates like the tiny locks of a miniature canal leading to under the trail culverts that obviously sent water to that far-off but lush-looking region. They were too far for Charley to see the groves, but the irrigation canals were unmistakable and she took Boday's word for the rest. Whoever that guy was, he was smart and he had smart people working for him, too. The odds were that the community over there was entirely self-supporting, but that made it doubly dangerous. They would be their own masters, paying only lip service to any central authority, and open to all sorts of influences.

After a while, Boday looked up, studying the vegetation that covered the river bank, and pointed. "Boday is *starved*!" she exclaimed. "And, look! Some of these trees and bushes have ripe fruit! They must be wild offspring of those farms, carried here by the winds!"

"Mistress, we fall more back if we eat," Charley noted in the only way she could.

"Bah! You can see that this canyon runs a very long way, and it is too late in the day for anyone to think of climbing out, so they are not going to climb out today. They, too, must eat, must make camp or reach a destination. If we do not eat ourselves we will be in no condition to do what must be done later."

There was no arguing with that logic, although Charley couldn't help but wonder what the hell they could do if they caught up to the riders. At least back at the rock arch she'd had guns and a well-armed and well-staked-out ally above, and she'd had eyesight well enough to use them. What were they going to do? Take on all those armed and dangerous guys with rocks?

Much of the fruit was overripe, but enough was still good or at least edible that they couldn't really complain. Charley managed to polish off two medium-sized *alu*, which was a lavender-colored fruit shaped like a bottle that looked inside a lot like pink apple and tasted more like a super-sweetened pear. The two of them stuffed her, although she'd eaten next to nothing for more than a day. She hadn't had much of an appetite since taking on this courtesan look, but she knew that she should be hungrier after this kind of fast and exercise than she was. Still, she felt neither sick nor particularly weak or dizzy and she was probably less tired than she should have been, so perhaps she was worrying too much. She was much more afraid of losing her eyesight than starving to death, anyway.

Boday ate well. That had been part of Sam's problem back in Tubikosa, really. Boday was the kind of person who ate all the good things in huge quantities and then complained that she could never gain any weight.

After a while, though, Boday picked up a last *alu* and got up. "Come, little butterfly! We wish to see if we can catch them before night, although Boday would *kill* to just sleep for ten or twelve hours!"

The shadows were getting long and the sun low before they got close. Boday put out a hand and stopped Charley. "*Habadus!*" she hissed. "Lots of them!"

It wasn't a word Charley knew, but the root indicated some sort of bird. She couldn't see but so far, but she strained at the sky and thought she could see some kind of dark, blurry movement. "What . . . ?"

"Carrion-eating birds. This is not good."

*Vultures!* They were some kind of vultures, these *habadus*. Giant suckers, too, if she could make out anything of them.

Following Boday's lead, they inched forward, a bit off the trail and using what cover they had, until they could see just what the big birds were feeding upon. Charley had a sudden fear that it was going to be very familiar bodies, and she almost didn't want to know for sure.

You could smell the death from here, all torn and rotting in the sun. Boday checked the whole thing out carefully, then stood up. "Come. There is nothing left living here except the birds, and even though they are as big as you are they will flee us. They have no stomach for living things." She paused a moment, then added, "Well, at least their Tubikosan relatives do not."

*Thanks a lot,* Charley thought sourly. There was cross-pollution, particularly of vegetation and birds, among many of the worlds of Akahlar, but there were vultures and there were vultures.

Between the flapping of enormous wings and the birdlike cries of protest, they walked among the scene of carnage and even Charley could see the very gory details and found them sickening.

Two dead horses, but no sign of the others. Lots of human bodies, though. Six, all male, stripped as naked as could be, their bodies and heads ripped open and mutilated, the blood merging into drying pools nearby. It was impossible to tell what damage had been done by the birds and what by the attackers, but it made no difference in the end.

"No bridles on the dead horses, no saddles or packs, the men stripped clean. These are the ones from whom we fled, little one. There is no doubt of that. And one of those poor horses is the very one Boday was riding! Pity. They were attacked suddenly, massacred, and stripped clean of everything of even the slightest value or use. If any had gold teeth they most certainly do not now. Boday is surprised they didn't skin them, too."

Charley felt as if she was going to be sick. "Sam . . . ?" she managed, moving out of the midst of the carnage.

"No. Rest easy, my pretty one! Boday will know if Sam dies. We are linked by potion and spell. No, since only the men died, it is probable that she and the others were taken by the attackers." Boday was suddenly very clinical and deliberative. "The blood and condition of the bodies put this at at least two hours ago. The attackers, they were very efficient, I think."

Charley was away from it. It helped, but not much. "Does Mistress think the—governor—did this?" She was beginning to have confidence enough to attempt a few needed words, as badly mauled as they might be.

"No, hardly, pretty one. They had our horses and probably their own since they would need to bring weapons and such. None of the men appears shot. Arrows, spears, that sort of thing. Not the sort that professionals would use, and if it were this governor, as Boday presumes you were attempting to say, they would have passed us on the way back. Nor were these the governor's men, Boday would wager. They had on plain black uniforms, not blue with gold, but they were uniforms all the same and thieves and scoundrels do not wear uniforms. They were army, but not *this* army. That was why they were attacked. The attackers had license to do what they would with invaders and how could this governor complain?"

"Yes, Mistress, but—where do they go?"

"Good question," Boday admitted. "Not back or there would have been a real racket. Not east, because that would take them into this governor's domain and they would probably at least have to share the booty. West is the river—far too deep here for horses. So—we continue!"

Charley nodded sadly and they got up and left the scene of carnage, none too soon for Charley's taste. It seemed to inspire Boday, though. She kept muttering, "Boday wishes she had some charcoal and paper. Such inspiration she is getting from all this! Such violence, such suffering, such travails she has already undergone! If this keeps up much longer, Boday will ultimately be acclaimed the greatest artist of her times!"

*Yeah,* Charley thought dejectedly. *If the great Boday lives to paint it. At least I don't have to worry that she's one of those artists who goes crazy. She was insane before we ever met her.*

The canyon was growing dark, the shadows long, and still they hadn't come upon anything still living except for a few insects and some distant birds circling high in the ever-deepening blue sky. It was hot and quiet, so quiet that only the sounds of their own movement and the rush from the swift-flowing river broke the stillness in the land and air.

Suddenly the rocks to their right erupted with forms and fierce cries. Before either woman could even see who or what was there they were overtaken and pushed roughly to the ground. Boday gave a good struggle; as two pinned her arms she managed to twist and kick another in the groin, twist away, and start in fiercely on her attackers. Charley had no such skills and reflexes and not much strength left, either. They had her quickly pinned facedown and then her arms were roughly brought behind her and tied with some strong, tight cord, and someone else pulled on her hair to make her face come up and then slipped a noose over her head.

They had to work hard for Boday, but there were too many of them and they were too strong for her in the end, and she suffered the same fate in the end.

Charley tried to look up and see just who or what their captors were, but once she caught sight of them she didn't want to look anymore.

They were as ragtag a bunch of filth as she'd ever seen; smelly, dirty, in torn and rumpled clothing, and not a normal-looking one in the bunch. There were eight of them, all well armed and tough as nails. One was huge and hunchbacked, his face contorted, and he snorted and dribbled from his twisted lower lip. Charley instantly dubbed him the Hunchback of Notre Dame even if he didn't look much like a football player.

Another was tall, muscular, with a tremendous, flowing bright red beard and nasty, close-set eyes above a pug nose, but he walked real funny and his arms and hands—well, they weren't *normal*. Thick, blue-gray and shiny, the arms terminated in a really nasty-looking set of lobsterlike claws.

The others were no better. They had all been human once, but all now had very different and inhuman parts to them. One was a sort of cyclops with weird hands that had three thick, curved fingers like a claw machine at the fire carnival. Another had tentacles growing from his back, and still another had a face that would have looked better on a toad. In fact, after seeing them all, the hunchback looked very normal and comforting indeed.

Redbeard with the claws was obviously the leader. With both women tied and held down, he walked slowly up to them and looked each over.

"Well, now, this *is* a pretty catch, and all decorated nice and fine like they's gift-wrapped or something. Who the hell are you, girls, and what in the name of the Nine Dark Hells are you doin' out here stark naked?"

Boday managed to look up. "Do you really think the designs are pretty? You are obviously a man of good taste to appreciate the handiwork of Boday!"

Charley groaned.

Redbeard turned to her. "And who might this Boday be?"

"She who speaks with you is Boday!" the artistic alchemist responded proudly, totally disregarding her circumstances.

Redbeard looked a bit taken aback by her attitude. "All right, Boday, so who else be you and why are you here?"

"We were flooded in a wagon train disaster, then taken by brigands who had their fun with us, then escaped to here only to be split up running from those dead men back there who stole what supplies we had. We seek our companions whom the men in black captured."

"These companions be men?"

"No, of *course* not! A young woman and two small girls."

"Weren't no females with *that* crew," Redbeard responded. "Your friends probably wound up in the clutches of that bastard crazy Duke. We got your horses, though, and your booty, and now we got you. Both of you now get up and shut

up! We's goin' for a little walk. Them's good nooses on your
pretty necks, now, so don't make no sudden moves or you'll
strangle yourselves. Now, we don't want'a kill you or damage
them pretty bodies, but Hooton, there, he's an expert at the
science of the noose. A little jerk just so and he can shatter
your voice boxes, and we don't need your voices. And any real
trouble and he's got a way of fixin' them so you don't strangle
all the way but just a little, so's you don't get so much blood to
the brain. I seen 'em after a few hours of his treatment. You
don't have enough sense left to remember what clothes was and
you might needs some help feedin' yourself, but your bodies'll
be just fine. So—shut up, do what you're told, and no tricks!''

*Shit!*, Charley thought sourly. *Back into the fire again, and
this time getting farther and farther from Sam. Damn! Damn!
Damn! Why didn't we go to that governor? Damn you, Boday!*

The horses were about a half mile farther down the trail,
held a bit off the track and upwind so that they hadn't made a
sound. Their own horses and the lone narga were among them,
still loaded with stuff. Four more ragtag and deformed nasties
held them, waiting. It seemed that Redbeard simply couldn't
conceive of six uniformed men with no protection just
marching in here, particularly past the Imperial Governor's
turnoff. He'd been convinced that more were following
behind, and he wanted to make very sure what he was up
against rather than risk fleeing with the loot with soldiers in hot
pursuit. Now, though, he felt his wait rewarded in a different
way.

Neither Charley nor Boday was allowed to ride; Redbeard
didn't trust them, even naked and tied, on the backs of their
own horses. They walked along at a steady pace, trying to
adjust so that those strangely tied nooses didn't have much
chance to tighten up. The gang made all sorts of lewd and
lustful comments about them but did not try to touch them or in
fact do much of anything to them. Clearly Redbeard was an
authority to be feared.

They reached a point where the river bent slightly, and two
riders came forward and stopped at the water's edge, checking
for something unknown. Then they rode right into the river, the
horses sinking only slightly into the water, and came up on the
other side with their riders not even wet.

"Now you, ladies, and don't slip," Hooton said in a low, menacing tone. "Right at this point it's right shallow with just sand and mud and small rocks there at certain times of day like now. Other times it's a killer. Just go on across."

It was an unpleasant balancing act, shallow though it was. The mud and rocks were slippery, the muck just under the surface felt just awful, and while it wasn't all that bad for Boday, tall as she was, it wasn't all that shallow for Charley at just a little over five feet tall. She felt tense, and the noose pulling at her throat all the way, and when she made it to the other side she gave a gasp of relief.

The others now followed without any trouble, and then the whole group turned not farther up but rather to the left, back the way they'd come. They went back down perhaps a thousand yards, then reached a rocky outcrop that seemed so solid that it blocked passage along that shore. A rider reached up and did something that couldn't be seen in the gloom, and the rock seemed to shift and the earth to shake a bit, and when it was done there was a narrow passage revealed in the rock itself. It wasn't wide enough for more than one horse and rider at a time, single file, and it seemed to go on for an eternity in near-total darkness.

They emerged for a moment, the lack of river noise meaning that they were now well away from the river, and the last man in the gang rode through, then stopped, and again did something that caused the same rumbling and the fissure to close with a nasty-sounding finality. It was a good way to escape if you needed to block pursuit, Charley realized. Even if you were tricked and they tried to follow, they'd be crushed along the way. Still, the mere fact that Redbeard had waited showed that they didn't want to have to rely on that trick. Ignorance on the part of their enemies that the passage even existed was far better long-term protection than just using it as a means of escape.

They went down a bit into the rocky jumble of the Kudaan landscape, hurrying a bit because of the growing darkness. Here and there they shouted some strange words and were answered by others, showing that this trail was well guarded. Charley's heart sank. Even if, somehow, she escaped this crew, how the hell would she ever get away, elude all of those guardians who knew the territory perfectly, and survive? These were dangerous men; fugitives holed up in the Wastes and living a different and primitive kind of life beyond the reach of any law. Men with no place to go, nothing to lose, and with nothing at all to hold them back.

Now, at last, a great glob of total darkness loomed ahead, and they suddenly stopped. Hooton, the toad-faced one, slid off his horse and came up to them. "Now you just walk right in front of me," he told them, "and keep your neckwear slack."

It was a tunnel of some sort—no, a cave. There was a blast of cool air coming from it, and as they entered they descended, although they couldn't see a thing. Hooton, however, could, and he kept giving them quick directions.

"Turn left. That's right. Ten paces forward, then left again. Fine. Now ahead until I tell you to stop. Now—right turn."

It went on for some time, made no easier by the fact that some of the mounted horses were ahead of them and leaving the usual horse droppings.

Within several minutes, neither Charley nor Boday had any idea of where they were or how they'd gotten there. It wasn't merely one cave, it was a network of interlocking caves going off in all directions including down, and between the darkness and the differences in the dark tunnels only one who knew exactly where he or she was and, perhaps, could see or read the hidden markings, would find their way in—or out.

Suddenly all was noise and light. It was the lights of thousands of torches rather than anything in nature, and the reverberant cacophony of great numbers of people and animals. The scene seemed to go on and on below them. Charley could see only the lights but the noise and smells were overwhelming. She realized that they had now entered some grand cave on the order of the Big Room at Carlsbad Caverns or even bigger. A giant cave, far underground, that held not tourists but a town.

This, then, was the outlaw capital, the seat of the unholy of the Kudaan Wastes. No wonder the worst could hide out here! No power could find such a place except by treachery, and the system didn't really care enough to even attempt that sort of thing anymore.

They moved now down into it, into a throng of people,

animals, changelings, and creatures, the discards of Akahlar.
Boday was entranced by the vision, so much so that she
seemed to forget her own situation. The cave was *enormous*,
and it seemed to go off in the distance a tremendous way. On
the floor of it were buildings, marketplaces, bazaars, a
tremendous life energy that knew no day or night; a town with
few laws and few limits that was a continual now, without
regard for yesterday or tomorrow.

They, however, could not explore it. When they reached a
central square, Hooton turned them abruptly and led them to a
squared-off building that seemed made entirely of glass that
was inches thick. Two guards, huge and somewhat piglike,
nodded and grunted and then gave way, and a jaillike door was
unlocked and opened. Hooton then carefully removed the
nooses, untied their hands, and while they were still rubbing
their raw wrists they were rudely shoved inside, so that both of
them landed sprawling on a hay-strewn floor. The door clanged
shut behind them, and the sounds of the great room became
terribly muted.

"That swine!" Boday hissed, and managed to roll over and
come to a sitting position. "Are you all right?"

Charley groaned, then managed to sit up and nod, feeling
her neck. God! It *still* felt like she had a rope around it! She
tried breathing hard through her mouth and tried to get hold of
herself. Then and only then did she take stock of the cubicle.

It was small enough for her to see all of it, if a bit blurry, and
beyond she could see the lights and activities of the city
beneath the ground. It wasn't very big—maybe six feet by six
feet, give or take, filled with a rotting straw floor that, when
you dug down in it, led to an unpleasantly sticky cold stone
floor. Over in one corner was a foul, rusted chamber pot, and
in another a clay jug of water that had a bit of scum on top.
Boday went over to it, frowned, stirred it with her finger, then
tasted it.

"It *seems* all right," she said dubiously, then sighed. "And
it is all we have." Still, she stared at it. "As an alchemist,
Boday would suspect that this water is somewhat drugged.
Still, she is *dying* of thirst, and what difference can it make
now anyway?"

It was a practical, pragmatic statement and Charley couldn't disagree. They both drank it, and even though it tasted flat and mineral-heavy, it was what they needed.

The door opened, and Hooton was there again. "I've made all the arrangements," he told them, then put a basket down. "Here's some food. It ain't much but it'll keep you going. Best make yourselves comfortable. You'll be on display here until the next slave auction, and that ain't for three days yet. There's a bunch that saw you come in got real interested in you. Ain't too often we get full-blooded Akhbreed down here." And, with that, he closed the door and the noises again faded.

Charley sighed and went to one of the walls. Transparent. There were already some people out there looking at them. Sizing up the merchandise. Not just men and half-men, either. There were some women out there as well, but from the looks of them even Hooton would be an improvement. She tried to imagine the kind of woman who'd do well as an equal in a society like this. These looked the part. The one with the wrestler's muscles, purple makeup, spiked green hair, and leather outfit looked just Boday's type.

She went over to Boday, who was ignoring the outside traffic and checking the contents of the basket.

"Slightly stale bread, moldy cheese, some slabs of some sort of meat that might not poison us, if we can stand to chew it and our teeth are strong enough for it. Not much else. And the amphora . . ." She uncorked it and sniffed it. "Ugh! The cheapest wine imaginable!"

Charley had not been able to tolerate meat since she entered this life and this look-alike existence, but she was far too hungry not to eat her share of the rest, including the wine. It *was* bad, barely drinkable, but it dissolved the bread enough to make it edible. The cheese wasn't so bad—all cheese smelled yucky anyway—if you just scraped some of the mold off with your nails first.

The wine was, however, definitely alcoholic to a much higher degree than she was used to. In a little while she felt light-headed, even a bit silly, and, somehow, not so horribly down anymore.

Boday, who usually had a high tolerance for alcohol, was feeling it a little bit, too. She got up after a while and pressed herself against the wall. "Boday feels like she is at the zoo," she muttered, slurring her words a bit, "but something is wrong. The people they are on the inside of the cage and the animals are out there looking in!" She seemed to find this thought funny and began chuckling.

The chuckling was contagious. For some reason the comment struck Charley that way as well and she started laughing. Then she went over and started making very graphic obscene gestures and moves to the crowd. This kept up for a while, until, finally, both women just sank down in the straw and, within minutes of one another, passed out.

There was no telling how long they slept; there was no way of telling any sort of time in a place like this. But from the way every bone and muscle in their bodies ached when they finally awoke, they had been out a very long time. The worst part, Charley thought to herself, was that she felt like she hadn't slept at all.

There was another basket of the same just inside the door. No telling how long it'd been there, but it was clearly what they got until they ate it and needed another.

Boday made her way, crawling, to it and settled down, back against the glass, looking glassy-eyed. "Boday feels like shit," she muttered wearily. "All of the energy, the fight, has gone out of her. What is the use of fighting anymore, anyway? She is sick of fighting, of running, of worrying. There is no escape. They can do what they want with her."

Charley was almost startled to hear Boday voice her own depression, as deep and despairing as the slight drunk had been manic. It was over for them, and something inside her just didn't care anymore. She felt so weak and small and helpless that she had no choice but to accept fate.

"It is the wine, you know, or perhaps the water," Boday noted in that still down, detached tone. "Not that what we feel is not the truth, the result of all that has gone before and all that is. It simply builds on that. Ah—Boday sees you do not fully understand. She is an alchemist. The caves here, they must grow a hundred different kinds of fungus. A minor potion, really. You drink it and for a while you have no worries or fears or inhibitions. Then it goes the other way, and the rest of the time you are passive, fatalistic, without real strength or will.

Just a way to see that we perform now and then for the customers and otherwise do not fight or resist or try and make trouble."

A potion? Charley stared at the amphora. The trouble was, while Boday was making sense, somehow it didn't really matter to either of them that they knew. What could they do but accept it? She no longer cared anymore.

Hell, inside her was another, simpler personality that was probably a lot more useful here. Hell, three words in English would bring up a spell that would banish Charley from her mind and bring forth Shari, an ignorant, servile, willing slave who could only think in the few hundred words of the Short Speech. Hell, she always wondered what would happen if she herself spoke the three simple words aloud, but she'd never tried because then there'd be nobody who would know how to bring Charley back. She wondered now if that even mattered.

Still, she could bring up that part of her without any spell. She'd had long practice at it. You just relaxed, put everything out of your mind, and began to think only in the servile Short Speech. *Mistress, I be Shari. How may Shari serve Mistress . . . ?*

So easy, so tempting, so worry free.

So damned cowardly.

The hell with it. Not yet. There was plenty of time if it became really unbearable, but, until then, where there was life there had to be some hope of something. If only she had a real command of this language! At least Boday had somebody to bitch to.

They had to have slept a very long time, since there were only two more "meals" and one more, and better, sleep before they came for them. When they did, they didn't bother to truss them up or chain them or anything. Charley guessed they already had proven that, at least for now, they weren't the suicidal type, and, down here, with this crowd, what the hell were they going to do and where could they go, anyway?

The crowd was like something out of a bad horror movie, with shouting and screaming figures dressed mostly in rags or patchwork stuff and many looking and sounding only vaguely human. They were pawed and pushed as their guards made way for them to walk through to the marketplace, and it was pretty unpleasant. There was almost a sense of relief when they made this little platform in a kind of square surrounded by broken-down stalls that was clearly the center of commerce, such as it was. The crowd was jovial enough, but somehow both women felt more like the unwelcome guests of honor at an execution than the objects of an auction.

Far back in the crowd, an unassuming figure in a full brown robe, looking much like an out-of-place friar, stared at them, then did something of a double-take and stared some more. The cut of his robe marked him as a magician, but its color and design did not denote high rank. He had a pudgy, boyish face, although he was more stocky than fat, and rumpled, thin brown hair to his shoulders that compensated only slightly for his massive but natural bald spot atop his head.

He was there almost as an afterthought; captives and slaves weren't of any real interest to him unless they were somebody important. In fact, he hated this crowd and would have timed his visit differently had he remembered about this, but here he was, and as he'd needed to purchase some essential charms at the bazaar he wasn't about to go back and make a second, later trip. This would be over soon enough.

At first he'd thought the two women an odd pair. The tall one with all those tattoos over her body was at once mean-looking and singularly unattractive; the small one, though, looked so frail, a courtesan far from her element, helpless and afraid.

That courtesan looked damned familiar. That long hair and those eye tattoos took away from it somewhat, but he was knowledgeable enough to see through them and overlay the familiar on her feature and form. Yes . . . Trim the hair and restyle it, remove the tattoos, add maybe fifteen or twenty halg to the weight . . .

*By the gods, they've captured one of Boolean's simulacra!* Perhaps the very one Zamofir had spoken of when he was through here!

Suddenly it all made lots of sense, but what to do? He couldn't deprive this mob of their show, that was for sure. Halting the auction at this point was out of the question, and he certainly had little with which to outbid those here. Calming himself, he got control of his thoughts and knew that there was no time to do anything here and now. The best he could do was to note the buyer and then get that information back to Yobi as fast as possible.

You could tell the Grand Auctioneer in an instant. For one thing, he was clean, well groomed, and dressed in a fine togalike garment and shiny leather boots and definitely had a lot more than most of this mob. For another, he was clearly in his element in front of the crowd and very much the businessman. He was accompanied by a woman who had once been beautiful, but her face and her silver hair told of a life where fate had been less than kind, and while she was clean and well dressed herself she walked with a pronounced limp. As she came up to the platform, Charley could see that the woman had two fingers missing on her left hand, and a small brass or copper ring through her nose. She also carried a small book and stylus with her, and propped herself to one side of the platform. The Grand Auctioneer came up to her and said something that the crowd noises made it impossible to hear, and she nodded. Then the auctioneer mounted the platform.

He turned, faced the crowd, and with exaggerated hand gestures pleaded for and then finally achieved a level of quiet.

"All right, all right!" he said in a penetrating, professional voice that seemed to cut through all noise almost as if amplified, yet not shouting at all. "Now, we don't have much today, but what we do have is well worth the wait. I know most of you can't afford either of them, but you can sit there quietly and drool and pretend you are. The serious bidders and their agents to my right, please. Let them through! Thank you, thank you!"

About a dozen people made their way to the designated spot. All were better dressed and obviously more affluent than the masses in the crowd, although many were as strange in their own ways as the rest here. Most were men, but a few were women, and perhaps two-thirds of them also wore rings in their noses.

"Ah!" said the Grand Auctioneer with satisfaction. "All set? Very well, then. You've seen this pair on display now, so you know pretty well what you're getting physically." He turned to Boday. "Do you have a name and any skills to recommend yourself?"

She glared at him. Boday always expected to be recognized, even here.

"You see before you Boday, the greatest alchemical artist of the age, and one of her finest creations!" she bragged.

The crowd roared, mostly with laughter, which seemed to infuriate Boday even more. She glared at them and they seemed collectively taken aback at the glare.

"There you are!" the auctioneer told the crowd. "An alchemist and artist of the body. Two for the price of one, ladies and gentlemen! A slave such as this can be *most* useful! Can I have a starting bid, please?"

Charley stared out at the crowd in wonder. Why were they all here and making so merry at this? These were the poor, the misshapen, the dregs of this underground society. Looking at the real bidders, it was clear that even slaves of such people would be better off than most of this lot.

And then it hit her. That was it, wasn't it? These were the losers, the dregs of the lowest society of Akahlar. The accursed and misshapen, without hope, without anything much at all.

But they were still better than slaves.

So long as there were slaves in this society, they were not the lowest, not the bottom of the ladder. So long as there were slaves there was always somebody to look down on, somebody so you could always say to yourself, "Well, I may be at my rock bottom but at least I'm not a slave." And if the slaves were pure Akhbreed, so much the better. She and Boday represented to these people that which had shut them out and cast them out, and just to see them sold into bondage was a sort of vicarious revenge.

The auctioneer was going well now, occasionally going fast enough to make a singsong chant in numerical units, although units of what wasn't clear. Surely money as such meant nothing to these people; there had to be some alternate value system here that was represented by the numbers.

The bidding slowed at eleven hundred and fifty, and the auctioneer began cajoling the bidders, alternately flattering and insulting them, trying to get another bid. It was now like pulling teeth, but he got another two hundred and then started his close.

"Thirteen fifty . . . once! Twice! Three times! Sold!" He

pointed to a huge pale man in a white toga whose head was shaved and who looked almost like a marble monument. The man had a ring in his nose.

Boday was told to step down off the platform and stand by the woman with the ledger, and the auctioneer brought Charley front and center.

"The girl speaks no Akhbreed!" Boday shouted to the auctioneer. "She knows only the Short Speech but understands much. She is Shari, a courtesan."

"Ah! You hear?" the Grand Auctioneer asked the crowd. "No need of breaking in this one. A courtesan, schooled only in pleasure and service. A beauty if there ever was one here. Never before have we had a jewel like *this* to sell! Who needs a hub when you can have *this* one forever at your beck and call? How much am I offered?"

Charley felt a sense of unreality about it all. The whole thing had more of a dreamlike quality to it for her, and she felt a curious intellectual detachment from the proceedings. She was curious to see just how much she'd go for in whatever it was they were using to pay.

The answer was a lot. In the first minute she'd passed Boday, somewhat to Boday's clear irritation, and the bidding was still quite spirited. When it passed two thousand virtually all noise ceased except the auctioneer's chant. When she went above twenty-five hundred the auctioneer was talking about a "new record" for any individual.

She felt a curious thrill at that, even though she knew she should be ashamed of herself for feeling that way. *What's happened to me in this world?* she wondered, more amazed than upset in spite of it all. *Yeah, I wanted to be senior class president, prom queen, college coed, and then found my own cosmetics business and make a million before I was thirty. And look at me now! First a high-class hooker who finds she likes it, then, standing here, mentally charged up at how much people are paying for me! Have I changed, or didn't I just know myself before?*

"Sold! Three thousand one hundred, a new record by far!" the auctioneer declared.

She looked over, hoping to see the same buyer as Boday, but instead it was a small, ugly character in a black robe and hood standing two away from Boday's new master. It was hard to tell if the buyer was male or female or maybe something else.

She was led off the platform and placed next to Boday as the auctioneer wound up his pitch, promised big deals in affordable merchandise and booty at the auction the next day, then stepped down himself. "Make way! Make way! Coming through! Successful bidders please follow!"

Boday shrugged and looked at Charley, then the two followed the auctioneer, then the two buyers, and finally the woman with the ledger book. They went across the square, through the crowd that was now straining for one last glimpse but was also beginning to break up, then down a narrow alley between two stalls and to a door halfway through to the next block. The auctioneer took out some keys on a big ring, opened the door with one, then walked in and they followed.

"You two sit on the divan there in the anteroom," he told them in a cold, businesslike tone. "No talking or moving around."

The other three now entered, and he closed the door and went over to a desk, while his female assistant took a chair to his right. The two buyers stood in front and were not offered seats.

"You have full payment?" the autioneer asked them.

"I have a draft bill, open," said the big man with the shaved head in a surprisingly soft and high voice. "Your client may redeem it at my master's place any time after it is registered." He reached into a hidden pocket in his toga. "I also have a draft for credits at any establishment you choose in the name of yourself, so there is no problem with the fees."

The auctioneer nodded and looked at the small, hooded one. "And you?"

The little one produced similar papers. "Pretty much the same, but the amount is high enough that you will have to dun the seller for your fees."

The auctioneer sighed. "Irregular, but, then, a percentage of that . . . I'll take the bill. The seller is Lakos in both cases, as you probably know. Best he not get his hands on this until he has settled with me. I understand that won't be difficult. He made quite a score otherwise in that raid. I'm selling much of the rest tomorrow. Yes, these will do. You may claim your merchandise. Vica—give them receipts and final bills of sale."

"Yes, Master Arnos," the gray-haired woman responded, and for the first time Charley realized that all of these people except the auctioneer himself were slaves as well—the ledger woman with the limp belonging to the Grand Auctioneer, and who knew whom these two belonged to? Who—or what?

The auctioneer went back to them. "Go with these agents," he told them. "Do whatever they say. Do not mistake the fact that they are slaves as some sort of license. They are bonded to their masters and have the power to do anything with you that they wish as if they themselves had bought you."

They both nodded and got up and went back out into the alley with the two strange slaves, but they didn't go far. There was a small arcade just before the next street and they were led into it and immediately into an establishment that clearly sold unusual merchandise. From the burners and dolls and strange designs and odd bric-a-brac both knew they were in a magician's shop.

It occurred to Charley that she'd actually seen little magic in this world beyond her own change into a semblance of, or maybe an idealization of, Sam, and Sam's own summoning of the storm. Almost everything she'd seen had been drugs and chemicals and maybe hypnosis, really. Oh, some of them did all sorts of wild things, like grow a foot of hair in minutes or make you fall in love or stuff like that, but it wasn't anything she was sure couldn't be done back home by some smart somebody. These kinds of shops with all the magic charms and incantation books she couldn't read and that kind of thing just hadn't looked like more than scams, and this junky place didn't look any different.

The proprietor, though, was something of a surprise. It was a woman, dressed in a brown magician's robe, perhaps fifty or so, with very short gray hair and deep lines in her face. There also seemed to be something odd about her eyes and her head movement, but it was hard to tell for sure.

"Yes?" she asked them.

The big man pointed to Boday. "She's enslaved to Jamonica. The other one belongs to Hodamoc. Both require bonding."

The magician nodded. "Very well. You have something I can use for each of them?"

The little one in the black hood and robe pulled out what looked to be a small, irregular stone and handed it to the magician. The big man reached in and removed a tiny box like a ring box that contained what appeared to be hairs. The magician examined both and nodded. "These will do fine. Wait here, and send the small one back first. Working from animate relics is far easier."

"I know, but Jamonica don't give no relics to nobody," the big man with the soft, high voice responded.

The magician smiled knowingly. "I understand." She pointed at Charley. "Come, little one. In back."

Charley hesitated, then followed, still in that somewhat detached state. The back of the place was a real mess, making the actual store look organized. There were all sorts of things around, making it look part chemical laboratory and part junk shop. She watched while the magician went into a drawer and took out a box containing a number of small bronze-colored rings. For the first time, Charley felt some panic. *Oh, no! You ain't putting one of* them *up my nose!*

The magician worked quickly and professionally. She took the hairs and put them into a small metal bowl, then began to add several other unknown substances, stirring and heating the mixture until it was a dull and sickly green paste. She then walked over to Charley and before the woman could say or do anything, the magician reached out, grabbed Charley's right hand, and she felt a sudden sharp sting.

"Ow!" she said, and tried to pull away, but the magician was surprisingly strong and had clearly done this a lot of times before. Charley's hand was pulled over the mixture, and her thumb squeezed enough so that two drops of blood fell into the bowl and green scum—and it sizzled. When that happened, Charley was released and stepped back, sticking her thumb in her mouth to stop the bleeding.

Now the magician took the ring and put it into the mixture, and more heat was applied, but this time the magician closed her eyes and began to wave her hands over the bowl and chant something in a low tone over it.

Suddenly there was a crackling and then a strange white

light, about the size of the magician's thumb, appeared in the center of the bowl and began to pulse a bit, bulging in the center. As Charley watched, the little thing moved, going 'round and 'round the bowl in lazy circles, each one a bit smaller than the one before, and as it did the sickly liquid seemed to be pulled up into it, as if the pulsing white energy were some sort of straw bringing that crap up to some invisible mouth—and maybe it was.

In less than a minute there was nothing left in the bowl but the ring, looking good as new. The little energy thing winked out with a zapping sound, and the magician nodded to herself, turned off the heat, and removed the ring from the bowl and put it aside, perhaps to cool. She reached over, found a small gourd, uncorked it, sniffed it, then nodded and handed it to Charley. "Drink some of this. One or two swallows, anyway."

Charley hesitated and wouldn't touch it, and the magician understood.

"I am a magician, not an alchemist. Unfortunately, most magic involves pain of one sort or another, and the last step is painful. Can you understand what I am saying?"

Charley nodded, but didn't like the message.

"It will be done either with or without your drinking it. You have no abnormal auras about you. I could freeze you where you stand with a simple spell but then you would feel everything. Two swallows of this and you will feel very little pain for just a few minutes. Go ahead."

Charley drank it. It wasn't at all like the alchemical concoctions—magic potions tasted like medicine. She handed back the gourd and the magician put it back on the table, then picked up the ring. She turned and faced Charley, very close, and suddenly made a sign of something with her left hand. Charley saw the right, the one with the ring, move up to her face and she tried to step back, but she could not. She was frozen stiff as a board.

There was a sudden sharp pain, like some needle being shoved through her nose, but it was dampened down almost immediately and she felt only a numbness there.

The magician made the reverse of her previous motion and this time with her right hand. Charley could move again.

"The spell now holds you but you are not yet truly bonded,"

the magician told her, taking on the same clinical manner as a doctor explaining a treatment to a patient. "It is quite loose and you will soon get used to it but do not allow it to be removed. You remember that little bit of pain you felt? If you remove it, that pain will be back, in full, and it will not go away over time. The spell compels obedience. At the moment, because you are not yet bonded, it compels obedience from anyone at all, instantly. Stand on your right leg only!"

Immediately Charley found herself standing storklike on one leg. She hadn't thought about it.

"All right, put it down and stand normally. Don't worry, you're not at everyone's mercy. In a moment Hodamoc's slave will touch your ring, and since he is bonded by the same spell you will then be attuned to it and will obey only those with the same spell. Once brought before Hodamoc, he will touch the ring and it will recognize him as the controller and then you will be obedient only to him. Control is transferable, but only by a master's command. If the master dies, control passes to his or her nearest of kin. It enslaves only your body, not your mind and soul. Accept it. Even a master cannot free you. From this point on, you, and soon your companion, will be someone's property for the rest of your lives."

That was a very chilling thought.

"Stand there and do not move," the magician ordered. "I will fetch the slave."

The little one in black entered, and when he looked at her she could see an oddly oblong face, huge, round nose, and beady little recessed eyes against a small mouth and lantern jaw. On him, the ring in his nose was barely noticeable, and she could understand immediately why he liked to wear the hood all the time.

He reached out and touched the ring in her own nose, and she felt suddenly a bit dizzy. It cleared almost immediately, though, and he let go.

"Good," he said in a thin, reedy little voice. "Now hear and obey our master's commands. Until you are bonded you shall obey all who are bonded to our master as if any of us were he himself and no others. You shall harm no one, not even yourself, unless ordered to do so, nor cause another to suffer harm. You shall not be out of sight of another bonded to our master or our master himself at any time until you yourself are bonded. You shall undertake no action on your own without permission. Slaves, even those above you in rank, will always be addressed as equals. All others will be addressed with high respect as superiors no matter how low their station. But only Hodamoc shall be addressed as Master, and only Hodamoc and those bonded to him or designated by him shall be obeyed. These are the orders of our master Hodamoc. Hear and obey.''

Well, she didn't *feel* any different, except that her nose felt funny, for all that.

"Now, follow me," said the little man, and she found herself turning and following him by a few steps back out to the front of the shop and then back out into the arcade, past Boday but unable to stop or signal or say a word. Charley found herself fixated on the little man, always keeping him in sight. Somewhere back there Boday would be getting the same treatment for her master, and boy! Would she ever hate *that*!

Charley didn't like the situation, but something deep down inside her liked that image of Boday. It was about time that somebody who turned lots of poor, trusting girls into mindless sex machines without a qualm got at least a taste of her own medicine. There was some small measure of justice in that.

For Boday, maybe, but what about her? Who or what was this Hodamoc, anyway? What was going to become of her now? A courtesan to the likes of Redbeard's crew, maybe? God, that was repulsive to think about! Now she was being led away to a strange place and people, severing her last link with anyone or anything in Akahlar. No more Sam, or even Boday, to fall back on. And, unlike Sam, nobody, least of all Boolean, even gave a damn about her.

Hodamoc lived well in the exile community, and he had good reason to be a major player in the underworld. It was said he'd been a general in the army of Mashtopol, assigned as commander of the Imperial Guard, one of the highest honors a soldier could attain and one of considerable political as well as military power and influence. He was of royal blood, but untitled, and those usually became either soldiers or magicians or other top secular positions of authority.

He had, however, overreached himself at last, as such

people sometimes do. Imperial succession often had less to do with who was firstborn than which son of the king was the most cutthroat politician, and alliances for such things were formed early. The seven wives of the old king had borne him twenty-nine children, of whom fifteen were boys, and of whom six were well into their twenties when the old boy passed away. Hodamoc, with visions of a conferred title of Duke or Lord and perhaps a cabinet post, had picked and backed the son who appeared the strongest, and he'd chosen wrong. His boy had not taken into account just how insane Warog, the Imperial Sorcerer, was, and when promised magical support did not materialize for anyone's side, it was over.

Barely escaping the purge that inevitably followed a new ascension to the throne, but smart enough to have hedged some of his bets just in case, he had fled to the Kudaan to reorganize and perhaps, one day, return in force and teach those bastards a bit of a lesson.

In the meantime, he and some of his loyal staff had set themselves up fairly well in the Wastes, using his influence with his bleeding-heart cousin, Duke Alon Pasedo, the Governor of the region, to broker between the outlaw and legitimate elements. The outlaws laid off Pasedo's own estates and people, and in exchange the Duke, via his cousin, transferred some products he had that were worth more than gold in the Kudaan Wastes.

Hodamoc, former General of the Imperial Guard, was now the fruit-and-vegetable king of the underworld.

It was a somewhat humiliating position for him, but it gave him great power and influence. His underground estate was in a fairly large cavern of its own with its own underground water source, and by harnessing some of that power he had a water-driven elevator of sorts that could take him and his people up to the surface, where his main house was built of and into the rock but was also open to the outside.

He proved to be a tall, strikingly handsome man in his fifties, with gray-black hair, intelligent brown eyes, and a trim graying moustache and goatee, who almost always wore his full general's uniform around the place. He ran it like it was his headquarters and he was still in the army, too, and all but slaves called him "sir" or "General." He also had the military man's mania for order and cleanliness, and while his household included some who were either not quite human or very strange, in his free staff he played no favorites.

Charley wasn't sure she'd ever be comfortable with this slave business, but she was becoming accustomed to it and had accepted it. There was no use resisting, anyway, and she knew that she could be far worse off than this. She no longer even thought about the ring in her nose and was only absently aware of it. She discovered, though, that its magical properties were quite strong. Once you were given an order, it *stuck*.

She had relative freedom of movement around the place, subject to a few areas which were forbidden to her, but there was no way she could leave its clearly defined boundaries. She had to work hard to get a bunch of Akhbreed phrases correct, because she was required to ask permission of whoever was in charge of her to do most anything, including taking a bath, taking a walk, eating something, or even going to the bathroom. It soon went from being resented to being automatic, and it sure as hell kept you in your place.

She had thought that for the money he'd paid—in good credits, as it turned out—she would be his personal courtesan, but that wasn't the case. In fact, after that first brief time when he'd touched her ring and she had been bonded to his will, she'd seen him very little and always from a prostrate position as he passed. She had wondered at first why a man like him hadn't had a family, but the constant companionship of young, good-looking junior "officers" around him, some of whom were *gorgeous*, told the story.

She was not for him or his boys, but rather for various others who came and went. All were Akhbreed, many were older men, and she got the distinct impression that most of them were old friends and potential allies still within the royal structure. The General still had some power, and maybe even eventually some hope of a comeback. Kings had been known to be assassinated in these lands by brothers and cousins and the like.

Charley was ambivalent about these liaisons. In one way she looked forward to them because there was very little else for her to do, and she did mostly enjoy it, although a few of these guys were *really* kinky. But they were also active big shots in

Mashtopol; as such, they could hardly be aware of the Storm Princess and the search for ones who resembled her, and that made each new liaison a potential threat as well. She just kicked into Shari mode as much as possible and hoped that the personality obscured any sense of the familiar.

The problem was, though, it was mostly *boring*. She'd be brought out a couple of times a week to "service" VIPs, and the rest of the time she was just, well, left. Her lack of any command of the language precluded her making any close friends or confidants or even having someone reasonably friendly and secure to talk to. Her restriction to the immediate grounds made it impossible to try to contact Boday or even gain any knowledge of what was going on in this crazy world. Nor was she expected to do anything but be handy if the General needed her for a guest.

She *did* get to wear some exotic and sexy clothing for a change, play with makeup and jewelry and all that, but there was only so much of it and nobody seemed to think she required any more.

If she could just get down to that underground town once in a while she felt she'd be okay. Go through those exotic bazaars and shops and all that. She wouldn't need money; shopping was far more fun than buying anyway. The answer, though, was always the same. She was far too valuable to risk in that city of scoundrels and ruffians, and the Master wanted no harm to come to his property. The tough and the ugly went to town, but never wearing the Master's precious gems. She was a one-of-a-kind possession, and, to Hodamoc, that's all she was.

Worst of all, her vision had continued to deteriorate. She spent as much time as possible up on the surface in the open air of day because she could see there. Darkness was total for her now, and even within the house she needed a bright light source to see anything more than dimly, and then only straight ahead. Her peripheral vision was shot to hell as well. The household knew of this, but didn't much care. You didn't have to see to do what she was there to do.

She was growing more and more tempted to see if she could summon Shari and leave her permanently in place and in charge. Shari, perhaps, could handle it, empty-head that she was. Charley, though, was hanging on through force of will but it was becoming harder and harder to hope for anything.

Unable to effectively communicate with her peers, she was essentially mute, unable to really make friends or join the slave subculture. Her future was looking pretty damned bleak. She was beginning to believe that she would spend the rest of her life in this godforsaken place, lonely, mute, blind, and enslaved.

# · 4 ·

## Some Failures to Communicate

*ENU* WAS A purplish fruit that tasted like a melon but grew on trees about ten or fifteen feet tall. The picking was tricky, since you could not pick them until they were almost ripe but if you guessed wrong and the fruit grew too large to remain on the tree and fell to the ground it was useless. It was also somewhat messy, since the trees needed a near-constant trickle of water gotten to them by a small but expertly planned network of irrigation ditches and canals and it was muddy right along the trees themselves.

The only reminder that this was not a totally normal farm or grove was the presence of armed uniformed soldiers riding back and forth. They would seem menacing but they barely paid any attention to the pickers; their concern was keeping the pickers from being rudely interrupted by denizens of the Wastes who might want anything from stealing fruit to stealing *them*.

The picking technique was to take a small wooden ladder and a basket, plant the ladder firmly, then go up it with the basket right into the tree itself and then pick the fruit. Due to both the heat and the mud, most pickers opted for what was basically a panty for the females and a jock strap for the males, a thick bandannalike headband to catch perspiration, and a pair of work gloves to protect the hands in the actual picking. Basically you walked along an irrigation ditch in the mud until you came to the first tree in a row not being picked, you planted your ladder, went up with your basket, then leaned and squirmed and picked what fruit was there, often going down to empty your basket into a collection basket—there were many spread evenly out along the work area—and then back up again, perhaps on the other side, until you picked it clean. Then you went to the next tree not being picked and did the same.

Each picker was assigned a quota of trees that he had to pick before the day was ended based upon his physical abilities or handicaps and done, from the looks of it, fairly enough. Few really *needed* a quota; the pickers all seemed quite happy doing their work and proud of it as well; they competed against each other to see who would exceed their quota and by how much.

It wasn't hard but it did wear you, and that was where the *makuda* came in. *Makuda* was some sort of potion guaranteed to do no physical harm—there were even some pregnant women out there—that was, nonetheless, a pretty good stimulant that also quenched thirst and helped retain body moisture. You could get it anytime you needed at the collection bins, and Sam definitely felt the need after less than an hour out there on that first afternoon. Living so long with Boday, she had no real qualms about such potions, not when they were obviously mixed to such a common and positive purpose.

And the stuff really worked. Not only did she feel the aches and pains vanish, but she felt very energized, willing to work, and much more comfortable. It also tended to lull the mind a bit, so grumps and complaints about working and worries of all sorts seemed to fade and you found yourself concentrating on and even enjoying the routine. She felt herself through the afternoon almost merging with the other pickers into a collective consciousness in which nothing else really mattered and there was an instant comradeship, even though the pickers were the usual settlement assortment of men, women, and, well, *whatevers*.

When she rode back in on the carts with them, she had done a reasonable afternoon's work and felt fairly satisfied as she saw the nargas pulling carts of the fruit along with them and thought, *Some of those are mine, picked by me.*

As she made her way from the worker's housing area back to the residence, however, the drug began to wear off and she began to feel her tiredness and all the aches and pains of the day. All she wanted now was a soak, some food, and sleep. Avala, however, had something different in mind.

"My Lord the Duke wants you to have dinner with him this evening," she told the tired refugee. "He always wants to meet anyone new who comes here."

She groaned. "Oh, I don't know if I *can*! I'm feeling every damned *enu* right now. I'm so tired I might fall asleep in my salad."

Avala gave a wry smile. "It *can* be a bit hard until you get used to it and your muscles get built up," she admitted, "but My Lord Duke knows this. That is why tonight, when you have worked only part of a day, and not later on. There is a potion similar to *makuda* that will give you energy and ease your aches but leave you with a clear head, and if he keeps you late you will not have to work tomorrow. Come, I will help you get clean and dressed, and then you will see."

The potion was slower to act but very effective. By the time she'd finished her bath and felt reasonably clean and presentable, she also felt very good, almost as though she'd just gotten up. She hoped that this stuff didn't wear off very quickly, either.

The outfit wasn't much—just the top from the cinnamon stretch suit and a patterned long but slit skirt that somewhat matched and the boots, but it felt, well, *civilized* after spending the day mostly naked in mud that tended to bake on.

The governor's quarters were upstairs, where the administrative offices were. The whole wing was rustic-looking but very nicely appointed, and you could tell immediately that you were in an upper-class area by just looking at the quality of everything and the perfection at which it was maintained. Never before had Sam been at this social and economic level on Akahlar, and it was impressive.

Avala left her at the top of the stairs, and Sam was surprised to be met by Medac, who was actually wearing a pair of trousers and boots, which looked incongruous on a man with wings and no arms.

"Hello, there," the winged man greeted her. "I am happy to see you looking so well."

"It's drugs," she responded. "I'm dead tired, really, but I could hardly refuse."

He chuckled. "I understand they had you in the *enu* groves. Yes, I have watched them from above. I wanted to, well, caution you a bit, before we go in. I have seen how tolerant you are of changelings and I think it is most admirable, but I wish to prepare you for my mother."

Sam's eyebrows rose. "Your mother?"

He nodded. "We were returning in a caravan from one of those silly ceremonial visits, to foster goodwill and all that, that members of the royal families have to suffer through from time to time. It was in Gryatil, one of our own lands, not a day from home and safety, when a changewind hit. It was sudden, unexpected, and brutal. We had Mandan cloaks, of course, but you are supposed to have some warning and seek the lowest point, then huddle beneath them until the Navigator signals all clear. That is fine advice if you have warning and can see it coming, but we were very near the point where the wind broke through into Akahlar from wherever such winds originate. We barely had time to get on the ground and pull the cloaks over us. It was in heavy grass on uneven land, and no one had ever warned us about the true force of such a storm. The Mandan cloaks are very heavy, but they must be just so. Mine was lumpy and had an opening. The great winds came straight at us, and my cloak actually lifted up as I was facedown and the wind went through, *under*, before falling back down on top of me again. I tried to reach up without looking up and bring it down but by that time I had no arms. I was fourteen, and the mere sudden realization that the wind had gotten me caused me to scream in panic and terror."

She nodded. Although she'd only seen one changewind, and that in a vision, she could imagine the scene.

"My mother was in front of me, facing me, and she heard my terror and could not stop herself from looking out to see what terrible thing had happened. Her face, and neck, were totally exposed. Each wind is different but it tends to have its own, unique, consistency. She will be present, not only because it is duty but also because I cannot feed myself in any sort of polite surroundings. She cannot speak, but her mind is still the same. I would not like her hurt."

"Don't worry. I worked with people far more bizarre today than any I had ever dreamed about and had no trouble. The men who attacked us and committed those terrible acts on us—they were Akhbreed. Their leader was a changeling, but they were what we would call 'normal' on the outside. Inside, they were hideous, evil monsters. I do not judge people on how they look. I will not embarrass you or your mother." *I hope,* she added to herself.

He smiled. "I thank you for that. Now, come with me if you will."

They walked down a long corridor filled with portraits and antiques.

"I am curious," she said to him. "Just curious. Only part of you was exposed, and yet you were changed in more ways than just wings. Hollow bones, and apparently whatever was needed to allow you to fly and have enough energy and strength to do it."

He nodded. "That is the nature of the winds. Consistency, of sorts, is always preserved. No one is ever left who is not put together as a functioning being, no matter how much or little the exposure or where it is, although only the exposed areas are radically changed. Although my mother has no wings, internally we are consistent beings. Were it not unthinkably incestuous, we could actually mate and produce similarly structured creatures that would either be her way or mine. Impossible for us, of course, but there are actually some very small races, the products of the winds, that breed true. Ah! Here we are!"

Two guards uniformed in full military dress stood at the large wooden doors and opened them for the pair as they reached the entrance. Inside, there was a large rectangular paneled room with a long table at its center capable of seating six on a side and one at each end. There were candelabras lit on the table, and the chairs were lined with satin. It was very regal, and Sam felt decidedly underdressed, although somewhat relieved that only a few places were set.

The Duke clearly sat at the head of the table; Medac showed Sam to one chair to the Duke's left and apologized that he could not pull it out for her. She understood.

Almost immediately the Duke entered from the rear of the dining room, followed by his wife and one other man who might well have been an aide to the Duke. The Governor himself was a strikingly handsome man, the kind of man who seems to grow even more handsome and distinguished as the years go by. He had thick, curly gray hair and a bushy but perfectly groomed gray moustache, and a rugged, aristocratic face and bearing. He was the kind of man who could command attention anywhere, and in any crowd.

So would his wife, but not for the same reason. It was difficult to say what she had looked like but not a bad bet that she had been a perfect match for the Duke. Even at her age, which was probably not that much less than her husband, she had a strikingly good figure and a formal dress that fit perfectly. The fact that the head that now sat upon those slender shoulders was that of a huge, falconlike bird of prey emphasized the tragedy of the family.

Sam stood silently as they entered, and reminded herself that no matter what she must not stare at the Duchess. Idly she wondered how you greeted a Duke. Did you kiss his ring or bow or curtsy or what?

"Please, please! Be seated!" Duke Alon Pasedo said in a friendly, low baritone that matched the appearance perfectly. "We do not stand on ceremony here unless we have to. It is one of the few truly bright spots to living out here." He saw his wife to her seat and made certain that Medac was also seated. Sam realized that the chairs were all designed to allow the winged man some comfort so long as he kept his wings in. Then the Duke took his place and the other man took his next to Sam.

The stranger was fiftyish, balding, with thick glasses, and his face showed signs of weathering and wear.

"I am Alon Pasedo, and this is my wife, the Duchess Yova, and the gentleman to your left is Kano Layse, the Director of the Refuge we have established here. My son you already know. He is quite adept at spotting and guiding those lost and in need to our establishment. But, come! Let us eat, and then we will talk."

It was a hell of a meal, even if Sam didn't know what half of it was and had never tasted the variations of the half she *did* recognize before. If most of the staff were refugees, as they seemed to be called here, then one must have been a master chef. Food was served by a team of two men and two women who picked up dishes from windows into the kitchen hidden behind decorative screens and then brought them to the table. The servants had the usual evening dress of the house staff, but their skirts and sarongs seemed to be of very high quality, their flower garlands fresh and exotic, and they were both made up and immaculate.

The Duchess took no food herself, nor drink, either, but spent the time cutting and then hand-feeding her son. Medac seemed to have outgrown any embarrassment for the situation, since he was in fact helpless in such a dining room, and Sam suspected that what that falconlike head could eat, and how it ate it, would not be suitable for polite company.

The Duke controlled the talk, which was light and generally directed at her.

"You are not from an Akhbreed hub," he said casually, "although you speak the language quite well. Were you born a colonial in Tubikosa?"

"No, Your Grace," she responded, figuring out the proper form of address. "I am not native to Akahlar at all. I am one of those people who—dropped in, as it were, to my very great surprise."

"Ah! Fascinating! And yet you speak Akhbreed so well. It is a horror of a tongue, in spite of its versatility as a language. Deliberately evolved, I suspect, because even the smartest colonial can't master it on his own unless raised with it. Tell me, how did you learn it so well?"

"Sorcery, Your Grace," she responded. That was no lie, although it wasn't the complete truth.

"Ah, yes. I remember my staff saying something about an Akhbreed sorcerer's curse. That explains it. Usually the only ones from the Outplane who can learn our tongue are natural sorcerers themselves. But the better sorcerers can endow it, to their own purposes."

He very suddenly dropped that line to Sam's relief. She did not want to have to lie or admit that in fact she was allegedly some natural kind of sorcerer and that was how she knew the language and why she was such a prize.

There was more small talk, and then the Duke asked, "Is your home world like any of ours that you have seen?"

"Not really, although people are people, it seems, both good and bad and even indifferent. We had far more machines, for example. Flying machines and even personal machines that replaced the horse."

The Duke nodded. "I have heard of such worlds. That is one of the pities of Akahlar, you know. We could build flying machines, but with the kind of conditions we have and our instabilities we would never be able to get them or any other high-speed conveyance where we wanted it, or be certain that complex mechanical contraptions would obey the same minute physical and chemical laws in one place as they did in another. Even communication is a problem here. We could have a system that might work inside this building, for example, or perhaps through the whole complex, but it would always have static and interference. As for any distance—it is impossible. The shifts and constant changes in our borders cause impossible static. Still, there is much to be said for the old, tried-and-true ways. Slow and clumsy at times, perhaps, but also reassuring no matter where you are. And they keep our weapons development, our armies, on a level that does not assure total destruction."

"Where I came from they could destroy the world with a push of a button," she responded. "It always hung over us like a cloud."

"Exactly my point! Single-shot guns and cannon and swords and the like are more honorable, and far easier to control. The argument for super weapons is always that they will stop wars. But, tell me, did they stop wars and conflicts in your world?"

"No," she had to admit. "They stopped the really big wars but not all the small wars."

"Yes. And in Akahlar the big wars are impossible—the same conditions I spoke about prevent them, and the equality of the kingdoms maintains stability. We, too, have our little wars but without any threat of a global one. Who, after all, could conquer thousands and thousands of worlds? And what conqueror could be safe if he did not? No, the drawbacks here are the sorts of things that make a place like this necessary."

"Your Grace means the intolerance of the different."

"Yes, exactly. We already have to deal with thousands of races, many of them only remotely what we think of as human, but each is, after all, the natural denizen of his world. You would think that with so much variety there would be little trouble in at least tolerating the different, the unique, the ones and twos of a kind. But the sight, the existence, of one who was once Akhbreed terrifies them. It is not like one who is born different—that is natural. But the thought that one of their own could become so alien a creature, that touches a basic fear in our society. The system discriminates against anyone who does not meet the basic standards. Not everyone is that way—I was never that way—but a few rational thinkers have no way to change something which is deep in the fears of a people and their culture and society. One does not need a changewind or a curse, either. Those two girls you have with you are a fine example."

Sam nodded. "I don't know how to handle that, really, Your Grace. In my world they would get guardians, the state would provide homes, and they would inherit. Here—they are outcasts, even by their own."

"Exactly. Minors cannot inherit here, and unmarried females have fewer property rights. Your system is far more humane, or so it sounds to me, but the rigidity of this system is its true curse. They do not have to change, therefore they do not. I would not wish the suffering of my family on anyone, but I often believe there was some purpose to it. I had money, position. I could shelter them until I could arrange to move here and gain this appointment. I could afford to seek out likeminded, progressive thinkers who were frustrated by the system and bring them here. If criminals and traitors could find refuge here, then I saw no reason why good, decent unfortunates could not as well. Here there is no reason for ones like your girls to be sold to brothels or turned into chattel, or for people crippled or maimed to wind up in the gutters and back alleys. Here those afflicted with curses and those unfortunates who were caught in changewinds but not mentally deranged could find some peace and purpose."

She nodded. "It *is* nice here, and the people are very friendly and seem to not mind the differences. The feeling of security here is very reassuring, considering what I have been through."

"A refuge," he responded, sounding pleased. "We provide not only security but a decent life."

They were finally through the sumptuous meal, and the Duchess stood up and cocked her bird's head at the Duke, who said, "You may leave if you wish, my dear, or remain. Please, by all means, do what you wish."

The bird's head nodded, and the Duchess walked out that back entrance to the dining room.

"So, they tell me that you are off to get this sorcerer's curse lifted," the Duke remarked casually. "Tell me honestly—is your heart in that? Do you really want to go to a foreign Akhbreed sorcerer and beg for favor? Truthfully, now."

She sighed, and decided that honesty was still the best policy. "No," she responded. "It is just something that is forced on me. From what everyone says about these sorcerers, even though they maintain the system they are as dangerous as the changewind."

"More," the Duke replied seriously. "Far more. The changewind is terrifying mostly because it is random. It is a thief that comes in the night and steals all that you take for granted, but it is an honest, capricious, random thief with no malice and no thought, no motivation. It just is, a force of nature. One with the power of an Akhbreed sorcerer cannot help but go mad from the sheer power at his or her command. But their madness has thought, direction, and also shows no mercy. Even the best of them is dangerous, unstable, psychopathic. We are their playthings, not human beings to them, if they decide to play. Only the changewind keeps them humble. It is its place in the scheme of things, I believe. For even the greatest cannot control, deflect, or even defend himself against a changewind or its effects. There is some suspicion that the sorcerers themselves foster and promote this insane policy of destroying any people who become victims of the changewind, because they have no power over those victims. Our own sorcerers, should they be so inclined, could turn me into a frog or a maniac or a monster with a single spell. Yet they could do nothing to my wife or my son. If any Akhbreed sorcerer is ever destroyed, it is by the product of a changewind, for their power ends there and only another changewind can affect them."

That was something to think about. No *wonder* they killed them when they could! The Akhbreed ruled by the power of their sorcerers and maintained their system and their position by virtue of that power. The changelings, then, would be the only things other than the winds themselves that the Akhbreed leaders would fear.

They wrapped it up with some more small talk, mostly about her and the refuge, and she had the sense to know that it was over. The Duke stood up, and so did the Director, and so she and Medac did as well, and the Governor said good night and the two departed out the back way. It was only after they had gone that Sam realized that this Director hadn't said more than a few words the whole evening. Perhaps it was just that when the Duke wanted to talk you didn't dare not let him talk.

Medac escorted her back to the head of the stairs. "You did quite well," he told her. "I want to thank you for it."

"I did nothing at all. Your father is a charming man."

"Yes," the winged man replied with an odd tone of voice. "I often wonder if I was not fortunate to become a changeling. I cannot imagine myself taking his place or having the ability to make so many hard decisions." He sighed. "Well, good night and good luck on the work the next few days. I hope your future brings happiness and peace of mind."

She was charmed by that. "Thank *you*. I don't know where I'd be or even if I'd be alive without you and your father. But I must go now. That potion is wearing off and I want to make it to my bed before I collapse."

Medac watched her go, then sighed, turned, and walked back by a different route to the living quarters. As he expected, his father and the Director were in the study, talking animatedly over cigars and coffee. They both looked up when the winged man entered.

"Ah, Medac! Come, relax and join us," the Duke invited. "I want your input on this. First, has there been any sign of this Boday or her friend?"

"Not really. The rebel band that was ambushed and massacred just east of here shows that a strong band of marauders was in the area about the same time. The two women did not turn in here, which suggests that they were tracking the rebels, either out of fear that their companions had been taken or out of some sense of bravado that perhaps they could get back their horses and belongings. Two naked, defenseless women definitely did not do that to the rebels, and there were signs of a considerable number in the attacking band. There were no women's bodies found, and they did not double back, and they did not meet our own patrol coming from downriver. The inescapable conclusion is that the same band that hit the rebels captured them. They are probably not dead, but are almost certainly beyond caring by now."

The Duke nodded. "I feared as much. Any luck on identifying the band? I do not like anyone operating independently this close to our lands here, although they appear to have only hit the rebels and not anything or anyone of ours. That implies at least partly a political act."

"Yes, but that's probably why I can pick up nothing of importance. Oh, I have a few details. Tracking down the horses and the booty was not difficult, but it was already through many hands and they were very closedmouthed about it. They had hoped, I think, to get away without paying our 'tax,' as it were."

"I also don't like any of Klittichorn's hordes in *my* canyon without *my* knowledge or permission," the Duke growled. "They had a small army in the region. Still do, I suspect. Brazen bastards."

"They are beginning to move off and away now," Medac told him. "You know, I wonder if there isn't a connection there. They put out the word that they would pay a tremendous sum to anyone who brought them a slender young woman with a superficial resemblance to the Storm Princess. Do you suppose that perhaps this Susama's young friend might have been that one? If so, we *know* what's happened to them."

The Director stirred for the first time. "Interesting. Your Grace, that might explain a lot. A double. A living duplicate of the Storm Princess, perhaps an *exact* duplicate, born and raised on another world. Somebody like Boolean, who has been crying for years about Klittichorn's threat, might go after such a one in order to make a switch or train her as a combatant. Those powers are unique. And the great storm that did in the train but also did in the raiders—it might be!"

The Duke scratched his chin. "And this Susama?"

"Obviously a friend, probably sucked along when Klittichorn or Boolean or whoever opened a hole and dropped the double down. That would explain the interest around here, all the events, and even why an Akhbreed sorcerer would be interested in them and give them language and a curse."

"But it was Susama who was cursed, not the other," Medac pointed out.

"Yes, sir, but who knows what powers, what resistance she might have? But if she were loyal to her friend, then curse the friend."

The Duke sat back and sighed. "Logical. And the fact that Klittichorn's men are now withdrawing from the area can have but one meaning. And that means this Susama is most certainly alone and stuck here. She'd have no chance of even getting that curse removed now. She has no future, gentlemen. She's without funds, has no family or tribe or anyone to fall back on, is bright but illiterate and has no meaningful skills."

"She also has no self-esteem," the Director pointed out. "You could see that by how she presents and carries herself. She'll wind up desolate, alone—I'd say there is a better than ninety percent chance that she would do away with herself."

"I don't believe there is any reason or mercy in waiting," the Duke said. "Even if her friend should somehow miraculously come into our hands we would have different uses for her than merely a reunion with a friend. You have our permission to incorporate them into the refugee program immediately."

"I will set it up for tomorrow morning, Your Grace," the Director replied.

The Duke looked over at his son, who seemed to have a disapproving look on his face. "You still have bad feelings about this. Consider, my son—if we left it up to her she would refuse and cling to a fantasy, a dream. She is someone truly without hope or future and she is insisting on jumping into an abyss. Would you gain her permission before you saved her from jumping?"

Medac sighed. "I see your point, Father. It's just, well, she was different and likeable. Totally without any reaction to me or Mother or any of the others except curiosity."

"And that will not change. That is the nature of this place."

When she first awoke she had, quite literally, no memories at all, nor any direct means of thought, although she was curious and aware, as a small baby might be aware. Then they began talking to her, not as before but in the peasant vulgar dialect of Mashtopol Akhbreed speech. As she heard each word and phrase and thought she understood it, as if it were being written indelibly inside her mind, and within a few hours she could think quite clearly in the Akhbreed tongue.

She lapped up everything they told her like a sponge, accepting it unquestioningly at face value. They had found her wandering lost and alone out in the dangerous, hot, endless desert and had taken her in. She was now a part of a great community under the leadership of Her Lord the Duke, who was kind and wise and provided all things for everyone that they would ever need or desire. All the people worked for the common good, and each had a vital role in keeping everything going. Each had a function which, when added to everyone else's functions, created a common, just society in which all were absolutely equal.

All products of the community were given to the Duke, the wisest and most just, who then redistributed them so that all received according to their needs. Beyond the community was only desolation, danger, and death. The Duke protected the community from it, and kept it safe. The community was a loving, sharing family of which the Duke was the wise, kind, and all-powerful father. All thoughts were towards the community's good; no one was above the good of the whole, and no individual should ever put him or herself above or below the group. All were brothers, all were sisters, and all were essential parts of an integrated whole.

She wanted to belong; she wanted to find her place, her function, and to contribute. She felt safe and secure within it, and wanted no part of anywhere else.

She was startled to find that she was a girl, although she would have been equally startled to discover she was anything but. It was a strange face and figure that stared back at her in the mirror, but she accepted it. Everyone told her how cute she was, how her big breasts were so desirable, how lucky she was to be so cute and look the way she did, and she accepted that as well.

They told her that her name was Misa, and although it sounded strange she answered to it afterwards because it was the only name she had. Then they told her that her function would be to work in the fields, planting and picking and tending the community's important food, and she thought that was wonderful.

Then they brought her to a long three-tier adobe complex and she climbed the ladders to the top level and then went into one of the "rooms" in the center. It was a one-room affair, with two sets of bunk beds on opposing walls, a worn but serviceable rug with pretty designs on the floor, oil lamps, and at the rear a long dresser that took up the entire back wall and contained areas for each of the occupants' clothing and personal effects plus some crude wooden stools and mirrors.

Water was rationed but there was a communal bathhouse two blocks of apartments down. There were also communal toilets there, but mostly you used a bedpan-type gadget and room-mates took turns emptying it and sanitizing it each day. Human solid waste was not to be discarded; it was placed in community bins and then blended with other things and spread in the fields, so that what was needed by the land was given back to it.

Her roommates were girls near her own age, all products of the system and true believers in it, all lifelong field workers. They embraced and took to her as if she and they had known each other all their lives, and it was from them she learned the rest of what was necessary to be learned.

She made a concentrated effort to model herself after them in all things; to talk like them, act like them, *think* like them, until in a very few days it was impossible to tell the new from the old. They talked and giggled and played silly games and compared the various men around and everything was open and shared. Mostly, of course, they worked—long, hard days, but nobody minded or complained because everybody had to work to keep the community whole. Without them, the community would not be fed and the groves would die. They were vital and that made them proud.

What little they had they shared freely. There was no lying, no cheating, no stealing, no thoughts of deception or shirking work or duty. There were also no questions. None. The entire world, its rules, and your place in it were clearly defined. It was the way it was, that's all. You couldn't change anything and you wouldn't want to, because it was good the way it was.

She liked field work because it wasn't the same all the time. After a time of fruit picking, you might do a tour elsewhere in the irrigation system ass-deep in mud making sure just the right water went where it was supposed to, and next you might be planting behind a narga-pulled plow, knowing that what you planted you would see grow and thrive and bear useful things for the community. Honest mistakes, even carelessness, were never punished; instead you felt terrible about it and everyone worked to reassure you and to teach you so that you did not make the same mistake twice.

And the work grew easier with time; she needed less to drink, felt hardier and more confident, and finished without aches and pains and tiredness much of the time as her muscles grew and her body conditioned itself. She grew no thinner, but her arms and legs began developing a hell of a set of muscles. It was not something she was conscious of, but it was noticeable in her neck and shoulders and when she flexed her arms.

Far from feeling self-conscious about her weight, she relished it as a reflection of power, the way a wrestler took pride in bulk, and no other girl had breasts so enormous; and because she could lose no weight the effect of muscle development in her neck and shoulders had the effect of pulling the breasts up and thrusting them out firmly so that there was little sag. She called them her "melons"—and she liked to flaunt them, never so much as during Endday, the one day of the week where they worked only half a day and threw a grand communal party and celebration that lasted well into the night. Then she would don her one fine patterned sarong and the traditional flower necklace and dance with the best of them. They took to calling her *Noma Ju,* which literally meant Big Tits, and she didn't mind a bit, taking it in the playful spirit that it was used.

She did, however, allow her roommates to do something of a makeover on her. There was a magic potion you could get from a friend or a relative of a friend who worked in the residence that would make your hair grow at a miraculous pace and they procured enough of the weakened formula to allow her to grow in a matter of weeks hair just below shoulder length, which set off her face and made her look much better. All the other girls had their ears pierced, so she did, too, even though it *hurt*, getting small rings inserted on which you could clip longer ones for special occasions like Endday Festival; and she started taking some care in her appearance outside of work and even in the way she walked and talked.

She found herself most comfortable around the women but the men seemed attracted to her and she *did* tease them a lot. Virtually all the Akhbreed peasant women were lean and muscular; her more padded form and largest attributes hanging out there seemed to turn some folks on. She found that she liked to be kissed and hugged and fondled but she didn't ever let it get too far. Although sex was rather casual among the peasant communes, a pregnancy meant an obligatory marriage and for some reason she just could not bring herself to take the risk.

And there were the dreams. Strange dreams, sometimes, of another person, another place, in some magical royal castle. A strange woman with a deep voice that was cold, eerie, aristocratic, and a fearsome nightmare figure in crimson robes and horns on his head. She felt that, somehow, these dreams were of the evil around the community, the evil from which they said she'd escaped, and so she did not talk about these dreams with anyone. Perhaps they were somehow shadows from her past, but she did not want to know any more. At least they were not common; she had experienced only four of them so far, and she could live with that.

Still, she was happy, *very* happy, and content, and she had no questions.

Up in the residence, however, where the peasant folk virtually never went and held in some awe, there were questions.

"This is a high desert," Duke Pasedo grumbled. "It has almost always been so and it stretches out for most of the continent. It rains for perhaps an hour every two or three years, and often less than that, and the land and the system, *our* system, is based upon it. And yet, in two months, just *two months*, gentlemen, it has rained heavily four times! Four times! Some of the crops are in danger, the irrigation system is a shambles in many places, and along the canyons there are now many landslides. I want to know how this can happen. What is causing it?"

The Director sighed and shrugged his shoulders. "Your Grace, these things happen. Some shift, somewhere, causes freak occurrences of all sorts of weather. You remember several years ago we had that freakish cold and actually a bit of snow over the night."

The Duke slammed his fist on the table. "That is one incident. This is more of a long pattern. My son has watched these storms, since I feared they might be Sudogs or some other sorcery, but they appear to be just storms—but localized. Very localized, and with no apparent source of moisture. It rains only on *us*! It collects from nowhere, rains, then dissipates. That is not natural, gentlemen. Not natural at all. When you begin to get such magical storms, can the change-wind be far behind, attracted to this very spot? Can you imagine what a changewind would do to this place, all our dreams? Yes, I see you are about to assure me that we are adequately protected, but the land is not! The river and canyons are not! The balance is delicate here."

"We are doing what we can to find the cause," the Director assured him. "Possibly a changewind deflection from some point. We will need to find it to see how or even if we can deal with it, though."

"I want the cause found. I want it stopped!" the Duke ordered.

Duke Pasedo was not the only one becoming aware of the phenomenon. When strong powers are exercised anywhere, those most sensitive to those powers grow aware of them, and with each passing incident the location and then the source grows more and more apparent.

Klittichorn, who liked to be known as the Horned Demon of the Snows although he was no demon and his horns were mere ornaments, was troubled. Several times now his concentration had been broken by a sense of activity somewhere far off. He liked it least because it was coming from a region where it should not be. The only one who had crossed through

Mashtopol had been that courtesan girl, and he had forces looking for her and he knew at least where she was not.

Was it someone new, someone he'd missed in spite of his best efforts? Or had that son of a bitch Boolean drawn him off with a decoy?

No, that didn't make sense, either. If the courtesan was a decoy, then the real one would be well away from Mashtopol by now and in another direction. Hell, it had been over two months since the showdown with his trusted agent Asterial, Blue Witch of the Kudaan Wastes, and all it had done was have her trapped in a nether-hell with some nutty demon Boolean had cornered and coerced into service. That had been a major blow, since she was the only really trustworthy one with any real power he'd had there. Damn! With thousands of worlds it was pretty damned difficult to cover *everywhere* with quality people!

That silly Duke with the messiah complex might have nabbed the real one, but he sure as hell wouldn't hold on to her. He'd play Boolean off against him for the best advantage and fast. But there had been a split-off somewhere. The courtesan and that lunatic artist were missing their friend, the other one who'd fallen through. What if that one had lost her mind and perhaps had fallen into the hands of some of the crooked characters out there? Hell, she could be some kind of mindless slave or bound by all sorts of nasty spells somewhere in the Wastes with neither she nor whoever had her even aware of her nature.

Could she be the one? Could he have been a sucker, maybe still a sucker? That other one had been reported a tub of lard wed to a lesbian loony, hardly the sort, and yet . . . If the duplicate were ever physically transformed her effectiveness would cease, yet would putting on all that weight qualify?

He slapped his forehead. *Shit! I've been a double-dyed idiot! I could do battle with a great sorcerer or a greater soldier, but I keep getting taken in by that bastard of a con man! Outsmarting him was like trying to find the escape clause in a Satanic contract!*

But if the other was a decoy, then the magic worked by the first might be out of dreams or emotional periods, not conscious acts. If she was still in the Kudaan, that meant that

Boolean didn't have her, either. He turned and shouted, "Adjutant!"

A man entered and bowed. "Sir?"

"I have reason to believe that Boolean's suckered us again and that the girl we've been chasing is a decoy. The one we want is the fat one, and I think she's under somebody's control and still in the Kudaan. Sooner or later somebody is going to notice the same things I have felt and find the source. I want her found first!"

The Adjutant looked thoughtful. "It won't be easy. Some of our patrols got massacred in there the last time, and if we take an army in they'll just go to ground and all we'll have is another Chief Sorcerer and perhaps a king as an enemy. To have any chance in that hole will require magic."

Klittichorn nodded. This fellow was a damned good man and he'd learned to rely heavily on his mind before going off half-cocked. "Yes, yes, I agree. And Sudogs aren't going to do it. We can't maintain them long enough there. We shall need Stormriders."

"But they themselves will cause some of the same disruptions as she would," the Adjutant pointed out. "And how are we to find her? A fat girl the same height as Her Highness isn't much to go on."

Klittichorn was thinking hard. "Their energy will be of a different sort. Still, you are right. Without a description all the spies on the ground and Stormriders in the air would be useless. And who knows what she looks like by now, within the limits? We'll just have to put people in there and wait for the next manifestation of stormbringer power. With the riders present it should be quite easy to localize it. That could possibly take weeks, but if Boolean hasn't found her by now I think at least we start even. Better than even, since he has nothing like my forces at his command."

"As you will, sir. Should I call off the ones hunting the artist and the courtesan?"

"No. For one thing, we can't be sure of the decoy. If they are anywhere close to making a run for it and need a diversion, it's just like Boolean to arrange something like this to draw us off. Besides, if we miss this time the artist will give us another chance. They foolishly married one another back in Tubikosa and that invoked a spell. They are linked until the death of one of them, whether they know it or not, and it has certain other attributes that might prove useful just in case."

"As you wish, sir."

"And, Adjutant . . ."

"Sir?"

"We cannot afford to allow this to drag on. One or the other and quickly. We are reaching the point where limited and theoretical tests are of no further benefit. The conditions under which a full-scale operation will work are quite precise mathematically and do not occur every day or week or even month. We must show our strength to retain our allies and gain new converts, if not through the demonstration that we could actually win then through fear of our disfavor. I should not like any wild cards out there, as it were, complicating matters, no matter how remote the possibility."

The Adjutant bowed. "We will do all that is possible, sir; of that I assure you."

The sorcerer chuckled. "This is Akahlar, where *nothing* is impossible!"

Heat shimmered off the desert floor and made the air dance in strange new patterns, distorting distance and rippling the few shadows. The small caravan made its way slowly and deliberately across the floor, following no road but only the experience of its Navigator, who sat then on a horse walking slowly beside the lead wagon.

He was a big man; not merely tall, although he was certainly that, but broad and tough, a mountain man's physique. He had a broad-brimmed white hat, creased in the middle, and wore light, almost cream-colored buckskins that showed his perspiration and the grit of the trail but also helped reflect the heat.

His face was broad and weathered, his hair and full beard long and strawberry blond, making him a striking figure in any setting. His odd, steel gray eyes, protected somewhat from the glare by swatches of black dabbed on beneath them, scanned the horizon, almost as if they sensed something not quite right. He reached down and took out his binoculars and looked again, then put up his hand.

"Hold up!" he called. "Break but stand ready! We have a

rider coming and I'd rather meet anybody out here on the flats where they got no place to hide."

Distances were deceiving in the desert, but this rider was clearly very close. The Navigator frowned, wondering why he or one of his crew hadn't seen the rider long before now. It was almost as if both horse and rider had materialized out of the desert shimmer. He didn't like that. It meant either a sorcerous enemy or an emissary from an old friend who was about as welcome news as the sorcerous enemy.

The rider approached to about a thousand feet of the caravan but then halted, standing there shimmering in the heat as if some bizarre apparition, waiting. The Navigator again looked through the binoculars, then sighed, and shouted, "It's all right. I know who it is, although I don't think I want to know what it's about. Full break and at ease. I'll be back in a few minutes." With that he spurred his horse onward to meet the newcomer.

The closer he got to the rider, the more ephemeral the vision. It was a man, or something like a man, astride a great black horse, but it was curiously flat, almost two-dimensional, and there were streaks or breaks in the vision that momentarily showed the desert beyond. Horse and rider almost merged into a black, streaking thing, but if you looked sharp you could see details, including the fact that the horse was standing not on, but slightly above, the desert floor.

The Navigator came very close to the apparition and stopped.

"Hello, Crim," said the dark rider, in a voice that was both ordinary and yet unnatural, with a slight echolike reverberation in it.

"I figured it was you," the Navigator responded. "You always liked to do things the dramatic way."

The dark rider laughed. "It is the only fun I get sometimes. I have an urgent problem that only you are in a position to help me solve."

"So what else is new?"

Again the laugh. "You are always one of the best I can turn to, Crim, in spite of your lack of any particular fear and respect for such as me. You have heard the rumors concerning the Storm Princess?"

Crim nodded. "Lots of 'em, and lots of activity as well. I can't say I approve much of the friends she has and the company she keeps."

"Nor do I, although from her point of view they are the only ones who would keep company with her so long as she persists in her prideful ambition. Klittichorn plays on it, and the military minds attracted to them know how to use all that power. I have spent years trying to convince the others to listen to me, but to no avail. My colleagues in the other capitals believe that I am attempting some sort of power play myself, or are too mad to care. The kings will unite against a common foe only when they personally feel threatened, and their minds are being expertly poisoned against me. I admit that I underestimated them, or, perhaps, overestimated myself. He is a great and cautious organizer and I am an opportunist. We were always that way. Now, perhaps, I finally pay for our differences, but it is not just me."

"You really think true empire is possible here?"

"Perhaps. Perhaps not. But it will not happen in spite of all their dreams, for Klittichorn is not interested in empire. He has an even grander design than theirs, and it could destroy all humanity everywhere. At the very best, it will eliminate civilization and most of the population of all the universes, not just those of Akahlar, in a form of devastation that would repel even him if he could see it. But he is blind to consequences, which is a common failing of his type. He is growing, Crim, but I can still stop him. Without the uniqueness of the Storm Princess both plans are doomed to failure. I found others in the Outplane. So did he, of course, but he killed them. I brought mine here, but they were ill-prepared for Akahlar or too easily recognized by Klittichorn's agents. They have me effectively boxed in, and I am running out of options. I believe I know where my most promising prospect is, but I dare not go to her myself or show any direct interest in her. This would be sensed."

Crim was intrigued. "Another Storm Princess? Huh! Think of that. And not far, I take it?"

"On your route. You recall the disaster that befell Jahoort's train?"

"Yeah. About three months back. He was a good man."

"Jahoort carried one of mine among his train, and another who precisely resembles the Princess. My doing—opportunistic again. It's worked fairly well, although I doubt if the young lady without the powers is exactly enamored of me or her role. I had arranged to separate them farther on, drawing off Klittichorn's people, but they were split in the disaster, or its aftermath. My people made the most thorough search of the whole region that has ever been made and could not find her. I believed she'd suffered some sort of injury to the head or fallen into one of the wild powers of this place. I would have known if she were dead. She has no real control of her powers and I have sensed her. It has already rained four times in the past eleven weeks on our august Royal Governor."

"The Duke? But why would he have her? I heard nothing about any survivors coming in and I've been through there twice since Jahoort's wipeout. If he didn't know who she was he'd have put her with me or one of the others who came through, and if he did he'd be trying to bargain her to either you or Klittichorn while keeping her buried. But he wouldn't hold on to her for this long. She's too hot to hold, even in this place."

"There is a third possibility that never occurred to me until now, lulled as I was by the same logic you just used. What if she was injured, perhaps in the head, and was found by the Duke's people? Or, possibly, what if she just kept her mouth shut and played poor little lone survivor? The Duke is a collector of injured animals and stray cats, as it were."

Crim whistled. "He'd give her one of their patented amnesia potions and she'd join the crowd. If she wasn't on staff or anything I might never have seen or heard of her. Those peasants won't hardly speak to an outsider. That means she'll have a new identity, maybe a new personality, and she won't remember anything of what she was. And they're almost never alone, particularly the women."

"The process is alchemical?"

"Yeah, I think so. They might use spells if they need to— they got a couple of pretty good magicians on the staff—but I'd guess it was alchemical. Their own concoction, though. And it's *permanent*. I never heard of a relapse."

"There is no such thing as a permanent potion if it leaves its taker alive and physically intact. I can deal with it, even from here, but first we will need her away from that commune."

"You don't know what you're asking! First I told you how it's nearly impossible to get one alone. One of 'em coughs and everybody in the group wipes their nose. And what if you could, and get out of the canyon district unnoticed—also no mean trick, by the way. You know he's got a small army there. You'd have a dull-eyed ignorant peasant girl fighting like hell and probably so mad and so scared that Klittichorn's men would only have to look for the permanent moving rainstorm and that would be me."

"You haven't heard the half of it. In order to make the decoy believable and the real one be overlooked, I took advantage of a situation she brought on herself and rendered her permanently quite fat. She is very short, and she almost certainly weighs at least a hundred halgs."

"Oh, great! Forget it! Klittichorn will just have to destroy civilization, that's all. It's impossible."

"I am an Akhbreed sorcerer, and not without power and resources. This is Akahlar. Nothing is impossible here."

"Then get yourself another sucker. This one values what he has."

"But you have unique qualifications of all those available, not the least of which is that you speak English like a native and that is her own old native tongue. I don't make that the primary qualification—the last time I did the bastard turned traitor on me and wound up cursed—but you are the only one I trust because I know of your distaste for Klittichorn."

Crim sighed. "I'll need a lot of help, and a lot of briefing as well. And I still need convincing. What are you offering to spring her?"

"Nothing. Not a thing. She is of no value to me merely 'sprung,' as it were. I need her *here*. The first one, anyone, who delivers her here, alive and physically intact, will gain the ultimate. One wish, and no funny business about the terms and conditions. Anything within the power of an Akhbreed sorcerer, Crim. *Anything*. But it's all or nothing."

Crim stared hard at the shadowlike horseman. "What's that sort of hovering there? A tree limb? You son of a bitch, you're riding in some nice park or forest all shaded and comfortable and I'm sitting out here in the middle of a desert hot enough to fry meat! You want her that bad, you ask the impossible, you give all the help and charms and information and everything else you have and you deliver three wishes."

"Two and it's done. One for you and one for Kira. Any more haggling and I'll make it a more open offer to others."

"All right, you bastard. But for that price you could just walk up to the Duke and get her."

"Perhaps, but he could not get her safely to me. And, of course, I cannot grant the only wishes that Pasedo would be interested in anyway, since even I cannot alter what a changewind has done. Nor could I trust him if he knew her value."

Crim sighed. "Very well, but this won't be easy. It'll take some time to figure out how to do it at all. I'll give you a preliminary list of what I think I'll need and soon. I'm only a few days from there now and we'll camp tonight at the river gorge. Take it up with Kira tonight at the gorge in the cool of the evening. If she still agrees, we'll make a good stab at it."

"This is the big one, Crim. Plenty for any whom you take into the plan, although of course the nature of the girl and my motives will be between us alone. Let the others wonder. But anyone who betrays us will find no refuge anywhere."

"Yeah. And we won't mention *my* reward, will we? Even the most trusted people can be tempted to knock me off and claim it themselves. No skin off your nose but plenty off mine."

"Agreed, for now. So long as you have and control the girl. If you lose her I reserve the right to broaden the offer. Now you are broiling and I have dallied long enough, so go, get a drink and make your time. All this riding fatigues me."

"Okay, you bastard. I'll see about your dirty work. At the gorge, tonight."

"At the gorge tonight," the strange dark rider echoed, then it turned and rode off.

Crim watched it go, away from him, out into the desert, until it was one with the rippling air. Only then did he turn and make his way back to the caravan, but he only idly gave the "ready to move out" sign with his hand. He was already beginning to formulate plans—not details, but a broad outline.

Some of this would require subtlety, and that was more of a Kira specialty. Still, you couldn't dream of a greater reward, but by damn they were going to earn every bit of it! And if Boolean had to be squeezed and sweated a little bit in the process, all the better.

# · 5 ·

## Of Slavery, Decoys, and Shadowcats

COMUG, THE CHIEF slave administrator of the House of Hodamoc, did not like to disturb his Master unless it was absolutely necessary. For one thing, the General often took out his irritation on the slaves closest to him, although he regretted it later. When you've spent hours in pain or are bleeding from terrible wounds, a sincere apology isn't all that appreciated.

Still, this had to be done. He knocked on the door of the Master's study, then waited patiently.

"Yes? What is it?" Hodamoc snapped irritatedly.

"Comug, Master. A thousand apologies, but there is someone here who demands an audience with you."

The door had not opened. "Did you say *demands*? Who is this who demands anything of me?"

"A magician, Master. Third Rank by his garb. He says his name is Dorion and that he is an urgent messenger from Yobi. It was because of this last that I dared to disturb you."

For a moment there was no reply. Suddenly the door flew open, and the General, looking more puzzled than angry, stood there. Comug bowed slightly and just waited, being one of the few slaves who did not prostrate him or herself in the Master's presence. Since he dealt with the Master on a day-to-day basis it would be rather impractical.

"Yobi . . ." Hodamoc mused. "What the hell does that crazy old bag want of me?" He sighed. "Still, she's Second Rank. It wouldn't do to piss her off without first hearing her out. Very well, Comug. Alert the House Magician and

Security. If they clear him I will see him, but you can never be too careful about his type."

"Master, he is as he says. Several of the slaves have seen him before in the bazaars and he is not completely unknown. He is a permanent resident and exile and does often do errands for Yobi. Had I not already checked on this I would never have allowed him even this far."

The General nodded, subdued. After all, that *was* why Comug was around in the first place and held the position he did.

"All right, then—show him up."

Dorion was not the sort of fellow to inspire awe and terror. Of medium height, perhaps five nine or ten to Hodamoc's six three, he was stocky, a bit chubby, with a pleasant, cherubic face that he'd attempted unsuccessfully to harden by growing a far too thin and wispy beard and moustache. His long reddish brown hair was thin and stringy and had vanished on top to a fair degree, giving him a monklike appearance enhanced by the rumpled wool earth-brown robe he wore. His deep blue eyes had that glazed look so common to magicians, and while he moved with confidence it seemed as if he were seeing by some method other than the usual sight. He had one of those brassy magician's baritones, though, which in incantations and spells might well sound commanding and authoritative but which in normal conversation often sounded either insincere or shrill.

Dorion bowed slightly. "Your Excellency, I bring you greetings from Yobi of the Sarcin Caves. I am Dorion, formerly of Masalur, a humble magician surviving here by doing services for others."

"An errand boy, you mean," the General responded, unimpressed. "Very well—you asked for my time and while I cannot spare it at the moment I am willing to grant an audience, so have done with it and dispense with the flowery and meaningless rhetoric if you have not lost your capacity for speaking plainly."

Dorion gave a weak smile and shrugged. "Very well, then. Someone important to Yobi was waylaid first by some rebel force that tried to penetrate the river valley and then in its aftermath was taken by raiders from Shorm. They were brought here, auctioned to the high bidder, and enslaved. You were the high bidder, Excellency, and you have her. Yobi wants her back.''

The General's eyebrows rose. "Indeed? You mean that pretty little whore?"

"Courtesan, Excellency. She is of some importance to Yobi, although I do not know the reason for it. *Very* important. Yobi understands your expense and is willing to be quite generous to regain her."

"The expense is irrelevant. She is a possession, part of my collection here. She was dear enough to buy in the first place; now you have added value to her. I collect, sir. I do not sell my collection."

Dorion cleared his throat a bit nervously. "Excellency, you know full well that while Yobi is of necessity banished to this place she nonetheless is a sorceress of great power and, in fact, some influence among the Second Rank. While she rarely gets involved in the affairs of the Kudaan, she can offer things of great value, and she is of the same sort of mind as Your Excellency regarding those things which she considers hers by right."

The General had to stifle a grin. It was the nicest and pleasantest threat he had ever received.

"And you, Sir Magician, know full well that the girl is bonded to me by blood and relics. I am not saying that you couldn't take her, but if she violated my will and left these grounds even involuntarily and could not get back she would simply die and leave you with nothing. Your Yobi might break that spell but only with full rituals, and she would never survive to get to those rituals. An attempt on me is also fruitless. I am protected from much by powers as great as your Yobi's, and even if you succeeded in a more conventional way I have no heirs. Upon my death my slaves will destroy all this, and then themselves, although even they do not know this. We have nothing further to talk about."

Again the magician did his nervous throat-clearing. "Uh, pardon, Excellency, but as a humble middleman I can but see two sides of equal will and determination. You are a soldier and great leader. A thousand pardons for bringing this up, but you exist outside your natural element here, in the Wastes, in relative comfort of exile I admit, but not as you would wish or should be. With Yobi it is different. She is no longer purely Akhbreed by the one power none can withstand. But neither is she retired. Are you truly content being retired here in the Wastes? If so, we can go no further."

The General sat back in his chair. "Just what do you have in mind?"

"As I am sure you are aware, Warog, the Imperial Akhbreed Sorcerer, is now so mad that he is beyond much of this world and, as is the eventual fate of all such powers, has become obsessed with the next world. It would take very little to push him completely over and remove him from the scene, but so wild and insane are his tempers now that only one of the Second Rank can even dare contact him. His acolytes are ruined as successors by this, so should he decide to seek First Rank status his position would become vacant. The number of Second Rank sorcerers capable of assuming the post and interested in it are quite limited. Should the successor be friendly to your own interests, it might fill in your one missing factor. Or, of course, it might well be someone inimical to your interests, in which case you will enjoy a permanent retirement."

The General stared at him. "Let me get this straight. You're saying that Yobi can push old Warog out of the picture and put a friendly young new fellow in the post who might be dissatisfied with the current political arrangement? Is that what you're saying? And all that trouble and work for a mere little whore?"

"I am but a messenger but I believe Your Excellency has at least a basic grasp of the message."

General Hodamoc sighed. "Well, first of all it brings up a sense of disbelief. I find it next to impossible to believe that Yobi or anyone else could pull it all off. But assuming against my better judgment and belief that this *could* be done, it brings up the question of just what makes this piece of fluff worth such work. You face me then with a problem, sir. If I give her to you, I must take on faith that all you say can and will be done. Not doubting that the old girl thinks she can do it, belief and accomplishment are two very different things. I know that well. It is why I'm stuck here. On the other hand, you have demonstrated that I own something of great value. If she is of great value to your mistress, then she is most certainly of great value to others. I believe I should see who else is offering something for her, then, perhaps of more certain value."

"That would be a mistake, Excellency," Dorion warned him in the same casual tone he'd used up to now. "One of your greatness should not make two grave mistakes in a lifetime. This is the business of sorcery, not practical men. Not merely Yobi but other high-ranking Akhbreed sorcerers are involved. Your protections come from Warog in better, earlier times, and they are formidable, but to have more than one of the Second Rank angered at you . . . Well, it would not be a clever thing for so brilliant a man to depend too heavily on those protections, particularly without Warog in his prime to back them up."

The General stood up straight. "You *dare* threaten me in my own house, in my own lands, in my own office?" he roared.

Sometimes the power of magicians stems not only from their supernatural abilities but also from their simple, nonmagical craft side. Having removed a small vial from a hidden pocket in his robe sleeve, Dorion deftly uncorked it without dropping that cork and even as he spoke to the General he turned the vial over and let its powdery contents fall to the floor of the office. The vial was then recorked and replaced in its hidden pocket, all in a matter of seconds, all in plain view, and all, thanks to manipulative skill alone, without the General seeing any of it.

"I do not threaten, Excellency, nor does Yobi. But this affair goes far beyond your own ambitions and interests, and involves the most powerful of people. I came here, unarmed and without rancor or malice or any evil intent, to convey to you an honest offer. My part is as an honest messenger only and that I have fulfilled. By your leave, Excellency, I will return and convey your sentiments honestly and truly to those who sent me. My part is now done."

General Hodamoc was having a hard time controlling his temper, but he felt he dealt from a position of power in this matter and the cooler part of his mind told him that it would not do to harm this insolent bastard. That would create a pretext for immediate retaliation by Yobi, and right now he needed time, both to find out just what was so important about this girl and to prepare defenses against whatever magic might ultimately be directed his way. He was of the Akhbreed blood royal, and even as an outcast and exile with a price on his head he had certain special rights and access by virtue of that blood.

"You tell your mistress I demand to know exactly why this girl is important and to whom, and then I might *discuss* the matter further," Hodamoc told the magician. "I make no promises, though. Now—get out of here! I am about to issue orders that if you are ever on my estate again you are to be killed on sight, and even your precious little whore will drive the knife into you if she sees you!"

The magician bowed, touched his forehead, then turned and walked out of the office at a brisk pace. The threat to his personal safety didn't bother him very much, but it was best to be out of this place as quickly as possible for—other—reasons. Hodamoc wasn't the only one who knew of the mystic bond that might be summoned by one of the blood royal, and how much time it would take, nor could Yobi afford to allow the General even enough time to start an inquiry on the girl. The General now believed himself in total control of the situation, and it was time to disillusion him by illustrating his one major mistake.

Back in his office, Hodamoc tried to think things through. Assuming that even a small amount of what the fellow said was true, this little bitch was of some major importance. Why? Perhaps she carried information in her empty little head even she did not know. A courier whose recorded dispatch could be extracted only by one knowing how. That would explain the foreign soldiers chasing her, but it didn't add up. Yobi would hardly need a courier to send and receive any sort of message. Those top sorcerers just sort of transported a part of themselves and talked securely and directly.

A sacrifice, perhaps? She was quite pretty, but hardly a virgin and not of much use in that regard. Perhaps the daughter of someone important, bound to the courtesan life as a runaway, whom Yobi had been asked to find. That made the most sense. Someone *very* important, since she'd be a pariah to the bulk of the population considering her current state.

He needed more information. He had a slave, Pocasa, who was a pretty good artist. A good, faithful drawing of this girl would be of great use, perhaps with a lock of that long hair for magical and alchemical analysis. Many of the troopers stationed at Duke Pasedo's were of his old guard, and they were handy go-betweens. Yes, that was the way to start.

"Comug! Get in here! I have some work for you!" he shouted at his loudest, which was very loud indeed. He expected an immediate response, and when nothing resulted he tried again, "Comug! Attend me! Anyone out there—attend me!"

He got up from his desk, suddenly aware of how still the air seemed in the office, and how deathly quiet everything had gotten. The office was well insulated from the rest of the estate but it wasn't a sealed room. There were always distant noises, shouts, muffled sounds and vibrations that one never paid any attention to until they were not there—and they were not there now.

Suddenly the entire floor of his office seemed to vibrate as if in an earthquake, and he made for the doors and tried to open them but they were sealed shut as if welded to the frame.

He turned and there was the sound of breaking wood as the very floor in front of his desk seemed to heave and push upward. Realizing instantly that the magician must have left something he missed, something that guided a more powerful magic, he made his way quickly around the edge of the office to a small cleared area and stepped within it, then made a few mystic signs. On the floor, barely noticeable unless one looked for it, was a true pentagram, created at great price by a master magician, and sealed with the ritual he performed.

The timbers gave way with a horrible crash and up, into the room, rose a strange and dreaded-looking figure. It was quite large, larger in all ways than the General by far, and it wore a broad black robe that seemed to conceal some great and gross inhuman body atop which sat a cowled head. Long, ancient fingers with sharp knifelike nails reached up to the cowl and threw it back, revealing the face of an impossibly old woman, a skull's mask covered with skin and punctuated with more wrinkles than there were stars, mostly covered with dull purple blotches and topped with only remnants of long, wispy snow-white hair. The long, broken beaklike nose sat below two blind eyes, yet the head and eyes fixed immediately on him and the toothless mouth twisted into a caricature of a wicked smile.

"Oh, I see you know you've been naughty and have fled to the corner," the creature croaked in a voice that was high and cackling. "And, oh, my! What a clever little pentagram! But, then, you always *were* ninety percent brilliant, weren't you Hoddy? It's the other ten percent that's made you a professional failure."

Hodamoc was not impressed. "Well, well. The great Yobi herself, who it is said has not left her cave in a century. This *is* an honor, even if it is a bit hard on the floor."

The sorceress thought that was uproariously funny, and cackled over it for several seconds. "Oh, my, always good for a laugh at that! Come, come—you expected something like this, didn't you? We are a lot alike, really. Both of us were big in our chosen fields, both of us made one big mistake, and both of us wound up in this asshole of a world. The only difference is that I do not make such mistakes twice. You seem to be bent on self-destruction."

"This display of theatrics is impressive but you know it will do you no good," he responded confidently. "The pentagram insulates me from your power and your presence, and even if you should kill me it wouldn't get what you want. And I am not afraid to die. I am a soldier."

"Oh, can the macho man bullshit, Hoddy! We're not amateurs, you and I, and I'm no third-rate shaman who thinks she can scare the big, bad general with a lot of demonic show and tell. The *last* thing I want is you dead, although I can't be absolutely sure that it won't result. How's your heart, Hoddy?"

She reached into the folds of her robe and brought out a small, grotesque wax figure and held it up to him.

"Look familiar, Hoddy? Oh, I know you brave soldier types only play with toy soldiers, but us girls, now, we get to play with dolls. Seems like a silly and impractical thing unless you're going to be a mommie, I admit, but dolls have their practical sides in a lot of areas."

He stared at the doll a little nervously. "I assume that is supposed to be me," he managed, trying to remain confident.

"Oh, it *is* you! I promise you that!" she responded with a cackle. "It has a bit of your hair and a bit of your nails and all that. No blood, but, then, I don't want you dead."

"That's impossible! All of my relics are destroyed or protected by spell and handled only by my bond slaves!"

"Except once. Bless you, dear, for being a total paranoid! You insist that every slave be relic bonded. That's smart, if you have a magician who can control an energy demon on a regular basis, but such ones are rare since those demons can ask a nasty price. But, you see, those demons can still be bargained with. They take your auric materials in with the relics. Not all is fused. Just leave out a hair here, a single small clipping there, and pretty soon you have enough to do some real mean stuff."

"Karella—the bond magician," he sighed. "But that's impossible! She is held by a Second Rank voluntary spell. She cannot betray her trust without destroying herself!"

"True, true. But she's only *Third* Rank, dear. She's not the one who betrays such as you. No, it is the demon who betrays, by not digesting one tiny little particle and instead depositing it very nicely my way where it can do the most good. I was dealing with that demon sprite before Karella's grandmother was born. I have *priority.*" Yobi sighed. "So, let's get down to business. You give me the girl, and I forget all about this encounter."

He stared at her, defiant. "You can kill me with that thing, perhaps, even in here, but you cannot make me bend to your will!"

Yobi shrugged. "But, dear, I wasn't talking about *killing* you. Oh, no. Suppose I just pinch one of these cute little feet here . . ."

General Hodamoc screamed in pain and dropped to the floor, suddenly holding his right foot. Anxiously, grimacing, he pulled the boot off and revealed a crushed, bloody mass where the foot had been.

"You see, dear? It's not nice to be impolite to old ladies," the sorceress said sweetly. "Now, what's next? The other foot, perhaps. Then the right arm, then the left. Then we can start on creative anatomy. I wonder what would happen if I pinched right here in the groin where the two legs meet the body . . . ?"

In terrible pain, mad as hell, but ever the pragmatist, he gasped, "No, no! A good soldier always knows when his cause is lost! That's why I'm alive here instead of dead in Mashtopol. You spoke of a deal . . .''

"Deal's off, doll. I told you we were a lot alike. You know you wouldn't offer a nice deal like that again after somebody turned you down and then put you to all this trouble."

"I paid thirty-one fifty for her! At least I demand a refund!"

Yobi held up the doll and went into a mocking version of the auctioneer's chant. "How much am I offered for a foot? An arm? How about the pride of the male? Do I hear a thousand? Two?"

That got his temper going and she suddenly realized she'd overplayed the scene. "Bitch! Do what you will! If you bring her to me I will order her to destroy herself! You cannot stop me, and I will follow in death no matter what torture you first mete out!"

Yobi thought fast. "Very well, General. I'll give you thirty-five hundred, a more than fair profit on the deal, and I'll also fix both your foot and the floor."

His hatred almost overcame him, but he saw a way to salvage his honor and bring things back to a more even keel and make the best of the situation.

"Not enough. I want the doll as well. And spells of protection so that my body and my home can never be so easily violated again."

She realized the opening and took it unhesitatingly. "Deal. But you forget all about this girl. Forget she was ever here, that you ever had her. Tell any guests who sampled her that she died or was killed and dismiss it. Betray the bargain and the spell that seals it will become undone. Time will curve, and we will be back here, as we are, and I will hold the doll. Be true to it, and it is done."

"All right. I will send for the girl."

"No need," said the sorceress. "I can handle that."

Charley was up top, on the surface and outside, just lounging in the sun and daydreaming about people and places far away, ignorant of all that was taking place. Suddenly she felt dizzy, and the whole outdoor scene seemed to blur, the heat of the sun to vanish, and in a moment she was inside a strange room beholding a strange and terrifying sight.

First she spotted Hodamoc and started to drop to the required genuflection position, but then she first felt, then turned and saw, Yobi just behind her, and even though the sight was terrifying the other automatic part of her slave programming took over. Someone was hurting the Master. Attack!

She rushed at the sorceress, but Yobi simply put up her palm and Charley felt as if she'd run into a brick wall and then fell to the ground, stunned. Still, she could not violate her standing commands and started to pick herself up, searching now for a weapon to use.

"No!" Hodamoc shouted. "Leave the creature alone and come to me!"

She immediately stopped, all standing instructions overridden, and turned and came to him. Or, rather, she tried to. When she reached a certain point on the floor very close to him she found herself unable to move another step.

"The slave bond can't move across the pentagram, dummy," Yobi noted, forgetting her spirit of reconciliation for a moment. "Have her bend down."

"Kneel and lean in as far as you can," Hodamoc instructed her, and she did so. He moved, painfully, and then reached out and touched the ring in her nose.

"Thy bond is transferred by my free will," he intoned. "That is Yobi. You will obey her as Mistress as you have obeyed me, and bond as she instructs. You are now her property, not mine, and all prior instructions and loyalties to me are canceled. Obey Yobi."

She felt dizzy once again, and then fell back a bit, but she also felt as if something of a weight had been transferred from her mind. She no longer regarded the man in the uniform as anyone special or unusual.

"Girl! Stand, turn, and face me!" Yobi instructed, and she did so with a sudden thought of *Here we go again!*

"Your former Master and I have some last-minute details to cover to seal the bargain. You will leave this place when I tell you, exit in the lower cave level, and at the boundary you will seek and find a magician in brown robe. His name is Dorion and he will introduce himself as such and then state that he is from me. You will go with him and obey him and no other as Master until we can modify that spell of yours. Now—go!"

She found herself walking to and then out of the door to do as instructed, closing the door behind her.

Yobi turned back to Homadoc. "Now, I fulfill my end of the bargain. I keep my bargains, General. I expect you to keep yours. The monetary part will be on deposit in town within the hour." With that, she lifted the cowl back over her head and began a chant, gesturing as she did so.

It was suddenly as if everything had been placed in reverse. Yobi sank into the floor with an odd sound, and the floor itself came back seamlessly to its original state. Hodamoc found the pain in his foot suddenly gone and looked down to see it whole, although he still had to put his boot back on. He did so quickly, then got up, unsteadily, and made his way out of the pentagram and over to the desk. It was another couple of minutes before he could get complete hold of his senses, and then he looked down. On top of the desk was the small, crude doll that Yobi had been holding.

He wasted no time in finding a copper bowl and then some lamp oil. Placing the doll in the bowl, he poured the lamp oil upon it and then used a flint to ignite it. The blaze was something fierce but localized, and when it was done there was nothing left in the bowl but a puddle of melted wax and some bits and pieces of things, charred and burned beyond recognition. That hold on him, at least, was now gone.

But his pride had been wounded by the encounter, and he was very bitter. Nobody, *nobody*, did this to him! Particularly in his own home and in his own quarters! First he would arrange for his protections and be ready for any retaliation, although it would take a bit of time. No more ninety percent here. Then, one way or another, he was going to find out just what was so valuable about that little whore, and then he would use all the influence he had to make certain that any value she might have would accrue only to him.

Dorion waited for her just outside the boundaries of the main cave of Hodamoc. She came swiftly, and he couldn't help but get something of an erotic charge just watching her approach. Her every move was unconsciously erotic, and he had never seen someone so totally sexual before who was a real person and not some sort of demonic succubus a good magician knew to avoid. She was wearing a beaded outfit; the lower part hung on her hips and formed a multicolored beaded loin covering in front, and another elaborate set of beads shaped and highlighted but didn't really conceal her breasts. Otherwise she was naked, and might as well have been anyway for all the good the beads did.

She stopped just at the entrance to the cave, the first time in weeks she'd been even a few inches outside of Hodamoc's territory, and began looking for this magician.

Dorion stepped from the darkness of the cave and approached her. "I am Dorion acting for Yobi," he said, sounding a bit nervous. "Obey me as you would her."

"Yes, Master," she responded in a really soft, low, sexy voice.

For the first time Dorion realized that she would have to obey anything he commanded. Somebody like that was completely under his power . . . God, he was so turned on, he only wished he had the nerve to take advantage of it.

"Take my hand and come with me," he instructed. "We have a very long walk and we're going to have to take the back ways to avoid running into anyone we don't want to meet. I am told that you can understand but cannot speak Akhbreed. What tongues do you speak?"

"English, Spanish, and the Short Speech, Master," she responded.

"English, huh? Well, we have something in common. I've never been able to manage to speak English so anyone else can understand, but I can understand it pretty well. So you speak English to me and I will speak Akhbreed to you and together we might understand each other. All right?"

She felt almost a flood of relief. *Somebody who understood her!* "Yes, Master," she responded in English.

"You are from one of the Outplanes, I guess. Brought here by Boolean?" he asked as they began to walk in what looked to her to be total darkness.

"Yes, Master. Almost two years now, I guess, although I have no way to judge the time." She didn't like admitting that—there was no way of knowing if this guy was a nice fellow or if he was one of Klittichorn's boys. That *thing* in Hodamoc's office wasn't reassuring. That Yobi looked like a

horrible version of the creature who had captured the others
and almost gotten her as well after the flood. However, there
were certain default conditions as it were built into the slave
spell. All could be countermanded, of course, but they existed
unless that was done. The first was total unthinking obedience
whether you wanted to or not, of course. The second was an
automatic subservience to anyone who could order you around.
One did not speak unless spoken to and one answered just what
was demanded—and absolutely truthfully. You couldn't lie,
cheat, or steal something from a controller unless told to do so,
and like a planet in its orbit you needed your controller as the
planet needed its sun. There was no running away. It simply
was not an option.

It was because of this that Yobi had been forced to act so
quickly after Hodamoc had turned down the initial offer. She
hadn't been able to afford even a questioning of the girl by her
then Master, or it all would have come out.

It *was* quite a walk, and, again, she couldn't have retraced it
if she tried, nor did she figure out how the magician knew the
way himself, but eventually they emerged outside and relatively high up in the mountainous crags of the Wastes. From that
point it was a narrow trail that wound around the top of a ridge
until eventually it entered a cave originating in the floor of the
rock itself and leading down a bit.

The place stank, kind of like the way Boday's lab had often
smelled in the old days. Lots of odd odors and unpleasant
fragrances, which identified it as a dwelling of either a
magician or an alchemist. There were several small chambers
and then a main one which looked, to put it bluntly, a mess.

A central pit was in the chamber, in which much was
obviously cooked, and over which a kind of metal web was
built on which could be sat large pots and bowls or from which
you could hang kettles and tureens. There was a pot of
something on, simmering, and from its look and smell Charley
prayed to herself that it wasn't dinner.

Most of the rest of the cave was taken with shelves filled
with all sorts of boxes, gourds, glass jars, you name it, as well
as apparently embalmed bats and lizards and such and even a
shrunken head and skull or two. There were also books—lots
of books, all huge and old and moldy looking. The only area of

the walls other than the entrance not so covered with bric-a-brac had an old and faded patterned rug hung on it right down to the ground.

"Not exactly comfortable looking, I know, but it's a lot better than most sorcerers' lairs," Dorion noted. "Just sit on the floor there. I'm sure Yobi won't keep us waiting long."

And she didn't. The rug suddenly flew up and the great sorceress entered the chamber, revealing an ancillary cave beyond that had to be her private quarters. Although Charley had glimpsed her back at Hodamoc's, it was not under the best of circumstances, and part of the sorceress had been stuck below the floor, as it were, out of immediate sight. She had not, for example, realized until now just how large the old one was, or how totally inhuman were her lower quarters, obscured as they were by a specially designed black robe. The face, though, was easy to remember. It kind of looked like the wicked witch from "Snow White," only without the redeeming qualities.

Yobi looked over at her with eyes that seemed glazed and blind, yet Charley knew she was getting a thorough examination on several levels.

"Shit!" the sorceress muttered. "All that trouble and all we got was a decoy. I thought you were better than that, son."

Dorion looked surprised. "A decoy?"

"Sure. Any fool can see that she's got Boolean's trickery written all over her aura. How the hell did you wind up looking like the Storm Princess wished she looked, child? You can speak English. I have been forced to learn the foul-sounding tongue."

"It is a long tale, Mistress, but it is as you say. The sorcerer Boolean did it by remote-control magic."

That struck Yobi as funny. "Remote-control magic! Wonderful. Well, speak, child. Tell us who you really are and how came you to this point. Take as much time as you wish—we are in no immediate hurry right now."

And, in general detail, Charley told them the whole story. Of how she'd been a friend and schoolmate to this rather odd girl in her own world and land, and how quite by accident and by not believing in this sort of magic she had wound up getting sucked down to Akahlar with Sam. She told how Boolean stepped in to save them from Klittichorn in the journey, in the process revealing himself as an active enemy of the horned sorcerer and making himself a target. How they'd been picked up and then betrayed by the mercenary Zenchur, but not before Boolean's magical device had caused her to appear to be an identical twin of Sam's.

And she talked of being sold to Boday, who gave her the beauty as well as the markings of the blue butterfly and changed her into a true courtesan, and how in rescuing her from Boday's clutches Sam had unthinkingly grabbed and made Boday drink a love potion that made the alchemical artist fall madly in love with Sam. And how Charley had volunteered to raise the money for the trip to Boolean by actually being a courtesan, and how Sam had grown fat and lazy and domestic under Boday. And, of course, how they'd finally made the money to get there not by selling herself but by creating and selling the patent to women's undergarments common back on their world.

How, then, they'd been attacked, and Sam's use of her power to summon storms to save them at the cost of a flash flood that had destroyed the train and killed many, with most of the survivors being captured, raped, and tortured by others of the gang led by Asterial, and how the demon prisoner of the Jewel of Omak had eventually saved them all. And, finally, how they had become separated and wound up where they did.

Both Yobi and Dorion listened intently, occasionally nodding but only rarely injecting a question to clarify a point they didn't understand. When she was done, she knew that her life, and Sam's, were now squarely in the hands of this pair.

Yobi was silent for some time, thinking it all over, and then she sighed and said, "Well, now we know where we stand, anyway. I'm afraid I'm going to have to get this Boday as well, which might be easier or tougher depending on Jamonica's mood and whether or not she's really of use to him. He's a trader and he buys and sells everything, unlike Hodamoc, who's a damned *collector*. The gods save us all from *collectors*! He does not use relics, however, so it'll cost, damn it." She sighed again. "From what you tell me, you *should* have been the one and not your friend. You have the spirit and temperament for it. But, we must deal with what we have, not with what we want. In the meantime, I sense that much troubles you. I would like to know what, one at a time, please."

"Well, Mistress, I do not like being a slave."

Yobi cackled. "Why, we are *all* slaves, child! We only kid ourselves if we pretend otherwise. Why, Akahlar itself is a source of massive power and wealth and nearly limitless resources, yet ninety percent of its people are at subsistence level toiling for the few. The ones that are leftover are subject to monarchies and governments in which they have no say even when some of those governments pretend that their citizens do have some say, and under a series of religions that oppress them even more. Wars and revolutions are always fought in the name of the dispossessed but always seem to really be about which side of a small elite shall be the oppressor. I envy you if you were born and raised in a different sort of place where this is not true. It must be strange indeed."

"Mistress, my land valued personal freedoms and liberties, although most of my world was as you say."

"Indeed? So your land was rich in a poor world, and so mere citizenship in it made you a member of the elite. Sounds like the Akhbreed here. Oh, there are poor Akhbreed, of course, but even the poorest in the hubs and colonies is better off than the average of all the thousands of races who inhabit the worlds they loot."

She wanted to protest that it wasn't really like that, but slaves weren't permitted debates with their controllers. But she remembered the visions of the migrant workers, the illegals from Mexico, who worked the fields in the Southwest, and the huge population of Mexico just out of sight of the tourist villas and fancy hotels. And how much say did anybody have in an election, anyway? Anybody could run, but only the ones with people and money and party support stood a chance. You got to pick between two people who were basically picked for you. And the seamy underworld neighborhood of Tubikosa where Boday had lived was not unlike that in any major city back home, nor, in fact, did pimps and prostitutes lack for business. Maybe it wasn't so great after all, but it was *comfortable*. And, for over a hundred years anyway, they didn't keep slaves.

"What would you have done, or thought you might have

done, if you'd stayed ignorant of all this?" Yobi asked her, giving her some clearance for an answer.

"Graduated from high school and gone on to college," she responded. "Most women aren't chained to families and child-rearing there because of easy birth control. I was going for a degree in chemistry, with the hope of getting into the cosmetics industry."

"Indeed? Wonderful liberation, that. Learn all that so you can better your fellow woman by making her look prettier. Lots of money, no commitments, total pleasure-seeking off the job. Perhaps an occasional march or donation to ease the con-science now and again. So long as you can live well and have fun, what the hell. I've got mine and that's all that matters. If you've got the brains, and the talent, and the connections, and not many scruples, anyone can become parasitic royalty. I'm surprised you don't all die young of pleasure potions and venereal disease. Or don't they exist, either?"

"They do, Mistress. Drugs, alcohol, and many kinds of VD. One was around when I left that was always fatal. It was scaring a lot of people. I have worried about whether such things were here as well."

"Of *course* they are, you ninny! You don't have to worry about *those* kinds of diseases, though. What alchemy can't create here magic can eventually control, or, if such a disease is created in the changewind, as has happened, the Akhbreed move to—sterilize—it. You're immune to the hundred or so venereal diseases we have now, so don't worry about it. That's what makes courtesans worth so much. Of course, the general population isn't so lucky, but it keeps the populations under control and in check. But even the highest of the Akhbreed can become addicted to the pleasure potions. That's Jamonica's real trade, and why he'd pay so much for an alchemist slave. And that's Hodamoc's hope for eventually controlling Mashtopol. Addict so many of the pleasure-loving and decadent royalty and the bored movers and shakers that he will enslave them in a way just as effective as he enslaved you. Do not feel so bad. That ring tells the world that your situation was forced upon you and not self-inflicted, and there is no dishonor in that. I sense you have a question on it anyway. Go ahead."

"Then—Mistress? It is permanent? I can never be free?"

"Oh, no! It's a complicated ritual and a real pain in the ass but any Second Rank sorcerer and even some of the Third Rank can undo it if you have the Master's permission. Finding one that *will* undo it, however, not to mention a Master willing to let you go, is the trick. Pardon, my dear, but there is no percentage in it. Don't look so crestfallen. You haven't exactly done very well on your own up to now or you wouldn't be under such a spell. Your value was, is, and remains as a decoy. Klittichorn might suspect, but so long as he does not *know* he can't take you for granted, and that means he must try and hunt you. Your value is to lead them away from your friend— without falling into their clutches, which you both have very narrowly escaped doing up to now. However, before we can make use of you we must first locate and redirect your friend. Since this Boday had the audacity to trick your friend into that marriage spell, she is essential to the task. I fear your friend has fallen into the clutches of Duke Pasedo and is even now happily and ignorantly picking berries somewhere many leegs from here. That we will have to determine. But you have other problems and worries. Speak."

"Mistress, I am still trying to make peace with myself over what this world has made me."

"A decoy?"

"No, Mistress, a courtesan. One who sells her body. In my world it is considered the lowest thing a woman can be."

"And you are bothered by the fact that it sinks you low?"

"No, Mistress. You see, I—I spent over a year at it in Tubikosa, and I *liked* it. I fear that there is something wrong with me that I did not suspect. That I would rather be a whore than a warrior or a queen or have my own business."

Yobi shrugged. "Many queens and sorceresses have done pretty good jobs. Others have been lousy—just like the men. We are what our destinies make us. To be otherwise is to be miserable. Most people are miserable. If you liked it, then there's no shame in that. Spend little time thinking of what other people demand that you be and please yourself. Consider—would you rather be a slave and courtesan or would you rather have fantastic power and look like me and live forever with *this*?"

With that Yobi pulled away the draping cloak, and what was

revealed made Charley sick to her stomach. The body was huge, bloated, and deformed, a pulsating and pulpy cream color like some sort of enormous monster insect larva or worm, and bits of slime and old skin hung to it or moved slightly with the pulsations.

Yobi replaced the cloak. "The Second Rank sorcerers are about as free as you can get in this or any other place," she told the still stricken-looking girl. "The things I can see, the kinds of things I can do, stagger even my imagination. I've lived six hundred years and I've seen and done most everything. Pretty soon the madness creeps in, and you begin to think and act like you're some sort of god. It happens to all of us sooner or later. And you begin to chafe at even the minuscule, meager limits still imposed on you. Your ego cannot accept them. First Rank or nothing! And eventually you dare, and you look in those places you dare not look and try those things you dare not try. The last barrier is the changewind, and you go against it. I was lucky. I managed to pull back with only this to remind me, and retaining—perhaps regaining is a better word—at least a hair of sanity. But, sooner or later, I know I will try again. It is inevitable. If one must live forever then one must gain and grow, or death is preferable. But—not yet, not yet."

Yobi sighed, then suddenly snapped out of it and bent down and looked at Charley's face closely. "How are your eyes, child?"

"Mistress, I was always nearsighted, and lately I have been so that my vision is quite poor. In the past weeks it had gotten progressively worse. I can no longer see anything except what is directly ahead, and without the sun or a strong light like your lanterns that I now face I can see almost nothing. I have been quite frightened of it."

The sorceress nodded. "You stood there, helpless, watching a knock-down-and-drag-out between a true demon prince and Asterial. There are—radiations—involved in most magic. That is why all magicians have very poor eyesight and Second Rankers are all blind in the conventional sense. It is unavoidable. But most in the magic arts have other means of sight that are not only as good, they're quite a bit better and more revealing. To be a decent magician, though, you must be born with the talent and also with an apitude for mathematics. It's quite precise or you don't survive long, which is why magicians are often powerful but rarely creative. You have no magic of your own to speak of and without that even a mathematical wizard would be helpless. Yet the dosage you received was probably quite intense. No, my dear, we must find some magical alternative for you. There is no way around it, but there are things that can be done."

Charley's heart sank and she was as depressed as she had ever felt at this. There was no way around it. She was being told that she would always be someone's slave, and, worse, even than that, a blind one.

"Boday is *crushed* by this!" the tall, tattooed woman grumbled. "First they make her a slave—a *slave!*—and set her to work in a happy-potions factory—me! A great artist! Hovering over what is no more than a soulless assembly line!"

*Yeah, well, at least you're not blind as well*, Charley thought dejectedly. Other than Sam, the only thing Boday ever thought of was Boday.

"And now they bring her here and duck both her and her finest creation into this moldy *slime pit*," Boday went on, oblivious as always. Charley had hopes that Yobi or Dorion would command her to silence at least but when there were just the two of them there weren't any limits on that sort of thing.

Two gray-robed acolytes, a man and a woman never introduced and so referred to only as Him and Her, entered and helped them out. Yobi, it appeared, had quite an operation here, and more people than had been immediately apparent. Some were students unable to apprentice to a Second Rank sorcerer in the hubs; others were exiles like Yobi and most of the others here.

Both women were now stood straight up and had water dumped on them in great quantities until the last vestiges of the goo was off. It had been worse for Charley than for Boday; for Charley they had prepared a sort of mud pack of the stuff and let it set and harden over much of her face.

Not that it had really mattered, except for the feel and the smell. Charley hadn't been at Yobi's two days before she woke up one morning on her mat and thought it was still completely dark. She had not seen a single thing, not even light and darkness, since.

It had been so gradual up to now that she had some suspicion that the sudden collapse of her eyesight was less natural than Yobi's doing, but she could not be sure and there was no way to ask and get a straight answer anyway. She resented it, but she could understand it. Yobi had wasted no time in having Him and Her begin training as a blind person. It was frustrating and boring and maddening, particularly since, with the slave spell, she couldn't take a break, couldn't give up, couldn't even complain as it went on and on, but it was now paying off. When you are ordered to walk you wind up walking with very cautious confidence after a while. Balance was more of a trick than she'd thought it would be, too, but she managed. You felt your way along the cave walls and you memorized where anything that might trip you up was, and you learned to use your other senses, and your feet as well.

Dorion entered the mud chamber and looked them over. He was still having a terrible mental problem over Charley, whom he was beginning to have wet dreams about, but there was just something inside of him that couldn't take that kind of advantage of anybody. If she was willing, that was one thing, but the master-slave relationship made that tough to figure out for real, and somehow actually having her would make him feel like a rapist.

"We've found your Sam," he told them. "Yobi's set to break her out of the alchemical traps she's fallen into and Boolean's set her up with somebody who's totally trustworthy, but we don't want to spring her completely until you're ready and underway. The trick is, we want them to chase you, but we don't want them to catch you. This is step one. Boday, your work is beautiful, but it's a beauty that is made to be seen. Frankly, the pair of you wouldn't last an hour in any hub with those tattoos, so off they come."

Using a thin razorlike instrument, Him and Her worked first on Boday, whose body below the neck was covered and thus was actually easier. Making sure not to cut the skin, they made a series of incredibly delicate incisions, and, thanks to the hours of soaking in the preparation, they then were able to peel off the tattoos from her body in segments. It was quite bizarre;

they came off, layer upon layer, like decals, most fully intact, and while Boday was less than pleased with the whole thing she was somewhat mollified that they actually laid the designs on a paper form and managed to preserve most of them. The result, when done, was not that bad, since Boday had natural brown skin.

Charley was more of a problem, partly because the designs were so delicate and intricate with few solids and also because she was naturally light-skinned. Her exposed skin had turned a dark brown with all the sun and exposure, but the tattoos had blocked the rays from where they covered, and now she stood there, mercifully unable to see the result, with the designs somewhat etched in outline in light skin against the otherwise suntanned complexion.

With Dorion they always had a certain amount of freedom to speak, within limits and subject to cutoff, of course. Boday looked over Charley and said, "Boday likes it. It is a fascinating abstract."

"We'll have to fill it in with dyes, I'm afraid," Dorion noted. "We want uniformity. We'll also have to do something with the hair. It's been alchemically lengthened and stabilized, but I'm afraid knee-length hair is not only a sure giveaway, it's not practical in the circumstances. The object remains the same—reach Boolean in the shortest possible time, but by a route totally different than the one your friend will take. Perhaps curled a bit, dyed a lighter color, and tumbling a bit over the shoulders. Boday, we have a different but no less effective set of ideas for you. I know you won't like them but you'd like Klittichorn's Stormriders less."

Boday thought a moment. "Permission to ask a question, Master?"

"Go ahead."

"Boday cares not for herself, Master, but—how is her darling Susama and what new curses does she bear?"

*Love potions conquer all*, Charley thought with amazement.

"Heavier than she was, but a lot more muscle. That curse kept her weight up, which is good—she's nearly unrecognizable as a twin of the Storm Princess—but she's been doing heavy farm work. She could probably lift the both of you and possibly a horse. Her hair's shoulder-length, and thanks to a tough potion she's amnesiac. That's what Yobi will work on. She's been quite happy, though, in her ignorance. And, well, it won't be certain until we see her, but Yobi's initial spells, now that we have her located, suggest—only suggest, mind you— that she might possibly be pregnant."

Both women gasped. "By whom, Master?" Boday asked at last, a bit shaken.

Dorion shrugged. "Who knows? We don't even know if it's true. But if it *is* and isn't just some byproduct of all those potions she was fed and the kind of life she'd been leading, it must be fairly well along, predating her current situation."

"Those filthy rapists," Charley muttered, then had a thought. "Or maybe it might be that friendly wagon train crewman she seduced out of curiosity. Poor Sam! It would be her luck to get knocked up the first time!" She suddenly caught herself, remembering that Boday didn't know about that one. Well, Boday didn't know English, either. "Please, Master, do not mention that one to Boday, though."

Dorion looked puzzled, but didn't pursue it. Boday, however, was now deep in thought.

"Pregnant . . . It could have happened to Boday as well just as easily, or those poor little girls. One wonders what the product of one of those—*creatures*—and Boday would have been? A great primitive artist, perhaps, or maybe an animist." She sighed. "No, with that mixture it would probably grow up to be a critic. Whatever, Boday will consider the child as her own. *Our* own."

"Yeah, well, it's just another complication now. We have to move, and fast. The word is old Horn Heart is getting set to pull something big. That's good in that it'll get him out of his citadel, but it's putting a lot of pressure on us. As soon as we get you two set up we have to *move*. We've been sitting on Hodamoc long enough anyway and it's been no end of trouble. We want to let him go, have him identify Charley as the Storm Princess's double, and draw them here. By that time you have to be long gone."

"Master, how can I do much of anything?" Charley asked him plainly. "I am *blind*. Totally so. And, out there, totally defenseless because of it. I was lucky once when I could see to shoot straight, but I didn't do really well with both eyes going. Now . . .''

"We are going to deal with that as well," the magician told her. "Of course it depends on whether or not you like animals—and whether any animals like you.''

Walking into the small room was a strange and unnerving experience for Charley. Unable to see, unfamiliar with the layout, she was nonetheless overcome with sounds. Screeching sounds, scurrying sounds, barking, and mewing sounds. Had she not been commanded, and therefore compelled, to enter, nothing that could be offered would have gotten her there.

"Nothing here should harm you," Yobi assured her. "Pets, strays, mongrels—the animal part of the Kudaan underground. Castoffs, like ourselves. Sit for a while on the floor cross-legged so you form a lap and see what might like you.''

She sat, but she didn't like all the implications of that one. A number of the animals approached her, but she tried to remain calm and not show fear. She remembered that animals could smell fear.

Suddenly something small and furry bounded into her lap and then tried to climb up her torso using sharp little claws. She cried out and recoiled and reached out—and knew that she was holding a cat.

Not a big cat, certainly, although it was no kitten. It struggled for a moment, since her blind grip wasn't exactly the best, but then she relaxed and so did it and she put it down in her lap and felt its form and started to pet it. The cat purred.

"It seems you have found a friend," Yobi noted. "That cat is a bit odd, very much like all of us here. It often seems to think it's a great tiger cat, taking on that which it cannot hope to vanquish, and other times it is a forlorn, mewing sort demanding attention. It's a bit scruffy and scraggly, but it is a tomcat through and through."

The cat seemed to snuggle up to her, purring loud enough to overcome the residual noises in the room. She found herself scratching its ears and stroking it and she liked it. She'd never had a pet before.

"A tomcat . . . Mistress, what color is it?''

"Gray with black stripelike spots, dirty white paws. Very ordinary."

Charley nodded. A typical alleycat, which kind of fit. Still, one thing bothered her. "Mistress—I like him, that is true, but I cannot see how this helps me. I have heard of seeing-eye dogs before, but not cats."

Yobi cackled. "Come. Bring your friend and attend me, and I shall work a little magic with you."

All had been set up ahead of time; the braziers were going, there was incense about, and Charley could feel heat from large candles. The big stuff.

"Bring your friend and yourself forward ten paces," Yobi instructed. "Then stop and wait, but do not let the cat out of your grasp."

The cat, fortunately, didn't seem to want to go anywhere except to scratch some primordial arboreal instinctive itch that made it want to climb up on her shoulders and perhaps her head.

"Many of us use creatures well suited to giving us information, culled from all the worlds of Akahlar," the sorceress told her. "However, they require special handling in most cases, or odd diets, or even controls of a sort you do not possess. For our purposes, the cat is fine."

She began a series of chants and Charley could hear a lot of sizzling sounds and smell odd odors wafting through the cave. Suddenly the sorceress broke into her heavily accented but quite understandable English.

"You shall have eyes once again, of a sort," Yobi told her. "There is also room in this equation for other attributes. Remain still. The cat will taste of you and it will hurt for a moment, but it is necessary. Do not move or drop it."

Suddenly the cat twisted a bit and she felt sharp fangs drive into her upper left arm. It hurt, and she knew instantly that it drew blood and she began to wonder just what was happening when the cat began to lick that blood from her arm and from the wound it had made.

"Mix, match, mate," said the sorceress. "The cat has become a familiar and shares your blood and a small part of your soul. Half in shadow, not in light, *link* ye two!"

Charley felt a sudden and uncomfortable hot flush, which

took a few moments to fade. She began to see images; strange
outlines and bizarre shapes and forms unlike anything she had
ever seen or imagined, and, somehow, she was seeing them
with her eyes. They were brilliant, dazzling, occasionally
scary, as they briefly turned and twisted and for a moment here
and there seemed to be not merely colored electrical lines but
shapes both monstrous and, somehow, evil. They turned, they
danced around her, reaching out, as if trying to touch her or
even come inside her, and she was powerless to recoil or
defend herself. Then, in a sudden flash that seemed to release
all the brilliant and eerie colors at once, all was dark again, but
only for a moment.

Then, slowly, incredibly, she began to see images in her
mind, visions that were quite dim at first and faded in and out
but which began to take on greater solidity, until at last they
were quite clear, if very strange.

She saw the central cave of Yobi's complex, but not with her
eyes, nor how her eyes would see it. The images were devoid
of color, but infinite in their gray shadings, and they were also
somewhat distorted, like the fish-eye lens of a camera, which
showed an enormous field of view but showed things in
perspective only in the center, and only a bit farther out. From
there the image curved out like an inverted mirrored glass,
elongating and distorting the images. Still, she could see Yobi
now, and the smoky braziers, and all the rest. the candles
momentarily smeared the view, and if you focused on them all
else was dark. The focus was general rather than on anything
specific, but if something moved, even the smoke or candle
flames, or Yobi herself, the vision instantly locked that moving
thing in at the center of vision. It took some getting used to.

Suddenly the image shifted, and she saw a giant human face
and neck. *Her* face, but not as she had ever seen it before.

*I'm seeing what the cat is seeing, the way the cat sees it!* she
realized suddenly.

"Yes, that is true," Yobi told her. "You and your cat friend
are linking together in a number of ways. There is a price, for
every so often he will need a drop of your blood to remain
active and alive and you must give it. But that will keep him
with you, inseparably if need be, no matter how far he may
roam. The blood link will allow you to see through him

whenever you wish, even if you and he are not touching, although always from his point of view, of course. It will take some getting used to. It's not as good as eyes, and you will still be blind, but you will now be able to see what you must."

The cat was now looking at Yobi's craggy face, as if also understanding the words.

"There is a side effect here that I did not negate, although it is a mixed blessing and curse," the sorceress continued. "While you hold the cat, your thoughts are open. Anyone fairly close to you, say as close as I am now, will be able to understand them as if they were spoken, regardless of language. You will thus be able to communicate with anyone anywhere in Akahlar, which is more than most can do, but you must be cautious. Your thoughts will be an open book to anyone looking at you or to anyone you are looking at or interacting with. You will have to learn to control your thoughts while you hold the familiar. I added that curse, for that is what it is, to enable you to communicate normally, and as a possible salvation should you be captured by the enemy. They will know immediately that you are the wrong one."

That was a strange and unnerving concept, but at least she didn't have to always hold the cat.

"Those—those shapes, Mistress . . . What were they?"

But Yobi didn't answer, and there was no other way to know.

Charley sighed. "Well, then. Well, we must have a name for you if we are to be so close, mustn't we? Half in shadow . . . That's not just a spell, it's me. All right, then, Sir Shadowcat, you and I will have to be very, very careful."

The cat purred.

# · 6 ·

## *Split Personalities*

THE GREAT GORGE was one of the most spectacular places in all the Kudaan, almost a fourteen-hundred-foot sheer drop to the rushing river below, unbridged and uncrossed. More than one animal had smelled that water and run to their doom, plunging over that sheer cliff so that by the time they reached what they craved from desert wanderings they no longer needed it.

To the west was the high desert itself; the river that ran far underground through stronger, tougher rock and only here, where the rock changed to the softer sedimentary variety, had its great tunnel been extended all the way to the surface, carrying away the collapsed material in the channel it dug over the eons, slowly enough so that it did not get dammed up but rapid enough to cause the impassable chasm.

The caravan stayed for the night just beyond the canyon, expertly limiting the animals so that while they could have food and what was left of the wagon they would not or could not wander off too far in the wrong direction.

She emerged from the Navigator's wagon and looked beyond the campfire to the starry darkness beyond. She wore only a thin, light robe tied at the waist, which was all that was required in the desert. It could get chilly here on occasion, but not tonight. Tonight she could almost sense that it would fall from broiling to merely hot; more comfortable but not exactly perfection.

Kira was perfection, or as close to it as a woman could

aspire to. Without makeup, jewelry, or any aids, just as she
was, she was almost a dream woman. The figure on her five-
foot-two frame was perfection, perfectly balanced and shaped;
her face an idealized, almost angelic one, the lips just right, the
nose perfect, the emerald green eyes large and dark, the
features giving just a hint of a playful, kittenish quality coming
through the beauty. Her hair was thick, lush, with a natural
body beyond the need of more than a regular washing, auburn
with natural streaks of a dark blond, cascading down from her
face, framing it perfectly, ending just below the shoulders. She
moved with a natural catlike grace that was no studied
affectation but simply a part of her, as totally feminine as
Crim's big, muscular frame and swagger was so masculine.
The word *sensuous* seemed invented for her.

The trail crew saw her, and nodded, but then went about
their work. Kira was one of them in spite of her appearance,
and while they appreciated her beauty she was nothing unusual
to them.

She went over to the campfire and took a small amount of
wine in a gourd cup and a couple of pieces of sweetbread and
nibbled on them, not feeling very hungry. She was thinking,
and waiting.

She felt, more than saw, him come. There was a charm they
had, one that allowed Boolean to know where they were, and it
seemed to have a sort of two-way effect. The feeling wasn't
absolute; it had more than once played them false, and it was
none too certain if it was Boolean or some other power from its
tingle, but she was confident now. She put down her meager
supper, got up, and walked out from the fire, out towards the
gorge.

She felt someone suddenly beside her, although it was quite
dark, and she found a rock and sat pertly on it. "So," she said,
in a soft, musical voice that could charm a tyrant. "Now we
shall talk."

"A pleasure to speak with you again, Kira," said that
slightly hollow voice again, the voice of Boolean somehow
both here and faraway. "I confess to preferring you to Crim
even though I feel more at a loss around you."

She laughed. "I thought the great Akhbreed sorcerers were
beyond all that."

"Some of them are, maybe most of them," he admitted. "Those who are have ceased to be human. Power can do that to you if you're not careful. Our kind of power." He paused. "You have considered the proposition?"

She nodded, even though it seemed a futile gesture in the darkness. "Crim prefers the more direct, fighting approach, which he is so good at," she noted. "But the mark of a great warrior is knowing when *not* to fight. As for myself, I could not even *lift* his sword, and the recoil from his guns would be as devastating to me as to whomever or whatever I hit. Crim is correct on one very big point, and that is no amount of force short of a total assault will get her out of there if she's in there under the conditions you surmise."

"Stealth, then."

"Caution, certainly. But the ideal method is extortion, if I had something to use, which I do not. We need the help of higher-ups in the Duke's entourage, that is definite. Access to them—the men, certainly—is no problem for me, but both cooperation and security cannot be secured by the basic methods. No, I will need something to trade, and with the entourage the magicians and alchemists are the most vulnerable. A sample of the potion used, I would think, would simplify matters a great deal."

"Immensely, even though analysis from this distance is going to be rough. It will keep me from falling into traps and making serious or irreversible mistakes."

"I thought as much. And we will need someone who can give us access to the girl. Finding her by hit or miss in *that* place might take forever."

There was a thoughtful sigh in the dark. "So we need something for each. A spell that any good magician might covet, particularly one of the sort that one who would spend his or her life there might value more than loyalty. The same in the chemistry department. The first one I can come up with fairly quickly, although I hate to give it away. It's a good one, and should be earned. Still, this is a prize for which the rules must bend. How about a spell that would regrow amputated limbs?"

"*Perfect!* They have much need of it and it will make them great in their little domain—and help a lot of unfortunates in the process."

"The one I have in mind is complicated as all hell and not very fast. It reads the genetic code and then slowly regrows what's missing over a fairly long period, but the results can still be spectacular. All right. But alchemy . . . That's tougher. They're apparently pretty damned good at that already, so the obvious probably isn't needed. I'll have to give that one some thought and perhaps some research." The sorcerer paused a moment, then said, "All right, so we use bribery. Now how the hell do we control the girl if she's been turned into a pea-brained grape stomper? With her build she'd probably be great at that."

"Surely if we can get to her there is some sort of simple hypnotic—"

"Yeah, yeah," Boolean muttered, still thinking. "But most of those are potions and I don't want to add anything that might complicate matters. I wish I had another equivalent of the Jewel of Omak. That was damned useful, but it also took me years. You don't trap demons every day. Your best bet, if possible, is to make some solution to that part of the bribe payment. They know what they're dealing with better than we do. I'll try some backup, but it'll be risky. Maybe theirs will be, too, but it'll be educated, not ignorant. The next step will be getting her out of there. She is not exactly unobtrusive."

"So you told Crim. No way to lift that?"

"It was demon imposed. I'd need her physically present to see what it did and how and they're tricky little bastards. Besides, it wouldn't matter even if I could. Once that thing's lifted she won't be any different. If she wants to be thin again she's still going to have to lose it. Any kind of spell that might restore her might also impair her. These things are all interrelated. Now if I'd had that weight put on by spell, or even the demon, it'd be a different story, but it's all hers. They don't check you much, do they?"

"On the way in it's pretty thorough," she told him. "They want to make certain that we harbor no surprises or are under no compulsions. Out is usually pretty casual, but even if there are questions I think we can deal with it. Once we are away, though, we shall have to restore her and I think we must break with the caravan. It would not do to draw attention to ourselves

by not keeping to routine. It's going to be rough and over-
land."

"By now she can ride very well, and she fights when she has
to. Don't sell her short because of her size or her looks. She's
kind of weird, though, even when she's normal. Most girls
dream of growing up and becoming princesses; she's got a shot
at princess and she desperately wants to be a floor scrubber or
grape stomper." Quickly, but in as much detail as he could—or
knew—he described Sam and her past in Tubikosa, sparing no
details. When he finished, he added, "Now I'll show you the
last vision I had available of her from the Jewel of Omak."

There was a slight spark and Kira felt her forehead tingle,
and suddenly in her mind there was a full, three-dimensional
vision of Sam, animated, even speaking.

"I can understand her low aspirations," Kira commented
dryly. "The others I see there with the painted bodies?"

"The tall, skinny one with the design riot is Boday. I told
you about her. The other one is Charley."

Kira gave a low whistle. "And this Sam should or could
look like *that*? I can see the resemblance, almost like sisters,
but you cannot really see the potential of one in the other."

"I know. Part of that is attitude. Even when she looked like
that she thought she didn't. You don't have to psychoanalyze or
cure her of her hangups, just get her to me in one piece."

Kira gave a faint smile. "That will be a most interesting
challenge."

Medac Pasedo did a low, lazy circle in the sky and then
descended towards the caravan that had pulled in and made a
basic camp near the supplies building just down from the
Governor's Residence. The men would stay in the residence
guest quarters tonight and sleep on real beds and eat decent
food.

Crim watched the big man land on the run and then slow to a
stop, get his land bearings, then walk over to the train. "Hello,
Medac," he said, using no formalities. When the Duke's son
had been changed by the winds he had forfeited all titles and
claims automatically; legally he was lower than a commoner,
although here in his father's domain he was certainly a
privileged person, a highborn. To Crim he was neither the

creature the Akhbreed considered him nor the near-deity that the people of the refuge regarded him, but merely an equal.

"Crim, it is good to see you," Medac said sincerely. "Did you have a hard trip?"

"Only the Kudaan, as usual," the Navigator replied. "If you all weren't here I'd skip this whole place, frankly. Ovens are for cooking, not for living. About the only good thing about Kudaan is that it dries up my sinuses and any cold I might have and keeps me from catching another for weeks. Even diseases know better than to live here."

Medac did not laugh, although he also was not offended. "I love this place," he said softly. "It has a beauty and an isolation that becomes a part of you. But, enough! We have gone through this many times before. What did you bring?"

"Some of the latest fashions of Court for your mother and her ladies, and some nice trinkets here and there for the rest. Morack coffee, which is the best as you well know, and the usual shopping list of chemicals and crap for your alchemical staff. I'll be glad to get rid of those. Two of those jugs break and mix togther in a bump and you wind up falling madly in love with a cactus and becoming a joyous pincushion when you embrace your love."

The winged man laughed at that one. "You are a little bit crazy, Crim."

Crim glowered in mock menace at him. "All us navigators are mad, sonny. Ain't ye heard? We gibber around campfires and howl at the moon and all that stuff. If you ain't crazy you wouldn't be doing this kind of thing, delivering all sorts of nice stuff to folks but never enjoying any of it yourself."

"You love it. You wouldn't do anything else and you know it."

Crim nodded solemnly. "Case for madness proved, sir. Only a madman would love it and do nothing else." He cocked his eyebrows and dropped his joking tone. "Now, anything I should know before we get all this unloaded and I pay my respects and let these characters have some fun?"

"Nothing that would concern you. We have had a few visitors in and out, some unexpected. One who showed up just yesterday was Zamofir."

Crim suddenly tensed. "Zamofir . . . here. I'd like to

have a real close private talk with that little bastard. He never just drops in. What's he want?"

"My father involves me in everything concerning the refuge, but nothing beyond it, which is how I want it," the winged man responded. "From what I hear, though, he's working as a ground man for a certain somebody from up north and his rainy girlfriend. They want something, I'm sure of that. There have been presences around—up there." He looked skyward. "I've felt them rather than seen them, and I think they're more powerful after dark, but they're there."

Crim was suddenly quite grim. "You make sure you steer clear of any of *them*, son. They don't care who or what you are. Interesting that Old Horny's still lurking around here, though. Guess he got frustrated when they used some of his patrols for vulture feed a while back, so they needed some heavy artillery."

"I have charms to keep us from meeting."

"Don't depend on no charms, boy," the navigator responded firmly. "They're okay so long as you aren't in the way or considered an obstacle, but no charm will keep them off you if you get between them and what they're after." He sighed. "All right, thanks. You happen to know where that moustachioed mouse is right now?"

"In the residence somewhere. He likes the mineral baths, you know. He usually takes a long one before dinner."

Crim gave a slight grin. "Thanks, son. I owe you one."

The Navigator went back and helped supervise the unloading, while lots of beefy members of the staff were ready with carts or to tote boxes to where they belonged. It took awhile, with a break for lunch, but Crim seemed quite businesslike. It wasn't until they were just about through that he turned to his trail boss and said, "I'm feeling a bit sore today, Zel. I think I'm in the mood to take one of those mineral baths." With that he walked off and up into the Governor's Residence.

If Zamofir had been any thinner or slighter of build he would have ceased to exist. He compensated to some degree with foppishly styled long curly hair and a waxed moustache that came out several inches on both sides and curled up into perfect rolls at the ends, and by dressing in a normally flashy manner. He had a long, thin face and a prominent Roman nose and would never be taken for handsome, but he certainly was unmistakable.

He called himself an "expediter," and that was what he was. He was never directly involved in anything, but if you wanted or needed something that was immoral, illegal, or fattening and paid him a fee he would make certain that Supplier A got what was required to Customer B. It might be drugs, human cargo, black magic, bribes—you name it. If you needed a criminal gang to attack a rival and put them out of business without any possible links to you, see Zamofir. If you needed someone assassinated, well, he knew a number of free-lance assassins. And if you needed slave girls, or beefy eunuchs, or your boss turned into a toad, well, he always knew somebody who knew how to do those things. And yet nothing was ever done directly by him, and his "consultant's fee" was a matter of public record. He was a businessman, a man who sold advice. You could never prove that some theoretical discussion of criminal activities was ever linked to the actual.

And now he sat there in Governor Pasedo's bubbling, soothing mineral bath, eyes closed, just relaxing and enjoying the experience and concerned at the moment only that the tremendous heat and humidity would wilt his moustache.

Suddenly something struck him, and he felt himself pushed violently underwater and held there by strong, powerful arms until he thought his lungs would burst. Then, mercifully, the pressure ceased and he broke for air, coughing and gasping. "Who *dares* do this to *me*?" he screamed shrilly between chokes.

"Hello, Zamofir," said Crim in a light tone. "Long time no see, but not long enough."

"Crim! How *dare* you . . . !"

Two strong arms came down again but did not push. "*Shut up, little man!*" the Navigator growled. "I'm going to say one name to you and then I better get a real convincing story from you or the next time I won't let up. The name is Gallo Jahoort."

"I—I don't know what you're talking ab—"

Suddenly he was dunked back under the water, and this time it was a very close thing. When he was released again, strong arms gripped him like a vise.

"Now you listen, you little motherfucker. You know damned well what happened to Jahoort because you were *there*! I *know* you were there. Public record, after all. You always do things on the record, don't you, shit licker? A whole train gets turned into mush and who just happens to be on that particular one? None other than Zamofir himself."

"I had nothing to do with that! It was a flash flood! You know that!"

"Yeah, and I suppose that Asterial behind a perch with a fucking hundred-round-a-minute automatic gun and a whole team of cutthroats working for her and trying to take over the train was just so much hot water too, huh? Why I ought'a—"

Zamofir felt the pressure and the anger and screamed "Wait! Hold it! All right, all right! Yes, I was on that train. I always travel that way, since I am always traveling in my business and I am no Navigator. I had no knowledge of Asterial or the raiders until they appeared, I swear it!"

"Uh-huh. And you just happened to survive that disaster that killed like three-quarters of the people and animals and you just happened to wind up in Asterial's camp with her friends and then you just sat there kind of nice and proper and watched them torture and rape and kill a lot of your fellow survivors because it was no skin off your big nose."

"Yes! I mean, no! They pulled me half-drowned from that place and took me with them. I'd done business with them before and they recognized me. What could I do but watch, Crim? Pick up a stick and beat them all to death? I could do nothing but survive and keep back, that's all! They were mad, Crim. The difference between me eating and sleeping and riding out with them and winding up myself on that torture pile was a word, a gesture."

Crim stared hard at him and cursed under his breath that time was running short. He was sort of enjoying this, and there wasn't anything even the mighty Zamofir could do about it. If the Navigator's Guild ever really even *thought* that Zamofir had deliberately aided that train and one of their own to doom there was no place in all Akahlar to hide and the dying would be horribly slow.

"They're all dead, Zamofir," the Navigator said menacingly. "Even Asterial, if not dead, sure as hell isn't anywhere

where she can do harm to Akahlar anymore. One little courtesan girl and a dying old man shot to pieces did it. But, of course, they make a hundred of you in backbone alone. And, now, here you are, alive and ugly as ever. How'd you get out of there, Zamofir?''

"Asterial zapped the sniper and she had the girl under her control, but most everybody else was dead and with magic around I didn't want to be there no matter what happened. While Asterial was preoccupied I slipped out and around in back of the wagons, loosed a horse, and walked out of the light. Didn't get on and ride for ten minutes. Even then, I only had on a damned sheet and was riding bareback in the dark. I almost died before I reached friends.'' He paused a moment. "But—how did you know I was even there, let alone that I escaped?''

"Two survivors. The gutsy courtesan and the nutty painted alchemist. They made a report to a Navigator and it didn't take long before that report was everywhere—and with your name in it.''

"*Those* two. Not the fat girl and the two kids, though?''

"Why do you want to know about them?''

Zamofir, still being held, tried to shrug. "Just curious. I didn't know if they made it or not.''

"Yeah? And it's not because you're looking for them for a certain horned wizard and acting as the point man on the ground for a horde of demon sky riders?''

"I know nothing of that. Just curiosity—I swear!''

Zamofir was so convincing it wasn't hard to see how the little guy survived in his world of evil.

"You're violating your own rules, Zamofir. Never be directly involved. That's a good policy. It's kept you alive and free and untouched.''

"What do they mean to you anyway?'' the little man wailed.

"They were passengers and they're still Company and Guild responsibility until they're found, gotten safe if they can be, and settlement is made. Now, if I find out you're actively looking for them for somebody else, then I'm going to think that maybe they were what the ambush was all about. And if I think that, and you were on the train, and now you're actively involved in this, then I'll have no choice but to spread the word. There won't be anyplace to hide. Even the Duke depends on the Guild and the Company, and maybe now I'll bring up those missing passengers with His Grace even though I wasn't going to bother. But when I heard you were here, and then I see your interest, well . . ."

Zamofir's eyes grew wide as he realized he was between a rock and a hard place here. Clearly he had already tentatively broached the subject to the Duke, and gotten no positive response, but it wasn't something that could be undone. And if the Navigators got the idea he'd caused the death of one of them . . . hell, even the most corrupt and evil of them held to a code concerning *that*.

"I didn't know about Asterial," he said slowly and sincerely. "I didn't have anything to do with Jahoort's death. Yes, I'm looking for her now, but that's separate. The price being offered is . . . *irresistible*, Crim! You've bent as many laws and flaunted as much authority as anyone, I'll split it with you, Crim!"

The big man was conscious of the clock and knew he could not remain. Still he said, "No. Not this time, Zamofir. Not for me, not for you. I have only your word on Jahoort and this now looks real bad. And I don't care what the price is or why, if you have anything to do with finding this girl and turning her over to Klittichorn's bunch there isn't a Navigator in Akahlar who will believe you." He gave the little man a violent shove into the water, letting go this time, turned, and walked out of the baths.

Zamofir, bruised and shaken, waited until the big man was well gone before painfully climbing out of the bath himself. He lay there on the floor for a moment, breathing hard, looking up at the ceiling. Damn it, he *hadn't* had anything to do with the destruction of that train! But Crim was right—if Zamofir found the fat girl and turned her over to Asterial's ally, who would believe that? He would have to risk the horned one's wrath and resign. It would be a terrible thing, but better a chance of quick, angry death than sure and certain slow death later on. No reward was worth *that* certainty . . .


"Kira, my darling!"

Duke Alon Pasedo went to the door personally and kissed

her hand, then drew her close and hugged her. "It is so *good* to see you so radiant!"

Kira smiled that man-killing smile. She *was* a stunner tonight, in a stunning sparkling burgundy slit dress and matching heels, golden jewelry and made up just right.

"You're just an old smoothie, Your Grace," she responded with a laughing tone. "You would swear we didn't meet like this every three months or so."

"Ah! It is because it is so seldom! You are the only one I have ever known who tempts me with lustful and unfaithful thoughts at the mere sight of you. Come—sit! We have a special meal in your honor tonight and we will sample our finest vintages and our best liqueurs."

"I doubt if Your Grace would still love me in the morning," she responded a bit playfully, then allowed her chair to be pulled out and then herself seated.

The Duke always outdid himself for her visits, and she thoroughly enjoyed them, too. She knew, too, that in his own way he was a man of great internal honor and would keep his lust platonic. Not so the other males in the overly large entourage that always dined with them. She was the object of every man's lust in that room and every woman's envy and she knew it and she loved every furtive glance and inattentive gaffe that situation caused. Even the Duchess kept one of those cold bird's eyes of hers always on Kira, not at all pleased with the way her husband acted when the beauty was around.

So far none of these people's fantasies had been fulfilled. Not that she was averse to a bit of sex when she was in the mood and really wanted the man, or when it was to her advantage for other reasons, but until now that situation had not come up in the Duke's refuge. The only really good-looking man in the court was Medac, and that smacked a bit of kinkiness. The others were the average dirty old men.

Tonight, though, she didn't brush off Director Kano Layse's clumsy under-the-table passes at her leg, and she paid him far more attention than she ever did, to which he responded by getting very, very hot in his pants. Layse was, after all, the Director, and he was also what Akahlar called a physician, although that term here meant more "healer" or "medical magician" than anything else. He was, however, a better administrator than magician, which was why he was Director. Better to have a man who could run things and understand what the smarter, more talented, more powerful ones below him were doing and talking about than to have your best magician wasted on administration.

The evening went quite well, and there were songs and poems and lots of gossip, and she never once brought up Zamofir or the fat girl. She didn't know if Zamofir had really been involved in Jahoort's debacle or not, and she didn't really care. Crim's anger and suspicion were real, but the major purpose was to convincingly remove the competition's man on the ground. If Zamofir was here at all for that reason, then they were just in time, and time was what Crim's fearsome explosion had bought. The mere fact that Zamofir, officially a guest and holding talks with the Duke, had skipped the banquet was evidence enough that, at least for now, the ploy had worked.

One of these days, though, she was going to stick a stiletto between the little man's ribs and twist slowly, or Crim was going to snap that bobbing neck, and therein rid Akahlar of at least one source of contagion.

At the end of the festivities, when they were going for the door, she whispered to Layse, "Director, I should like to speak with you privately. Will you walk me to my room?"

"Delighted," the magician responded, certainly meaning it. They made their good nights to the Duke and the others and walked out and down the hall. It wasn't until they were in the quiet of the residence wing and in fact in front of her door that she said, "Director, I'm afraid a bit of a problem has arisen and you are the only one who might help. Would you mind coming in for a minute?"

The Director, who clearly had a totally different line of thought in mind that included that invitation, responded, "Of course."

She sat in the chair facing the mirror and he sat on the bed, the only other place to sit. She kicked off her shoes and began removing her makeup while watching him in the corner of the mirror.

"Director, I'm afraid His Grace is in a very awkward

position, one that will cause him certain embarrassment and perhaps far more.''

"Oh—what? Yes?"

"About three months ago, a certain young woman wandered into here who was under the protection of an Akhbreed sòrcerer, and was mistaken for just another poor injured girl needing help. She could not tell about this because she did not know whom to trust."

The Director was now partly listening, even though it was hard to keep his eyes off her. "The fat girl with the two children."

"Yes. I am happy we do not have to play games," she added, while loosening her dress.

"That scoundrel Zamofir was also asking about them, that's all."

She sighed. "Then we *do* play games after all. I am not a patient woman—Kano. Unlike Zamofir and his employer, we *know* she is here. I was sent—ahead—to see if something could be done to keep disaster from befalling this nice place."

His voice was trembling, but he replied, "I will not betray my Duke even for a night with you." She stood up and the dress fell away. "*Oh gods!*" he almost sobbed.

She reached for a robe and donned it, although taking care not to conceal very much, and perched down next to him on the bed and gave him a seductive pout.

"My darling Kano, there is no betrayal here. There would be to Zamofir and his crew, but not to *me*. You see how it is. The sorcerer Boolean *knows*. If we can't settle this, then he'll have to contact and make public demands of and embarrass the Duke, and the Duke, to retain his honor, will have to deny it all, and then the full fury of an Akhbreed sorcerer will be brought on all within and this will all be destroyed. No more refuge. No more governor. Nothing but all the changewind victims who survived wandering the ruins. And even honor and reputation will also be crushed, for her mate is still alive and will lodge a formal inquiry with the Kingdom."

Sex wasn't off Kano Layse's mind, but it paled before the vision she was so softly and gently painting, a vision he could fully accept when he heard the name of the sorcerer involved.

"Good lord! W—what can be done? You know His Grace

can never admit to anyone what was done, even though it was an honest mistake made out of compassion and nothing else. No! If this were true surely she would have told us."

"Uh-uh. You remember that train that she was from? The one that got attacked and finally destroyed? They were after this girl. Just her. To kill her. You think she could just wander in here, ignorant of the Duke and the nature of this place, and *trust* anyone? Better to just leave and then contact the sorcerer."

He was sweating now, and he nodded, absently. "But—she got the strongest potion. We—we knew she was from the Outplane, so it was full treatment. Absolute obliteration and hypnotic compulsions to conform."

"Boolean says that there is no such thing as a potion that magic cannot undo."

"Yes, yes. In the strictest sense that's true, but this formulation is powerful because it goes to the heart of the affliction, as it were. The pain, the loneliness, the fragile ego and poor self-image . . . Our diagnosis was correct, damn it! She *wanted* to forget, wanted to become someone else, to be loved, to feel important, needed, for herself, and she didn't care if it was on the level of a base peasant. If she had, she would have developed differently. Many of our staff here had the same potion and all began as base peasants, but they could not find happiness at that level, so we allowed them to rise until they were at the level that met their basic inner needs. Not her. She loves the communalism, the tribal identity, the basic life with few demands and no responsibility. And the longer she's been there the more thoroughly she's become one of them."

"It is no longer her choice—it was *never* her choice, which is part of her problem I suspect—nor yours, nor mine, nor the Duke's. The freak rains that have been doing so much damage here will continue and increase in severity."

His head snapped up and he stared at her. "*She* is the cause of that?"

"The magnet that draws them, anyway. Klittichorn has Stormriders above, just waiting for it to happen again, and you have not had a nightmare as bad as the Stormriders running roughshod through this place to get at her. She cannot remain, and if you give her to Klittichorn then Boolean will destroy this place in his fury."

He was thinking now, all thoughts of an assignation gone. "But how do I know you are from this sorcerer?"

She got up, went over to an old, weathered leather saddle pouch, rummaged through it, and withdrew a small piece of paper. On it was a complex mathematical formula, written in the Akhbreed characters. She handed it to Layse without a word and he stared at it for more than a minute and his mouth dropped slightly.

"Do you know what this is?"

"I can't make sense of any of it," she admitted, "although it is in my hand. But I know what it is."

"But there is something missing! A variable not provided!"

"I have it. And you shall have it if we can work something out."

His hands trembled as he held the card. "This is the highest level of Akhbreed sorcery, far beyond anything lessers could manage. But—what would you have me do?"

"We need the girl, and we need a means of getting her safely and quietly out of here when we leave at dawn the day after tomorrow. A sample of the potion and whatever records you have on her would also help. Remove her and you remove all threat to the Duke or this place. She never was here after all."

He nodded. "I can pull her after work tomorrow to the clinic for a medical check. It's routine, although she's not really due as yet. We could keep her on a pretext, sedated perhaps. The most obvious way to have her voluntarily go would be a love potion, but that would have to be compounded—we do not keep any here—and I'm afraid of how it might mate with the present alchemy. It might cause even more dire personality changes, particularly in combination with that spell of legal mating she already has. Mild, transitory hypnotics might not give you enough time, since they wear off unevenly depending on the individual. Only a strong hypnotic, one requiring an antidote, is sure. She would be an automaton, requiring that you tell her everything to do, without thought. And if you lost the antidote, she would remain that way unless you returned here, since all of our preparations are proprietary."

"That will do," she told him. "I've had experience with that sort of potion before. But can her mind be restored?"

"It's only been three months. The potion does not actually erase—there is no known way to do that without damaging a lot more, actually turning an adult into a mental infant. What it does is block *access* to any past memories. The new personality is built by simply being in and around what you want them to be. Access is by exposure. She has been around only peasants of our sort, so she was able to retrieve and use all the words and phrases and such that they use and she hears. Then she adopts that culture, that belief system, that mode of speech, that way of life. The longer the period that this lasts, the more permanent it becomes and the brain, not accessing the old information, begins to stick it where it cannot be found, like memories of infanthood and fine details of our past. The more she wants what she has, the more she is comfortable that way, the more rapid and total the process of eliminating the past and its knowledge becomes. Eventually, it is irrelevant and irretrievable."

"How long does that take?"

He shrugged. "It varies. There's the age—the less to forget the faster—and various psychological and physiological factors. Those girls who came in with her, for example. They're happy here now, they're placed with loving families, and they are much better off. By now both are probably irretrievable. Your girl—I don't know. She's young, which works against her, but she's also from the Outplane, which makes it an unpredictable factor. You might well get all, or at least most, of the memories back to one degree or another, but the personality—that is a different matter. She had a very weak ego and self-image before; she has a very strong one now. I can only guarantee she will be different."

Kira nodded. "That's all right. I was asked to bring her in, not turn back any clocks." She leaned over and kissed him on the forehead. "You have been a *big, big* help. I won't forget it."

He stood up. "I'll need to have an alchemist in on this. We keep antidotes around but none of the strong potions, for safety's sake."

She stood, too, went back to the bag and pulled out another

small card. "I think this will silence any alchemical questions. I trust you to be able to fake any convincing reasons that might also be needed."

He looked at it. "Some sort of chemical formula. Not my line. What is it?"

"A compound that can be made from common materials. It hardens and can be colored and then molded into flesh, and while there is no feeling I am told it will make the biggest scar look and feel like a tiny scratch—and it can be permanently bonded to skin, even breathe like skin."

He gave a low whistle. "Yes, that will be most—helpful. But there is one more condition to my doing this for you."

"Yes?"

"All of them upstairs saw us together, saw us leave. The porter saw us enter together. Please—could we just—pretend—that something happened here?"

She gave him her sweetest, sexiest smile. "It'll be our little secret," she whispered.


"That's *her*?" Kira asked as she peered into the low and primitive adobe clinic used by the field workers from a safe office. Layse nodded.

The young woman they were watching was the proof that both *short* and *large* could be used to describe the same person. She was certainly quite fat, and no area from the face to the hips, thighs, ass, stomach, and breasts had escaped excess. And yet she was certainly muscular—the arms took very little work to exhibit an amazing set of muscles, and the legs when they were tensed showed much the same.

Her face and skin were burned almost black by the long periods of hard work in the sun, and the skin also had an almost leatherlike toughness to it, as most of the peasants had. It also seemed that her lips had been sun-bleached to an unnatural pale, almost colorless point like her nails, but that might have been just the contrast. At least something in her ancestry had protected her from the most dangerous horrors of this climate, at least for now, but no one who had been out that long could remain totally unaffected.

She had long, straight dark hair down below her shoulders, which did in fact give her a more impish appearance and make her look more human. It was not well trimmed and curled up at the ends, but the sun had created an odd and shifting pattern of light streaks in it that might well be white.

"Nobody grows that much hair in three months," Kira noted.

"A potion. It's a common one and harmless, since if it doesn't work you can always cut it again. It's one of a number of innocent things we allow them to think they're stealing or lifting from us that does no harm and makes them happy. The rest is natural, a consequence of spending over a thousand hours in the sun. You can see it on the others, too."

She nodded. *What a life,* she thought sadly. Still, "She certainly seems bubbly and outgoing," she noted.

"Yes. She was rather quiet and somewhat withdrawn with us before, and I suspect with everyone she didn't know well, but without pressures and with a large tribal family she's been quite extroverted and extremely uninhibited. Physical differences aren't a minus here, you see, and there's no pressure on her. She's strong as a bull, too, which gives her complete self-confidence. My people have seen her hold up the end of a wagon while a wheel was fixed for quite some time without breathing hard, and at Endday she picked up a big, bruising fellow built like a stone tower and head and shoulders bigger than she."

"How'd you get her in here?"

"Slipped a small powder in the field drink today that gave her a nicely timed case of the runs. The treatment potion she'll be given as soon as the last of the other patients leaves is the hypnotic. It will cause some dizziness and she'll be told to lie down. Then I'll dismiss the staff."

She nodded. "We must get her out tomorrow. Zamofir is certain to be around somewhere, just more circumspect, and we have our heavenly host to consider as well."

Layse went over and opened a small case and removed two sealed containers, each with a label on it. "This gold one is the antidote," he told her. "The marks on it represent degrees of recovery. Half dose will represent the more classic hypnotic trance, where the subject is aware but suggestible. All of it should be swallowed for complete recovery, although she will go into a very deep sleep for a couple of hours while it flushes out the remnants. The light red potion is about forty percent of the dose of the amnesia potion that she received. Don't let anyone drink it and particularly not her. That kind of dose on top of the one she had would probably produce a childlike individual with no memories, no self to speak of. Basically an animal."

"Don't worry. We're not out to steal your formula or use or abuse it. We just want a means of getting her back without harming her."

"Where will you take her?" he asked, curious.

She smiled. "That is something it is better for you not to know." She looked back out through the peephole. "I think everybody else is gone. She's taken her medicine like a good girl and they're helping her over to a cot."

Layse nodded and was out the door. Timing was crucial here; there was no sense in having to convince the medic here that there wasn't anything untoward going on. He and Layse talked in animated terms for a while, then seemed very chummy, and finally the medic picked up a file on his desk and handed it to the Director, who went through it absently, then told the man to go, he'd take care of this.

The medic looked uncertain for a moment but didn't really want to argue for more work. It had been a long day, and he had staff privileges at the residence. He left, and Layse sat looking through the file intently, almost forgetting Kira. She waited patiently; no sense in showing up and then have the medic or somebody come back because they forgot something and see her.

Finally he sighed, put down the folder, and motioned for her to come in. She did so, then looked over at the young woman who was out cold on the cot, dead to the world. "Anything the matter?" Kira asked him. "I saw you studying the folder."

"Medical history. Environmental adjustments were the first priority so we didn't do much of one when she joined us, just the usuals to make sure she could stand the work and was as healthy as she seemed. There was supposed to be another one, a more thorough follow-up, a few weeks later but she seemed to be adjusting so well and the case load is huge, so it wasn't done. This was the first physical she had. She's gained eleven and a quarter halgs, which sounds high until you realize it's all muscle and some of it is fat into muscle conversion as well. If that's not allowed to go back to fat it won't be serious.

"Enough for me. I only weigh forty-three myself. Even Crim weighs only ninety-two. It's a good thing we won't have to *lift* her. Any medical problems we should know about other than that?"

"Only one, but it is really going to complicate your situation if you have a very long journey."

Her eyebrows rose. "Yes?"

"She's three months pregnant."

That was a stunner. "Oh, *great*!" Kira muttered. "Just what we needed. Does she know?"

"I doubt it. If she underwent any morning sickness she didn't report it, and who would notice any of the other minor symptoms out in the fields? It probably won't start to show until the end of the sixth month, and who's going to notice a bigger belly on *her* until it's well along? But it will weaken her, slow her down, there will be biochemical changes, that sort of thing."

"Yeah, but what you're telling me is that I've got six months or less to get her where she's going." She sighed. "Any idea whose? Somebody here, perhaps?"

"Possible, but doubtful. They don't usually take advantage of newcomers here, and it's normally a few weeks before there's any real social activity. From what you say it's unlikely she had any earlier male trysts on the move, so that leaves the rape."

Kira sighed and looked at her. "Poor kid. No way to get rid of it?"

He looked a bit shocked, but recovered. "Um, not without lots of work and recovery, no. Not *safely*, anyway, and the other, cruder methods at this stage risk infection, even possible death. If you take her tonight, either your sorcerer has to come up with something or she's going to have the kid."

The woman nodded. "Well, I'll let Boolean decide that one." She turned. "Think she's ready now?"

"Oh, yes. And the loose bowels was a one-time thing, really. Just a super laxative. However, she'll have no bladder control in this state, so remember that. Have her try going often."

Kira turned and walked over to the unconscious woman. She had come in directly from a day in the fields and she was filthy and smelled like shit. There was no way around that for now. "Misa, open your eyes, sit up, and sit on the side of the bed."

The eyes opened, but they were blank, as if still asleep, and she did exactly as instructed.

"Now listen to me," she said carefully. "You will hear only the sound of my voice and no other voice, so my voice is all that you will obey for now. Tomorrow, a man will come to you and say the words, 'I am Crim, obey me as well,' and you will hear him say that and then obey him as well as me and hear either his voice or my own but no one else's. Do you understand that? Answer."

"Yes," she replied dully, in a voice that was startlingly low.

"All right, now stand up. You will follow me, three paces behind me, and whatever I do you shall do until I tell you different. If I sit, you sit. If I walk, you follow. If I stop, you stop. Understand? Answer."

"Yes."

Kira checked to see that she had the antidote and the sample. "Does she have anything to wear except those filthy black panties she's got on?"

Layse shrugged. "Sorry, not here. Back in her room, yes, but there's no way to unobtrusively get to it now."

"All right, all right, I'll have to make do. Getting out of here is the only real priority right now, and putting some distance between us and the forces above. Can you put out all the lights?"

"Of course, but it will be pretty dark if I do."

"I am a creature of the darkness," she told him. "Still, there's enough residual light from other sources for her to see me. Do it."

He killed the lights, and she waited for Misa's eyes to grow accustomed to the dark.

"Misa, can you see me now? Answer."

"Yes."

"Then follow and obey."

Kano Layse suddenly had a thought. "Wait! What about the missing variable in the formula?"

"You have it now. It is on the same paper as the rest of the formula. If we leave this jurisdiction the variable will fade in and be like the rest of the ink. If we are betrayed, or caught while still in the district, the paper will burst into flame. That is fair enough."

Layse sat back down in the dark, disgusted. He had every intention of betraying them on this. He felt like a traitor to the Duke in this matter, but that formula—when he saw it, and knew what it was—was, well, irresistible. Tomorrow he'd go down to the labs and start tinkering. In a couple of weeks he'd come up with it, and his star would really shine and his position would be quite secure. But the price he paid still made him feel guilty. Creating Misa was the right and moral thing to do; he was still convinced of it. And while restoration was theoretically possible, he had never seen or done it, and no one he had known could do it, either. The gods knew what poor Misa would become now.

Getting out of there had been the easy part, although finding a shipping crate that would fit her without harming her was a real pain. The next morning, just at dawn, Crim had the caravan put together and everyone was ready to move. The cases of the Duke's private wines provided nice cover, and would bring a decent profit at some point.

Crim was not yet ready to feel safe, but as the mileage built up between him and the Duke he began to feel a little bit better.

They followed the river trail, as they always did, at neither a faster nor slower clip than anyone would expect, but with an eye to the canyon walls and particularly to side canyons and old slides which might hide ambushers. Thanks to agreements between the wilder denizens of this area and both the Duke and the Navigators, there was generally little risk so long as you were known and official and all that, but there was always the chance of newcomers and some of the folks in this country were just plain crazy.

By nightfall they were camped at one of the safety zones, a campground that was agreed to be neutral territory of sorts and thus safe. It was only a theoretical safety, of course, and they would have guards and spells and all sorts of things for insurance, but in all these trips they'd never been hit anywhere in this area. Anybody inclined to violate this place would also

be too afraid of Yobi to actually do it. Only the crazy, and
Klittichorn's bunch, might try it, and the latter only if they
suspected something.

They were about thirty miles from the Duke's now, a fair
distance in these parts but not really comfortable, not when the
Duke's son flew with ease over great distances by day and there
were Stormriders about at night. The latter was not strong
without a storm from which to draw energy, but they could see
well enough and if one could get a message off, they had a
mistress who could whip up a storm of any fury desired. And
even though the canyon now was broad, nobody on the caravan
wanted to think about a real gully washer in the area.

Kira couldn't risk going out alone into this in search of who
she wanted. Not even Crim would be really safe in this place,
not alone, or not particularly with the girl.

They had checked on her from time to time. The crew knew
better than to ask questions about such things; they all had
hands in one shady thing or another now and then. Every once
in a while Crim would climb on the wagon, crawl back to her,
open the side of the crate, check her condition, have her eat
and drink, and, using a bucket as an ersatz chamber pot, have
her go if she could as well. They didn't catch that last need
every time, and she was getting pretty gamy in there, but there
was no way around it. To command someone to hold it invited
forgetfulness, and you could cause a kidney to rupture or
bowel blockage by doing so.

Now, Kira could only wait, although she decided to take the
risk and attend to one matter. She brought her obedient woman
to the river, and commanded that she remove all clothing left
and discard it and then bathe completely. "Misa" was no work
of art when she was done, but at least she didn't smell so bad.

Everyone was fast asleep except for Kira and one other
guard, both of whom kept pistols on their hips and rifles at the
ready nearby just in case, when someone came. It was the
guard who first saw or heard or felt something, drawing on a
near–sixth sense born of long trail experience. Kira had
expected someone, but not old Yobi herself, who never left her
cave. Yet, here she was, with two very inhuman attendants,
slithering in, long ears twitching, pulling herself with the aid of
two strong-looking canes.

Kira looked over at the rather stupefied guard. "It's all right, Garl. I know them and I've been expecting—someone."

Yobi came straight for her, and stopped when she saw "Misa" apparently asleep under a tree. The dark woman was hard to see in the shadows, but Yobi didn't use the same sight as normal people did.

"So," she rasped. "That is the source of all our machinations. My, but there is little that hasn't been done to that poor girl. I see the demon spell, with its inhuman mathematical insanity, and the marriage bond as well, thin as it is, trailing like a spider's web. And the potions, layered this way and that. The hypnotic is easy, then the memory one. Oh, my! That's a nasty one, that is. And under it all, what strange and unnatural *power* lurks! The threads that run wispily to the north are firm. Yes, yes, she is definitely the one, poor soul."

Yobi sighed and looked up at Kira. "Kid, this one's gonna be a real bitch to do."

Kira stared at her. "Do you think you can bring her back?"

"Not me. Mister Smartass Greenpants, maybe, with my help. You have the sample and the antidote?"

"Yes, in my bag. I'll get them."

"Bring that idiot sorcerer's calling stone, too. We're gonna have a long night here."

"You think it is wise to do it here? This close?"

"Of *course* it's not, you silly, blithering idiot, but if I can't recover from old Horny the Fart and his minions as long as I need I don't deserve to still be here!"

# · 7 ·

## *Stormrider*

"THE TIME HAS come to run swiftly and well," Yobi said to Dorion. "Just today that little shit Zamofir is due at Hodamoc's. Once the moustachioed twit hears the description of Charley and all that transpired, the full hue and cry will be out. They will even come to me to try and make a deal or somehow threaten me if they think they can. I'm pretty well invulnerable, I think, but they can cause a lot of trouble."

"We've worked on the disguises pretty well," the magician responded. "It's a delicate thing to figure out something that's effective but not *too* effective. That crazy one, Boday, is also pretty good with many kinds of weapons, including the whip and crossbow. Charley, of course, is much more limited, but she'll make it."

The sorceress nodded. "Yes, they are a strange pair, this Charley and her Sam. Charley has already overcome things that would have beaten many a lesser person, but never have I seen such a determined and survival-oriented ego. She adapts incredibly. Already the blindness is simply accepted as an inconvenience and she is using her other senses more and doing much with confidence—including knowing her limits. She uses the cat's vision sparingly, when she needs it, instead of trying to make the animal substitute eyes. Yes, she is incredibly strong and yet the irony is that she believes herself to be incredibly weak. Somehow her ideal is to be a man with a better tailor and more clothing options." The old one sighed.

"Now, this other one—this Sam," Yobi continued, "she's a

real mess. Charley does not understand that it is perfectly fine to enjoy being a courtesan so long as it was a valid choice on her part. Few men have the courage that she showed in tracking down Asterial and her whole gang in hostile country with only two pistols. This Sam, though—I'm beginning to wonder if the breakthrough will ever really come with her. She wants to run and hide. She wants to be docile. She'd be perfectly fine as a slave or some peasant. She wants to avoid all responsibility and all pressures. Even if I can pull her back from Pasedo's mental acids, I don't know if she'll *ever* have the will and temperament to take on the Storm Princess. That is another reason for keeping Charley alive, Dorion. The only act of bravery and will, the assumption of risk and danger, was when Sam rushed to save her friend. She draws strength and resolve from Charley. So it is not just as a decoy that our girl is important. I think she will be essential in the ultimate battle."

Dorion nodded. "I think I see what you mean. So how do we work this and who does what?"

"I, obviously, can go nowhere in the flesh, and I don't have an acolyte I'd trust on something like this. I've made arrangements with some various people who owe me in ways they dare not refuse my will to get them through, but they will need a native guide and helper, as it were, preferably one with some magical talents, odd and arcane as those talents might be, and a full Akhbreed citizen able to move freely throughout Akahlar."

Dorion stared at her a moment, then gulped. "You mean—me?"

"Oh, good! I'm happy you volunteer. Saves me the trouble of putting pressure on you."

"Hey, wait! I'm not—I mean, damn it, Yobi! You know the limits of my magic! That's why I wound up here in the first place! I'm in lousy shape; I'm a poor shot and even poorer with any other weapons. What the hell good would I be?"

"You're streetwise, as they call it in the cities. You think fast when you have to, sweet Dorion, and you're basically trustworthy and with a strong sense of honor that is almost nonexistent around here. That is worth more than muscle. I can command muscle, but never honor."

Dorion thought about it. "You mean—me? Alone, with those two, for all that distance?"

Yobi gave her cackling laugh. "Yes, indeed. I'm transferring complete control to you, but their Master will be Boolean himself. That means that even if someone should get to you, they would be useless and always driven to Boolean. Frankly, I'd remove their slavery if I thought it would be productive, but Boday needs discipline or she'll be more hindrance than help, and Charley needs the same external discipline because of her beauty and her blindness. And so long as they have those rings no one is going to abduct or make off with them, since they know their prize is both useless and dangerous. Nor do I want her wandering off lost somewhere, particularly out of fear. That's a very real possibility when she discovers, as she must, that she is not exactly blind."

Dorion, whose eyes were also little use because of the magical radiations of his apprenticeship but who was of sufficient power that he saw, as Yobi did, by other means, understood what the sorceress meant. This kind of blindness shifted the eyes rather than destroying them. As Charley would discover, there were many things she could now see that before she either could not or could not see properly, nor could any sighted person. But seeing on a magical plane often meant one saw what one wished one could not see.

Dorion sighed. "All right. When?"

"Tonight. After dark. I have horses ready capable of taking you into Mashtopol itself in just a couple of days. From that point I have a list of contacts and methods along the route that you must memorize. You'll have sufficient supplies for the initial journey and sufficent money along the way for whatever you need. Since enslavement of an Akhbreed is technically illegal, although nobody really cares, I've had papers drawn up showing them to be indentured under a spell certified by a ranking sorcerer—the sort of thing everybody makes up to make this kind of thing legal and proper. Officially, you and your superiors performed a service of magic the price of which was indenture. That makes their enslavement a consequence of their own free choice, and thus legal. Gad, how I love bureaucracy! You can commit murder and pillage so long as the paperwork's right!"

He nodded soberly, thinking of the job. "All right, so what if we somehow manage, and I admit I'll be shocked if we do, to get them to Boolean? What do I do then? I mean, I'm not exactly a stranger to Boolean, and he wasn't too thrilled with me the last time I saw him."

"All is forgiven and forgotten if you deliver them," Yobi assured him. "After that, it's up to you. You can transfer their control to Boolean and get out with a whole skin from this mess—and with a nice reward to boot—or you can stick it out if you prefer and if you and Boolean can stand each other for that long. That's the other reason why it must be you, though. Others might be able to shepherd them to the boundaries of Masalur, but you are from there and you know the region better than any other that I have. If anyone can sneak them in right past Klittichorn's nose, you can."

"Yes," the magician sighed. "That is true enough. If I live that long."

Both women looked very different from the way they had looked in years. To eliminate the butterfly design outline, they had treated Charley with a potion that triggered the release of all melanin within each cell and added it if it wasn't there. The result was a uniform chocolate brown complexion that suited her quite well. The process could be alchemically reversed but was otherwise stable, permanent, and self-renewing. Her hair had been cut to shoulder length and given a great deal of curl, and it had also been colored a reddish blond that contrasted greatly with her skin tone. She was still sexy and gorgeous and all that, but she was no longer obviously a courtesan but rather an Akhbreed colonial who probably had her hair dyed.

The physical disguise was a deliberate and subtle choice. There were a lot of pretty girls in Akahlar, but the blind blonde would not be recognized without a very close inspection as one of the wanted women—but she would be remembered. The object was really to be recognized, but too late to do any good and not without a lot of work.

Because she was "indentured" to a magician, she wasn't a free agent and thus wasn't as well expected to live up to the local dress codes. This was a relief to her, really; it had been so long since she'd worn a lot of clothes that she wasn't all that sure she could abide a complete and cover-all type outfit, and she certainly had doubts that she could ever again stand to wear a pair of shoes.

The clothing thing didn't bother her—she always dreamed of having the body to dress lightly and sexily—but she remembered spending many fond hours shopping for shoes.

In point of fact, she knew that slaves were fairly common among the Akhbreed nobility and many others important enough and rich enough to afford to create them. It was somewhat ironic that the very colonial system made them inevitable. Since none but Akhbreed could enter the hub cities, all non-Akhbreed were excluded if you lived in a hub. But the level of obedience and service slavery provided to feed upper-class egos was simply too tempting to ignore, and the strictures of the society were such that if you didn't fall into the hands of the criminal element but were still outcast from tribe and clan, you could wind up commercial property. As erotic as Charley was, and blind to boot, there was only one assumption possible as to what sort of slave she was, and she would have to dress the part. Bare breasted, with the little beaded bottom she'd been wearing when taken from Hodamoc, and with a loose robe of semitransparent gauzelike material worn generally untied. To those were added dull bronze earrings, matching bracelets and anklets, and a thin necklace of braided chain.

Boday was still tall and lean, but she didn't look so exotic when shorn of her elaborate mass of tattoos. In fact, she really didn't look all that bad. She had nice curves, a tight ass, and surprisingly smooth skin, although without all the artistic pyrotechnics her breasts looked rather small for all their firmness.

The absence of the tattoos caused such a dramatic difference in her that they didn't feel they had to do much more. The only thing they worked on was her hair, although she hadn't forgiven them yet for not allowing her to dye it some nice rainbow colors. Instead it had become thick, wiry, and incredibly curly, and they had grown it out almost to a manelike stature. Through Shadowcat's eyes, Charley was able to see at least the basics and thought Boday resembled nothing so much as some *National Geographic* shot of some African warrior woman. With her Mediterranean-type features and all those tattoos and straight, short black hair she'd looked very different; it took this to see the real Boday—more black African than exotic Lebanese, for example.

Boday even admitted that this was how her own natural hair had looked. She had straightened it and lengthened it alchemically before.

But if she could no longer look so exotic, Boday was determined to dress that way and had designed and helped make most of her outfit. It was kind of a revealing leather bodice with silver rivetlike studs, long leather boots with fairly high heels, and a matching headband. Charley thought she looked like something escaped from an S & M porno movie, but, somehow, it suited Boday just fine. The whip, and the leather holster with its pistol, only completed the impression. Charley thought that when Boday started to sweat and move around a lot in that outfit it was going to become very uncomfortable, but the mad artist was not to be denied at least this much unless commanded to do so.

Dorion dressed in a mud-brown cotton outfit that matched his robes but was a more conventional shirt and trousers, along with a broad felt brown hat with a crease in the middle. He had his robes and his magic paraphernalia with him, but the regulation outfit wasn't practical for a long horse journey. Neither, of course, was either outfit the two women were wearing, but right now that couldn't be helped. The first object was to get them through the tightest squeeze, which was Mashtopol, with the place surely swarming with Klittichorn's agents. Once through the bottleneck, they might be able to change not only clothing styles but a lot else—perhaps might be forced to do so.

"I want to get a few things clear at the outset," he told them. "First of all, keep the abject slave stuff for the public, when strangers or any others are around. When it's just we three, you can dispense with the Master stuff and just talk to me pretty much as you would anyone else. Feel free to make comments and ask what you need. If I get sick of it I can always just order you to shut up, so don't abuse it."

He looked at them and at the horses and knew he really didn't want this shit but, somehow, he was stuck. Well, he'd been the one who'd started all this rolling—even though she wasn't even the real Storm Princess double, damn it!

"Now, Charley, I know you've been practicing but you're not going to be great as a free rider and you know it," he continued. "Your horse is old friends with the other two. It'll follow me, and that's where you'll be—just behind me. Boday, you're behind Charley and since you've got the weapons it's up to you to use your own judgment unless I countermand it specifically. Don't wait for an order if an attack or real threat appears, and make Charley's protection your first priority. Remember, I have some magical powers and they've gotten me this far alive and whole, so Charley's the one who needs your help. If I need it, I'll yell loud enough. Understood, both of you?"

Charley nodded, as did Boday. Charley was a bit fascinated by something that hadn't been so until now, but which was both inexplicable and intriguing. She found that, somehow, she could *see* Dorion—not with Shadowcat, with her eyes. Not really him, but an odd, wriggling glowing shape that was mostly deep reds but occasionally showed or flashed other colors as well. This against the eternal gray nothingness was disconcerting; she could not see Boday or any of the landscape or the horses at all.

There were, however, a few other things in view. An odd yellowish glow from a point about eye level and off to the right—Dorion's saddlebag, maybe, with the magic stuff in it? And Shadowcat—Shadowcat was a small deep lavender fuzz. She sent her mind to the cat's, and saw, from a very low perspective, that Dorion was where the deep red was, and that there was certainly a horse where the yellow came from.

There was also a curious wispy light red string, almost like a single strand from a spider's web, that continually twisted and turned and seemed to go off into the distance. She realized suddenly that it came from Boday, but what it was and where it went was a mystery. Boday herself was in no way visible—but the wispy strand helped locate her.

She was still blind for all practical purposes, but she began to realize that the radiations that had taken her sight had perhaps given her another, stranger one. Was this, then, what the magicians and sorcerers saw with their own eyes, or did they see clearly what she saw as only bizarre and pulsating shapes and colors? It didn't matter, but it was at least something she didn't have before, and it would allow her to keep Dorion in sight no matter what the light. She could not use the magic, but she could see it, and somehow that gave her a lift.

They helped her on her horse and she settled in like the lifelong horsewoman she was. When they were down on the ranch many times when she was but a girl they had used their familiar horses and closed their eyes and tried all sorts of games and tricks that way. This wasn't so bad, as long as you didn't have to gallop for your life.

They had made a sort of sling for Shadowcat, which the cat had taken to right away. Clearly there was some magical thing now residing within or controlling the cat, for he was quite loyal and willing to submit to a number of indignities.

"I am surprised that Mistress Yobi did not come to see us off," Boday noted, taking advantage of the new freedom of speech.

Dorion chuckled. "Mistress Yobi is pretty damned busy right now, and part of it is making some arrangements for our future security—if we get that far. We've already delayed too long and it's going to be tight. One of Klittichorn's agents is right now a guest at Hodamoc's, and it won't take that little moustachioed son of a bitch too long to put two and two together."

Charley's head came up. "Moustachioed? Is that the word I understood in translation? Can this one you speak of be called Zamofir?"

Dorion looked surprised. "You know him?"

"The spineless swine of a mud demon!" Boday spat. "He was with our wagon train and then with the animals who tortured and defiled us! How much would Boday *love* to get his balls in her grasp and squeeze hard—if he has any balls."

"He's a free-lance scum," Dorion told them. "Expensive, though, careful, effective, and, most important, he stays bought. The Horned One has offered him a bundle for you two and your friend, it's said, and he'll work like a demon to find us. If they've given him a bottomless money account, as they probably have, he can be a pretty nasty enemy, although, as I said, he's careful. He must have slipped up on that wagon train business, because he almost never gets close enough personally to get caught in anybody's hands." He sighed. "I'm not too worried about here to Mashtopol. I know this territory well and few will dare risk Yobi's wrath. But pray that your new look fools them in Mashtopol. It's so damned corrupt we can't count on anybody or anything."

Riding by night and sleeping by day made the journey much easier, since they didn't have to contend with the hot sun, but they could never have done it on their own unless they'd stuck to the road. Dorion, however, seemed to know every back trail and crack and crevice, and seemed to see as well in the dark as Boday did in daylight. Charley envied him that kind of second sight.

She liked Dorion, too. Oh, he was chubby and he got out of breath in a hurry when he had to do anything energetic, but, what the hell. So he wasn't Mister Wonderful with the body of a barbarian and the head of a Greek god. He seemed a pretty nice, levelheaded guy, and it both impressed and somewhat puzzled Charley that, with them subject to his every whim, he had taken no advantage at all of that situation. She wasn't sure about Boday, but she sure as hell wouldn't have minded a therapeutic fuck or two in the wilderness. She began to wonder if the magician might not be as gay as Hodamoc.

Still, when you can't even see the sights and you're strung out in a line so conversation's pretty limited, it gets pretty damned boring pretty fast. Charley began to imagine herself, as she sometimes did, going back home at this point. It had been so long, and she'd gone through so much.

*Hi, Mom! Hi, Dad! I'm back! I found a career I really like as a high-class hooker. I'm blind, and, oh, yes, I'm now black, and I'm a slave girl who dresses like a porno belly dancer, but other than that, everything's just fine. Oh, I almost forgot. You remember my best friend Sam? She got real fat and married another woman . . .*

Their parents' sense of loss would still be there, of course, and maybe she and Sam had their faces on a million milk cartons, but there was no going back. Not now. The trouble was, it remained to be seen whether or not there was any real going forward, either.

This whole period, both the dull sameness of Hodamoc's place and the more active but still strange and isolated time at Yobi's, had left her for the first time with a lot of time for introspection, and she had come to some conclusions about herself while still wrestling with others. Part of it was this last stay with people who knew both alchemy and magic and who had taken away some of her mental props by separating what was really her from what had been imposed upon her. Many could be made into courtesans, for example, by the kind of alchemical magic Boday used to wield, but few truly enjoyed it. The distinction, in purely Akahlarian terms, was between what you *did* and what you *were*.

For example, she realized that she really loved men. Not in the sense of being heterosexual; it was a more encompassing, even generic sort of love. Oh, she liked those cute little asses and there were some that were simply *gorgeous*, but it wasn't just that. She liked them young, old, tall, short, fat, thin—you name it. She couldn't explain it, but she knew what her ideal was and she missed it. That wasn't alchemy; it was deep.

And she loved sex. Not just the screwing, although that was the hot fudge on the sundae, but all of it. She had liked it the first time, back home, but it had scared her as well, perhaps because she had liked it so much and it had dominated her fantasies and daydreams. Now she couldn't get enough of it, not anymore. It wasn't enough that she got off; she had to give as well as get in equal amounts. Now, having done it so much with so many, there were no inhibitions left, only a deep craving. Something that had always been there had been loosed by circumstance and now here it was.

She began to understand what Yobi had said to her. It didn't mean that she wasn't smart, or that she didn't want independence and control of her own life. She was proud of that rescue operation, and if she could somehow get this ring out of her nose she'd be overjoyed. She didn't want a husband; she wanted twenty years or more of one-night stands that would make her also wealthy and totally independent of others.

She wasn't gonna let this blindness hold her down, either. She missed her sight, sure, but it was only one sense and not the most important. She was already learning quickly how much she could do. A lot of it was just plain common sense, like putting your thumb inside a cup where you want the fill line to be and pouring until it reached that point; others were trial and error, or just doing things a bit slower and more cautious than before.

She liked Shadowcat, and appreciated what he could do for her, but she was sparing in using him. Dorion, after all, understood English, which left Boday out rather than her, and she'd much rather talk to Dorion than Boday anyway, so she didn't want that telepathic thing unless she needed it. And when the cat was let free to roam, she discovered quickly how you didn't really want to see what he was doing. The first mouse and insect kills kind of cured the romance right out of her. But it was convenient to be able to look over a campsite and memorize it, or to check on things when she had to. But she was determined from the start not to use him as a crutch.

Blind, she could saddle and unsaddle a horse and ride with confidence. She could prepare her own food and drink to a fair degree on the trail, and she could attend to her own personal needs. She managed her own sleeping bag from unpacking and setting it out to repacking her gear. She would rather have her sight back, but she wasn't about to give up living because it was lost or wallow in self-pity waiting for it to somehow miraculously return. It would be nice to have it, but it was something she could live without.

Perhaps this Boolean could restore it, although they said that most all magicians and sorcerers lost real sight so if they could get it back they would. Dorion was a bit vague on it, admitting that his eyes were shot and yet he could see with remarkable clarity better than he had with them. He was not blind, but his methods were those of sorcery denied to her.

The strange things she *could* see puzzled her. Why was Boday nonexistent save for that odd and fragile red strand, and the horses and the landscape a seamless deep gray, but Dorion this strange, fuzzy red blur and Shadowcat that lavender blob?

"Your eyesight, like mine, has been shifted, not canceled," Dorion told her. "It is very hard to explain to a lay person, but you can read a lot into the shapes, colors, and types of patterns you see. You are seeing perfectly well, but in dimensions beyond the capability of normal eyes to ever see. It is like being in a haunted house and being able to see the ghosts but not the house they haunt. Still, if you could see fully into those other dimensions you would probably go mad. Only that which is in this world but gives off radiations into the others is visible, and that's for the best. Some things of the magical world are best not seen, but you might see them. Be prepared for it, but control yourself as well. It is better to see those who would do you harm from that realm than to be at their unseen mercy."

On the third day they rejoined the main road very near the border of Mashtopol, but Dorion decided to camp yet again in the Kudaan before going through. "Best we move still by night, at least for a while," he told them, "and be fully awake and alert going through there."

"Boday does not understand what risks there might be," the artist noted. "Surely this pig Zamofir is behind us, and after all this time those still alerted for us must be mere hired hands and ruffians, not the sort who will keep a steady watch or be difficult to fool."

"Yeah, perhaps," Dorion responded, "but it's best to take no chances. Zamofir has birds and other means of communication that are far faster than we, and he has access to a magical network with near-instant communications. We have to assume that they're expecting us. From tomorrow until we're clear of this place we're going to have to depend on all aspects of the disguise, including our cover."

"You mean the slave business," Charley said, nodding.

"Yes. You will have to be total slaves and act the part at all times, even when it seems as if no one is around. Charley, you're going to have to be the slave girl Yssa, the total and uninhibited sex slave who's also subservient and docile to my will—and mute unless I say otherwise or unless we need to be alerted to a danger, since you can't speak the language. And you, Boday, will be Koba, and you will have to be different. Do not use your name at all except to answer 'Koba' if asked what it is. If you must speak in the third person, then use humble and self-deprecating terms like 'this unworthy one' and 'this humble slave.' I know that will kill your ego but it's essential. You are our defender, a warrior slave. If anybody asks too personal or specific questions just tell them it's not permitted for you to answer or that your past life has been wiped out. In all cases you are *my* slaves and there will be no references to others."

"Boday has spent her life seeking recognition," the artist noted. "This will not be easy for her."

"You don't have to be inconspicuous, but you must eat, sleep, think, act the part at all times," he told them firmly. "Only if we are discovered and unmasked are you on your own, using your own discretion. And I will have to treat you as my slaves, too, acting my own part. I'll apologize later. I never liked this slave business, and I'm uncomfortable with it."

"Use us as you must," Charley told him, "and don't worry or feel guilty. We have already been through so much, and what you ask me to be is a role I very much enjoy playing."

The Kudaan exit station was unusually crowded, with a number of tough-looking men about, mostly armed, and to no apparent purpose, but both the officials and the men spent most of their time looking at Charley and not very much looking at the documents or anything else. She gave them a good show, lounging sexily on the saddle and doing offhanded obscene things in a playful way. They would remember her, all right, but not a one of them seemed to entertain the slightest thought that she was anything more than she appeared to be. In fact, you didn't have to read minds to know pretty much all the thoughts those guys had.

She couldn't see them, of course, but she didn't have to. The comments and the sounds and the panting and the many attempts to bribe Dorion for a little while with her said it all.

Shamelessly, she loved every minute of it. In a way, this was a different kind of power and no less real for all that.

And beyond the gate was what looked like a great yellow wall rising from ground level as far up as the eye could see. It looked amazingly solid, and imposing.

"Each null zone has a shield like that," Dorion told her. "It is a great shield of an Akhbreed sorcerer, and it prevents any but Akhbreed from going through it to the land beyond. In that way all non-Akhbreed, all changelings, all the ones who don't fit the definitions, are prevented from ever moving from world to world. It's not absolute because you can't ever be smart enough to write a spell that covers everything, but along with the entry gates it keeps things so manageable it may as well be impenetrable to all others.''

*Maybe not as impenetrable as they think,* Charley reflected, remembering that when she'd first entered this world there had been a centauress hiding out in a cave within a hub itself. But, as Dorion had said, nothing couldn't be beaten, but that centauress *was* hiding out and would have been killed instantly if discovered.

For them the boundary was paper thin; they passed through it with no sensation at all and went into the null zone itself, and that was something else again for her. She could not see the ever-present thick white mist, but she found she could see the massive spurts of energy that had previously looked like occasional sparks here and there. It was a forest, a fairyland of color and light and constantly shifting patterns, and there seemed to be a kind of yellowish rain connecting it to the unseen clouds above.

As they entered and passed through it, they interacted with it, causing the area around them to become intensely more active and to constantly change colors as well. This was the beauty and wonder of the magic sight. Outlined against the darkness of her conventional blindness, it was breathtaking.

There was no magic to see beyond, in the hub itself, but far off in the distance, she couldn't guess how far, there seemed to rise a single pencil-thin beacon of brilliant gold, like a searchlight beacon breaking the night.

"That comes from the city," Dorion explained. "It emanates from the royal Akhbreed sorcerer himself. We're going to avoid that and try and stick to the borderland, although we can't avoid some civilization. All roads really lead to and from the capitals, and the crossroads are intended for local use only and we'll have a very crooked path to follow because of it."

Dorion worried about Boday, no matter what the commands, but he wondered about Charley. He was the first to admit that he never really understood women, not even if they were six hundred years old and built like a cross between a crone and a slug. Charley was bright, resourceful, adaptable, everything— and yet he got the very strong impression that if she were free of him, of the ring, and of all obligations she'd become a full-time professional whore, a seller of her flesh. She wasn't just acting back there; he had the distinct impression she would have been delighted had he taken any of those men up on their offers. Yobi had said as much and had seemed to find nothing wrong with it. You never argued with Yobi, but it sure as hell seemed wrong to him somehow.

Both Charley and Boday were relieved to reach the Mashtopol entry station. Finally, at last, the Kudaan was behind them, with its merciless heat, its strange denizens, and its bizarre risks. It had taken so long to get through it that it was only by great luck and a hairsbreadth that they'd not wound up spending the rest of their lives there.

The duty officer at the entry station found both women fascinating, but he was also far more officious and more steadfast in his duties.

"Indentures, huh? Permanent?"

"Yes, sir," the magician responded. "Neither originally to me, though. I was in the service of a great sorcerer who saved the tall one's people from a demonic attack and got her because the old boy outgrew his need for servants. The other, well, you see her. I had to pay a high price in spells and services to talk her owner out of her, as you might guess, but you can see why any price was good enough."

The duty officer looked at Charley and nodded. "Yes, I can see why you would want her, but not why anybody'd sell her."

"She's blind. That made her inconvenient to her old owner, but there's no problem with what *I* wanted."

The officer *tsk-tsked*. "Too bad. So pretty. What about the cat? We have to check on all animals, you know."

"I have it on the documents here. The cat is mine and used with some of my magic, but it's just a cat. The girl took a real liking to him, though, and he to her, so they stay pretty well together when I don't need one or the other."

The duty officer sighed. "All right, sir. All in order. Big festival in the city the end of the week, you know. Lots of folks in town, so you might have trouble finding rooms if you haven't already booked them. Also, this time of year, there's a lot of the bad element creeping in to take advantage as well. Been some girls disappearing here and there, and some murders. You watch your pair there, sir."

"I will," he promised. "But in Koba's case they better watch out for *her*."

The officer stamped the documents, and Charley wondered just how easily those things were forged and just how few were real that came through these stations, anyway.

"All in order, sir," said the duty officer, handing back the papers to Dorion. "You're cleared for as long as you wish to stay, exiting either here or at the Northwest Gate. Have a pleasant stay."

Dorion thanked him and remounted, and they were off into Mashtopol. Charley, in fact, felt suddenly very relaxed. When they had gone about a mile inside the hub city, Dorion stopped and drew them close and gave Charley permission to speak this once, since she seemed dying to anyway.

"Master, there is no danger here to us," Charley noted. "Could we not take a room with a *bath* and perhaps purchase more useful clothing? I should like to feel and smell the life of a city after all that time in the Kudaan."

"Sorry, no, it's not that easy. We have problems," he told them. "I just didn't think of it, but if Zamofir talked to Hodamoc he knows you both came in together and that you were both auctioned and enslaved. I don't think the word's gotten here yet, or that officer would have taken us on some pretext, but it's sure to draw the wolves in a day or so. There's not much open country but we're going to have to stick to the side roads if we can stay out of any real civilized areas. They'll have all the gates covered, and the odds are good they'll have the nulls covered somehow as well. With everybody drawn to this city festival we might make it across okay, but we might just face a fight in exiting. I'm afraid your bath and city feel will just have to wait."

For two days they traveled through the outer periphery of the Mashtopol hub without much incident. There were some curious farmers and some negotiations for overnight camping rights, but clearly they were keeping well off the main drags. There was also a lot of curiosity and some very high-moral-tone commentary about the two women; the conservative farmers and small-town types weren't at all anxious to have *those* kinds of women around, and they were forced to buy what they needed and move on fast—which suited them just fine.

Shadowcat was delighted with the region, where the rodents were very tiny and apparently pretty stupid and the bugs were big and crunchy. She let him roam and have some fun, knowing he would not stray far and that somehow his link with her would call him back if they needed to pick up and move. She was even getting used to the occasional tiny prick he might make to get just a small bead of her blood to lap up and renew that link. He was good to take it unobtrusively and take only the minimum required, and while it stung for a second it healed over in a matter of minutes, almost as if when he lapped up the blood drop he somehow also undid the hole.

And maybe he did. This was magic now, in a land where the difference between black and white magic was strictly in the motivation of the magician. If the magic of Akahlar had any coloration, it was gray.

But the land was not rife with magic, even though the locals thought it was, for she could see magic if nothing else and, aside from the magic in or attached to her companions, there wasn't much here.

It was a pleasant land, though, for all that. It smelled of flowers and new-mown hay and the sun was comfortably warm rather than broiling hot, and when on the second day they ran into a brief shower it took an order by Dorion to get either woman to take shelter. It had been a long time since they had seen rain or felt it fall on them, and it was *wonderful*.

Here was the magic that all could see and few ever did. The sound and smell of a gentle rain on field and forest were true magic and life and full of promise and wonder.

By the third day out, even Dorion was beginning to think he was being overly paranoid. No secret agents were about, no attacks had been made, and there was no sign of any real pursuit. It was only because he was beginning to relax that Boday, in particular, got worried. When things went *too* well in Akahlar, you'd better watch out, something was lurking there ready to bite you.

"We will have to exit by night through the fence," he told them. "I don't want any record of us exiting at any exit station along here. There will be patrols, but it won't be any big deal I don't think. Once in the null, though, we'll have to be patient and pick and choose with care. If I do a Navigator's trick and force a world on my own at this point, it'll be noticed by everybody and they'll have a perfect trail. We're going to have to sit and wait out there and hope something decent comes up that I either know or can handle and cross at that point. If we can cross a colonial wedge undetected and cross from there into Quodac, there is no way they can find us except by luck. If Klittichorn had enough agents and wealth to cover all the possibilities he'd be in charge already, and Quodac's officials aren't nearly as corrupt as Mashtopol's. Quodac means a breather, and then we can plug in to some of Yobi's muscle.''

They approached the border with little trouble, but Dorion didn't want to cross at any point close to civilization. He suggested that, after dark, they move a considerable distance from the gate along the border until the land would no longer support the horses without having to turn inland or force them into the null zone.

It was an eerie sight for Charley, who could see all along her left side the enormous power and energy of the null while all elsewhere was dark nothingness to her. They rode for about thirty minutes, and then Dorion called a halt.

"Construction equipment here," he explained. "They appear to be building a fence completely around this region. Wonder why?"

He got down from his horse and walked over to it and examined it.

"Huh. Copper wire. Looks like enough on that one reel to run from here back to the exit station. Insulated fence stakes, odd post fasteners . . . It's as if they're going to run something through the wire and they don't want it grounded. Very odd. Oh—you two can speak freely now. Pretend time is done.''

Boday jumped down and looked at the stuff all laid out there. "Clearly it is more than a mere fence," she noted. "Boday has seen small areas for security that are electrified with materials such as this. They would kill anyone who touched them. Could that be what they are doing? Although it begs the question of who they would be doing this against.''

Dorion nodded. "Yeah, that's a real question, all right. A lot of the hubs have fencing, but it's mostly to keep animals from wandering in. It's easier and cheaper to barrier the small section of overlap with the colonial worlds than entirely ring a hub. Besides, where would they get the kind of power a fence like this would require? They can barely power the central district of the capital with what they have.''

He thought a moment, then mused, ''But if there was a very low-level charge, a trickle, of any sort of energy, even a bit of the null bled into it if somebody figured out how, then it would be enough to close a circuit. It wouldn't keep anybody in or out, but you'd know when your border was breached, and roughly where. Yes, I'll bet that's it. Probably just a test section now, but nobody goes to all this trouble to prove a theory. I wonder who or what they're suddenly afraid of.''

''Does it matter?'' Charley asked him impatiently. ''Let's get someplace where we can cross out of this place and begin to relax and maybe have time enough to sleep in a real bed and— take a *bath* . . .'' She added the last less wistfully than reverently. She knew how she had to look and she knew how her hair felt and she certainly knew how everybody smelled. These Akahlar people didn't seem to take too many baths, but that was an area too gross for her to compromise, and gross was the word for all of them by now.

Dorion thought it over. ''Well, here's as good a place as any, although who knows how long we're going to have to wait out there until a world we can live with comes up? If we go any farther north we'll hit the exit station area, and if we go south we're going to probably wind up cutting holes in their nice, shiny new fence that isn't even ready yet. *That* would sure tell them where we exited and give them something of a lead. All right—here it is. Boday—mount up and stay behind Charley as usual. We're going across!''

They went in; Dorion in the lead, Charley almost slipped once as the horse tried for a decent balancing act, but she hung on and felt the horse suddenly level out and speed up as they went out onto the null.

She liked the null because she could see it, and, more to her surprise, she seemed to also see the sky, although it looked kind of weird, like some trick photography or something, the swirling clouds outlined in dim and unnatural colors and hues and crackling with a dark, demonic energy.

Shadowcat, in his harness and perch, gave a sudden yowl that would wake the dead, and Dorion whirled and yelled, *"Stop! Turn around and head back for the bank! It's a trap!"*

Charley didn't react at first; the demon clouds seemed suddenly to take on a shape, and then out of those clouds, or perhaps of the clouds, a giant and horrible vision formed.

The gaunt was outlined in hellfire; a great pterodactyl with hollow, burning eyes and a mouth that seemed filled with flame. The rider was even more terrifying, outlined boldly in whites and crimsons, a gigantic figure who rode the flying beast as comfortably as they did horses. The Stormrider was easily ten or twelve feet tall and proportioned to match, and there was a semblance of armor in the magical energy outline, and of a helmet with visor up inside which burned deep crimson flame out of which two dark, demonic eyes peered.

She didn't need any more encouragement. She couldn't see the hub itself but the very lack of vision was enough of a visual cue. She kicked the horse and let it take her back.

The great gaunt screamed at them, its cry echoing off the land and piercing their very souls as it did so. Charley could only hang on for dear life and pray that she could make it back before that thing could single her out and its talons take her.

Clearly, though it was a creature of sorcery, this was no invisible monster to anyone, cursed with the magical sight or not. Boday tried to keep pace with Charley and keep her on the right track, but she turned, watching the great Stormrider on his gaunt pivot, turn, and start to dive in towards them; and she reached for a gun, turned in the saddle, and, certain she couldn't miss something that big even at this distance and under these conditions, fired.

The bullet found its mark but it had no effect, cutting right through the fearsome apparition as if it did not represent anything real.

An incredibly deep, resonant male voice filled the air with mocking laughter.

Furious but frustrated, Boday watched Charley's horse make it to the edge of the hub once again and scramble up that short but irregular ledge. The horse slipped, and Charley suddenly found herself thrown, falling into the mist and hitting the soft, mossy ground of it hard. She managed to get up quickly, adrenaline pumping and masking any pain or injury, but she was shocked, confused. Turning, she watched as the great horror swooped down on her, perhaps only seconds away.

Suddenly she felt herself being picked up and held against a horse, then bounced as the horse made it up the side of the hub to the ground above. She felt something touch her, sting her thigh, and there was a rush of air and a foul stench, and then suddenly she was dropped onto the dirt of the hub.

Boday was breathing hard. "Hurry! Do not delay! We shall find your horse later, but, for now, come up with me and get away from the edge!"

But Charley just lay there, hurting, unable to move. She looked down at her thigh and saw it shining a burning crimson, the same as what had been inside that creature's armor. Her leg was suddenly numb, paralyzed, without feeling or the ability to move except for the burning.

She could only sit there and look out and watch the horrible thing finish its circle and come in close again. There was nothing she could do, no place she could run, and she just watched it come closer, ever closer—until it was virtually at the hub border.

Suddenly the rider pulled up, and the gaunt and rider remained suspended in the air just a few feet away from the border, the great flying creature's wings going gently up and down in an apparent attempt to keep it there.

Charley abruptly realized that for some reason the thing couldn't come in. Perhaps the same power that kept out the colonials and the nasties prevented even this form from crossing into one of their sacred hubs.

The two deep, burning eyes fixed upon her.

"The power of the storms in a null is great," said the Stormrider in that low, resonant bass. "Because of the mixing of the air masses and the constant shift in access to the colonial worlds it is always turbulent. Even now forces obedient to me have cut off access and soon will be closing in on you from all sides but this. You cannot win. You cannot escape. Rise and come to me!"

Charley felt will in her burning leg, but it wasn't her will. It tried to stand, tried to force her into motion, but it was simply not enough.

Suddenly Boday was there, pulling her back from the edge, pulling her back behind cover.

"I have fifty men who have no morals or scruples at all and whose reward is great when they bring you to me," the Stormrider chided them. "They also do not care for the lives of your companions. You cannot cross except through me, and your pitiful weapons mean nothing to a prince of the clouds."

Dorion came up beside them, crouching low. "Damn it, he might be right," the magician muttered.

"What *is* that thing?" Charley asked, scared.

"Stormrider on a gaunt. Creatures of the Inner Hells, beyond Akahlar where no humans may exist. They can cross, though, into our existence if there is sufficient energy and if they are called by a sorcerer, and they very much want to cross into here."

"It's that horny bastard again, isn't it? *He* brought that thing in!"

"Yeah. He's got something going with them. It's all tied in with the same plot somehow, if we knew what it was. Never mind the history lesson now, though. I don't think he's bluffing about those men, either. Damn! I should have thought of this! Their powers are lessened in daylight."

"Enough to get across through it?" she asked.

He paused. "No. Not that lessened. Damn! I wish I could *think!*"

"You are a magician, oh mighty Master," Boday said sarcastically. "Can you not divert it so that we might cross?"

"I'm not *that* good a magician! Besides, the cure might be worse than the disease."

Charley felt something furry brush against her and looked down to see the shining lavender fuzz that was Shadowcat. The cat went to her burning leg, climbed on it, and seemed to rest there. She felt a sudden tingle and watched as the cat began to take on some of the crimson coloration of the magical wound. It was incredible, but, somehow, Shadowcat was absorbing the spell, restoring her leg!

She began to think furiously. "Look, didn't you say that the fence they were building was mostly copper? To conduct some magic energy?"

Dorion stared at her. "Yes, but what of it?"

"How was the fence wire stored?"

"On a big reel. That's the only way they can handle it." He was beginning to get interested.

"Hollow core?"

"Yeah, but it must weigh like lead."

"How far are we from it?"

He looked out. "About a hand. Why? What are you thinking of?"

A hand was around 125 feet or so. "Something impossible, probably. If if you could turn that copper wire coil and mount it somehow on a spindle so it'd turn, and if you could pry off the end from inside and fix it to something iron here, in the hub . . ."

Dorion's eyes lit up. "I think I *see*! Yes, it's worth a try!" He turned and explained it as quickly as possible to Boday. "Stay here," he ordered. "Boday and I will go see."

There were several reels of the stuff at the work site, and the two of them could barely move the smallest one on its side, but they managed. Boday looked around at the rest of the work site and the tools and equipment there, found a number of things, and began to improvise.

"Ha! Not a mere *winch*, a sculpture that shall enter into legend!" she muttered, and began to assemble a very strange-looking device from bits and pieces of boards and equipment she found lying about.

The activity took time, and did not go unnoticed by the Stormrider.

"What is this? A fence of magic, perhaps? Effective, to a degree, but hardly a good defense against bullets and knives and swords I should think," he noted.

"Silence, pig!" Boday shouted back at him. "Boday is creating and she *detests* critics enough later on; she cannot *abide* them looking over her shoulder as she creates!"

The Stormrider seemed somewhat taken aback. "She is truly mad," he muttered, almost to himself. "But this avails you nothing."

Dorion suspected that he might be right, but it took less than fifteen minutes for Boday to come up with what might just be a workable winch—if they could keep the damned roll on the spool or even lift it on there in the first place. However, after failing for a few minutes to convince Boday that decorative carvings and shaping of the edges into artistic forms was a luxury they couldn't afford and finally commanding her as a slave to obey, they managed with great difficulty to get the reel up onto the spindle, which sagged just a bit but seemed to hold.

Boday fed out several yards of the wire while Dorion reached in with a knife and finally found an end piece; then, with a knife and with Boday steadying the reel, he got enough out to be manageable.

The artist looked at the inner end. "You will have to hold that down and firm. When this reel turns, it will want to pull that end back up into the reel."

He nodded. "I'm going to loop it around this iron fencepost and then jam it into the works of the bonding device here. It must weigh a thousand halg. If the wire is tied and the post wedged firmly enough it should hold. Can you shoot such a stiff wire, though?"

"Boday would prefer a cannon, but she will manage. See, she has already taken off at least two hands of wire, and that is about as far as the crossbow will reach with any accuracy. Still, we shall have to bring him in a bit."

He nodded. "I'll get Charley and the horses. Either this works or we're going to be in deep trouble. I think I can hear riders in the distance now."

Shadowcat had somehow completely absorbed the evil from her leg. She had some feeling again, and managed, somewhat wobblily, to stand. She reached down and picked up the cat, who seemed all in with the effort.

"Don't you worry, Shadowcat. You just earned whatever you want from me," she told him.

Dorion came, startled to see her standing. "It's done—I think. Boday may be crazy but in her own way she's a real genius." He paused for a moment. "So are you," he added softly.

She handed him the cat. "Here. I don't know if that bastard can understand English but the last thing we want is for him to read my mind right now. Bring me around until I can see him and he me, and pray that Boday gets the idea. Be ready in a flash, because that might be all we have. Even if this works, who knows what'll happen?"

He sighed. "Yeah. Nobody's ever even hurt a Stormrider before in all this time."

"Yeah. I'm counting on him knowing and believing that, too."

With the magician's help, she stepped out from behind the rock-and-bush cover and saw the edge of the null and the great, fearsome, hovering shape that waited.

Boday had the crossbow rigged, but she was still too far away to be effective. "Over here! Towards the sound of Boday's voice!"

Charley shifted, and, keeping just a few yards in from the edge, she managed to cautiously move towards the fence line where Boday waited.

After what seemed like an eternity, she felt and heard Boday behind her. "Good enough, but you will have to bring him in," the artist whispered.

"I have to admit I am curious," said the Stormrider. "Just what has all this been about? Do you think you can somehow sting *me* with that crossbow and some puny wire? Sticks and stones can't break *my* bones for I am a creature of sorcery!" he mocked. "And that half-baked magician of yours is no match for me no matter what magic he intends shooting up that wire."

"Yeah, well, if you want it, come and get it," Charley said in English, and walked slowly towards the edge of the null.

"Ah! The bait for my trap! Come, come, then, my pretty one! Come to me and try your worst. Here, mad one, I will make it easy for you!"

With that, the Stormrider slowly moved down and in, until he was perhaps twenty feet, no more, from the hub's edge. Thunder rumbled ominously and Charley could see the energy from the null storm transferred not to rain or mist but to the Stormrider, energizing him, making him more and more solid.

Suddenly Boday bolted past Charley and went right to the edge. "Very well, sir! Try *this* stick!" she screamed at him, aimed, and fired the crossbow.

Boday didn't allow for the wire that was suddenly shooting

out and she felt a sudden sharp pain in her back that knocked her over and sent her tumbling down into the null itself, screaming curses. In the same time that it took Boday to fall, the arrow struck low into the Stormrider's gaunt.

The laughter stopped abruptly, and there was a sudden, piercing scream from the gaunt. Instantly, creature and rider were turned into a giant ball of flame like a miniature orange sun, and what happened next was so fast that Charley could not follow it. It seemed as if the sun raced towards her, and she fell on her face and felt a burning sensation and then there was nothing but a terrible crackling sound and a monstrous roar of thunder so close it rattled her eardrums and knocked her senseless.

Dorion was out in seconds with the horses. He didn't wait for Charley to recover, but picked her up and somehow got her on the horse, where she sat, stunned and confused, only half-aware. He led the horses and their lone rider down into the null, stopping just inside.

Boday was still cursing, and he helped her up. "Are you hurt?"

"Boday's ears are stuffed with cotton!" she screamed, although it was no longer necessary to do so. "She is bruised and sore and perhaps hurt, but not as much as that flying son of a bitch!" Unsteadily, she mounted the same horse as Charley and held on to her. Dorion led the procession, with Charley's horse carrying only a dazed and very tired Shadowcat out into the null mists.

The riders were now very close, and some could be seen in the distance. There was no time to waste and Dorion knew it. No matter what, they had to ride like blazes across the null and hope that something decent came up before the riders caught them.

# · 8 ·

## A Chase Down Memory Lane

YOBI HELD THE potion up, studying it. "Interesting stuff," she muttered in her raspy voice. "There's some real creative people there."

Kira gasped, horrified, as the old witch suddenly drank a small portion of the memory-erasing potion. "No! Wait!"

A toothless grin spread over Yobi's face. "Smooth . . ." she whispered. "Good stuff. Oh, don't worry, my dear. I just want to see what it does and where it goes. I'm in perfect control of it. It's a foreign substance by my spell and will."

They waited for what seemed interminable minutes in the darkness.

"Fast," said the witch. "They must have put it in her morning breakfast juice or something. It'd knock you over before you knew what hit you, and then it goes for the jugular, as it were. Forces the victim to cooperate with it, it does. Fascinating. It sort of gets to know you. Then it finds your lowest common denominator, as it were, and allows those feelings and impulses to remain while it blocks all nonessential memory, anything keyed to 'self.' It appears to actually displace, even replace, certain chemicals or enzymes in the brain itself. It has a very long life and it doesn't get thrown out as a foreign invader, but eventually it does wear out, but not before the new pattern is reinforced and there's been some rewiring, as it were. It establishes Misa as the mind, the identity, then it wires in a whole new set of connections so that only those things relating to 'Misa' as 'self' are referenced. By

**191**

the time it's learned 'Misa' and worn away, there's no connection with the old self. Needed memories—language and the like, common sense about not sticking your hand in the fire, all that—are duplicated as new 'Misa' information and then the old references are replaced by the potion. When it wears away, there's no more connection to the old. Fascinating.''

Kira nodded. She didn't follow all the mechanics of it but she got the general idea. "In other words, whatever they tell her she is when she wakes up is what the potion takes as true. It then takes whatever the new personality needs from the old and cuts off the rest. It almost sounds *alive*."

"No, no, merely a wonder of modern chemistry, my dear. Dangerous, too. You could make an army of devoted, soulless killers with the same stuff. I hope Old Hornass hasn't got hold of this." She sighed. "Well, it's gonna be rough. The tricky part is that the only thing that's holding any of her to her old self is the potion. We can get rid of the potion easy enough but then we'll just be stuck with Misa. If we leave it we just get Misa because it's blocking. The worst part is, we can't wait. There's been damage done now, and every day that passes does more. I hope the mighty Akhbreed sorcerer who bills himself as nearly a god can figure a way around this 'cause I sure can't. The only reason we got any crack at it at all at this stage is that marriage spell, which only a magician's court can fully dissolve and provides a connection of sorts with the past, and the link to the Storm Princess. But even they wouldn't matter if she'd been there another couple of months. Better call out the gods on this one!''

"I'm afraid I'll have to do," came a pleasant man's voice, sounding slightly hollow with a trace of echo. It came from even further into the darkness, and from no clear fixed source.

" 'Bout time you showed up, Smartass," Yobi commented.

"I was here. Your analysis was just so interesting I didn't want to interrupt. Kira, give her half the antidote and let's bring her up to a trance state. I can't deal with a zombie and, frankly, that mental blankness only makes that potion's work easier."

Kira got it, poured to the measure in a small cup, then went over to the apparently sleeping fat girl. "Open your eyes, take this cup, and drink all of its contents," she instructed.

"Misa's" eyes opened, she took it, and drank obediently. While they waited for it to circulate through the system, Boolean discussed the problem.

"It appears that we have to take what's left in there and replace that potion with something equally good that doesn't block. If we can, then she may be missing parts of her old self, some permanently and others temporarily—the brain's pretty good at finding alternate routes if given half a chance and some time—but she'll be basically back. You have the formula?"

"I think so," Yobi told him. "Here—catch!" Blue-white sparks flew from her head into the darkness, yet did not illuminate anything around them.

Boolean whistled. "Wow! No human mind ever worked out something that complicated on its own, I'd bet on it. This was developed somewhere in the upper Outplanes, out where they have very big computers for our nasty-minded people to use. It could take *months* to break this sucker down and understand what's doing what! We're going to have to try some desperation patches, slow and easy, trial and error, and see what we can get. The only way we're going to break through is for her to do it herself. Maybe try and convince *Misa* that *she* needs this information. Well, let's see what we can do. Kira, open her up to us."

Kira knelt down. "Misa, listen to me. Just after I say your name again, you will hear two other voices. Hear both voices, answer, and obey them as you would Crim or me."

"Yes, ma'am," came the slightly slurred response.

"Misa—now."

"Hello, Misa," said Boolean gently.

"Hello, sir," she responded, not sounding as blank as before she had the antidote.

Boolean allowed Yobi to repeat the process, then asked, 'Who are you, Misa? Tell us about yourself?"

"Ain't much t'tell," she responded. "We be peasant girl. We helps t'plant things 'n help 'em grow so's they gives t'fruit and stuff, and then we helps pick'n pack 'em so's folks can eat and drink and wear good stuff. It be hard work but when we sees the seeds b'come the trees and give th' fruit we feels real good like magic, almost."

"Do you ever think you'd want to do anything else?" he

asked her. "Maybe be on the staff or even somebody important in the Duke's office?"

"Nay, we be happy. For som'thin' else y'gots to get th' schoolin' 'n learn all that readin' and writin' shit. And we's borned t'do what th' gods made us t'do. Ain't no bad thing to grow stuff. We wasn't meant t'be but what we is, an' ain't no shame in bein' no peasant. We's *proud* of that. If we don' do it then som'body got to or there ain't nothin' to eat."

"What about your personal life, outside of work?" Yobi asked her. "What about boyfriends? Would you like to get married, have children? Tell us the truth, now."

"Oh, we got lots'a frien's. Th' boys they always tryin' t'fuck us, 'n we guess sometimes we'll let 'em, 'cause y'got t'have kids if y'can, y'know. Truth is, though, we don' get hot 'n juicy with th' boys. Dunno why, but we ain't th' only girl what feels like that. Ain't no big deal, nohow, though. We take th' boy 'cause we gotta 'n the girls 'cause we wanna and it's all right."

"There's not enough access to her old self for that to be a factor," Yobi noted clinically. "It's got to be the marriage thing that's holding her."

Boolean thought a moment, then asked, "Wouldn't you like to have riches, all that you needed? Fine, pretty clothes and a fancy place to live and servants of your own and the finest foods and wines? Maybe use some of it to help others?"

The fat woman thought that one over. Hypnotized, totally honest, she was giving very plain responses without consideration for her audience.

"No, sir," she responded. "We guess them things might be nice f'r them that needs 'em, and we likes th' pretty things, but we thinks a lot of 'em is not so good as horse shit. They don't really do nothin', ain't good f'r nothin' 'cept givin' the lords 'n ladies ways t'show off to each other. Anybody cares more 'bout how they look than how they act ain't worth shit nohow, 'n all the pretty shit won't make a pig a lord, sir. We's just as soon work a good day 'n be friends with them what does, too, 'n get what we really needs in pay. Ya owns stuff ya got to worry 'bout it 'n keep it 'n try'n be better'n the rest and we don't wants that shit. Horse shit's an honest thing. Ya give it to the ground 'n it gives itself to th' plants and th' plants gives ya food. Ya eats the food and ya gives the shit back. And if y'don't want nothin' but friends 'n food 'n work, ya don't wants nothin' nobody else got. An' any friend who's friends 'cause of what ya got or what ya work at or how ya look ain't no real friend nohow.''

"My God!" Boolean exclaimed. "She's been turned into a saint!"

"We're getting some threads," Yobi noted. "Want to go for more?"

There was silence for a moment, and then Boolean asked, in perfect, clear, American-sounding English, "But you're married to a woman, aren't you, Sam? And what about Charley?"

She did not react, and instead looked very confused.

"Looks like the English is cut off, Boolean," Yobi noted. "She's still understanding good Akhbreed, but clearly her mind-set is such that she doesn't believe it's her place to speak or think except in that peasant garbage. She has gone too far."

"She *can't*," he responded firmly. "There's not enough time left and I need her. They're planning something big, Yobi, and within the year. Something horrible. I haven't quite gotten exactly what—not the full-scale thing at this point—but something so terrible it scares the hell out of even their own who have hints of it. They've just about stopped their small testing, and that means preparations for something more ambitious. I've *got* to have her!"

"Then you've got to be drastic," the witch responded. "You have to give her something that will force a break through that block."

"I know, I know. I was just hoping we could undo without doing more to her than has already been done." He sighed. "All right, then. Kira, I want you to put the little amulet of mine you carry with you around her neck. That will establish a direct link here. Maybe I can jolt her out of this."

Kira, fascinated by all this, did as she was instructed. The small, green gem was an ordinary-looking stone set in a rather drab setting and fixed to a thin brass chain. It wasn't intended to look like very much, but those who had it, or similar stones, throughout Akahlar were those who had either done Boolean a service in the past or were known to be trustworthy or mercenary enough to call upon if needed.

"Ah! Now I see you, little Misa Susama Sam," Boolean whispered. "Now I can truly deal directly . . ."

She felt a series of soft blows inside her head, and because of the potion she could do nothing and could not resist.

*You are married already, Misa!* said a voice.

"No!"

*Yes! Look at your hand. See that mark there, the witchmark? See the thread flowing from it, out and away into the night? You must believe what I tell you. You must believe all that I tell you. You are married, and your mate is worried and wants to find you. You know it is true! Now, who is your mate? What does your mate look like? What is that name?*

Flashes . . . Intermittent, fleeting visions of a strange, tall, thin woman with short black hair and a painted body . . . The potion fought to suppress these visions, but the belief command together with the reinforcement of Boolean's will was more than it could stand. This was now a part of Misa, required information. A process began.

"Boday," she whispered, sounding amazed. "We's married to a girl named Boday . . ."

*Who is married to Boday? Picture the marriage. Where was it? Who was there? Who is Boday? Why does she love you? You must answer me. You must find the answers to these questions in your mind!* The questions and commands came fast, thick, furious, compelling.

"Susama Boday . . . is Sam. . . ." Scene of her rushing Boday in some oddly half-familiar setting, like a laboratory only not, and when she was knocked down feeding the painted woman something, something . . .

"Artist . . . Alchemist . . . We is married to an alchemical artist . . . Boday . . . Love potion . . ." It was like a brick wall that first crumbled in only a spot or two, revealing only a tiny part of the view, but the more view it revealed the more it began to crumble.

"He's a pretty powerful bastard at that," Yobi noted approvingly.

*How? Why?* All pressure, all commands, no let up.

"Save . . . Save—Shar-lay . . ." Visions of a pretty girl with artwork around her eyes and on her beautiful body like an azure blue butterfly . . . "Friend . . . *Best*

friend . . . Name was . . . Shari. Yes, but also . . .
Char-lee. Charley."

*Remember. You must remember. Charley, Boday,
Sam . . . Fill it in. Break it down. Remember . . . remember . . . remember!*

Things began to fill in quickly now, as her new personality
was now told to want, even require, that information. There
was too much, far too much. She couldn't sort out the details,
or make sense of it all. It was also being filtered through the
Misa personality as the controlling one, and evaluations were
being made involuntarily as the information was accessed or
copied to where it could be accessed. This Sam was parasitic,
unhappy with herself, unsure of anything. But *she* was Sam,
but she didn't like Sam very much, either . . .

"Quickly!" Boolean snapped. "The rest of the antidote! All
of it and now!"

Kira poured it, praying she wouldn't spill any of it, and said,
"Misa—take this and drink it all, to the last drop!"

It was an automatic gesture, and Kira held her breath when it
looked as though the girl was going to spill it, but she obeyed,
almost absently.

Suddenly her eyes opened wide and she stared out not at
them but at something beyond that only she could see. The
cup, empty, fell to the ground. "Oh! Oh! *Oh!*" she said, and
then collapsed in a dead faint forward and lay there silently on
the ground.

"I'm not sure what we'll get when she wakes up except a
woman with a headache," Boolean told them, "but that's as
good as I can do by remote control, as it were. It's crazy,
though. The most whacked-out part of her was the only way in
that I found. If she'd liked boys, if she hadn't gone along with
Boday in getting that thing formalized, it might not have been
possible. If we had to actually break that stuff down and find an
antidote there would have been nothing left at all to grab and
hold on to. I owe you one, Yobi, for your analysis, your
insight, and for keeping the Hellhounds off. I already owed
you for the other two. If Boday had died out there, then the
spell would have broken and that would have been that."

"You bet you do," said the witch. "And one of these days

when the time is right I'll collect. For now, screwing that madman is enough of an excuse."

"I dare not risk remaining any longer," the sorcerer told them. "Already, even with Yobi's excellent blocking, they know I am roaming the ether and they're trying to track me."

"If you're so all-fired powerful why don't you just will yourself here?" the witch wanted to know.

"Because it would invite a power down that canyon that even I am powerless against and would finish us all," the sorcerer responded. "Why the hell do you think I'm stuck here? In my own hub, I have power to draw on and acolytes to marshal. Outside of it, I'm just another Akhbreed sorcerer no stronger or weaker than the others. Our side's losing, Yobi. It's weak and fragmented while Klittichorn grows stronger and bolder. This girl isn't a pawn, she's a last, desperate chance."

"Go, then," Yobi responded. "I'll get them at least on their way."

You could sense almost immediately that Boolean had gone, even those without any magical powers of their own like Kira.

The pretty woman looked at the witch. "What did he mean by that, old one? What are they planning in the cold north? What is it that even ones such as yourself and Boolean fear it? And how does she fit? The Storm Princess has great and unique powers, but hardly of a world-shattering sort—or have I been missing something?"

Yobi cackled. "That's what's so slick about them, my dear. Klittichorn is marrying the sorcerer's power to that of such anointed ones as the Storm Princess, each complementing and aiding the other. You know that the changewinds have been blowing more frequently and a bit more violently of late in certain parts of Akahlar?"

"Yes, but what of it? We have always had to live with them and in fear of them."

"The whole of a world is greater even than a changewind which affects only a small part of it," the witch explained. "Even the changewind is subject to the forces that make up a world, its greater patterns of wind and sun, gravity and centrifugal and magnetic forces. No matter how great a change the winds may wreak on an area, it is relatively small and the rest remains and partly recovers the damage. All the factors that affect weather and climate affect the changewind too, you know. It even enters Akahlar through a combination of transitory weaknesses at that given point. Klittichorn, it is said, has found that combination. He can summon the wind, but he cannot control it. The Storm Princess, however, can influence its local factors, its course, and even to a degree its intensity and duration here. They don't even like each other, but they need each other. Together, they have the potential to be a god of wrath."

Kira nodded. "I can see it as a horrible weapon, but not what good it would do. They still cannot determine what changes the wind will make, nor make good use of it except as a weapon of terror. In the face of it, the armies and sorcerers of the Akhbreed kingdoms could destroy Klittichorn and kill the Princess no matter where they were if they tried to use the weapon as blackmail, and that is all it is good for."

"Perhaps," the witch responded. "But I hardly think that the opposition is stupid, my dear. The Princess's end is politics. Klittichorn sees the politics as a means to a darker end we cannot yet fathom, but will know well to our horror if he manages to pull it off."

Something exploded inside her head. She didn't understand it and it frightened her, but she was helpless to resist it or to cast it out.

At first it was beautiful, like staring into infinite facets of the finest diamond, all colors shimmering this way and that, the triangular shapes turning and twisting, but soon it was all around her, enveloping her, trapping her suspended there in the midst of chaos.

Suddenly, near her, there was a tiny black dot, also suspended, and the dot grew into a long black line and the line suddenly turned and revealed the shape of a man. No—not a man, but the shadow or outline of a man, all dark and featureless and somehow as thin as paper.

She cried out and thousands of triangular facets seemed to echo her cry and make it something terrible.

"You are right to be afraid," said the figure, "but not of me. I did not make you or have a hand in the destiny you must follow, but I can help save you from it if you'll let me."

"Go 'way! I want nothin' t'do with you!" she shouted, and the twirling facets echoed and mocked her.

"You don't really fear me," said the shadow man. "I'm so thin that if I turn I'm not even here at all. I can't harm you, and I have no wish to do so. You didn't choose to be what you are, but you are what you are and you cannot change that. From the moment you were born you were set on a path that gives you no choice but to follow it or die, and only at the end can you gain your own freedom."

"What—what do you want of me?"

"Look into the center of the gem and see the source of your destiny," he told her.

She looked, and as she did images formed: clear images, as real as if they were there, although something told her that they were not. They could not see her, but they were real . . .

A tall, gaunt figure in robes of sparkling crimson, who either had two cowlike horns growing out of his head or was wearing some crazy kind of crown or cap with them. He was an old man, and there was hatred and bitterness in the lines of his face, in the glare of his cold eyes, in the way his small mouth twisted naturally into ugliness atop a lantern jaw.

"Behold the one who calls himself Klittichorn, the Horned Demon of the Snows," said the shadow man, "although he is no demon but a man, a sorcerer of tremendous power and learning but without wisdom. A man from another world and another culture whose intellect was so great that he became almost godlike in Akahlar. He schemes to destroy all Akahlar, all its people, its cultures, all its worlds, and all the other worlds as well. He does not mean to destroy them particularly, but he is beyond caring if he does—and he will. Everyone you know, everyone you have ever known or might ever know, will be destroyed by this one man."

She was appalled. Maybe it was magic, but, looking at him, she couldn't help but believe what she was being told was true.

The view shifted. No longer was there a crimson-robed sorcerer, but instead a young woman, perhaps no more than twenty, a bit chubby but not at all unattractive, with long black hair and in beautiful jewel-encrusted furs, wearing a tiara surely made of pure gold encrusted with every great gemstone ever known. The girl was very different from anyone seen so far in Akahlar, but, somehow, she was also very, very familiar.

"She is known only as the Storm Princess," the shadow man told her. "Klittichorn found her among common stock in one of the colonial worlds. Much like you, she wanted neither power nor position, but she had it thrust upon her because she was born different from other girls and because something happened to her that changed it all. She was a witch and the daughter of a witch although she'd never asked to be born that way. Her people farmed the land in a place where the mountains kept the rains away and where no natural rivers flowed, and they did so because of her mother. She was born with a gift; a magical gift, perhaps a reward for some intelligence we might call supernatural because we cannot understand it or know it to an ancestor who did some service or made some bond. A gift passed down from mother to daughter—one child, no more, with the gift, and always a female. A power beyond those of the Akhbreed sorcerers. For she could call the storms, call the rains, and they would obey her. She alone could summon the waters of life and tell them where to drop their most basic gift of liquid life, and in what amounts.

"And the child wanted for nothing that was truly important," he continued, "because she and her mother gave the people of the valley the waters of life, and they in turn returned a part of that bounty to them."

And she saw the place in the center of the facets; saw the beautiful, lush valley and the small peasant village and farms that dotted it, and she understood just how rich and beautiful it was.

"And then the Akhbreed soldiers came," the shadow man went on, "and they marveled at how they had missed so rich a place. The people had no army and no lords to protect them, yet they resisted as best they could, and even when easily subjugated they refused to recognize the soldiers' king as their lord and to give much of their bounty to him and his armies. And when the witch, her mother, called down lightning and struck down many of the army and turned their camp into a quagmire so that the people of the valley could set upon them and kill them, those valley people rejoiced. It was a short-lived celebration.

"For the king had more soldiers alone than a hundred times the population of the valley, and more came, this time with sorcerers and mighty magic as well, and they showed no mercy. They were more than mere lightning or the creatures of the storms could count, and they slew without mercy. The girl saw her own mother slain before her eyes, and found herself captive to a sorcerer of terrible power. He understood that she, too, knew the secret of the storms, and he coveted that knowledge and took her. But, of course, there was no secret and there was no knowledge She was what she was. And the valley became dry and barren, as lifeless as stone, and she was the last of her people, and she hated them for it. Hated them all."

Tears came unbidden to her eyes as she saw what the valley had become and the stains of blood still there after several years because there had been nothing more to wash them away.

"By the time the sorcerer understood the girl's ignorance of her powers," the mysterious one told her, "and knew that such powers were somehow forbidden those who had all the others, Klittichorn had heard of her. So powerful was his magic that he was able to spirit her away from the very palace grounds of the king and his sorcerer. He used her hatred, and fed it. He showed her the Akhbreed empire, with its subjugation of the races, its feudalism and slavery, its cruelty and oppression. In his northern palace, in the land of eternal snows, he crowned her the Storm Princess, and convinced her that, together, they could end this cruelty, revenge her mother and her land and people, and liberate all of the oppressed. Many who were terrified of him, more terrified of him than of remaining under the Akhbreed kings, rallied to her. They have now not one army but many armies, trained, hidden among the vast colonial worlds, waiting for the call to liberation."

She understood what he was saying, understood and believed it all, but she did not understand her place in it. "She is good!" she shouted at the shadow man. "Her dreams are noble and proper!"

"They are," he agreed, "but life is not that simple. She and all her armies cannot overthrow the Akhbreed sorcerers in their hub citadels or hope to match the great armies of the rulers. She needs the power of true sorcery behind her, and that Klittichorn brings. He has convinced her that he shares her dream, but he does not. For if the power of the Akhbreed sorcerers is somehow halted, and if the Akhbreed themselves are destroyed, there will be no controls. Instead of all hating the Akhbreed, the thousands of races will begin to suspect and hate and then war with one another. And out of this chaos will come the only remaining, untouchable source of great power, which will be Klittichorn. This he believes, but he, too, is wrong. To destroy the Akhbreed and their sorcerers he must loose the terrible changewinds themselves, the only things against which no Akhbreed sorcerer has power. He will loose them by the score and the Storm Princess will guide them.''

"Is that—possible?"

"Klittichorn thinks so. *She* thinks so. He has somehow managed to summon many small changewinds to the places he commands, although how this is done is a mystery, and she has managed to shape and turn them. But those were small, and one at a time. To control great ones, all at once, and all over Akahlar—that is something reason says cannot be done. Reason and experience also tell that such an event, done all at once, would create such an instability that the worlds themselves would collapse upon each other, that the changewinds would roam unchecked and over vast areas, and none would be safe. Such weight alone might draw all of creation down to the Seat of Probability and to oblivion. All that has ever existed, all that exists, and all that can or will exist will be no longer."

"But—surely she knows this, or senses it!"

"She is a farm girl the same age as you; a peasant girl, really, with an inherited power she can wield but not comprehend. Seven years ago she was ignorant that anyone or anything outside her valley and people even existed. Since then she has been a victim or a dupe. How can she know, or even comprehend? Certainly she has seen the winds and knows the risk, but such is her thirst for revenge and so skillfully has her hatred been fed that she would prefer oblivion to inaction, which are the only choices she has. Those who follow her blind themselves to the risk for they see no other choice but eternal subjugation. They would rather risk the end of time and space and all within than accept the permanence of their condition. Understand well that Klittichorn is prepared for either event. He believes that should the end come in such a manner he will be left, alone, to re-create the universe, the one lone supreme being. Lord of Akahlar or the one true god. He feels he has nothing to lose."

She was appalled. "Can he—might he really become *god*?" That man, that ugly man with the ugly soul that showed?

"Perhaps. He is one of the strongest sorcerers ever known. Together, however, the rest, even a relatively small number, might defeat him. But if they are removed, if the changewind crumbles the Mandan castles themselves and sucks the very air from the shelters, then who is to say what he might become? Either way, the Storm Princess's dreams are hollow and stand on no foundation. She will replace a bad system with pure evil, or with oblivion for all. Not just death—the nonexistence of the universes!"

It was a terrible vision. It was worse than terrible, for it gave no hope. It was a choice of lesser evils over greater ones and there was no way out.

"But why me? What has this to do with me?"

"Search those memories that are slowly returning to you. Search within yourself as you gaze upon the face of the Storm Princess. You recognize her. You certainly recognize her. Remember back, remember before you gained your weight, remember the face and form in the mirror. *Remember!*"

A face, a form, reflected darkly in some wall of glass in some far-off place. A strange vision, with storms all around outside, yet a great deserted village totally enclosed . . .

A face and form reflected in a window. *Her* face. *Her* form.

"My god! She looks a lot like me . . ."

"No," responded the shadow man. "She *is* you. The Storm Princess is you."

"But how can that be?"

"There are many worlds encompassing Akahlar. Each is its own complete and unique world. The people of those worlds differ, usually, in some major or minor degree from Akhbreed purity, but a few do not. The same is true in the vast Outplane of millions of universes all stretching out from here. Almost anything possible has happened in one or more of them. Given that, it is not surprising that not just one but many women were born in those universes who, by chance, are genetically identical with the Storm Princess even if they have nothing in common with her, not even genetically identical parents. It happened. One of the ones so born was you."

"But I had no power over storms!" *How did she know that? She couldn't remember . . .*

"No. But Klittichorn worried about this, about such doubles being discovered by his enemies and brought here. The gift, or curse, of the power is keyed to a particular person—the Storm Princess. But it is a power, not an intelligence. It cannot tell the difference between you and so it endows you both with that power. Once the way was opened from Akahlar to you the power knew you and of you and it became yours as well."

"If there are many girls, then let me be! Use one of them!"

The shadow man sighed. "There are—were—not many. There were some. Klittichorn, using the Storm Princess herself as the object, was able to seek them out ahead of his enemies and kill them. They died, never knowing why or how. Only a very few were saved, such as yourself, and brought here by other powers. They were nothing like you—except physically, of course. Oh, they preferred the same things generally and they tended to like and dislike certain things and do things in certain ways the same, as twins might, but they were products of different parents, different worlds, different cultures. Like you, they were subjected to the rigors and strange magic and powers of Akahlar. Most succumbed."

She was shocked. "They're all *dead*?"

"No. Some are. Others have been changed by the change-winds or by demonic sorcery. Others have been rendered useless by falling into powerful and evil clutches. You are the one most likely to make it as of now. You are the only one we know the location of, and condition of. We did not choose you, and, frankly, had we been able to choose we would have selected someone different. We have no choice, just as you have no choice. Klittichorn is hunting you. He has more difficulties here, in Akahlar, than he did in the Outplanes because he cannot locate you by sorcery. The presence of more than one of you destroys the effectiveness of all such spells. He must do it the hard way, as must we. If you fail to reach the safety of Castle Masalur in the hub of that name then you will die, and others around you will die. It may also be that hope to thwart Klittichorn will die. If you succeed in reaching Masalur, and if you then are able to aid in the defeat of Klittichorn— something not assured by your merely reaching the castle or even fighting—then, you will be free. There is no other choice. There is no other way."

It was a sobering, flat-out statement. No choice, no other way.

"What do you want me to do?" she asked, resigned.

"First decide who you are and what you want to be."

It was an odd comment. "What do you mean?"

"Who *are* you?"

Who indeed? The question was in its own way more unsettling than what had preceded it. She wanted to be Misa, but she couldn't be Misa. Misa could not do this, could not stand against such powers, and would only bring down horror on her people.

There was—another. Sam. Vague memories, disjointed thoughts, many grave gaps. She remembered the Sam of Akahlar, although still with some gaps here and there, but there had been yet another Sam before that and that one was hazy, strange, impossible to focus.

Who did she want to be? That was easier. Both Sams had been unhappy. They had reacted, never acted. Everything they had done they had done either to try to conform to others' expectations, others' standards, never her own. They had made fun of her low voice, her liking for sports and competition, her grades, everything . . . That first Sam had rebelled, but in the wrong ways. Constant diets, to keep super-thin. But forget pretty clothes and cosmetics and all that. Wear boys' clothes, take on a boyish manner, talk tough and dirty, play rough-house.

But her body turned female anyway and when the boys shot up she stayed very short. To be with the boys now took something else.

*Sudden scene in the mind: she and a boy named Johnny out back of a bowling alley after dark. They were both sixteen and had grown up pretty much together. He was big, though, and she was short and slight. He made some passes. Scared but curious, she responded. From the way he acted it wasn't his first time, but she knew what to do only from the romances and the soap operas. She liked the feelings, the hugging and the kissing, but she didn't want to go all the way. That was too much. He had a different idea. He dropped his pants and revealed his—his thing. It was big and stiff and enormous and not at all like she'd thought they were, although she didn't really know what she had thought. And he wanted to put it in her mouth, to suck on it, for god's sake! It was ugly and, and, he peed out of it! She had been revolted. She thought she was going to throw up. This wasn't like it was supposed to be at all! She'd run away from him, away from all of them . . .*

She could not put together the world or frame or life around that experience, not even at the moment remember what a bowling alley was, but she could remember that, and she could still feel the revulsion. If *that* was what guys wanted and what girls were supposed to do then she wanted none of it.

*Scene: she and another girl, frightened, alone in a remote cabin someplace. She was scared to death. She clung to the girl friend—to Charley—the only real friend she had in the world at that time. And Charley had responded to her need and they had made love and it had been wonderful, for a time. She knew that from Charley's point of view it had been an act of compassion, not love, but it hadn't seemed wrong.*

*Scene: Boday, who loved her because she was the first one the artist had seen after inadvertently taking a love potion. Boday's sexual tastes were bizarre and her appetite insatiable, but it was also secure. No worry about what her Sam looked like or sounded like. The love and the strength were absolute, unquestioning. Sam had grown very fat and lazy under such love and security, but she still was insecure inside. Because Boday's love was chemical, she could not bring herself to think of it as genuine and so give some of it back. Because Boday was a woman, it was, somehow, still wrong. She was no damned freak!*

*Scene: on a big wagon train in Akahlar. She had compelled by the magic of a hypnotic charm, out of jealousy, guilt, and curiosity, one of the trail hands to make love to her and he had done his best. And she had felt little but disappointment. Nothing he had done was nearly as good as what she had gotten from Boday, and the end for him came all too soon and was nothing much to her.*

*Scene: Tied down on the rocky ground as three ugly, brutish, foul-smelling men had at her, over and over, as she closed her eyes and tried not to feel the foulness . . .*

But Misa had been accepted. Misa had to conform to no standard in the refuge. The men had made passes but that was okay and the girls had been earthy as well. No one had made fun of her low voice or her fat or her lack of knowledge or anything. So long as you worked hard and did your share it didn't matter at all, and there hadn't been any guilt or shame or pressure, and she had enjoyed being female and all that meant. Nobody had judged, and nobody had cared except one equal to another.

*And the fucking Storm Princess was fat, too!* Maybe not as fat as she was, but really a chubbette. Charley was a lie, a "duplicate" made not to reality but to an ideal and kept there by sorcery and alchemy. She could never be Charley. Left to her own devices the best she'd look like was that Storm Princess! More, why in hell did Sam ever *want* to be Charley? To be seen only as a body, a sex object, a fly trap for men?

Her reflection came up to her in a huge facet and she stared at it. Okay, so she was fat. But she was still kind'a cute, damn it, and she didn't really *feel* uncomfortable this way. *Comfortable*, that was the word. She was comfortable and she didn't give a damn what anybody else thought. Sam had never liked herself but Misa had liked herself just fine.

By god, she was gonna *keep* liking herself just fine!

The facets whirled, became less reflections than a maelstrom, and she felt herself falling, falling . . .

And suddenly she was aware that she was on her back on something hard and moving, and that it was incredibly hot.

She sat up in the wagon and opened her eyes. It was odd; her mind had never seemed clearer, her senses never more acute than now. That included the basics; she was damned thirsty, and starving to death.

She crawled out of whatever she was in—a box of some kind!—and looked forward. She was in a wagon being pulled by a narga team; in back she could hear the sounds of one or maybe two horses, possibly tied to the wagon and walking with it.

The driver was a big man in Navigator's buckskins with a broad-trimmed felt cowboy-style hat on his head, and beyond the landscape was unmistakably still the Kudaan but back out in the harsh desert land far from the river.

She felt distrust of Navigators. One—when and who?—had supposedly been her friend and had tried to betray her. The memories were kind of fuzzy, hard to hold on to and make sense out of, so she didn't try. Maybe it would come back to her, maybe it wouldn't. But for right now she was crawling out of a box in a wagon in the middle of nowhere, stark naked and with a big guy the only human in sight.

He heard her but didn't turn around. "If you're awake and feeling all right, there's drinkable water in the cask with the water sign on it and warm ale in the one with the mug on it. There's also hard rolls and dried trail meats in the box just to the right of them with the diamond on it."

She jumped, then caught herself. Uh-uh. No more of this "poor little old me" bulishit. She was naked, thirsty, and hungry and this guy could have done anything to her by now but hadn't, so relax. The beer sounded great but not when it was hot enough to take a bath in. The water wasn't much better but at least it didn't surprise, and the food wasn't exactly great but it did fill. Only when she was done did she climb forward to see what this new man was like and what the situation was. She was still naked but it didn't matter to her. Let the guy have his jollies if he was that way.

He *was* a big man, well over six feet and with the look of one who is trim and lean but still had muscles to spare. His face and hands showed weathering and evidenced hard work and that said a lot about him as well. He was about as solid and all-around masculine a man as she'd ever seen in real life.

"I'm Crim," he said in a friendly tone. "And who are you today?"

"I—I'm Misa," she responded. "But I'm also Susama and Sam and some long name I can't really remember right now." Her tone and inflection was strictly peasant and bottom class, but her grammar and general vocabulary and structure was more standard, sort of like a peasant girl who'd spent a fair amount of time as the servant of somebody high up. It was kind of folksy, but nobody would ever mistake her for an aristocrat. The accent was strictly Mashtopol sticks—down home, *way* down, on the farm. "I'm sort'a all mixed up inside my head."

He nodded. "That's understandable. Hopefully it'll sort itself out over time. In the meantime, do you know who I am and where we're heading, sooner or later?"

"I guess you're somebody hired by the shadow man to bring me to him," she responded, then frowned. "Seems to me somebody else dressed like you was supposed to do that a long time ago but he double-crossed me."

Crim nodded. "I heard about that. Well, like most of the independent Navigators I have my problems and my hangups beyond the normal kind, but that kind of thing isn't one of them. For one thing, I'm being paid only on delivery and the pay is so high nobody can outbid it and be trusted. Boolean may be as crazy as the rest of 'em but he always keeps his word. For another, it's not just the pay. There's no way I'd ever work for the other guy, and he's the only one who really wants you other than Boolean."

"Boolean." She repeated the name. "Yes. I remember that name now. Is he the shadow man?"

"I have no idea, not having seen any shadow men. He's usually either a voice or a vision, though, so maybe that's as good as any. Hell, even his name's a joke. In the tongue he uses when he thinks, it's not a name at all but a number system. Algebra, I think. Invented by an Outplaner named Boole a long time ago. I think he took it as a sort of private joke."

She stared at him. "You know the Outplanes? And the languages?"

"Well, some. It just happens to be some knowledge I—acquired along the way, as it were. You're from the Outplanes, too, originally, I'm told."

She hesitated. "I—I know that I am, but I don't have no real clear memories of it. Just bits and pieces here and there, some making no sense at all."

He turned to her and said something that sounded like an ugly string of monotones. She stared at him and shook her head.

"You understood none of it?"

"Didn't sound like nothing at all."

"That was English," he told her. "I was told it was your native tongue. We'll try and work on it and maybe it'll come back to you over time. It's a handy language to know when dealing with Boolean. That's *his* language. One of them, anyway."

She sighed and shook her head. "There's just so much—missing. I remember all sorts of scenes, but they don't make no sense and don't go together. Kind'a like memories from when you was real small. Some basic shit, maybe, but no details."

"What *do* you remember clearly?" he asked her, probing a bit.

"Well, all of bein' Misa, that's for sure. All but that last night when I had the runs and went to the clinic. Ain't much after that, 'cept I can, well, remember a real pretty woman, maybe the prettiest I'd ever seen, and she was takin' me someplace. That's about it. Or did I dream her?"

"She's real," said Crim. "That's Kira. You'll meet her before too long with a clear head. But is that it? Just Misa?"

"No, no. But the more you go back from there the fuzzier it all gets. I lived a while in Tubikosa. A long time. Not in the straitlaced world of most of 'em, but in the entertainment district where them hypocrites snuck down to blow off steam and do all that shit they preached against. My lover's an artistic alchemist. Creates beautiful girls for the courtesan trade. I remember all that, too, only it's a little bit fuzzier. No dates or real order, just the whole thing sort'a running together in my head. Old friend of mine was a courtesan. Me and Boday we sort'a lived off her and doin' stuff for the other folks down there. She didn't mind none and that was the funny part—my friend, I mean. She's smart and she was gonna be the big wheel, the queen of big business and all that, and she found out she loved bein' a whore. Most of the girls either hated it or had no choice or were under drugs and all, but she really liked it. Crazy."

Crim shrugged. "Maybe. Maybe everybody's so busy trying to be what everybody else tells them they should be that they never have time to be themselves. No offense, but it's the people who enslave and victimize those girls that are the real criminals. It'd be a pretty victimless crime if only the ones who wanted to do it did it and got to keep the profits. Nobody ever held a sword to somebody's throat and said, 'Go fuck a prostitute or I'll kill you.' They buy what they want and need but for some reason, like pleasing all the others, never can get in normal life. It's not my thing, but I can't condemn somebody who does it for herself and because she wants it. Problem is, you mostly can't keep the crooks out of it—and, of course, when you get past your prime you haven't got much of an old-age job.''

"Maybe. I guess maybe I been so busy tellin' myself that I don't much care what nobody else thinks about me that I kind'a forgot not to do the same thing to other folks.''

"Do you remember even further back? Before Tubikosa?''

"Not clear, anyway. I didn't have much fun or much of a life back then, I don't think. It's like I said—a scene here, a scene there, and some funny memories of things that ain't in Akahlar or not the way I somehow think they should be. I ain't tryin' too hard to remember, truth to tell. I don't think I'd want to go back there, somehow. I know where we're goin', sort of, and I know why I gotta go and what I gotta do—sort of. I know I got to go if I can and I got to do it—if I can. And I want to find my lover and my friend. Any sign of 'em?''

"Oh, yes. They would have wound up where you did except they thought you were captured by the rebel troops. They got captured by a witch gang who took your friend for you and hauled them off to their camp. With no word about you, Boolean wanted them to lead the enemy away from the Kudaan, so they set off ahead. If both they and we make it, then we'll meet them in Masalur. Not much hope of meeting up ahead of time, and I don't think we want to. The enemy suspects the trick now and they're off hunting both them and us. If we link up it'll be all the easier for them.''

She nodded. "I guess so. I just, well, don't want to screw it up at this point, not when I finally got myself a little put together. The Misa in me wants what Sam had but doesn't want to be Sam, if that makes any real sense. Sam was such an asshole. She didn't know what she had or what she wanted and let everybody else do her thinking for her. Hell, she even lied to herself. I'm done with that. You got to make the most of what you are and not waste it all tryin' to be or dreamin' of bein' what you're not and can't never be. For the first time in my life I'm damn happy to be what I am and I don't give a flying fart what nobody else thinks. I can't free myself from this job, and if I can't do it then this is all the time there is, but while it is I'm gonna make the most of it. I liberated my mind and now I'm gonna liberate the rest of me as much as I can."

She suddenly got up a little and looked out and around the wagon and to the back. "Are we it? Nobody else?"

Crim nodded. "Just us. My train had to keep going on its scheduled route in order to keep anybody from noticing and pointing a finger right at us. They're all around, even here. They're looking, and many of the lookers aren't human in any way. Just be sure you don't make it rain. *She* has more experience with that than you do and she's got a sorcerer right next to her to use that energy and send things through."

"Don't worry about that," she assured him. "But what about the pretty woman? Are we gonna meet up with her separate?"

He cleared his throat. "Uh, well, not exactly. Aw, hell, I'd better explain the whole thing to you. In about four hours you're going to know it all anyway."

She stared at him. "Huh?" From the looks of the sun that would be about sundown. "What is she? Some kind of vampire or something?"

Crim chuckled. "No, although you're not the first to suggest or suspect that, and there are many, I think, who believe it. It began a while back now. She came here accidentally from one of the Outplanes, like you did."

"Oh, yeah?" She was getting very curious about this now.

"I didn't start out to be a Navigator. When I was very young, I worked as an apprentice to a shady trader named Yangling. I had some natural magical talent—that's where the navigating comes in—and Yangling had high hopes for me as a tool, more or less. Then Kira quite literally fell into his hands—at least she was found, unconscious, near his place and taken to him by those who found her. As soon as I saw her there I think I fell in love with her, even before she recovered. I was assigned to find out from her all that was possible, since Yangling had made me study an Outplane language which was her native and only one. I spoke it poorly, awkwardly, and probably made only a very little sense, but she seemed appreciative that I could speak to her at all and that she could be somewhat understood. This was particularly important because the language here was an illegal one. A number of the younger and newer Akhbreed sorcerers had taken to using it as a sort of standard for some reason. It was thought that some knowledge of it might prove useful."

She nodded. "All right, I'm following this so far. Sounds kind'a romantic."

"It was, in a way. We got to know each other quite well. She improved my English immeasurably, but she never could get the hang of Akhbreed. It's that sort of tongue. She was a wonderful person, but tragic, too. She had not many months before been in an accident that was not even her fault. It had broken her neck and spine. She had some jerky movement, nothing useful, in her arms and fingers but not much else, and no real feeling below that. That beautiful body was useless and unfeeling and she was basically no more than a talking head."

"What little memories I have seem to show her pretty lively."

He nodded. "Anyway, Yangling was furious. He called in a bunch of top black magicians he had on his payroll and they went to work on her. Didn't do any good, though. Nothing short of a changewind or some terrible magic would have her mobile. Well, Yangling was more interested in the fact that she could read intercepted communications from top sorcerers with ease and then I could translate them to him. They thought of changing her into an animal, using a curse of some sort, but there are few animals that can read and speak in human tongues and nothing was certain there. The changewind option, if chance provided it, might alter her mind or her sanity. Yangling had a garden filled with erotic statues, and with her face and body there was talk of turning her into stone, her soul imprisoned, and animating her head only when her services were required. I couldn't have stood that, and I told her enough that she seemed to just want to die. I had to do something."

"You got your own magician?"

"Sort of. The blackest of the black, really. A grotesque figure who wandered the mountains there filled with hatred. No one dared seek him out, or could conceive of wanting to, but I did. I offered to trade information—many of the complex and totally incomprehensible Akhbreed spells we had been intercepting. To my surprise, he agreed, although he said I would have to raise my own demon and do my own bargaining. At that point I was ready for anything."

She was shocked. "You sold your soul to a demon for her?"

"No, no. That's for fairy stories. Demons might like to eat you, for they hate all humans, but they couldn't care less about souls. I did the ritual, scared to death, and I raised the demon in the pentagram just right. It was a horror, worse than any nightmare imaginable. There were only two ways to make him do anything he didn't want to do, and one involved human sacrifices—this one of children. That was sure, but I could never do it. The other was risky and involved a way of threatening a demon with being trapped in the netherhells, regions of nothingness between the Outplanes. That's possible, but when a demon is doing something under duress, particularly for a human, he's not honorable. This one basically gave me one choice or it said it would rather spend eternity in the netherhells—and you believed it. I took the choice, and while he was mean he wasn't very bright. They often aren't. It's worked out."

"Yes? And the choice?"

"I wanted not just her body restored, I wanted a way for her to get out, to escape becoming the inevitable courtesan or slave. We became—fused, in a way. All that Kira was, is, is inside me, inside not just my head but all of me, yet it isn't a part of me. I have her memories but they're somebody else's memories, not mine. I'm still the same as I ever was, and maybe a little more. In some ways it's been quite—useful. My command of English is absolute, and my knowledge of Outplane science and devices is improved. More important, I understand the feminine outlook, which is both a more similar and more different view of the world than I'd ever thought. I also know what attracts them and what turns them on, what they want in a man. That's been—useful. Not just in the way you think, but in various dealings as well."

"But—I saw her!"

He nodded. "It's my turn from sunup to sundown. That's the way the curse works. Then it's her turn. For me, it's just going to sleep, and she takes over, physically and mentally. Like me, she has all my memories, and so she knows what went on during the day—she will know about you and this conversation as I know about last night—but she will not be me. She likes men, by the way. Sorry. Apparently more now than before, and for the same reasons I gave about women. She's formally registered as a citizen of Holibah, the kingdom we were in, which took some bribes and connections. This business seemed perfect, since any kind of permanent relationship with anyone is kind of out of the question for either of us, and because she's sleeping all day and I sleep all night there is a presence here who needs no sleep at all, which is quite handy, particularly out here. In most ways she got the better of it. She gets to be wined and dined and romance men in the dark, and I get to do all the shit work during the day. I pay a bit by not having a night life and she pays by lonely nights standing guard at four in the morning, but we are best at our appointed times. Still, the joke is really on the demon. It was going to keep us lovers forever apart, unable to kiss or embrace, but we are closer than if we could."

She whistled. "And I thought *I* was havin' identity problems!"

"No, no!" he laughed. "There's no conflict. I'm not Kira and she's not Crim. Just remembering what the other said and did isn't the same as being them. Still, as I have her English, she's got my native command of Akhbreed and my knowledge of its people and its territory. And, there's an odd by-product. We age only when we are 'alive,' as it were. Each of us is aging at half the rate."

He paused. "It's hard to explain, but when you talked I couldn't help thinking that in a way that's what you've got to come to grips with yourself. Sam doesn't pop out at sunset, but she's still a part of you that you have to deal with. You're not the Misa we saw last night. You're totally different. You're Sam with a Misa outlook and maybe that's not so bad."

She considered it. "Well, we'll see. I got to see this change, though, before I'll believe it."

"You'll see it. Or, rather, you'll be around many times when it happens. It's *very* quick. But we, all three of us, luck willing, will be with each other for quite some time. Months, probably. It's a long way to Masalur."

"You're a Navigator. How come we just can't go straight there?"

"Because the Earth is round. All of them are."

"What? I don't see . . ."

"Akahlar intersects with thousands of worlds, but the only common points are the hubs, the points of greatest force and power. The rest are compressed around the hubs and only intersect at certain random intervals. But when they *do* touch, they are worlds touching round worlds—so that actual point of overlap is very narrow. Kudaan is a world, not a desert. This is the Kudaan Wastes, a large desert on the planet, but not all of the planet is this way by any means. If we go outside that narrow overlapping strip then we'll simply wander the face of Kudaan and never intersect a hub. The only way to go is along the strips and through the hubs. We're being a little roundabout in our routing, but we're still going to head for the border of Mashtopol and we have to go into and through that hub to go farther. There are no short cuts, for anybody. At least there I have a number of contacts. We'll get you new identity papers—as Misa, I think, a colonial peasant of Kudaan whose services are bound to me by your liege lord as a favor because I'm short some experienced animal tenders. That won't be citizenship or anything—you'll be little more than a bound slave I can't sell but that's about the only restriction—but it'll explain your appearance, ways, speech, and the like."

"That's okay. I don't mind."

"We'll probably play a bit with your appearance, too, just to make it even harder for them. Maybe dye your hair and a few other simple things. The real colonial women of the Kudaan, as opposed to the refuge people, have certain cultural things about them and we want to be right just in case. They're considered primitive and terminally crazy from the sun and because they generally like to live in that sort of place. I wouldn't worry about the dialect—your class dialect is okay and there are probably dozens or hundreds around just the dry continent."

She nodded. "Okay, but I want to keep myself up as well. I don't want these muscles to go, 'cause once they're gone I got an awful feelin' they'll never come back. I'm gonna lift weights and put myself through a pretty damned hard routine and stick to it. And I want some training from you, too."

His eyebrows rose. "Training?"

"You're a pretty big guy. I seen the swords back there, and the rifles and pistols. I want to learn how to use a sword. I want to learn how to shoot and hit what I aim at. I want to know about and practice with just about every kind of weapon and defense thing there is. If it's gonna be months, then we have time for some of it. We ain't gonna be movin' all the time."

Crim liked the idea. "If you're really serious, I can run you through swords and other heavy weapons every morning before we start out. Give you as much as I can. Don't expect to be a master—you haven't the height or agility for it—but maybe I can have you hold your own. We'll do some horsemanship, too, and everything else time permits. Kira—she can teach you as well. Pistol shooting is a close-range thing and she's good at it. She can also fence, which is something I never had the control for, and she knows a number of ways for somebody relatively small and weak like she is to throw a heavy attacker across the camp. It'll be frustrating for a while and it'll take practice, but if you really want to learn it's a very good thing. If anything happens to me or Kira, or if there's any kind of a fight, you'll be much more valuable."

She nodded. "I was just thinkin' 'bout what you said about these worlds only touchin' at narrow strips and us havin' to go through the hubs at the gates. I mean, the enemy's gotta know that, too, right?"

He nodded. "And that's why we have to turn you into someone else as quickly as we can."

# · 9 ·

## On Dangerous Ground

THEY HAD A pretty good head start but it was a very long distance across the null to the colonial boundary, far more than you could expect a horse already well traveled to make with maximum effort.

Still, Dorion, Boday, and Charley did not have quite the pressure of an armed mob after them. Some had been close enough to the border to see the Stormrider destroyed or whatever they did to him and it had a major effect. There had been no immediate pursuit, and when the rest of the gang had gathered and been told how the Stormrider had been defeated and possibly killed, something considered impossible up to then by anyone, there was a lot of debate and hesitation about going after them. Anyone who could take on a Stormrider and win had powerful magic, and what were guns and swords to that sort of power?

Still, nothing builds courage like greed, and a few of them were still game for the chase no matter what. Perhaps they didn't believe the large number of witnesses, or perhaps they had little to live for unless they got a very big score, but finally a half dozen men broke ranks and galloped off into the null.

By this time, however, the fugitives had built up a lead of more than two miles, and Dorion, thinking as fast as he could, had angled them well off the straight-line path to the colonial boundary. He knew well that at some point the horses were going to need a rest, and if they were out of sight then the null became a fairly large place indeed to hide in, one also shrouded

in dense electrical fog and covered by incessant heavy clouds
and occasional rain, and in which darkness was a great ally.

Charley rode like she had always ridden this way, with
confidence in spite of limited vision. In fact, her vision was far
worse here than it was back in the hub, since the magic of the
null spread out all around her and obscured somewhat Dorion's
own form. It was fortunate that his aura or whatever it was was
a different and contrasting color, and that it seemed to float
over the mists. For a while, though, it was nearly too bright, as
Dorion took them for a long stretch at right angles to the
boundaries and thus created the mist ahead of her as far as
anyone could see, sighted or not.

Finally, after an interminable number of zigs and zags and a
lot of all-out riding, the magician slowed and shouted for them
to stop.

"We'll stop here and rest the horses," he told them. "Boday,
stay on guard in case those bastards somehow spotted us, or
start this way. I think we can relax for a little, though. Feels
like it's going to rain through here any minute, which will
discourage them and cool off the horses, and we won't be easy
to spot in here until daylight."

Charley slid wearily off her horse. "I said I wanted a bath,
not a storm," she noted tiredly. "Still, I prefer anything to
those men or that *thing*. It went so fast I can't be sure what
happened to it, though."

Dorion shook his head in wonder. "How in the world did
you get the idea of *grounding* it?"

She shrugged. "Well, you said they were gonna power the
fence with some kind of magic energy, so when Boday said her
bolt just went right through it I figured the thing had to be made
of some kind of magic energy. Magic energy, I figured, had to
work kind'a like regular energy—electricity and all—because
of the fence."

"You were most certainly right," he responded, still not
really believing it. "I wonder why no one else has ever thought
of it, though?"

"Maybe 'cause nobody else happened to have a mile-long
roll of copper wire handy when they met one," she suggested.
"It's not exactly something you keep around for the right
occasions. We were damned lucky there to have it."

He nodded, mostly to himself. "Lucky—or something else. Maybe that's why Yobi was fairly confident we'd make it."

"Huh?"

"Destiny. It is a difficult concept to explain to anyone not versed in the magic arts and probability theory as well, but I'll try and boil it down. Everything, not just life but mountains and flowers and air and fire and water, is or contains energy. It—you, me, Boday—is a collection of mathematical equations that make us what we are and who we are. From the moment we're born, perhaps even conceived, this energy construct interacts with everything and everyone around it."

"I can't figure if you're talking astrology or genetics," she responded honestly.

"Neither. Both, sort of. But we each have a thread, a destiny, that we follow. It is layered, from primal to inconsequential. Some people just seem to be naturally lucky; others seem to always have a little black demonic cloud over them causing them untold and undeserved misery. It is not dependent on intelligence or courage or anything else, or its lack. That's why so many rotten people get all the breaks and so many good ones still suffer. Your destiny pattern is randomly assigned by so many factors that one can only influence a few of them. Magic is really an attempt to alter or change some of those patterns. The more powerful the magician, the more factors for more people or places or things he or she can influence."

She thought about it and didn't much like it. "You sound like we're actors going through somebody's script, only we don't know and can't really read the script."

"Well, it's not quite that bad," he told her, "but that is one way of looking at destiny. You *can* change some things, of course, and the fact that your destiny is so complex that no one can ever completely figure it out gives things a certain amount of spice, but basically the script idea is valid. Magicians can read a few lines and directions of the script; sorcerers can read whole pages or scenes. But no one can grasp it all. The First Equation, which set all else in motion and created the universes and all they contain or will contain, created the complexities of everything's destiny. If you believe that was the product of an intelligence, then that is your religion. If you believe that it was random, then you're not religious. Religion has little really to do with magic for all its trappings. Even the gods and devils and spirits are creations, like us, of that destiny and not lords of it. Only the changewind, being of the same sort as the First Equation, can actually alter those equations. It's the random factor that keeps everything from becoming scripted, so to speak."

She was fascinated, but felt a bit uncomfortable at the idea nonetheless. "And you're saying that it was our destiny to beat that thing and its destiny to die or dissolve or whatever? That it wasn't chance or even somebody's design but destiny we just happened to show up where the wire was and I figured out how to use it?"

"Not quite. What Yobi felt, what the others might be learning now, is that it is your destiny to survive. You are a survivor, and probably your friend, too. That's what attracted Boolean to your friend in the first place. In fact, it makes sense. If she's created genetically the same as the Storm Princess, then the two probably share much of the primal parts of destiny as well, and the Storm Princess is a true survivor. It means that you will always have the means of a way out. It doesn't necessarily mean that you have the will to take it, but it is there. Consider that flood that destroyed your wagon train as an example. Most died, yet all three of you survived. The rest, for the most part, were killed later—but not you three. You survived. You fell into the wrong hands but somehow eventually fell into just the right ones. They do their worst against you, and you are still going. You see? That is what Yobi could see. That is why the copper wire was there, and that was why you had the knowledge to put it together."

"Damn!" she sighed. "And here I was feeling real good about how clever and smart I was to come up with that."

His tone softened. "But you *were*! I—I can't tell you how— impressed—I am. To have been so cool and calm and analytical under such pressure, to have put it all together—it was *brilliant*. You are a very remarkable young woman."

He said that sincerely, and she liked the sound of it a lot better than that destiny crap. She was brilliant, he said, and brave, he said, and she was also every heterosexual guy's wet dream to boot. What more could you want? For a minute it might turn your head and take your mind off the fact that you're starting to get rained on in the middle of literally nowhere, you have guys with guns looking all over for you, you're effectively blind, and you're a hell of a long way from anyplace safe.

"Hey! Magician!" Boday called, and the other two tensed, wondering if she heard something. "Boday caught your half of that discussion. Her destiny is unknowable so Boday does not think about it. If one is ignorant of it, then what good is it? But if you magicians can see even a bit of it, then why are we cowering here in this shower afraid of a bunch of brigands? Why did we all wind up in such a spot to begin with? Where are your powers? Why is it that you cannot whip a spell up that would curse our enemies and protect us all?"

It was a fair question, but not one Dorion liked talking about. He cleared his throat nervously.

"Well, uh, it's true I know the stuff and it's also true I have a fair amount of power, but my powers are a bit—odd—and restrictive," he replied uncomfortably.

"So? If those hordes of men show up now Boday can take only a very few with her. She would need your magic or all is lost."

He sighed. "I'd use it if I had to," he said carefully, "but not unless I do."

"Your power is not great?"

"Oh, it's great—potentially," he admitted. "It's just, well, *unpredictable*." He sighed. "All right, then, I guess I may as well tell you. It's control. Some say concentration. Some have said I've got some kind of brain damage or something that makes it happen. Others, well, they have been less kind. That's why I was out there in the Wastes with Yobi and a few others. I was scared to get back into civilized company where I might do more harm."

Charley, too, was interested now. "Harm?" She paused a moment, sensing his embarrassment. "It's all right. We should know, and we won't tell."

He thought a moment, trying to figure out the best way to explain. "I was born the child of magicians and a grandchild of a great sorcerer," he told them. "The power in me is strong. And I know how to use it. Really, I do. That's what is so tough about it. The ability to tap magic is inbred; you are either born with it or you're not. But it's not enough. You also have to be able to use what great power and energy you can draw, and that means you have to have a tremendous mathematical mind. There are set spells, simple things, that anyone with the power can learn to do, even me. And if you have the memory and years of study, you can memorize even huge spells and make them work. I know a couple but I was never that good at rote memory. I get bored too easily. An acolyte is one with the power who can work the simple spells. Third Rank knows enough of the big ones to demonstrate it and get his or her ticket. Those are the craft ranks. Second Rank, like the Akhbreed sorcerers, are mathematical genuises who can size up a situation they've never been in before and create complex spells in their head and impose them, improvising as they go. Me, I knew enough to reach Third Rank, but just barely, but I can't help *improvising* and it just doesn't work right."

Boday shrugged and Charley looked blank.

"Look," he tried, talking to Boday, "you're an artist, I understand. If somebody learns enough to copy great paintings and sculptures perfectly, they have perfected their craft but are they artists?"

"Of course not!" she huffed. "Art is not something one *learns*, it is something one *feels*."

"Okay, so I'm a barely talented craftsman but I have the urge of an artist. I keep improvising in spite of myself, even with the simple stuff. I had to take a hypnotic drug to pass the Third Rank tests. Only I don't have the mathematical ability to build equations into infinity on the fly. Even if I work 'em out, or have time to, somehow they don't stay that way when I use them."

"You mean your spells don't work?" Charley prompted.

"No, no! I've got great power, but no control. The mathematics is wrong, or fuzzy, or incomplete. The spells work, all right—they do incredible things. But they don't do what I designed them to do or want them to do. Sometimes they only half work. A spell to take us all to a desert island might take us to a desert instead. A spell to make us invisible or invulnerable might well make everyone *but* us invisible or invulnerable. No matter what I try or how careful I am, it goes wrong. I work a spell and gold is transmuted to lead. I once accidentally turned a handsome young fellow into a toad. Stock spell, but not the one I was trying to do. Rather than try to undo it I decided on the usual remedy, got a pretty girl to kiss him. She turned into a toad, too. I am a danger and a menace. I've been exiled by many governments for their and my own good. Don't you see, I don't *dare* use any magic if I can help it. Particularly when it involves Mashtopol. I only hope Boolean will understand my service without killing me first."

Charley's head shot up. "Boolean? You *know* him?"

"All too well," Dorion admitted sadly. "How do you think I got to know English? Several of the newer Akhbreed sorcerers are English speakers. For a long while, before my time, it was something called German but they're pretty well gone now. Boolean speaks English and German and a lot of other languages, too, and not all by spell, either, but he *thinks* in English and he's most comfortable using it, so everybody around him has to learn it."

"There's a world of Akahlar, then, that speaks English?" Charley asked him. "That's why he does?"

"Uh-uh. There's thousands of tongues, and probably a few close to English or one of the others, but none that really speak it. Boolean and many of the others, they aren't originally from Akahlar. They're Outplaners, like you. Some of the best are Outplaners. They were born with the power but either never knew it or were too far away from the Seat to really use or draw on it or something, but they were whizzes at mathematics and real geniuses. They get here and put it together in a flash and do in a few years what it takes ones like Yobi hundreds of years to attain. Boolean says that it's because Outplaners don't have to unlearn a lot of the crap and mysticism that we're brought up with. That they have a different perspective. Maybe. How could I know?"

Charley's mind flashed back. Long ago, so long ago now, in the maelstrom that brought both her and Sam to this place, Boolean had saved them from Klittichorn, had stalled the horned sorcerer to get them past and out of his clutches. She hadn't understood Akhbreed at all at the time, not having Sam's mysterious link to this world, but she realized now for the first time that she'd understood that exchange between the sorcerers. They had spoken in English!

Boolean—from the Outplane, maybe from her own world or one very much like it. And maybe this Klittichorn, too? Jeez! To be dropped here, suddenly, and find that somehow you could learn to have godlike powers . . . No wonder they all went nuts!

Dorion was obviously uncomfortable discussing his own magical past and abilities and she decided not to press it. Still, it gave him a more human dimension. He was a pretty nice guy, and smart, and he sure had guts. His guilty secret, his embarrassment, was actually kind of sweet.

Dorion sighed. "I think we've gotten wet enough," he told them. "Let's mount up and make our way carefully over to the colonial border. If those guys didn't spot us by now then they're not going to."

Boday nodded. "Still, if Boday was in their saddle, she would have men riding up and down the border area hoping to spot us, and if she couldn't prevent us she could at least signal the others to get into the same world that we did."

"Right, and so we're still going to have to be careful," the magician agreed. "You can only take this destiny business so far. Maybe Charley will somehow get through, maybe destiny will take you in sight of the goal only to thwart you—we can't know. But even if it's your destiny to reach Masalur, it might not be mine. I'm not taking any chances."

They rode along in relative silence for more than an hour. Dorion had to bring them in a bit; they had wandered so far north that they risked the true null point, where they might well fall into the void or into a netherhell. Only a strip of each world was touching Akahlar, and all those worlds were round. There was a point where the curvature of each earth rolled off and another rolled up and on, and in that region many things were possible, none of them desirable.

Dorion thought of this, but his thoughts were most of all on Charley. She was unlike any woman he had ever known, even for an Outplaner. She was beautiful, sexually uninhibited, almost every male kid's private fantasy. Only they were just sex objects, not real people, and the beautiful and sexually uninhibited women he'd known were generally ignorant, dumb, broken in spirit, or had a screw loose somewhere. Charley, though, really was brilliant, imaginative, and as strong-willed and independent-minded as a queen or sorceress might be. Slave ring or not, nobody, particularly no man, would ever be her real master, that was for sure.

Hell, he knew as much about electrical properties as she did, maybe more, and he also knew far more about the nature of Stormriders. He had seen and known about the same materials that she had suggested using, but it would never have occurred to him to use them, or that they were of any use except as a barricade for a last stand. He, and probably Boday, would have stood and fought and died back there, or at best been captured and held by an enemy too powerful to defy. Not Charley.

She didn't need any magic, or regular sight. Her own abilities were far stronger than that. If she understood that, if she ever saw herself the way she was instead of just a pretty girl with common sense, there was nothing she could not do or have. The fact that she did not realize that her mind was far more exceptional than her body was the only thing holding her back.

Damn it, he was falling in love with her and he didn't know what to do about it. Hell, he didn't even have any real experience with women. It wasn't for lack of desire, it was just, well, he'd never exactly been handsome or athletic or had the kind of personality that attracted women. Now, here he was—and, as usual, he was a comrade, not a lover. He hadn't had much attraction before, he knew, but now that she also knew his terrible secret about his magic he felt he had no chance at all.

They were all surprised to find the colonial border essentially peaceful and undefended, not knowing that only six of the small horde of gunmen had gone off in pursuit of them. Still, crossing in this far from the entry station was not without its risks. Roads were deliberately engineered so that they led only to entry stations; people in general were not allowed to live close to a border or have access to it in order to make it more difficult for anyone coming in the back way, and there was much use of natural as well as artificial boundaries to make anyone coming in far from the gates very miserable.

Dorion was nervous. Knowing all this, he didn't want to take the first reasonable world that came along, but he was also conscious that the longer they remained there, poised at the boundary but still within the null, the more likely that someone would come along. *They* might hide, but not the horses, and without the horses their chance of crossing a strange colonial world undetected was much slimmer.

Charley had always been fascinated by the ways the border changed—very abruptly, as if it was a colored slide of some place that just faded out as another faded in—but this scene was no longer possible to enjoy. She could see only the energy part of the null's mists and the fuzzy colored shapes of Dorion and Shadowcat and that wasn't much. She got down off the horse and from her pack located the box with a preservation spell on it in which there was ground meat for Shadowcat. The cat ate like a pig, and even though it wasn't that old she was already running low.

The cat ate with his usual gusto, then crawled into her lap for a pet, oblivious to the wet conditions. Well, she was wet herself. The cat climbed up so its head was looking over her right shoulder, body limply down and held, and purred like an outboard motor as she scratched and petted him.

Charley was conscious of the curse of holding and stroking the cat by now. It was nice to be able to project yourself to anyone, regardless of their language, but having your forward, surface thoughts broadcast whether you were trying to communicate or not was unnerving. It was impossible to lie under such circumstances, and at least once already Boday had become offended by a stray thought of Charley's. The trouble, really, was boredom, which had allowed such stray thoughts to creep in, and she found that the technique she'd developed from those nights as a courtesan and refined further during her interminably boring stay at Hodamoc's helped a lot in both regards. She had two personalities inside her head, and by just relaxing she could push her real self well into the background, almost on standby, and allow the simple courtesan Shari to assume forward control. Shari didn't think very much, and she was quite content to just sit there blankly petting Shadowcat and awaiting some order or instruction.

Dorion watched the slowly changing procession of worlds and tried to stave off boredom once one came up that was obviously unacceptable. High granite walls had greeted their approach. The next two, at roughly twenty-minute intervals, were both seascapes; vast stretches of salt water without land or dock in sight. Even land didn't mean much, really. The average world was three-fifths or more covered with water; it wouldn't do to step out into a fairly nice-looking place only to discover you were on an island. That was a favorite of this particular region as well—islands big and small.

In a way, it was a tempting fantasy. Marooned, the only man on a tropical island with two women, one of whom was Charley, and both with the enslaving rings bound to him. He knew it was egocentric and self-centered and didn't take the women's interests into account, but, hell, it was *his* fantasy . . .

In the end, it wouldn't even matter to the scheme of things or the shaking of events. It was the other one, this Sam, who mattered. It was such a tempting thing, he and Charley, romping naked in the surf of some tropic isle . . .

He was so lost in his own dreams that he almost failed to notice the sudden change in the colonial tableau. It was speeding up, taking on almost a blurry appearance. After a minute or so he suddenly realized what was happening and jumped to his feet.

"Mount up fast!" he shouted. "A Navigator's working on the border! That means that whatever comes up will probably have people and some kind of civilization, so we're not likely to get stuck in some monster-infested swamp or another Kudaan!"

Charley suddenly snapped back to control, jumped up, and with a little trouble found Shadowcat's socklike carrier and slipped him in, then mounted up. She was getting very good at this now, she thought to herself with satisfaction.

The view that suddenly came up and locked in looked quite pleasant but it wasn't a hundred percent encouraging, either. A wide landscape illuminated by bright moonlight lay before them, covered with thick grasses going down to a white sandy beach and a beautiful bay beyond with some dark areas showing a light or two that might have been islands. The beach wound around the bay, and on both sides there were low rocky mountains that on the right came to a major promontory and on the left seemed to stretch out into the darkness, a few small lights showing that it went for a considerable distance. That meant shoreline, and the possibility that if this was an island it was a damned big one—and it was possibly a main land mass. Hot, humid air struck them.

"It appears to be the start of an ocean," Boday noted. "Are you certain that this is the one we can use? We will have to cross that, you know."

He nodded. "We'll have to cross some ocean anyway to get where we're going, so it might as well be where can see a lot of land. Move in now! We don't know how long whoever it is will be able to hold this position!"

They went forward, and suddenly the air seemed very thick and heavy and there was the smell of salt spray in every breath and the sound of small but steadily advancing waves striking the shore. Somewhere ahead Charley could hear the clanging of bells, possibly markers out in the bay itself or even beyond. She just kept her eyes on the crimson blur that was Dorion.

Now there was the feel of the horse in sand—fairly hard-packed, wet sand at that, and she could both feel and hear that they were within the reach of the waves themselves.

This was one of those times when she was really hit by her lack of sight. They were out of the null now, and all was just that deep gray with those few fuzzy colored smudges she'd come to recognize as Dorion and other magical things.

They rode for quite some time at the water's edge, although at a slow pace to keep the horses from collapsing. She wondered why, and finally shouted the question out to him.

"I can see the high tide mark, and the tide's coming in," he yelled back. "It's vaguely possible that somebody might stumble on our tracks entering this world, but even now the waves are totally wiping out our new tracks and our direction. If we can find some place, like a shallow stream cut, to go inland with the same effect we'll do so and make camp. We can do with some rest and I think we can risk a campfire for some decent food. I think we want to explore our situation in daylight."

He eventually found what he sought, and they made their way away from the sea, although not terribly far, the horses making their way in the shallows of a rock-strewn stream, until he found a place with reasonable cover. The ground was fairly hard, but the stream water was fresh and drinkable, and the small fire would not be visible from the beach area and wasn't likely to be observed from the bordering junglelike forest.

Charley barely touched her food; Shadowcat wandered out after they had finished to explore the area, and she found herself basically wet and grimy and all-around miserable but, most of all, she needed sleep. The bedroll wasn't the most comfortable place on such hard ground, but it didn't matter. She was soon fast asleep.

The next morning she awoke feeling a bit guilty. She'd slept solidly and well, not being able to share in the duties of being a camp guard which kept the other two from enjoying a long and uninterrupted sleep. It wasn't so much that the blindness limited her activities, since she was learning to deal with that and barely thought about it now, but the fact that it limited her usefulness in such a situation to the others. She checked for Shadowcat and found him curled up sound asleep at the bottom of the bedroll and a little miffed that she had the temerity to wake up and move and spoil his comfortable bed.

Boday saw her rise and came over to her. "Boday has been exploring the area a bit, and has found a large pool just inside the bush which the stream has dug deep," she told Charley. "It would be breast-high on you, and it is a bit colder than one might like, but Boday thinks you might want to use it as she did."

Charley did—and *how* Charley did. Boday was right—the pool was fairly chilly relative to the air, but the water seemed clean and smelled okay and there was enough of it. She might have liked some soap, and particularly some shampoo, but even as basic as it was it was *wonderful*. Somehow it made her feel human again, even though she wondered if her hair would ever dry in this humidity. Not only that, but she could wash out her really smelly, filthy clothes, although again the drying would take time. For a while, all she'd have was the never-before-used cape, which was kind of sexy without anything under if a potential modesty-preserver. Any saddle sores that might develop in the interim had developed long ago; she was pretty toughened now to riding bare-assed in the saddle.

Dorion could not wake up without his thick, super-strong coffee that could be smelled a ways off, so Charley had to wait until he and Boday had drunk their fill of the filthy stuff before she could get the pot cooled, cleaned, and boil some water for her tea. Then it was time for discussions on what came next.

"We must go east," Dorion told them. "That's the only way to Quodac and that in turn is the way we must go. It's going to mean a boat, from the looks of it, and that means finding civilization. The main road from the entry gate's got to be no more than thirty or forty leegs tops from here, probably closer. The odds are good that if we can find it it'll take us to a coastal city or town."

"Well, aren't we gonna be a little conspicuous?" Charley asked him. "Even if they aren't on the lookout for us, which they might well be, three strangers showing up not even knowing what the world is called are gonna raise a few eyebrows. At least somebody'll check and see that we didn't come through that gate. And you said some Navigator called up this place, so they're likely to be there waiting for a boat, too. They got to have heard about all the commotion over us back there, and they'll put two and two together."

"I know." Dorion nodded. "Still, I can't wave my arms and materialize a boat for us with a knowledgeable pilot aboard. I can *try*, but I'd probably wind up with a sea monster working for Klittichorn. I don't think it's going to be as bad as you say, though, and there's always the age-old method of bribery." He sighed. "Well, let's saddle up and see if we can find this town or port or whatever it turns out to be. We can't know how to solve our problems until we find out what the problems are." He thought a moment. "There were some lights last night farther on up the coast where we're heading. Not enough for a town, but maybe some private dwellings, maybe even native. Just stay loose and relaxed and we'll see if we can find somebody to give us the information."

That somebody was a good two hours' ride away up the beach. It was a strange-looking shack made out of native woods with the design looking like everything had been compromised. Certainly the oddball lumps, deliberately sagging roofs, and very small additions sprouting out from it made it look very strange indeed.

Stranger still was the creature who peeked out curiously from a trap door in the top of the thing as they approached and watched them come up to the place and stop.

It was totally hairless, a very pale green in color, with a leathery skin and wide, somewhat webbed feet that ended in very mean-looking claws. Its arms were rather short and ended in hands with three gnarled fingers and an opposing thumb that terminated in a sharp, spikelike nail. Although a tailless humanoid, its face was more reptilian than Akhbreed human, its nose just two indented nostrils above a wide, flat mouth, its eyes bulging from its head and covered with thick, rubbery lids that barely moved. It wore some sort of necklace but no clothing, and yet its sex was impossible to determine just from looking at it. It did not, however, seem afraid of them, merely curious.

"Uh-oh," Dorion said in a low tone. "Looks like this world has a very different set of natives. Maybe *too* different. I'm not sure that mouth could form Akhbreed words or sounds if it knew it. Still, no harm in trying."

"If it does not try and eat us," Boday responded nervously, putting a hand on her pistol but not drawing it lest it provoke an attack.

"Good day," Dorion attempted, a bit nervous himself. "Do you understand my tongue?"

The creature stood there a moment without responding, then let loose with a string of sounds that were a cross between a hiss and an impossible collection of all consonants.

Charley couldn't see the creature and so picked up Shadowcat who deigned finally to look at the native. Even with Shadowcat's strange vision, the native was something of a shock, as alien a creature to humans as Charley had seen in Akahlar, even stranger than Ladai, the Ba'ahdonese centaur. Suddenly, though, she realized that she could communicate—if one way. She stroked Shadowcat.

*"Please,"* she thought, directing it at the native, *"I know you can read my thoughts with this spell although I cannot read yours. We are strangers in your land and we are lost. We seek the main road and perhaps a place to get passage west. Is there any way you can help us? We do not know your language, but while you can understand me we have no way of understanding you by speech, I fear. Can you help us?"*

The thing looked very surprised. It was amazing how much very human emotion came through that reptilian form, although you never really knew if the reactions meant the same thing. At least it seemed to understand and thought a moment. Then it turned, went back into its house, and returned a moment later with a strange barbed spear, although it didn't seem menacing with it.

The creature leaned over, smoothed some sand, and began to use the spear point to draw a crude design.

"A map! It is making a crude map for us!" Boday exclaimed. "How—primitive—the style."

Dorion got down to study the design, finally having to turn the other way when he realized he was looking at it upside down. Yes, there *they* were, and there was the coast, and there was a road or trail or something leading inland a bit farther on. It appeared that this was some sort of peninsula, and that the town was on the opposite side and a bit before the point.

"I think I've got it!" he told them. "If we can find the trail. Charley, thank him or her for the help and let's be off. I can't tell from the sun how much time we might have left, and I'd rather be in a town used to Akhbreed travelers than in the middle of a strange jungle by nightfall."

She did so, and they started off, leaving the native standing there and watching them go.

"At least the language barrier keeps us from being asked embarrassing questions," Boday noted.

"True, but not from *thinking* them," Dorion responded worriedly. "I hope after this world we'll be able to keep in areas closer to Akhbreed types, though. Keep a sharp watch, too. Remember, we're Akhbreed and we aren't exactly the most popular folks in the colonies to the colonials no matter what our personal opinions are. It was probably being legitimate and nice, but you can't tell when one of them will direct you right off a cliff."

While the trail wasn't easy to find and wasn't really designed for people on horses, they *were* able to spot it by going slow and having Boday check out every likely access, and they were able to use it single-file, although Charley had some tough time avoiding low-hanging branches and the like that she could not see ahead of her and which were low enough to unhorse anyone not ready. Finally, after falling off and getting bruised, Dorion took her horse as a lead while she climbed onto Boday's

mount, riding behind her doubled up in the saddle. It wasn't
very comfortable and made her aware of her limitations more
than she liked, but she preferred that to breaking her neck or
even getting permanent rips in her face and body.

The trail was a bit over eight miles long and slow going, but
at last they reached the downward slope and the jungle gave
way rather suddenly to thick grasslands and a picturesque view
of a second and smaller bay below. The town was easy to spot
and not much; one main street, some warehouses, a two-block-
long row of facing buildings, none over two stories tall, and,
most important, a dock.

"Remain here and relax," Dorion told them. "I can't see
any sign of a train down there and the place looks more
Akhbreed than what we saw on the other side, but you never
can tell about anything. If I go in alone at first I can get the lay
of the land without rousing too much suspicion. A magician
can always travel between the worlds on his own, and without
you two I won't stand out so much." He looked around. "I'd
go back up close to the woods and off the trail and just wait.
From the looks of the sun we've got about three hours to
sunset. A half hour down, one or two in town, and then maybe
three-quarters of an hour to an hour back up here. You are
commanded to hide, wait, and make no contact with anyone
until I return. Avoid contact unless it's forced, defend yourself
in that case if you have to, but avoid being seen. Understand?"

Boday nodded. "Yes, we understand. But it will be very
inconvenient if something happens and you do not return."

He thought about that. "Well, I don't think it'll be that
serious, but if I don't return by sunrise you are to consider me
dead and are to make it on your own to Boolean by whatever
means you wish. Your one overriding command is to reach
Boolean. In that case you, Boday, will be the warrior slave
Koba and you, Charley, will be the courtesan slave Yssa, as
before, and no torture, no spell, will prevail to get your true
identity. And while you will do anything you must to reach
Boolean as fast and as safely as possible, you will not reveal
the name of your Master, only that you must go to him.
Understand?"

They both nodded. "Take care of yourself," Charley told
him sincerely. "Don't make us go off on our own again."

He grinned. "I don't intend to." And, with that, he was off and going down the trail towards the town.

"Come," Boday said firmly. "We must get off the trail and hide ourselves." There was no hesitancy or thought of disobedience in any way. Although they were quite casual with Dorion, they were bound to carry out his commands.

They found a spot about a hundred yards off the trail that had a means of getting into what Dorion called the woods—more like a jungle, really. The horses could be brought to cover, however, and still have something to graze upon, and they would be able to monitor the trail without being seen.

"Boday is uncomfortable with this situation," she growled, sitting as guard just behind a few trees and with a clear view of the immediate trail. "She is an artist, not a slave and a warrior, although there are many she would love to kill right now. Still, she perseveres for the sake of her beloved Susama."

It being still daylight, Shadowcat had no interest in being anything but a lump, and Charley disturbed him and then sat petting him, making a sort of conversation possible so long as she watched herself. The distance to the trail was much too long to carry her thoughts.

"You really miss Sam, don't you?"

Boday seemed surprised and also surprisingly soft. "Yes. Boday loves her. Do you think that anything else would have brought her forth from her comfortable studio, her art, and keep her going through all this?"

"But—it's due to a potion. One of your own potions. You know that."

Boday shrugged. "What difference? One feels what one feels. Boday dreams about her, thinks about her all the time. It is real. It is now a part of Boday, the most important part. All those husbands, and all those lovers—male, female, and other—over the years, and Boday never really loved any of them, nor felt any love really from them, either. It made her heart cold, her art surface and cynical. Now Boday both loves and suffers. One day she will create art that none will deny is great and glorious and immortal—if she lives. The potion was perhaps part of Boday's destiny." She paused a moment, reflecting. "You, however. You have never loved. You have lusted, as Dorion lusts for you, but never loved."

Charley was startled. "Dorion lusts after me? But he could take me anytime he wanted to! I'd have to obey! Hell, he could have *both* of us if he wanted to, and you know it."

Boday gave a slight smile. "Yes, but he is from a cloistered youth, and he has never learned how to approach women properly, nor read them, as most do when they are just teens. What he did learn during that time was a strong sense of honor and propriety which is keeping him dull and miserable. His status as a magician is the only thing that gives him any sense of self-worth, and he feels flawed in that. Far worse when he has to admit it, worse yet when he must admit it to women."

Charley was stunned by this. "How did you figure all this out?"

"You are too young, my precious flower. You may have had hundreds of men, but they were just a commodity to you, all the same after a while. You mistake your expertise on sex for expertise in people, but they are not the same. Most men see women more as objects than equals; do not make the same mistake in reverse or you become like what you hate in them. Boday is close to twice your age, and, she suspects, has lived four times your lifetime. Boday knows these things."

Charley made no reply, but the words hit home and were very uncharacteristic of Boday. Perhaps she, or maybe all of them, had missed something in the woman, seeing only the flake. And, of course, that's just what Boday was accusing *her* of doing. Seeing only the surface and never looking beneath. Her two-level personality she had mostly taken for granted as, like Boday's love for Sam, it was alchemically induced. At least, she'd been telling herself that all along. But was she kidding herself, really? It wasn't magic, it was drugs of some kind, permanent or not. Wasn't that really the difference between magic and alchemy? Magic created and destroyed; alchemy only enhanced or depressed what was already there.

Now Boday was saying that most, maybe all people acted on several levels, the public one being perhaps the best perceived to others but the least important in terms of really understanding the person underneath.

"You are learning, my sweet," Boday commented, and Charley suddenly realized that while she held Shadowcat her inner musings were basically public knowledge.

Boday looked out and frowned. "It is growing dark now and there is no sign of him. Boday begins to be nervous. Each of these paths so far has led to a bottleneck that has spelled trouble."

Charley began to share the nervousness. "What happens if he doesn't come back by dawn?"

Boday sighed. "We have our orders and we must obey them. First we go back across the border. Then we use some of the valuables in the saddlebags and we buy incongruous clothing and create for ourselves still other appearances, and then we bribe our way across or hire aid or we make it alone. If Boday can get some alchemist's supplies she can change us yet again. We can do only that becuase we can do nothing else. Our free will is limited to improvising how we carry out our commands."

Charley knew that Boday was right, although she didn't relish it. There was still a long way to go and a lot that could go wrong.

Later on in the night someone did come up the trail on horseback, and Charley peered out and looked in the general direction of the sounds approaching from below. Boday was instantly at her side.

"It's Dorion," Charley said with some relief.

Boday didn't know English but she could understand that much. "How do you know? There are clouds tonight and the moon is either hidden or not yet up. Boday sees little."

The dark, however, was the same as bright daylight to Charley. She groped for the Akhbreed words. "Shari see Dorion *melagas*," she tried, fumbling for the word for "aura" and settling for the one for "soul." She had stared at little else for quite some time now.

Boday was still worried. "I hope he is still in control of himself," she muttered. "Still, what could we do if he isn't? If he commanded us to surrender to the enemy we would be forced to do so."

And that summed up their dilemma and their frustrations all at once. They were subject to Dorion, and dependent on his own wit and independence.

Dorion stopped at the top of the trail at the edge of the

woods. "Come out! Bring the horses and packs!" he called. "I think we might actually have gotten a break this time!"

Charley gave a mental summons to Shadowcat, and they got the horses and saddled them, packing up with a mixture of apprehension and relief. Charley worried when they made their way slowly out into the open because the cat had not yet shown up, but suddenly there was a flying fuzzball of lavender jumping up on the saddle, barely holding on with all claws. She helped him up and then stuck him in his makeshift riding sling.

"Don't cut it so close the next time," Charley warned the cat. "Remember, you need me as much as I need you."

The cat reacted with typical indifference.

Dorion was patient but seemed excited. "The town's an Akhbreed colonial town, although it's got a fair number of natives working there," he told them. "The thing is, I ran into an Imperial courier down there who's somebody I used to know. Somebody I was a kid with way back when. He's the one who brought this world up, by the way—carrying dispatches to Covanti. This is one of the fastest places to cross over, it seems, which is why it came up."

Boday wasn't so certain that this was a good thing. "How much does this person know?" she asked him. "About what happened back there, that is? Or about us? And how trustworthy might he or she be?"

"He," Dorion told them. "His name is Halagar. When we were kids we all looked up to him. He was a natural leader type. The kind you admired and hated all at the same time. You know—he was stronger than you, better-looking than you, always smarter than you. That kind. He's gotten older, just like me, but he hasn't changed all that much. As for what he knows—well, I've never known him to betray a confidence or an old friend. He might if he had direct orders, big pay, and believed in it, but I don't think that's the case here."

Boday still wasn't so sure, even as they made their way slowly and carefully down the trail to town. "If he is so Mister Wonderful how is it that he is a mere courier?"

"Oh, couriers are highly paid and highly skilled," the magician assured her. "And you're on your own and pretty independent of bosses and the like. They might have to be anywhere. He says he's taking it easy for now after some experiences that were a lot more harrowing. He talks about being in the military but whose and where I don't know. I think he might have been a mercenary, and ex-mercenaries don't like to advertise that. Some folks think a mercenary can always be bought."

Boday was clearly thinking along those lines as well, but there was nothing to do but follow Dorion's lead.

"There's a ship due in here tomorrow," Dorion continued. "It's a freighter but it'll carry passengers as well. A few days' sail and we'll cross the null into Covanti. When we do that we'll be buried enough that it'll be a lot easier to move, and we can rely on some of Yobi's people to take the load off."

"Sounds good," Charley responded, sharing some of Boday's doubts but not voicing them. "Maybe too good to be true."

Dorion had apparently been talking over old times with this Halagar in the bar of the small inn there and carefully getting what information he could about the town and the situation before figuring out a way to introduce and explain the two of them. His cover story here was pretty close to the truth: that he had been conned by an Akhbreed sorcerer into taking two female slaves consigned from one sorcerer to another.

"He knows that there's a whole mob on the lookout for three women wanted by Klittichorn," Dorion told them, "but the general word is that one's short and fat, one's got a painted body, and the third resembles the Storm Princess but has the butterfly tattoos. Neither of you now matches any of those descriptions, really, and if you just keep your slave personas from this point on I don't think anybody's going to associate you two with them."

"That Stormrider did," Charley noted. "And those guys chasing us . . ."

"Not the same. The Stormrider no more 'sees' in the conventional sense than you do—or I do, for that matter. The patterns he saw are invisible to those without full magic sight, and I don't think he had much of a chance to have reported them to anyone. None of those men ever got close enough to get a good look; they were being summoned by the Stormrider by magical means. Now, that doesn't mean I want to stay around here any longer than we have to. The sooner we've crossed into Covanti and even beyond the more obscure all trails will be and the less likelihood of even a smart guy figuring out what's what there'll be. If Halagar is what he says and still basically honest, he can be a real help as far as Covanti hub itself."

"And if he is not?" Boday pressed. "If he turns out to be an enemy?"

They were coming right into the town now, and Dorion looked around, then sighed. "Then we will dispose of him as discreetly as possible. Any old friend who would betray me deserves no more respect from me than he gives."

Boday smiled. That, at least, was unambiguous, but left her with a great deal of latitude.

"There won't be many people in the inn," Dorion told them. "I think we're the only ones other than Halagar with a room there, which is a good thing since I don't think they can have more than four rooms total. They don't use this world much; mostly it's used by people like Halagar who want speed over all else, and for shipping emergency and highly perishable stuff. Ah! Here we are! Let's get the horses stabled and then we'll get some real food—not great but a lot better than what we've been eating—and sleep in real beds."

Until now Charley hardly remembered that she was wearing just the cloak, but now she suddenly felt self-conscious, not only about that but about how rotten her hair and her overall appearance might be—and she had no way to improve on it. Boday sensed her sudden feeling.

"We can not do much about the clothing—the old outfit never was much and is a mass of shrunken wrinkles right now—but we can at least comb the hair and get it looking somewhat presentable . . . so. Both of us would prefer a true bath and a wider choice of wardrobe and perhaps some slight makeup, but we do what we must with what we have. There! Not as lovely as you could look by half, but more than good enough."

It was no longer enough to simply follow Dorion's crimson aura; now there were steps and obstacles about which she could know nothing, and it was up to Boday to take her hand and guide her as well as she could.

Charley had never particularly liked Boday, but she was beginning to see why Sam had stuck by her. Boday was more and more showing her other, more hidden side, at least to Charley, and, most of all, she was totally trustworthy in a world where everybody seemed against Charley, Sam, and all that was good and holy. There was certainly no getting around the fact that Boday felt no guilt for turning young girls into mindless courtesans and whose only objection to slavery was which end she was on, but that wasn't all her fault, either. This world had bred Boday, and Akahlar bred harder, harsher people with ideas and standards formed in a quite different world than Charley's home. And even back home, there were people brought up to believe with all their heart that suicide for god was the best thing you could do so long as you took enemies with you and lots of equally weird stuff. Didn't the same guy who wrote "All men are created equal" own slaves? You couldn't blame them so much as you could blame the system that created them.

If nothing else, Charley was beginning to learn perspective.

The inn *was* small; a bar and back kitchen area opened onto a relatively tiny room with just five round tables. There was no electricity or other modern conveniences; even by Boday's standards this place was pretty primitive. In back and opposite the bar was a steep wooden staircase and rail leading upstairs. If the top floor wasn't any bigger than the bottom, then the four rooms up there were pretty small and the bathroom had to be in the back of the place.

Boday described it softly to Charley, who sighed and said, "Well, there goes the dream of a nice bath."

The inn was run by a couple of middle-aged Akhbreed types, the man of medium height but with bushy red hair and moustache and a great belly that no tunic could disguise. The woman, presumably his wife, was a bit shorter but of equal girth, wearing the traditional baggy dress and sandals and with short graying hair. They appeared to be in their fifties and they looked well suited to this sort of job in this middle-of-nowhere location.

The man greeted Dorion. "Well, I see you are back with your charges, magician," he said in a gravel voice that suited him. "You'll need two rooms, you know. No way to put three of you in one of ours."

"That's fine," Dorion responded. "I think the best thing to do would be to get settled in as best we can. Do you have any facilities for bathing? I think after so long on the trail that's a top priority."

The innkeeper scratched his chin. "Well, sir, we got one tub and heating the water's no problem. You understand, though, there'll be a charge."

"Just add it to the bill. If you can get started on that now, I'd also like to find some more suitable clothing for this pair. The elements have pretty well wrecked what they came with."

"We usually just go over to Quodac for that," the innkeeper responded. "No use in keeping much stock here, being so close to the border and all. Benzlau, he runs the dock and warehouse, keeps a stock of things, though, in case there's need. Might not be much of a fit, or much at all in women's clothes, but I'll get down there when we're through here and see if he can get a wub to open up the company supply store there. Closed now, of course."

"Wub?"

"The lizard folk. That's what we all calls 'em. They ain't too bright but they does a lot of heavy labor with no complaints around here. Most folks use 'em for most everything, but I don't allow 'em in here. For one thing, they get really nutty in the head when they get some booze in 'em, if you know what I mean, and they'll steal that sort of stuff. Best to keep 'em out of places like this."

*The good old Akhbreed colonial mentality strikes again,* Charley thought sourly. For people who weren't that bright that one back on the beach sure got the message fast and had no problems with a map. The fact was, they probably had more interaction with the "wub" than this guy did who lived and worked here simply because he treated them as the animals he saw them as being, while they'd treated the one as an equal human being. She couldn't help but wonder what most of this world, inhabited by only its natives, might be like. There might possibly be "wub" cities and "wub" kings and all the rest. The government probably knew, but to these people who lived here it was not only irrelevant, it was unimaginable.

"Thank you, that will be fine," Dorion assured him. "Have you seen my friend?"

"The courier? Yes, sir, he went out a little while back to check on the shipping and just take a walk down by the water, he said. He'll be back at any time."

As Dorion predicted, things began to work out, at least for a little while, in their favor. Dorion decided to try for the clothing problem first, while the bath situation was percolating, so to speak, and one of the wubs came after a while with a bunch of keys on a ring and led them to a door in the side of a big warehouse and then into the structure. At the rear was a separate room containing clothing, shoes, hats, boots, you name it. Most were in men's and boy's sizes and clearly were designed as replacements for clothing of the Akhbreed who lived and worked here and perhaps who lived and worked on the ship or ships. The women's clothing was mostly the sack-like dresses and, as slaves, they weren't allowed to don "respectable" clothes, something that distressed neither of them.

Nothing really fit Charley, but they found that large men's cotton T-shirts came down almost to her knees and they provided some protection and improvement over the bare nothing she really had. Boday found a couple of pairs of boys' black work pants that were okay at the waist although the legs weren't long enough. She decided the effect was all right, and went with them plus the same kind of shirt situation as Charley. Since Boday was so tall, the shirts were large and baggy but didn't come down nearly as far as they did on Charley, which made things work out.

"We will win no fashion awards, but it is acceptable," Boday pronounced.

The baths were crude but compared to the lack of them for so long Charley was not about to complain. With water a bit cooler than she liked it but with a big bar of soap she managed pretty well on her own, impressing the innkeeper's wife with her ability to manage without sight very well indeed. She didn't really want to get out, but considering that it was also Boday's turn she reluctantly did, now recapturing what it was like to actually have towels to dry off with once more. There was no doubt about it; no matter what else she was, Charley wasn't the wilderness-trail type. If there wasn't a good hotel every night, decent food, and the other creature comforts, she really wouldn't be happy.

As expected, there wasn't any indoor plumbing, but the inn's lone toilet was inside and reminded Charley somewhat of the port-a-johns back home. It had a regular seat and seemed to be made of metal, and it had a tank of something that kept it from smelling up the place and which took the crap to a holding area. She had the uneasy feeling that the contents of that tank wound up fertilizing the local gardens from which the inn and others got their fresh fruit and vegetables, but she didn't want to think on that very much.

Finding the cotton shirt acceptable and after then spending some time walking about and memorizing the general layout of the place she had it down pretty pat. She knew that many people might have a terrible time with this sort of thing, but somehow she just had this unsuspected talent. Give her an hour and she knew a place at least well enough to navigate if need be. Of course, with chairs moving, things changing as other people went in and out, and the like, you had to be cautious, but if need be she felt that she could leave her room, make her way down the stairs, find the john in back, do her business, and return to bed without help.

Dorion was right on the food. It wasn't all that great, but after what they'd been eating it seemed like fancy cuisine. Charley decided that her inclination to vegetarianism served her well here; the fruits and vegetables and even some nuts were quite good and fresh, leaving Dorion to grumble and Boday to sigh when eating the cooked parts. Charley did try a piece of the pie, but it was gummy and far too sweet and she didn't eat much of it.

They were just about done when Halagar entered the inn. Boday immediately saw what Dorion had meant in his description of his friend: Halagar was tall, broad-shouldered, muscular, and extremely handsome. He carried himself with the confidence of a professional soldier and officer at that, and what age and experience had added to his face and hands had only added to the effect. He was clean-shaven, with thick, black hair perfectly cut, and dark complected but not deeply so. His rich, baritone voice was just what you expected, and it had a melodic, almost hypnotic quality about it. This was the sort of man heads turned to see whenever he entered a room, and who was automatically the center of attention. Boday thought him perhaps the most attractive man she had ever seen, and immediately made a note never to turn her back on him for a moment. He might be all right, but people like this were always dangerous.

"Well, Dorion! Returned, I see, and with your two lovely charges!" Halagar's twinkling blue eyes fell on Charley and he paused for a moment. "And you vastly understated the little one's beauty," he added in a low, appreciative tone.

Charley felt suddenly very strange. She couldn't see what he looked like or get the effect Boday got by looking at the man, and yet she *felt* him, *felt* his gaze and sensed his instant attraction, and his voice just seemed to reverberate through her. There was something indefinably magnetic about him that instantly drew her attention and to some extent turned her on. He'd spoken perhaps twenty words in the minute or two since he'd entered the room and yet already that other side of her was in control, the irrational and emotional one, and she was thinking of nothing but him. She'd been horny as hell for a couple of weeks and something in this guy just tapped that and drew it out.

Halagar walked over, took a chair, and leaned back. "The wine here isn't fit for salad dressing," he muttered. "Innkeeper! A tankard of dark draft, if you please!"

"Yes, sir! Coming up, sir!"

As the tankard was delivered, Halagar sighed again. "What a pity that such beauty can not gaze upon itself, even in a mirror," he said, sounding totally sincere. "Her very manner is—magical."

Charley felt a tingle go through her. It was only the hold the slave ring had on her that kept her from responding or seducing him right on the spot.

"She is not magical," Dorion assured the man. "No powers at all. Some alchemical enhancements from when she served her trade, but that's all."

"Incredible."

She could feel him staring at her even though she could not see.

Dorion cleared his throat. "Both of you go up to the room now," he ordered. "Wait for me there."

There was no argument even though Charley in particular wanted very much to stay. They got up, said, "Yes, Master," and made their way upstairs. Once there, however, Boday exploded.

"Just when Boday thinks you might be learning something you turn back into the silly, immature sexpot again! You know nothing of this man and he is potentially as dangerous to us as the devil monster we slew!"

Charley sighed. Without Shadowcat around she could only be lectured to, not respond herself, but she did not feel apologetic. *I'm what you made me, Boday,* she thought angrily. *It's what I am. It's who I am. It's also the one thing I can be good at here.*

Dorion entered not long after. "I saw how you reacted to him," the magician said to Charley. "And I sure saw how he reacted to you. He asked me—well, whether or not you could be with him tonight."

"You refused, of course," Boday responded sharply.

"No. I have to think of the objective. I can't let my own feelings or anyone else's get in the way. Free, safe passage all the way to Covanti, and connections once we're there. He knows he can't have you forever—he's well aware of the fact that you belong to a high Akhbreed sorcerer and nobody crosses them. He doesn't know which and won't. If you hadn't been so damned hot there, I might have said no, but if you want him and it helps us then I can't see how I can't go through with it."

Charley didn't hesitate. "It would please me very much. Is he as good-looking as he sounds?"

"Yes," Dorion sighed. "Damn his soul. Go to him, if it's of your own mind and will to do so. He's two doors down. But don't let him pump you for information. Be dumb and ignorant. Short Speech only. You understand?"

"Yes, I understand." She turned and went to the door. "Do not worry, either of you. This will be strictly—physical."

She walked out, knowing that Boday would probably have to be ordered into silence but not caring. She felt down the hall—one door, two . . . Here it was. She made to knock, and suddenly there was a strange, eerie, inhuman voice in her mind, saying the one phrase she firmly believed that only she and Sam knew in all of Akahlar.

"Charley be gone," said the inhuman voice in perfect English as she knocked. And, in that instant, Charley ceased to exist as an active or accessible personality in her mind, leaving only Shari, the girl of pleasure, who knew nothing but service and wished to know no more.

From the darkest part of the hallway, two unhuman eyes watched as the door opened and Halagar bid her enter. For a moment the light caught the eyes, causing them to reflect it back and making them shine, but it was not noticed, and soon the door closed again leaving the watcher in the darkness it preferred. Satisfied, it crept silently to the top of the stairs, then went down to the inn. It went over to the open window, judged distance, then leaped up to it, then went out into the small port town.

Shadowcat had a lot to learn about this place.

# · 10 ·

## *Some Self-Reevaluation*

IT HAD TAKEN some adjustment to get used to the idea of Crim and Kira, but the actual changeover was a letdown. Oh, Crim would make camp before sunset and then slip out of his buckskins and into a robe, but even if you watched real close it wasn't any spectacular thing. One moment Crim was there, the next it was Kira in a robe now very oversized. The same thing happened in reverse at sunrise.

It was also difficult to accept that this was no transformation; they really were two entirely different people, and had they been able to walk side by side you would have thought them a near-perfect couple but hardly each other. Crim had literally given half his life to Kira, and that's the way it was. They shared some sort of existence, but they described it as dreaming; each "awoke" at his or her appointed time with vivid yet dreamlike memories of what the other had experienced. But the innermost thoughts and feelings of each were separate and closed to the other; they had information, but were not merged.

The hardest thing for Sam to get used to was that they never slept in the usual sense of the word. Even so, it made Sam sleep a little better just knowing that Kira would not. Still, there was a feeling of guilt in going to sleep on her out on the trail. This was a very lonely existence for her. In the towns and cities, Crim was often frustrated that he could do the heavy work but not partake of the night life, and Kira, so pale even here, longed for the feel of the sun now and then and more of the day-to-day activity and friendships that would not come with this kind of life. Each had clearly paid a price for the bargain, but it was also clear that neither regretted the price and thought it was well worth it.

There had been many rumblings in the sky, particularly at night, as they traveled circuitously around the Kudaan Wastes to the main road once more very close in to Tubikosa. Sam had managed a measure of clothing using one of Crim's undershirts, and it was casual enough to get them through the checkpoints, but as soon as they actually entered the hub Crim had arranged for them to be put up at a roadhouse while he used his contacts to get what was needed.

For all the bureaucracy, so long as you met the basic physical requirements for being called Akhbreed you could get hub documentation. The small black passportlike folder said she was Misa, an indentured field servant of Count Bourgay, Prefect of Allon Kudaan, which was within the rough boundaries of Duke Pasedo but far from the canyon regions and far to the north and east of the refuge. Allon was an oasis built around a solitary but fruitful well where water from streams far underground made its way to the surface and provided an arid but workable farm environment. The Count was actually a warlord of unquestioned criminality and highly questionable nobility whose alliance with Pasedo had allowed him some measure of respectability and kept the law off his back, but he was not a popular man in the region and was rarely seen and little known, which suited their purposes just fine.

For cover purposes, the story was that Bourgay, who was on Crim's regular route, had "loaned" Misa to the navigator while he broke with the train to do some business in the northwest. This wasn't an altogether unusual arrangement when Navigators were off on their own, since it was assumed that the trains must keep their schedules and to take a paid—highly paid—member of the train crew would be ridiculous. In effect she was a slave, expected to do the cooking and washing and tend the horses and nargas and even drive the wagon if Crim wanted to sleep. The peculiar nature of Crim and Kira was not public outside his regular areas, since such a thing would have disqualified Crim as an Akhbreed and prevented access to the hub and produced an instant loss of citizenship at the very least. By now, Crim and Kira were pretty adept that keeping their duality a secret. Sam's certification as an Akhbreed was necessary for hub entry at all, and unless you were Akhbreed you couldn't go from world to world at all, leaving the colonials isolated and separated and thus helping maintain the system.

Sam not only acted the part, she enjoyed it. She was a quick and eager learner, and had no trouble learning how to cook over an open fire, what things would keep—and how—and what would not, how the animals were cared for, hitched, and unhitched, and even elementary carpentry and mending of the wagon area. Her strength surprised and delighted her, and she was eager to keep it up. The broadsword that Kira could hardly move seemed rather light and easy to manage when Sam picked it up, and she worked out a regimen using heavy iron pieces used in the wheels and other things picked up along the way to keep those muscles. By rarely riding in the wagon but mostly walking or running beside it her leg strength and endurance not only maintained itself but actually increased, providing she had some oil on her inside thighs to keep them from rubbing themselves raw.

The practice sessions with Crim each morning and with Kira each night didn't turn her into an expert swordswoman or marksman or a great archer, knife-thrower, or martial arts expert, but they helped. She had the feeling that if she worked on any one exclusively over many months she could become pretty damned good at it, but for now all she wanted was a working general knowledge for defense. As Crim was fond of pointing out, the vast majority of people who used such weapons and techniques weren't very good at them, either— but they were far better than those who knew nothing.

The most frustrating part, at least from Kira's point of view, was Sam's continuing inability to relearn English. She had much from that period, including a habit of using archaic English measures like pounds and feet and miles even in Akhbreed, yet she had no clear-cut, specific memories of her old home world, only major, usually traumatic, scenes from there. After a while, Kira got the idea that Sam was actually fighting it; that the old memories and old life might be there, at least most of them, but that Sam unconsciously or otherwise didn't want them to come back, didn't want to even think of that place.

Although there was lots of paperwork and connections with Crim's underground friends, they stayed well clear of the Mashtopol hub's capital city and even camped outside of the small towns. This didn't prevent either one from going into those places when and where necessary, but it was thought best to leave Sam in a less obvious, less exposed position just in case. This was partly because Mashtopol was the most dangerous point, theoretically, until they reached Masalur, since if the enemy suspected that she still lived and was hunting her, as seemed obvious from Zamofir's comments back at the refuge, then here was where there would be a plethora of spies, mercenaries, and opportunists mobilized to look for anyone new or suspicious. Also, while Mashtopol looked to Sam to be physically a carbon copy of Tubikosa, its government was far more corrupt.

In Tubikosa, only "bad" women would go about without the long, baggy dress and bandanna on their heads, and only "wicked" men would be seen not fully and formally dressed at all times. There *were* some like that in Mashtopol, particularly in the small towns, but the majority of people were far more casual, with women casually wearing colorful print skirts hanging on their hips and comfortable tops, and men in more casual pants and shirts, usually of dark, somber colors, and wearing vests of various colors over their shirts. Hats, however, seemed to be out of fashion for either sex inside the hub. Social norms still hadn't progressed here to the point of seeing women wearing pants, but it certainly was a lot more casual than back "home" and some of those skirts were hanging pretty low and some of those tops were pretty damned tight. It also beat those stretch outfits that always felt like they were cutting her and grabbing her in all the wrong places.

The Kudaanese fashion, though, which Sam was expected to wear for consistency, was for light solid colors in the skirt and a halter-type top, sometimes set off with a matching blanketlike cotton garment that had a hole in the center for sticking your head through, but there was also a small pocket on just one side that contained a pull-out integrated hood with tie strings. Wearing it that way you had your head pretty well covered and the rest became something of a cape. The light colors, design, and all-cotton nature reflected simple attempts at dealing with the horrible sun of the Kudaan region. Sam's hairy legs and underarms were also reflective of a colonial origin; most hub women shaved them.

The last touch wasn't so much fun but made the most dramatic change in her. Kira had mixed a nearly alchemical mixture of foul-smelling chemicals and had thoroughly and repeatedly treated Sam's now long black hair with it. It had taken most of the color right out of the hair over repeated rinsings, giving Sam what she thought of as "dingy gray" hair. Kira called it silver and tried to be nicer about it. Still, Sam's sun-darkened complexion and weathered look combined with the long and full "silver" hair to provide a striking change in appearance. Only Sam didn't like it, but she preferred it to meeting Klittichorn face-to-face.

She had just the right image, which was why the fake origin was picked, but there was still a real risk. Agents of Klittichorn might not know her appearance very well, all things considered, but Crim had had that run-in with Zamofir who had told him pretty much everything, and somebody was certain to be suspicious of the fact that the Navigator had now suddenly left his train and was heading in a general westerly direction in the company of a Kudaanese woman.

Sam came back up from the woods near where they camped to see Kira checking supplies. "Something up?" Sam asked her.

Kira nodded. "The hub's filling with all sorts of strange and not-so-strange faces," she told her. "There's also a rough sketch of your face making the rounds, unofficially. It's not very accurate or very good but it won't stop them from looking hard at every—heavy—young woman they come across. You look different but it's a no-questions-asked reward and many won't bother to ask questions. A number of short, fat women have been reported disappearing, and the police and militia here are as corrupt as the rest. We have what we need and we've been here long enough. Once we get into the colonies on the other side they'll have a hard time finding us. There are just too many possibilities, even if they know our direction. It's only in the hubs that we have to really worry. Get a good night's sleep. How are you feeling?"

"Pretty good," Sam told her, " 'cept it seems like I got to pee every twenty minutes. Maybe that's the price of girls havin' muscles. I dunno. Why do you ask?"

"Because this is still a big place and it's our turf, as it were. We have as many people bought here as they do and we know the land better. That's why we haven't run into ugly scenes so far. But those who hunt us know that as well, and they also know that the one place we have to show up is at the exits. There are only eight possibilities there and you can bet that there's a ton of people looking over the most likely exit points and enough looking even at the out-of-the-way ones."

"Can't you just avoid the guard posts?"

"Not without ditching the wagon as well and cutting our way through fencing. Then we'd have to take random choice on whichever colonial 'petal' was up and we'd be reported there sooner or later by any officials or Guild trains we might meet. And, going west and north, we're going to be out of our normal and familiar grounds ourselves, and that means we have to watch it. Some of these places are pretty dangerous."

Sam looked at her. "You got any bright ideas?"

Kira shook her head. "No, and I've been thinking of little else. Maybe Crim will come up with something in the morning."

"The problem," said Crim, "is the wagon and supplies. Two of us on horseback wouldn't have much trouble sneaking out of here, although we'd have to take pot luck on which petal happened to be up. When you start getting into unfamiliar territory, though, it's best to stick close to the main roads and have the bare essentials with you, and for this type of journey I don't want to ditch the wagon and head for the hills until we have to. The worst thing this rebellion business has done is to bury honor. There are lots of possible friends and allies out there but we can take none of them for granted. That means going legitimate whenever we can. And that means going right through one of these checkpoints."

She stared at the map. "What about doing a go-'round?" she mused aloud. "I mean, you go through *there*, alone, with the wagon, and I go through on the side, here, by cuttin' through the fence and meet up with you out in the misty zone. I know there's bound to be a border checkpoint wherever we're goin', but there's a pretty long distance between the hub and the colony."

He shook his head. "No, it's not that easy. First of all, they stamp your identity papers when you go through. Yours wouldn't have the exit stamp."

"Then maybe I go all the way myself. You know, like paralleling you, keepin' you in sight but off a bit. I sneak in the other side when you bring up the right world and meet on the other side of the border."

He frowned. "I don't like it. First of all, that's over forty leegs to cross, and you'd have to be pretty far off me to avoid being seen. Maybe a lot of magicians could make a horse invisible but I never got that far in the course. Second, things seem to have a way of happening to you. If we get separated at this point and you wind up in some other, nastier world all alone, I might never find you, and while I wouldn't help the other side on a bet I'm doing this for profit, remember."

She was undaunted. "The big thing is just to be close enough to you to be sure I can get over to you but without them guys seein' me on either side. How close could I get in that mist without gettin' caught up in the wrong world?"

"Fairly close. You can see where the connection is made because the mist doesn't sparkle and it's darker. Why?"

"Well, why can't I try it on foot? I got myself built up pretty good."

He sighed. "That's not across the street, you know. I know you've been running a few leegs a day and walking more, but it'll take you some time to make it that far. Too risky."

"Not near as risky as goin' through a hole where there's bound to be a bunch of tough guys waitin' for me who'll take no chances, maybe with the guards lookin' the other way and you with a bullet in your head. Uh-uh. I been in that crap before. It ain't so bad. Just gimme a canteen of water and some candy for energy and I'll make it. You said it yourself—once we get clear over there we'll be harder to catch, and once we cross out of this turkey of a kingdom it'll be even harder."

He still wasn't convinced. "That's the region where two

alien air masses meet, remember. There are always clouds and sometimes storms. If they get any idea at all that you're there, the Stormriders will be on you."

She thought about it. "What are these Stormriders?"

"Creatures. Some say they used to be warrior magicians who went too deep into the black side of their arts and became inhuman. Others think they're renegade demons. Whatever, they're Klittichorn's protective guard and they're fiercely loyal to him."

"Can they be killed?"

He shrugged. "Nobody knows. Unlike the Sudogs, which are minor spirits requiring the storm's energy to feed them and the clouds to give them shape, they're independent and only draw additional energy from the storms. They can exist by day but are far more powerful by night. I've seen one, once—there aren't many of them, but you don't want to meet them."

She fumbled and brought up the white cotton hood. "Well, with this on and short as I am I ought'a be pretty hard to see in daylight, and if they got less power then it's when we should cross. I'll take a pistol and a spear. The spear's light enough to carry easy and I'm gettin' pretty good with one. And don't worry so much. Up to now I been a pretty naive kid lettin' other folks and events push me around. Now it's my turn. How in hell am I gonna take on that Storm Princess or anybody else with power if I can't even manage this?"

It was a good point. "Okay, then, we'll adjust to camp just before the border tonight. That'll give us a chance to see what we're up against. If it looks in any way bad, then you'll be off just before dawn. I can't give you but a few hours' head start, though, or *I* won't get across in daylight at the speed I can go with this rig, and I can't stall much in bringing up Briche, which is the land we're going to use. You must be there when I get there. Understand?"

She nodded. "I understand. What's this Briche like?"

"Not too bad. Heavily forested, a number of small towns and one or two big trading centers, but pretty peaceful. The natives are formidable-looking, I'm told, with hair all over. They're supposed to look something like giant apes only with a more human build. Civilized, though, and pretty peaceful, really. I was warned not to eat with them, though. Among other things, they make soups and pastes out of hordes of insects and flavor them with tree leaves and grasses."

"Yuck."

"There's also a lot of fog and rain in there, but seldom a thunderstorm. As soon as you enter start heading for the road and come into it as close as you dare. It's pretty easy to get lost fast in a forest, particularly when you can't see the sun and you don't know all the rules in force there."

She nodded. "Let's do it, then. And I'll put in extra hours today gettin' myself up for this."

The edge of any of the worlds of Akahlar was always an eerie sight no matter how many times you saw it. The land just ended, and below and stretching out far into the distance was a flat plainlike region covered with a thick white mist that rose perhaps three or four feet from the ground, and within which were little flashes like hidden Christmas lights turning randomly on and off under the white shroud. In the distance, on the other side, you could see another land rising up out of it, but every few minutes that land would change. Where there were mountains there were suddenly valleys, and where there were farms there might now be the shore of a vast sea. It was almost never sunshine on a border, either; clouds always boiled and churned as two alien and incompatible air masses met but, somehow, did not quite mix.

From time to time there'd be a crossover of insects or birds or other such things, even rarely some plant spores, but nothing actually lived for long in the transition zone. There was nothing really to feed or nurture life, and nothing at all would grow there.

A small wire cutter was the only thing needed to breach the long fence that surrounded the hub. It wasn't really there to keep people in or out; those who were not of the Akhbreed were prevented from entering by the spells of the chief Akhbreed sorcerer. Crim and Kira could enter and leave the hubs only because they were truly two different people who were both Akhbreed. The spell might exclude a curse or changewind-induced departure from the norm, but when Crim entered he was just Crim to it.

The fence was basically there to bar wild animals who might

wander across from getting in, and as a political statement. Colonial races who could not enter a hub could never attack, let alone overthrow, a seat of power.

Kira was as dubious about all this as Crim had been, but just a casual visit to the border station convinced the both of them that this was the only way. Mashtopol was corrupt as hell; the guards had a picture of the Storm Princess herself hung in their entry station, and around and nearby were a number of shifty types apparently idling in the area for no particular reason.

So it was that Sam, when it was just turning light enough to really see but before dawn broke, had received a kiss and hug for luck from Kira and slipped through the opening in the fence and down onto the mist-covered floor. It felt as wet and spongy as she remembered it, but it was firm enough. The far horizon was still dark, although you could occasionally see isolated lights here and there when one or another world would come up. Looking back from perhaps half a mile, Sam could see the lights of the entry station for the hub, and even farther out that glow always kept her oriented.

As the sun rose she conserved her pace and repressed the urge to sprint or hurry along. Forty leegs was about twenty miles, give or take.

Once she felt she was out of sight of any but someone looking directly at her through field glasses, she stopped and removed all her clothes and put them in the small backpack Kira had fashioned for her. Better not to have to deal with a skirt and top until you had to.

Crim had worried about her ability to cross in the needed time, but she was having no trouble and feeling very proud of herself for that. The big problem, which they'd also discussed, was the lack of a far reference point in the ever-shifting landscapes beyond. That meant, as soon as it was fully as lit as the cloud-shrouded nether-region ever got, picking an area on the fixed hub and checking back every once in a while to keep herself in line with it. She picked an odd-shaped bluff just beyond the entry station that was shaped kind of like the face of a fat guy doing a big pout. It was fairly easy for a while, but the farther across she got the harder it was to make out that feature or distinguish it from the other bluffs and crags of Mashtopol's end. She began to get a little worried and disoriented as now the far "shore" appeared closer, and she slowed to an easy walk.

Ahead of her now was the shore of a vast ocean, filling the horizon and making orientation even more difficult. There was no entry station in sight, either, which didn't mean much. If you were coming along here you'd better have a boat waiting or you'd be stuck anyway.

She took a drink and decided to walk diagonally to her right and wait for something better to use. She was walking for some time when the scene flipped, showing some barren, yellowed hills leading down to an ugly-looking lake. The air coming from it reached her, smelling foul, sort of rotten-egg type, and both hot and humid. She could hardly wait for *that* one to be out of the way.

Suddenly she heard noises of animals and equipment and shouts of people and stopped dead. For a moment she couldn't see them, but then, suddenly, they were there, coming almost right at her! One of the wagon trains, damn it! She was too far over, maybe right between the two stations!

There wasn't a whole hell of a lot of time, but she dashed back the way she came at top speed and the sprint, after all the rest, finally got her winded and feeling a bit dizzy. She collapsed to her knees, breathing hard, and tried to let the mist cover her, peeking up just enough to see how close they'd come to her.

It was pretty damned close. The outriders on this side almost trampled her, and she could see the wagons clearly and the people in them. This was one of the passenger types like she'd started out with, and it contained a fair number of families and tough-looking men and women dressed in various garb. One man sat on a wagon seat holding a furry creature that seemed all eyes and teeth. The thing seemed to sense her presence and its cold eyes looked where she was, then as the wagon got closest it tried to leap from the man's grasp and come after her. Instinctively, she grabbed the spear and crouched down.

*My god, it's all mouth!* she thought nervously.

But the man held on, and the pet or watchdoglike thing or whatever it was finally gave up.

Then the train stopped. The Navigator, she knew, was going to pull his magic trick, not tremendous as the sorcerer's went but one hell of a trick nonetheless. She turned and watched it, always fascinated.

The scene changed. First slowly, then more quickly, worlds flashed by, mountains rose and fell, seas stretched out and receded, trees grew and then shrunk, summer turned to snow and then to torrential rains. Suddenly it slowed again, settling on a peaceful-looking meadowland with lots of flowers and gum trees and plenty of green. It looked like a pretty nice place, and off in the distance the sky was even blue.

There was a series of shouts echoing up and down the train and then, slowly, it began to move once again, off the mist and onto a nicely maintained road, and within ten or fifteen minutes tops the whole train was out of transition and into the new world.

Almost immediately after the traditionally buckskin-clad Navigator made his final checks and rode in himself, the world was lost, but this time not to just another scene. Like a deck of playing cards bent partway at a cut point to expose a single card and then let go, the rest of the worlds held there now began to snap back as the vast worlds piled upon worlds of Akahlar sought equilibrium once again. Scenes, whole worlds, flashed by, dark, light, cold, hot, wet, dry—all the combinations, going by too fast for the eye to gain more than a general impression of the place before it was gone. She had never seen this end result of a Navigator's magic before and was fascinated by it.

Suddenly, all around her, was the sound of thunder very close, and lightning split the heavens again and again. She whirled and looked up to see ominous black clouds and a tremendous display of energy, and then *something else* before sheets of pouring rain hit her. *There were things up there!* Things with great, leathery wings and heads on long necks that looked like chisel-points, with glowing coals for eyes, atop which were strange, wraithlike giants in saddles riding them as if they were horses. The riders were transparent, outlined by pulsating borders of energy that seemed to form both body and some semblance of armor.

*Stormriders!* Made visible by the Navigator's work and all the turbulence it set up and now drawing on that tremendous energy.

The rain was still driving, but the lightning was no longer striking the ground but rather seeking out those great black things with their ethereal riders, who grew brighter and more horrible as they absorbed each bolt.

She dropped down below the mist, the rain so hard it was almost stinging her, afraid to look up, afraid that one of those *things* up there would instead look down and spot her with those cold, empty outlined eyes. Above, there came the noise of horrible screeching that pierced even the noise of the storm as the ghastly black mounts screamed their defiance of storm and all else in creation.

And the strange thing was, she didn't *have* to see. In her mind, throughout her body, she felt the storm and its deadly occupants in ways she could never explain, almost as if she and the storms were one and the riders were tearing at her. Somehow, she and the storm were one, and she felt almost violated that they were draining the energy from her even as she lay there, frightened. She wanted to lash out at them, order them to stop, or, at least, to divert some of that energy to herself, but she dared not. If they knew, if they so much as *sensed*, that she was there or anywhere about then the talons of the leathery-winged creatures would be upon her in an instant.

It seemed to rain for an eternity, although it probably wasn't more than a few minutes, but even after it tapered off suddenly, then stopped, she lay there, in what was now a couple of inches of water, listening for more of those screeches and afraid to stick her head up.

There was a slight but steady current to the water, and it began to recede quickly, going off towards the nearby land. Soon there was little left, save that the ground was kind of squishy, like a sponge, and oozed water wherever it was pressed.

After a while, she knew she *had* to risk looking, and fumbled in her now thoroughly soaked pack for the white hood that might give her a little extra camouflage. It was soaked through, but so was she, and she wrapped it around her head and then, very cautiously, peeked up.

She could still see them, but they were not close and seemed to be going away from her. She decided not to move, though, or do anything, so long as any of them were in sight, and the clouds, going back to their usual swirling gray, now seemed more menacing, as her mind feared a great black shape with an electrified neon warrior atop it hovering just above, waiting . . .

The "petals" of the worlds had stabilized once again, and she looked back in hopes of seeing a lone and familiar wagon. She could see nothing, hear nothing, but the world that now was locked in, at least for its time, contained an entry station not that far in and with a number of uniformed men and horses there.

It was impossible to see the sun through the cloud cover, but she had the impression that it was getting quite late in the afternoon. At least, as far as she could see inside the revealed world, the amount of light was more consistent with afternoon than any other time, and she began to worry. *Was I too late? Did he have to go without me?*

She rejected that almost immediately. If Crim had dialed in whatever that world was called there would have been the same kind of thing she'd just gone through almost surely. So where was he? Stopped at the border? In some kind of trouble? What?

She didn't want to spend a night out here, alone, particularly with those *things* around. Almost nobody crossed at night. Not even a Navigator could see all the landmarks and keep dead on at night, and it was generally only done when it was some kind of military or medical emergency or in the case of urgent diplomatic dispatches which would be aided and guided by sorcery. Night crossing wasn't a real option anyway. Kira couldn't navigate—it was a talent you had to be born with, or so they all said. You could only learn to control and develop it, not bestow it on someone else. Besides, while Kira was real smart in a lot of ways she'd been a female jock. Something called the Biathlon, she'd said. Crazy kind of thing that had to do with cross-country snow skiing and rifle shooting. That was why she was such a good shot, but the deserts of the Kudaan were a hell of a place for a snow skier to wind up!

But it *was* beginning to get darker, though, and not from any impending storm—she could tell that now—but because of the lateness of the day. Her hair and everything she had was still soaked through, and there was a chill wind blowing from whatever world was up right now.

She was still trying to figure out what to do when she heard the sounds of others approaching from the hub. *Crim!* Or—was it? Not one wagon there, but two! She moved off a bit so she wouldn't be right in line once again, but she wanted to stick close enough, risk or no risk, to make sure just who was in what.

The lead one *was* Crim! She felt some relief at that, but what the hell was the second, trailing wagon? Two tough, weathered men in front, on the seat, and probably two more in the wagon since four horses were trailing behind them. This didn't look good, and it was unlike Crim to take this long to get across. Hell, what if it was sundown before he could clear the entry point? What if it was sundown *while* he was at the entry point?

She shadowed them at a distance, taking a wide semicircular route around them. Wherever Crim was going, that's where she was going, and to hell with those other guys. If he was being shadowed by suspicious characters, maybe with too many guns, figuring on just what they were pulling and hoping to catch her when she caught up with the Navigator, then that was a problem, but not an insurmountable one. She was sick and tired of being hunted like an animal and kicked around by the fates and something within her had hardened her. If she was mortal then they were mortal, too. She'd rather take her chances with Crim and Kira, even if it meant taking these men on, than wander around another unknown land until she bumped into another Duke Pasedo or worse.

After you saw the Stormriders, four guys with guns didn't seem half as frightening as they might have.

Crim had gotten a bit ahead of her, but now he stopped, very close to the border region, as the trailing wagon crept up to him and then passed him, allowing her to draw roughly even but maybe a few hundred yards down. It was risky being this close, but this was a new circumstance. She was going in with Crim, no matter what Crim did.

The Navigator looked nervous, maybe even tense. There were two more guys looking out of the back of the wagon and they had guns of some kind, that was for sure. So why had they decided to pass him?

Suddenly she realized the reason. He was the Navigator—none of them were. He had to be behind to bring up the world and stabilize it for them to cross. It would also hold only a couple of minutes after he let it go at best, so she had to be really ready now. It was maybe a quarter of a mile to the border. She didn't feel much like more exercise, but she was prepared to *float* over if she had to. She took off the backpack and let it fall. The hell with that waterlogged dead weight. She had other clothes in the wagon. Besides, some cruel god or fate seemed to like her naked for some reason. At least this time she was armed.

The worlds began to flip, faster and faster, and, after a couple of minutes, they stopped on just what he had described—a great forest, in the first throes of dusk, with another good road leading up to an entry station carved out of the forest that already had some lights on.

She started to go in, for some reason, held herself, as she watched the men in the wagon proceed in and then up onto the road itself. Something, perhaps in Crim's manner or perhaps a sixth sense she hadn't suspected and which hadn't been very useful until now, warned her.

Suddenly the forests vanished and several worlds flipped past before slowly coming to a stop again. *He'd gotten rid of them! He'd dumped them in that world and then let them go!*

"Misa! If you're out there *run like hell now!*" Crim called at the top of his lungs, and she ran as if the Stormriders were right on her tail.

Crim slowly edged forward as she took off. He was buying her all the time he could, but it was still an ordeal for her after the rest of the day and no picnic at all. She was going on sheer determination, every muscle aching, not even seeing what kind of world had come up.

Suddenly there were trees and leaves batting her face and she grabbed some limb and brought herself to a stop, then dropped on the ground, gasping for breath. It was several minutes before she could get hold of herself, and when she did she knew that Crim had crossed the border. There was lightning and the start of a storm out there in the void.

She took stock of her surroundings. It was getting pretty damned dingy, but they *were* going west, after all. This sure wasn't the world Crim had planned on, though, and she wondered if he had any more idea about this place than she did or had just picked it as the first decent-looking one that came up before he lost control of the "deck." Probably the latter, but the odds were he'd spotted a road or something, so her best bet was to head back over towards that road—if the land allowed her.

The humidity was tremendous, and the vegetation was incredibly thick and seemed to reach almost into the mist itself. She worked herself around as best she could, using the spear as a probe and walking stick. It was getting *very* dark *very* fast, and she wanted that road. If it was dark and nobody crossed late, then the odds were it was a pretty safe area so long as she avoided any entry station.

It wasn't easy. Several times she almost slipped off the slick floor into the mist, and while she had no fear of the transition zone as such she had no desire to lose Crim now that she'd kept up with him. Or maybe Kira by now. She hoped that after all there hadn't been some kind of awkward embarrassment ahead.

Finally she made it to a cleared area that was most certainly the main road. It was more than a little muddy, although none of the rain that she could see had escaped from the transition zone, but she wasn't going to be on it, anyway, but rather walking along it.

About ten feet inside there was a strong and very high fence with a kind of barbed wire on top, and she realized that when she'd dropped the pack she'd also dropped the wire cutters. Smart. If she *had* tried to press in, she wouldn't have been able to get through. The road was open, though, and the gate there was a simple wooden slab on a hinge.

Just beyond was the entry station, a pretty small affair by its look, with just room for a couple of people. There was a small cottage made of bamboo or the like nearby with a thatched straw roof, kind of looking like a fairytale house, and a couple of horses grazing in a nearby clearing.

Crim's wagon wasn't there—he had to have cleared the place and gone farther up, maybe to wait for her. By now it was sure to be Kira, and Sam didn't want Kira out in a strange place alone right now. Kira was skilled, but this wasn't her kind of element, and against a gang or perhaps animals of who knew what variety she was just one woman alone.

The lights for the entry station and outside the hut weren't electric but plain old torches, but they gave off a good amount of light and definitely lit up the entire gate area. Suddenly a dog started barking over the hut and Sam didn't like that at all. It was definitely a dog, and maybe a big one. She tightened the grip on her spear.

*Funny,* she thought. *Like a half hour ago I was ready to kill four human beings, but I'm not sure I can kill a dog.*

A woman came out of the hut and said something sharply to the unseen dog, who quieted down but only a little. She went on over to the guard shack and called in. A man came out, then reached back in and turned off his inside light. Sam couldn't tell too much about them from this distance, but they both looked kind of average. Thin, though. They looked like the kind who could eat a chocolate cake apiece and still lose weight. They were also kind of romantic, as if they hadn't been married long—if they were married now. He said something, she laughed, said something back, they kissed, and then walked hand in hand back to the hut. Sam thought it was kind of sweet.

But that damned dog better be on a chain or something.

She suddenly sensed an odd building of energy, and almost immediately after there was a crack of thunder and it started to rain. It wasn't the kind of very hard, driving rain like out in the mist, but it was a steady rain with pretty good volume, the kind that soaked everything through and turned the mud to worse. She risked at least a bit of a bond with the storm, trying to sense if it were normal and natural or if some ghostly airborne riders were within it, trying to use it. There was nothing but the storm, though, and she relaxed. If it was a normal thing, then it could be used. She doubted the dog liked it any more than anybody else, and it was noisy enough to mask most sounds.

She went to the fence, then to the gate, and squeezed through. The horses made irritated sounds, not at her particularly but at being left out in this crap, and she walked back into the shadows sinking in mud to her ankles now.

Within a few hundred yards of the entry station it turned pitch dark; so dark it was impossible to see a thing, only feel the rain and mud. She slipped a couple of times, but it meant little, since the rain was giving her a rinse. She was, however, beginning to long for very short hair again, and mulling over the virtues of shaving her head. Hell, considering how she looked now what difference would it make? Boday would still love her, and Charley would still be her friend, and Boolean would still need her. Still, she had the uneasy feeling that maybe looking like some freaked-out Hunchback of Notre Dame might not be something *she* could live with.

Odd to be thinking of Boday and Charley at a time like this, but she really missed them. They were the only two people she really cared about in this godforsaken place, the only two who cared anything about her. Oddly, and particularly these past few days, she missed Boday more than Charley.

Charley had changed so much Sam wasn't sure she knew or understood her old friend anymore. Jeez—she didn't have any more to do with working as a hooker than Sam had with getting fat, but Charley *liked* it.

Boday—Boday was security. Hell, it was more than that. She'd lived with the crazy artist for a real long time now, and she knew her better than she knew anybody. Oh, not that you could *understand* Boday—that was probably impossible—but you got to know her real well. She admired Boday's egocentric confidence, her real genius at almost any art form she wanted to tackle, her inner strength and toughness in a world that was far more of a man's world than anything Sam had known before.

That was something. It was starting to come back after all. She was starting to remember "home," or at least the Earth she'd come from. There were lots of gaps, mostly personal ones, but she remembered the music and TV and cars and all that. She could remember Boston, and Albuquerque a little, but she couldn't remember any faces. Not even her Mom and Dad. No faces.

It bothered her, but only that. She hadn't ever been happy there, and God knew where she'd have wound up if she hadn't gotten pulled here. If only they would just leave her alone here. If only she had some time and some peace to find out about herself once and for all . . .

Where the hell was Kira with the wagon? She couldn't have kept going far in this weather. She *knew* Sam would be along, and it wasn't out of friendship that the strange two-in-one couple was helping her, but for profit. She was *sure* that Crim or whichever had made it to this particular world, and equally sure that customs or whatever had been cleared because there was no sign of the wagon or any problems back there.

Clearly something had gone wrong *after* clearing the gate, and that something was almost certainly not related to the entry gate itself—that couple hadn't looked like they'd had anything unusual happen back there.

So now there was just the rain and mud and darkness of a strange world, and she began to feel miserable and alone.

*I'm sick of this!* she thought sourly. *Sick of running and hiding and being chased and abused, sick of having everybody crap on me in this world and having everything go wrong to boot! Damn it, I've been nothing but somebody's Ping-Pong ball since we got here! This has just gotta end! There's just gotta be an end to all this!*

The storm rumbled, and there was now thunder and lightning. She had been conditioned to fear such storms, first by the dreams, then by the reality of being hunted by ones who used them, but suddenly she began to think things out. She was a clone or something of the Storm Princess, or the Storm Princess was a clone of her. Who cared? And the Storm Princess was being conned or was going along with this Klittichorn clown who wanted to kill her, right? But why did this big-shot sorcerer who had enough power to find her back home and chase her here need the damned Storm Princess at all? It wasn't just a big plot, it was something that Boolean guy had said long ago.

Klittichorn didn't have any power over the storms! That's why he needed this Storm Princess! Sure, he used those ugly creatures of storms, but *they* were dangerous when they were around, maybe, not *him*. And she'd actually *called* a storm once, here, to save them. It hadn't turned out so right, but it saved their personal asses anyway. But it hadn't worked out so right not because of Klittichorn or those monsters. Why was he trying to kill her, anyway?

*Because for some reason he was scared of her.* She was a wildcard he had to kill because he couldn't control her and her power was dangerous to him! That wasn't putting down the real threat from killers and sky creatures and changeling

witches and all that, but she was running into them *anyway*.
And—why were they all chasing her?

*'Cause he's just as scared of me as I am of him!*

She stopped dead in the middle of the muddy road, closed
her eyes, and took a number of deep breaths. There, in the
dark, in the rain, she let her mind go, let it rise up to the clouds
and turbulence above.

And she felt *power*.

She was one with the storm, and the storm was hers. She
was where she stood but she was also everywhere touched by
this great tropical storm. The winds were hers to command, to
bend branches or whip through the treetops; the lightning was a
plaything, a toy, a weapon if she wanted it to be.

She was aware, suddenly, of a *presence* in the storm, a thing
not of it that hid within it and took from the storm's center a bit
of its power to give it form. It used clouds to form a skull face,
a demon face, and electrical energy to feed it and give it
strength and solidity. She did not know what it was, but she
knew immediately, somehow, that it was looking for her.
Looking, but not seeing, because the rest of the storm was hers
and she would not permit it to see.

The Sudog felt resistance, felt its will being blocked, but the
force against it was too strong. It looked anxiously in all
directions for the source, but the source didn't seem to have a
center, a locus. The storm itself was somehow alive in the
same way as the Sudog was alive, and the storm was much
larger and greater than it could ever be.

Winds whipped around it, creating an upper-air twirling, a
tornado within the clouds, and with it came the force and
power of a vacuum, tugging and pulling at the Sudog as it
strove fruitlessly to break free. Sucking it up, tearing it
apart . . . It gave a mournful, anguished moaning scream as
it came apart, on a level few could hear, and then it was gone,
leaving the storm to her alone once more.

*My God!* she thought, feeling both exultation and disgust at
herself. *Boolean should have told me! All this time I been
runnin' from storms, cowering in lonely rooms, scrunched up
in dark corners. All this time I've been afraid of the thunder,
and it was my greatest ally, my one true friend!*

She felt the soaking rain on her body and found its touch no longer terrible but instead a friend, a lover's caress.

She shifted her mental focus again to the storm, using it now, directing it. Lightning within the storm could be used as well, could illuminate the very road ahead, if only briefly . . . *There!* Off to the side and not too far ahead, partly hidden by the tall trees! Horses!

Just whose horses she couldn't be sure, but so long as she had the storm, and she knew now that she could have it if she needed it, it wasn't as important. She started walking again, this time using the illuminations as a guide in the rain and mud and darkness.

Yes! There! It *was* Crim's wagon and the familiar team, still all hitched up as if waiting for the rain to pass. The wagon wheels were sunk deep in mud, and even she was now struggling in the mud of the road, sinking down well past her ankles and going on only because of her hard-won great strength. Clearly, though, that wagon was going to have lots of trouble unless things dried out.

She approached the rear of the wagon cautiously, unable to figure out why she had been forced to walk so long a distance. Satisfied as well as she could be that there was no one lurking under it or in the nearby trees, she stood there and shouted, "Kira! It's me! Is there anything wrong?"

There was no answer, and so she climbed up and started to look inside.

Something lashed out from the dark interior of the wagon, catching her on the head and knocking her back, stunned, into the rain and mud. Confused, she made her way painfully to her feet, slipping a couple of times before she made it, and looked up.

A dark figure stood there just beyond the tailgate, a figure that wasn't of anyone she had ever seen. The occasional lightning illuminated it slightly, showing a mean, scarred face with deep-set, wild eyes and a frizzled gray beard, and he had a pistol in his hand like he knew how to use it. He reached down and came up with something—they looked like chains or maybe manacles.

"Ye just stay right there, Fat One," he shouted menacingly at her. "Ye ain't worth nothin' dead, but I'm a dead enough shot even in the dark at this distance to hit one of them fat drumsticks of your'n with a high-powered slug that'll keep you there. No funny moves, now. I'm comin' out in this crap but there ain't no way ye can move or take me without me gettin' ye bad, and if it's my life or your'n I'll drill a hole right through ye.''

His accent was strange and low-class but she had no trouble understanding his words. Her head throbbed, but this was no time to worry about a headache.

"What have you done with Kira, you pig?" she shouted back at him.

He laughed as he reached down, let down the back board, then sat on it, all the time his eyes and pistol never wavering from her. He was definitely a pro, all right, for all the rest he might be.

"Yer pretty friend's inside, all trussed up like a stuffed goose. She tried to give me some trouble when I popped up and ordered her to pull over, so's I had to whack her one good. She won't pull her changeling trick again, neither. I seen the big guy turn, but it won't do her no good if she tries it. Got a wire noose on her pretty neck. She turns now and that little neck gets big, well, she's gone and hung herself is all. Now ye turn 'round, back to me, hands behind ye, so's I can stick these things on ye. No tricks, now. I know 'em all and by the gods you'll feel a bullet rip through ye like ye never dreamed.''

*Think! Concentrate! Got to get him farther away from the wagon! Move back a little. Make him come to you!*

"Gad it's awful in this miserable hole," he grumbled, easing himself down into the mud. A sudden gust of wind whipped the rain right into him, and he was momentarily off-balance. Not enough to jump him, but when he recovered she was several steps back.

"Oh, no ye don't! Ye don't move a muscle 'cept I tell ye," he said menacingly. "Ye been warned. Do anything but what I say just *'xactly* as I say it and I'll plug ye through and do it myself while ye writhes in pain in the mud! Now—*turn around, hands behind your back! Now!*''

It wasn't far enough, but it had to be. She reached out to the storm, surprised at her lack of fear. Fear was irrelevant now. She was too damned angry to be afraid.

"Go fuck yourself, Deadeye!" she shot back defiantly. "Don't you know who I am, *what* I am, to be so valuable to them?"

He hesitated, not expecting such defiance and, frankly, pretty curious about the answer to those questions.

"Ye look like a fat peasant pig t'me," he growled.

She felt a sudden, total coldness within her, a cold and calculating dangerous part of her she had never known or suspected was there.

"You know the Storm Princess? That she knows how to bend even storms like this one to her will?"

He frowned, now thoroughly soaked himself. "Yeah? What of her?"

"Well, *so do I*," she responded.

The lightning bolt was strong and powerful; it came in an instant from the great clouds above and struck him dead on and went on through him to ground. The displaced air caused a loud thunderclap and went off with such force she was momentarily thrown backwards, landing again in the muck, but there was no shot. The moment it struck him it so heated the powder in the bullet that the gun had gone off, but she wasn't aware of anything except an ass full of mud.

It took her a moment to collect herself and get up again, and when she did she looked at where the man had been. He was man no longer, but instead a charred and gruesome-looking corpse, still smoldering, the manacles and pistol still sizzling as the rain struck them where they lay.

She felt momentarily grossed out at the sight, but ran quickly to the wagon and hauled herself in. "Kira!"

She looked around, fumbled with the lantern, found the flint and, removing the glass, struck it at the wick until it lit. Replacing the glass, she waited for the flame to stabilize and then looked around.

Kira was bundled up really good. Since the man had seen the change but hadn't realized it was involuntary, he didn't want Crim suddenly popping in, breaking bonds, and coming after him. He'd tied her hands and feet with wire, then stuffed her into a sleeping bag and tied that off as well. He'd also stuffed rags in her mouth to gag her. Finally, he'd rigged the wire noose he'd spoken of and nailed it to the wagon floorboard.

She was awake now, but she didn't look any too good, and there was a nasty welt on her forehead and a small cut that had bled a little before drying. Kira's beauty was going to be tempered, at least for a few days.

Sam pulled the rags from Kira's mouth and she started to cough and gag.

"Stay still!" Sam told her. "I've gotta find something that'll cut you out of that thing. I sure as hell can't undo that stuff. Never seen nobody who could do that with wire."

She went and got the trail shears. "This'll probably screw these things up, but I think I can get through that stuff with 'em." She knelt down and first tried to cut where the noose was fixed to the floor but that seemed to strangle Kira and she stopped, first cutting the bonds around the sleeping bag and then getting it off her as gently as she could. She got the tight bonds off Kira's legs, but the woman was face up, arms beneath, and that noose just had to go first.

Sam looked at the hammer but it had a back kind of like a pick instead of a pry groove. Another invention to file away for future profit. She sighed. "Turn your head a little to the side and hold on," she warned Kira. "I'm gonna have to get in there around the neck and cut. There's no other way."

It was tricky, nervous work, but she was careful, and with her powerful arms she managed to apply enough pressure to eventually snap the cord, although Kira was also going to have a bruise around her neck and particularly on one side for a while as well.

Kira sat up, coughing and gasping, and Sam quickly freed her hands and then got her some water. Kira felt her throat and gagged a few times, but seemed at last to recover enough to try talking.

"Sloppy on Crim's part," she managed. "But I wouldn't have thought of it, either. They—suspected—somehow, or—at least—this one did."

"Take it easy," Sam cautioned her. "No rush now."

"He—you—got him? How?"

"Tell you later."

"He crawled—into the wagon—must've—during the long wait. Just lay there—quietly—in the back. Probably got in when Crim took a crap. The border guard either—didn't look—or didn't care." She kept stroking her neck, but she had to talk. "Caught me—by surprise. Tried to—take him—but he had—something. Long weight on a chain, I think. Got me good." She suddenly stared at Sam. "You, too?"

Sam was so muddy and cruddy in general she hardly realized it, but when she touched her forehead it hurt like hell. "Ow!" Suddenly she felt a stinging in her left thigh and looked down. There was a gash there, and blood not fully clotted. "The son of a bitch still shot me!"

"Sit down! I'm all right, now—honest. Better than you," Kira told her firmly. "Let's get that cleaned out and some salve put in there. Then I'm going to put a tub and the cistern on the wagon sides. If it's going to rain like this, the least we can get out of it is drinking water and a bath."

The pain was starting to rise up with a vengeance, but Sam managed a satisfied smile. "Don't step on the mess outside," she warned. "And don't worry about the rain. It'll rain just as long as you want . . ."

Klittichorn, the Horned Demon of the Snows, fumed, and those around him quaked in awe and fear.

"Who are these girls who survive every torment?" he thundered. "One burns our agents with fire and strangles the Sudog in its cloudy lair, and the other—the _other_—manages to destroy a Prince of the Inner Hells, a _Stormrider_! They avoid our armies, exile the Blue Witch to the netherhells, and we seem powerless to lay hands on them! Well, this will have to stop! They cannot both be magic, yet they do things even I had not dreamed to do! No, my lords and ladies, this must not be permitted to continue!"

Suddenly his fury seemed to vanish, replaced with cold calculation. "We can never hope to snare them both and we have lost them as well. Let the mercenaries keep trying, but otherwise pull back. We have failed at stopping them so far, so let them through. Ease their way. But marshal local allied forces off Masalur hub. I want them ready to act when we are ready."

"I see, My Lord Klittichorn," said one of the generals. "Let them grow confident and then grab them where we know they must go."

The sorcerer whirled. "No, idiot! I care little now if they reach the place or not. Too much time and energy and expense has already gone to that goal without result. It would be convenient to know their location, of course, and even more convenient if they both made it to Boolean within a few weeks' time, but it will not matter in the end. Without him they are not relevant."

They all looked shocked. "You mean, after all this, you intend to let them reach Boolean?"

"Let us just say I no longer care to prevent it. But double our spells upon Masalur, concentrate our magic, poll and deploy our demons and allies so that the bastard remains where he is. Lose him and we might as well be lost. No, my friends, let us not combat fate any longer. The mathematics of destiny appears to protect them. Let it. But whether they meet or not, we shall cheat destiny and alter their heads by the one means that neither destiny nor Boolean can fight. We must have one final test. We must know if our calculations are correct, our dreams realizable."

"My Lord, you don't mean—"

"And why not? We must know if it works. What better target is offered, that rids us of the only enemy that might defeat us? If they get together in time all the better—we shall eliminate all threats at once. But no matter, the time will be set and fixed and the one most dangerous will most certainly be there."

"But the girl—she might . . ."

"Might what? Without Boolean she is helpless, without training, without direction. A wild talent, no more, soon without anyone who knows how to use her properly. Remove the canny Boolean and they will fall victim to the fates they have so narrowly cheated up to now. No Storm Princess, but merely a girl who can play tricks with the weather."

"But, My Lord—a *hub*! We are the strongest single force it is true, but to attack a single hub and eliminate a single powerful sorcerer is to confirm all he says! The other kings and sorcerers will band against us! It is tipping our hand too soon!"

"Ridiculous! They are mad fools. One they will put down to the same chance as they put down all the others through history, not only because it is most logical but because they *want* to believe it is mere chance! A few might suspect, but out of fear they will tip our way. The rest will cry a few tears and make sacrifices to their gods in thanks that it did not happen to them. Come, my friends, this is not boldness but caution! If we cannot murder Masalur and Boolean with it, what chance do we have of ever accomplishing our wider, grander dreams?"

He turned on them, eyes blazing. "Now the changewind shall come to Mashtopol! And soon, my friends, upon that disaster and with that blood to feed us, the Akhbreed empire will cease to exist!"

## The *Changewinds* saga continues with *War of the Maelstrom*.

# Fantasy from Ace
## fanciful and fantastic!

# CAPTIVATING TALES OF FANTASY WORLDS BY TODAY'S BRIGHTEST YOUNG AUTHORS